D0960282

FIVE DARK FATES

Also by Kendare Blake

Three Dark Crowns

One Dark Throne

Two Dark Reigns

Queens of Fennbirn

Anna Dressed in Blood

Girl of Nightmares

Antigoddess

Mortal Gods

Ungodly

FIVE DARK FATES

KENDARE BLAKE

HARPER TEEN
An Imprint of HarperCollinsPublishers

HarperTeen is an imprint of HarperCollins Publishers.

Five Dark Fates

Map of Fennbirn by Virginia Allyn

www.epicreads.com
Library of Congress Control Number: 2019941397
ISBN 978-0-06-268617-6 (trade bdg.)
ISBN 978-0-06-295506-7 (special edition)
ISBN 978-0-06-293756-8 (int.)

Typography by Aurora Parlagreco
19 20 21 22 23 PC/LSCH 10 9 8 7 6 5 4 3 2 1

First Edition

CAST OF CHARACTERS

THE QUEENS

Queen Mirabella, the great elemental
Queen Arsinoe, the Bear Queen
Queen Katharine the Undead, the Queen Crowned

THE CROWN

THE BLACK COUNCIL

Genevieve Arron, a poisoner
Pietyr Renard, a poisoner
Antonin Arron, a poisoner
Lucian Arron, a poisoner
Paola Vend, a poisoner
Renata Hargrove, giftless
Bree Westwood, an elemental
Rho Murtra, a priestess
Luca, the High Priestess

Elizabeth, a priestess

THE REBELLION

Jules Milone, the Legion Queen
Emilia Vatros, a warrior
Mathilde, an oracle
Billy Chatworth, a mainlander
Caragh Milone, the Midwife of the Black Cottage
Cait Milone, a naturalist
Ellis Milone, a naturalist
Luke Gillespie, a naturalist
Matthew Sandrin, giftless
Gilbert Lermont, an oracle
Camden, a cougar familiar
Braddock, a bear

FIVE DARK FATES

Fennbirn
BEVELLET
VALOSTRA
N
W
E
S

Mainlands
CENTRA
TORRENSIDE CASTLE
ENNBIRN
DOWLING BAY
SALKADES

SUNPOOL

Arsinoe, fugitive queen of Fennbirn Island, sits stone-faced before the desk, surrounded by crumpled balls of parchment. She has not slept but a few hours, and the light spilling in through the cut-stone window hurts her eyes; it shows the dark hollows beneath them and the gray hue of her face. Not that anyone is there to see. Her only company is a tan mountain cat with a black-tipped tail, chained to a wall. And the occasional thump from behind the closed door of the inner chamber as the tonic she gave to Jules to keep her in a stupor starts to wear off.

Arsinoe turns her head and stares through the wood. Jules Milone, the Legion Queen of Sunpool, lies behind that door. Her hands and feet are bound. The broken blood vessels in her eyes from the force of the legion curse being unleashed have begun to heal. But Arsinoe will never forget what her friend looked like when Emilia brought her home from battle. Jules with bared teeth and bloodred eyes will always be there, lurking behind Arsinoe's eyelids when she goes to sleep.

"But she will get better," she whispers, a promise to the mountain cat. Camden's only response to the promise is a deep, low growl. "She will," Arsinoe says again, and rubs her face with both hands to try to summon the last of her energy. "Not fast enough to suit you, I know. But she will."

In the meantime, there is the business of the letter. The reason she dragged the small writing desk up into the seclusion of the tower to begin with. She touches her pen to the paper and watches the ink gather. How can she tell them that their daughter was taken hostage and then murdered by Katharine the Undead? How would she tell anyone that, let alone Cait and Ellis Milone, who are like her own grandparents?

Footsteps sound in the stairwell and Arsinoe groans. She nearly picks up her ink pot to throw before she sees that it is Billy, smart enough to lead with a tray of food and poke his head in second.

"I've some oat cakes and honey. A few boiled eggs. And tea."

"Strong tea?"

"So strong it may as well be whiskey." He comes in and wedges the tray onto the side of the desk, spilling the small pile of crumpled parchment. Then he runs his hand through her hair and kisses the soft skin of her temple. "You look terrible. Maybe I should have brought actual whiskey."

"How do I write this letter?" she asks. "How do I tell Cait

and Ellis that Madrigal is dead? How do I tell them that Jules is out of her mind?"

"Leave out the details about Jules's condition." He pours the tea and drips honey over the oat cakes. "That's better done in person. But you have to write to them, and soon. They'll want to be here for their daughter's burning."

When the sun rose, she had wandered to the window to look out over the beach. The flat, gray stones and rocky shore of Sunpool do not resemble the sand of Sealhead Cove, but they will have to do. "Is Emilia still grumbling about the location?" The warrior had suggested they hold the funeral in the square. Arsinoe insisted that Madrigal be burned by the water. A naturalist should be burned in the wild.

"No. She's stubborn, but she trusts that you would know best about this. About what Jules would want, if she could tell us."

Arsinoe snorts. "Stubborn she is. Yet what bothers her most is that it was my suggestion. An order, from a queen."

"Only, that's not what it was," Billy says, a little too carefully. He, as much as Emilia, does not want to see Arsinoe step back into that role.

"No. That's not what it was." She places her hand on his, then sighs and reaches for her teacup. "But until Jules is well again, who else is there but me and Mira? Speaking of Mira, I should go to her. We'll need her gift on the beach, to calm the winds and embolden the flames." She stands up too quickly and jostles the tray, spilling tea across unused parchment. "Damn it all!"

"Cursing like a mainlander, I see," Billy says as he helps her mop it up.

She smiles. "You do have much better curses. We never should have come back. We should have stayed there."

"No. Daphne and those dreams were right. You and Mira are needed here. What would be happening to Jules without you and your poisoner potions? What would the mist have done if not for Mira's wind and storm? You're needed. Just not forever."

"Not forever," she says, and takes his hand, her touch like a promise. They turn at the sound of rushed footsteps up the stairs and break apart when Emilia bursts in, her face flushed and long strands of dark hair hanging down her shoulders.

"Jules is still resting," Arsinoe says. "And I've nearly finished writing these letters."

"Forget the letters." Emilia strides across the room and slams a flattened scrap of parchment down on the desk. "You have a far larger problem."

Arsinoe picks up the paper and reads.

It is elegant, scrawling script, written in an unfamiliar hand.

We have spoken with the queen, and we, too, believe she is true. We have departed for Indrid Down. The decision is yours, but we will be here if you need us.

—B&E

"That was discovered in Mirabella's room this morning."

"B and E?" Billy asks, reading over Arsinoe's shoulder.

Arsinoe swallows. "Bree and Elizabeth." She looks up.

Emilia's expression is as triumphant as it is angry, validation written over every line of her frame. The warrior curls her lip and spits the words as the note falls from Arsinoe's fingers.

"Mirabella has defected."

INDRID DOWN

Mirabella wakes to the thumping of the driver's fist against the carriage roof. She does not know how long she slept. Judging by the light, she thinks it seems near midday, though it is difficult to tell beneath the low, gray clouds.

"Coming up on the capital," the driver calls, and Mirabella wipes her eyes. She moves to the window and drops it open. Ahead, the twin black spires of the Volroy rise into the sky.

She has seen the Volroy before. As a girl, she saw it a hundred times in weavings and paintings, in books and in her own imagination, when she thought she would rule there one day. She saw it for herself when she arrived in Indrid Down for the Queens' Duel. But this time is different. Queen Katharine reigns there now, and though Mirabella comes under an offer of truce, it may not be true. She may arrive and find a block prepared, ready for her head. She may have to fight her way out of the capital for a second time.

In her hood, the small black-and-white tufted woodpecker trills. He is excited, sensing he is close to Elizabeth, and Mirabella strokes his head feathers. Katharine said she would be safe. Bree and Elizabeth thought that she meant it.

Back in Sunpool, they must know by now that she is gone, and it pains her to think of Arsinoe, and Billy, when they realize what she has done. They would not believe it at first. They would defend her. Maybe they would even send out a search party, or a rescue party, thinking she was taken against her will.

After that— Well, there is plenty of time to worry about what she will say the next time she has to face Arsinoe. For now, her mind is on Katharine. One sister at a time.

When the carriage last stopped to rest the horses, the driver asked Mirabella where she wanted to go. It would have been easy enough to go to Indrid Down Temple, where she might send for Luca. Or to Bree's household, where she could be sure she was safe. Instead, she asked to be taken to the Volroy gate.

"The big gate, then," the driver had said, and for the first time, looked carefully at Mirabella's face. After that, she did not speak much to her and began addressing her as "Mistress" rather than "Miss" when she did. She dared not say "Queen" so close to the castle.

In the back of the carriage, Mirabella listens to the horses' hooves clack along the road and watches the Volroy grow larger. The approaching sight of the castle has banished all thoughts of sleep, and she fidgets with the folds of her cloak and the skirt of her light blue dress. The lace edge has come loose and turned black with dirt after dragging across the ground, and she considers tearing the whole of it away. Instead she clasps her shaking hands in her lap. She must be calm. Katharine is her little sister and will not see her tremble.

Two guards stop the carriage before the main gate and approach to question the driver and peer inside. All the other passengers have been let off elsewhere. Only Mirabella and the cargo remain, trunks and crates loaded onto the roof and lashed to the back.

"What business do you have at the Volroy?"

"None of my own. I'm bringing a passenger. And I think you'll find that she has plenty." At the driver's words, both guards lean back to look in through the windows. Mirabella gazes evenly at them. It takes longer than she expects for them to realize who she is, but eventually they open the gate, and shout for more guards to attend the carriage.

"Our coming must have been kept a secret, Pepper," she whispers to the little bird, who watches with his head cocked. "But of course it would be. Katharine would not want to lose face if I refused her offer."

The carriage stops, and Mirabella steps out into the shadow of the fortress. The moment she is clear, Pepper darts from inside her hood, flying off to find his Elizabeth. Mirabella tries not to feel abandoned. But as the guards glare at her warily, she wishes he would have stayed.

"Will you be all right, Mistress?" the driver asks, and

Mirabella turns to her with a grateful smile. "I will be fine. Thank you. It has been a pleasure."

The woman makes a reverent gesture and clicks to the horses. Mirabella turns back to the queensguard and is greeted by the blades of their spears.

"Do not point those at me," she says. She sends a crackle of dry lightning through the sky and the blades drop. "Take me inside. To the queen."

GREAVESDRAKE MANOR

Katharine sits beside the bed, surrounded by whispers. Her old bed in her old room, only this time it is not she who lies upon it but Pietyr, as the three healers she has summoned from the capital and one from Prynn mutter near the open door.

They are the finest healers she could find. Poisoners all. But none of them has been able to help Pietyr. None is even able to say what is wrong with him.

Of course, perhaps they could if they knew what truly happened. But Katharine will never tell them that.

"Please wake up," she murmurs for what feels like the thousandth time. She touches his cheek, then his chest. Both warm, and his strong heart keeps beating. The slow bleeding from his eyes and nose has finally eased, and his face and neck have been wiped clean, the pillow and bedding beneath him changed. Only the barest bit of red seeps from inside his ear.

"Let him wake," she growls, but the dead queens do not respond. She can feel them staring at him through her eyes. Perhaps she can even feel a little remorse.

No. Regret, perhaps, but not remorse. They did what they had to do to Pietyr to keep him from sending them back into the Breccia Domain. With his bumbling, flawed, low-magic spell that caused them so much pain, he gave them no choice. And every day and night since then, they have reminded Katharine by raising their rot to mar the surface of her skin, by humming through her blood and her mind in soothing, comforting tones. They are part of her now, and they will not be moved.

He would have harmed us. Weakened you. We would protect us. Protect you.

"Be silent," Katharine whispers. "Be silent!"

"Our apologies, Queen Katharine," one of the healers says, and bows his head.

"We will take our counsel into the hall so as not to disturb you," says another, the one from Prynn, and motions to her colleagues.

"No." Katharine stands. "Forgive me. This accident—his illness—I cannot think." And it seems that Greavesdrake is always full of whispers. At the end of every hall. Behind every closed door. "Speak plain and tell me your thoughts. What is wrong with him? When will he recover?"

They straighten nervously, huddling and rustling like a flock of birds.

"I know there is no good news," she says, reading their

faces. "But I would have your opinions."

The healer from Prynn steps back toward the bed. She was the one who took the most aggressive approach to Pietyr's examination, prodding his gums, pulling on his fingers and toes. It was hard for Katharine to stand there and watch him be poked at, lying unresponsive while a stranger turned his head back and forth and peered inside his ears. When they peeked under the bandages wrapped around his hand, Katharine held her breath. It had been ugly business when she sliced into the rune, mangling it to hide it from discovery. She had made so many cuts that his palm looked like it had been torn apart. But sweet Pietyr had not been awake by then. He had not felt it.

"The wound on his hand continues to heal. Though it is still impossible to tell what caused it. And it does not seem to be the source of his illness. There are no dark lines stemming from the cuts, no foul odor—"

"Yes, yes," says Katharine. "So you have said before."

"We think it likely a trauma inside the skull. An unlucky vessel that burst or became clotted. It would leave no outward sign and would require no external impact. You said you found him lying on the floor. It is likely that, when the vessel burst, he simply fell there. There was probably little pain or what there was would have been brief."

Katharine stares at his sleeping face. He is still handsome when he sleeps. But he is not himself. What makes Pietyr Pietyr is the glint in his eye, the clever and cutting curve of his mouth. And his voice. It has been too many days since she heard his voice. Nearly weeks.

"When will he wake?"

"I do not know, Queen Katharine. That he continues to breathe is a good sign. But he is unresponsive to stimuli."

"So much blood . . ." When Katharine returned to her senses after the failed spell and found Pietyr lying beside her on the floor, his face was a mask of red.

"There is no way to tell the extent of the damage," the healer says. "We can only wait. He will need round-the-clock monitoring . . . care and feeding—"

"Leave us," Katharine says, and listens to their footsteps shuffle into the hall. She takes his hand and kisses it gently. She should have banished the dead queens when he gave her the chance. If only she had not been such a coward. They know she cannot oust them now, not with her reign assailed from all sides: the mist, the Legion Queen, her sisters' return. She used to think that the dead queens had made her strong. Now, too late, she knows the truth: the strength was theirs and theirs alone. And they would see her weak forever, to keep her as their puppet.

"I did not know," she whispers against Pietyr's cheek. "I did not know that this is what they would do."

When Katharine walks out of Pietyr's sickroom an hour later, tired and dazed, she stumbles directly into Edmund, Natalia's old butler, carrying a tray of tea.

"I thought it might be welcome," he says softly.

"It is," Katharine says. "But I have had enough of sitting in that room. Perhaps in the drawing room or the solarium." She trails off and puts her hand to her eyes.

"Perhaps right here on the floor. It is still your home if you wish it. A tea party on the carpet."

"Just like we never used to have," Katharine says. But she smiles at him, and they step aside as a maid enters Pietyr's room. "Where are the healers?"

"They have clustered in the library," Edmund replies. "And are demanding lunch."

"I suppose that they will need to eat." Katharine and the butler fall in step beside each other down the hall. "Poor Edmund. I have turned your household upside down."

"Nonsense, my queen. It is good to have heartbeats in Greavesdrake again. Even the heartbeats of new staff and strangers. Since Natalia was killed, it has not felt like a great house so much as a shrine."

How right he is. As they ascend the stairs, the sounds of people in its farthest corners, the bustle and occasional laughter of servants, make Greavesdrake feel alive again. Still draughty and dark, of course. But alive and no longer haunted.

It will feel haunted forever if Pietyr dies upstairs.

In the main floor dining room, they find Genevieve, reading a book over a half-eaten bowl of soup.

"How is he?" she asks, and sets the book down.

"Unchanged." Katharine sits across from her as Edmund readies the tea.

"Unchanged," Genevieve repeats, and sighs.

Katharine watches her carefully. Katharine was the one

who "found" Pietyr, unconscious and covered in blood, just as she was with Nicolas the night her poisoned body killed him. Two lovers, one dead and the other unable to wake. Though Katharine was careful to dispose of all evidence of the low magic, Genevieve must still have her suspicions.

"He will wake," Genevieve says, and tries to bolster Katharine with a smile. "He is too meddlesome not to."

Katharine nods. She is about to bite into one of Edmund's excellent crumbly shortbreads when they hear the front door open and the servants speaking in raised voices. Soon enough, a breathless messenger arrives in the doorway.

"Well?"

"She's at the Volroy," the messenger declares, her eyes wide.

"Who?" Genevieve asks. "Were we expecting someone?"

Katharine stares at the girl. She knows, by the way the messenger avoids speaking the name and the fearful wonder in her eyes, that she means Mirabella. Her powerful sister has come. The strongest of the triplets. The strongest queen in generations has come at her request.

Katharine's legs twitch beneath the table. She is so eager to meet Mirabella, to look her in the eye under an offering of peace. But she is careful to control her reaction.

"Who?" Genevieve asks again, losing her patience.

The messenger opens her mouth but says nothing, trying to decide how to phrase it without breaking decorum. "The queen's sister," she says finally.

"Mirabella," Katharine supplies, and Genevieve gasps.

"She—? She would come here?"

"She was invited."

"By who?"

"By Luca," Katharine says. "And I suppose, by me. Where is she now?" she asks the girl.

"Waiting for you at the Volroy. The guards are holding her in the throne room."

"Has anyone seen her? Spoken to her? Anyone from my Black Council?"

"No, my queen."

Katharine rises. "Then ride quickly back there ahead of me and make sure that no one does. No one is to see my sister before I do. Not Antonin or Bree Westwood. Not even High Priestess Luca. Is that understood?"

"Yes, my queen."

"Good. Hurry. Take a fresh horse."

Katharine and Genevieve share a carriage to the Volroy. Genevieve's jaw has not unclenched since receiving the news, and she holds her arms crossed tightly over her chest.

"I am to be your eyes and ears. How? When you tell me nothing!"

"Luca and I told no one of this," says Katharine. "Honestly, Genevieve, I did not think she would come." She turns back toward the receding bulk of Greavesdrake and to the window of her old bedroom, wishing that the curtains would move and reveal Pietyr standing there. He would love to be at the Volroy for this meeting. And she does not know how she will fare without him.

"Why is she here?" Genevieve asks. "What good can she do?"

"She is another queen. She can help me win the war," replies Katharine. "If I can trust her."

"Neither of you are queens," Genevieve says, her voice thick with disgust. "If you were, there would only be one of you left."

THE VOLROY

"We have received word that the queen is on her way."

"Thank you," Mirabella says. They have put her in the throne room to await Katharine. The guard nods and leaves, closing the heavy doors. No doubt they are stationed three deep on the other side, afraid Mirabella will blast the door open with a gust of wind and set fire to the entire castle.

She snorts softly. She could, she supposes, be free of the Volroy within minutes if she chose. Her gift, now that she has returned to the island, has come back even stronger and quicker than it was when she left. Though she still may not be able to blast through the door. To do that she might need a different kind of gift. A gift like Jules has.

She unfastens her cloak and drapes it across a chair before the long, dark table beside the throne—the table where the Black Council must sit on days when the queen gives audience.

She runs her fingers along the back of the chair. Who does it belong to? Bree? Or perhaps Luca? Probably not. This seat, directly to the right of the throne, is probably reserved for one of the Arrons. The eldest woman. Or that pale-haired boy of Katharine's, Pietyr Renard.

Mirabella's eyes roam over the room. The walkways of the stone and wood floor have been overlaid with carpets woven in designs of black and gold. The hammer-beam ceiling shows intricate carvings representing the gifts and many of the great queens, the wood itself very dark and the ceiling painted in stunning black and silver. Luca used to tell her about it all when she was a girl. She sat by Luca's knee and daydreamed of the time when she would rule in the castle beneath all that history. She looks up and tries to spot the carving of lightning and thunderclouds for her favorite, Queen Shannon. And of course it does not take long to find the plaster and wood plaque crafted for Queen Illiann, as it is the only part of the ceiling painted blue.

Mirabella wanders to the throne and steps up beside it, her fingertips just grazing the gilded arm. Even now, it feels like it is hers, this thing she has been directed to, pointed at, since the day she was born. But it is not her portrait that hangs behind it. No portrait of fire and fierce storms, no elemental queen with her gown billowing behind her. Instead, the portrait that hangs there is Katharine's, dark and still, and full of bloody bones.

"Do you want to sit in it?"

Despite herself, Mirabella jumps. And when she turns,

there she is: wicked, deadly little Katharine, who slipped inside silently, without so much as the creak of a door or the rustle of a skirt.

"To pretend for a while that you won?"

"No," Mirabella says. "Of course not."

"Then get away from my seat," says Katharine, and smiles. "Come and greet me properly."

Properly, Mirabella thinks. Is she expected to kneel and kiss her ring? She could not bring herself to do it. She does not know if she can even steel her spine enough to touch Katharine at all, for fear of a poisoned blade quickly buried in her neck.

Katharine walks slowly forward. Her black eyes glitter. Unlike her guards, she seems not the least bit afraid.

Mirabella steps down and away from the throne, forcing her legs to move across the carpet. The sisters stop in the center of the room, no more than an arm's length away from each other.

"Do not ask me to bow," Mirabella says. "I am here as an ally, not a subject."

"I will not ask you to bow any more than I will ask you for embraces." Katharine's mouth crooks. "Not yet."

Mirabella relaxes slightly. They have not been this close since the banquet before the Queens' Duel, when Katharine dragged her around the dance floor like a marionette shortly before Mirabella was poisoned by Billy's father. But she remembers well the coldness of Katharine's grip and the strength in her fingers.

"I am surprised that you came," Katharine says, and crosses

her arms. "You could not have been pleased that I cut that naturalist's throat."

"It was supposed to be a trade. The Legion Queen for her mother. No one was supposed to die."

"And no one would have, if not for the mist. And if she had not tried to run."

Mirabella swallows. Her mouth has gone completely dry.

"I did not turn to your side," she says. "And I did not turn against Arsinoe. I turned against Jules Milone when I saw what the curse had done to her." She narrows her eyes. "Or, I suppose, what you turned her into when you cut the blood-binding loose from her mother's neck."

Katharine cocks her head, indifferent. "All that did was reveal the monster she always was underneath. And what a monster she was. She will be a handful, even for you."

She will be more than that, Mirabella thinks. The war gift that Jules hurled at her in the valley knocked her clean off her feet. And Jules had not even truly been aiming.

Katharine walks around Mirabella in a slow circle, and Mirabella straightens as she is appraised. The queen looks over the stains in the blue fabric of her dress, the torn and dirty lace. It is a rather poor fit as well—too tight in the bodice and bosom, cut for the thin, wiry figure of Billy's sister, Jane. Mrs. Chatworth had brought in a tailor to make alterations, but the fabric had its limits.

As Katharine walks behind her, Mirabella is careful to keep her in her sights.

"Is that all?" Katharine asks. "All it took to make you desert the rebellion?"

"It was not all." Mirabella looks down. "I am a queen. A true queen, in the blood. And the line of queens should not be set aside so lightly. Not even if the future of it resides in someone as terrible as you."

Katharine whirls. She holds her hands together so tightly that they shake.

"An interesting choice coming to the Volroy dressed as a pauper," she says finally, her voice light. "Was it intentionally symbolic, or could you just not manage anything else?"

"On the mainland, this dress was one of the finest in the city."

Katharine raises her brows. "No matter. We will have you dressed in proper blacks and looking yourself again soon enough."

"Would you want that? Should I not be dressed in a penitent cloak of gray? To show my shame and my deference to the crown?"

"The people do not need to be reminded of who wears the crown," Katharine says. "And if you are here, I would have them see you. You, the great elemental queen, come to fight by my side. If you are here, you will be of use. But only when I choose. Guards!" The door to the throne room opens, and in moments, Mirabella finds herself surrounded again by the points of spears.

"Take my sister to the king-consort's apartment." She turns

to Mirabella. "My sweet Nicolas did not have the chance to enjoy it before he was killed in the fall from his horse, and I will not have such fine furnishings go to waste. And of course, there are no chambers designated to hold a Queen Crowned's sister." Katharine pivots on her heel, and shining black curls bounce over her shoulder. "I will send Bree Westwood and the priestess Elizabeth to see you. I am sure you would be comforted by their presence. And then I will have a small meal sent up. But do not eat too much. Tonight you will dine with me." She stops at the door and smiles at Mirabella broadly.

"We have much work to do."

Katharine goes from the throne room to the Black Council chamber and shuts herself inside. The moment she is hidden from view, she begins to tremble as she hugs herself and paces.

She had been face-to-face with Mirabella again, and she had done well. The black crown emblazoned across Katharine's forehead had acted like a shield, giving her courage and lending righteousness to her words. It had been hard not to shout. Not to strike out preemptively. Everything about Mirabella put her on the defensive: the way she stood in the throne room, beautiful and regal, even in that hideous wreck of a dress; the lingering bonds of affection she still holds with many members of Katharine's Black Council.

Perhaps it was a mistake to bring her here. Perhaps she is falling right into Luca's trap.

Even the dead queens, as they hissed and sniffed around her, also tugged against Katharine's edges, drawn to the strength of the elemental gift that flowed off Mirabella in waves.

"You would leave me for her."

Never, they whisper. *You are ours. We are you.*

But Katharine feels them pull against her skin. She feels them rise up and nearly slip out of her mouth. The dead queens had a taste of being outside her, of moving through another person when they left her to rush into Pietyr. And they liked it.

We are with you, always.

"Always," says Katharine as a plan begins to form in her mind. She could be free of them, and free of them for good, if she is careful, and if she is more clever than they are.

SUNPOOL

Wolf Spring arrived in time for Madrigal's burning. Cait and Ellis Milone, their backs straight and rigid as knives. Luke, cheeks wet, in a deep crimson vest and coat he was sure to have sewn himself. And much of the city came with them. Madrigal burned, in the salt spray and wind, atop the chest-high pyre of wood that the workers of the rebellion had built. The priestesses of Sunpool had wrapped her in crimson cloth and covered her in crimson petals. The rebels left offerings of wreaths and colored shells. Birds' eggs to crack and sizzle in the heat.

Together Wolf Spring and the rebellion watched as the pyre blazed, turning to ash the body that was not really Madrigal Milone any longer but merely the very pretty shell that could barely contain her.

Madrigal, Arsinoe thinks now, in the echoing whispers of Sunpool's great hall. Madrigal was the sum of her actions. She was a laugh in a quiet room. In life, she had never liked for anything to be easy, and in death she was the same.

"I thought you were dead, too."

At his voice in her ear, Arsinoe turns and grasps Luke around the waist. "I'm so sorry," she says, over and over, and only lets him go when his black-and-green rooster, Hank, begins to flap and spur holes into her only good pair of trousers. They sit down together at the nearest open place.

"Where's your boy?" he asks.

Arsinoe gestures to Billy in the crowd, where he spoons meat and gravy onto plates. All through the burning he let her lean on him without being seen to be leaning. When the flames touched the crimson cloth, he held her close.

"Getting you food, eh?" says Luke. "He knows you well." Then he lowers his eyes. "The funeral was well attended."

Arsinoe nods. "You would think she was someone important." Luke clears his throat, and she knows that Cait and Ellis are there.

"We wanted to wait," she says to Cait. "But we didn't know if you would be able to come."

"Your letter reached us," Cait says. "That is what matters. What of her sister? Has no one told Caragh?"

"I sent a letter to the Black Cottage, but—" Arsinoe shakes her head. "Maybe travel is slower . . . with the baby. . . ." She closes her mouth and looks to Ellis. Cait will be all right. She was made to bear. But Ellis—gentle, scholarly Ellis—he has doted on Madrigal since the day she was born.

In the crowd, Arsinoe spots a slew of familiar faces. A few of the Paces, and the Nicholses. Shad Millner and his seagull. Even Madge, who sold the best stuffed fried oysters in the Wolf Spring market. And Matthew. Of course Matthew.

"Matthew," she says when he sees her, and he walks forward and scoops her up, almost like he did when she was a child.

"Hello, kid," he says, and sets her back down on her feet. He wipes a tear from her cheek with his thumb and adjusts the knot of her crimson scarf.

Billy returns to the table with food and greets them all, especially Matthew, who he views as extended family through his connection to Joseph. His eye lingers on the crow on Cait's shoulder. "Is that Aria?" he asks, speaking of Madrigal's familiar.

"No," Cait replies. "This is Eva. Aria flew away from the smoke. Where is Jules? In your letter you said she was unhurt but still unwell. What did you mean?"

Arsinoe rises. "I'll take you to see her. But only you two," she adds when Luke and Matthew move to join them. It would be too difficult for Luke to see her in that state, and Matthew—Matthew looks too much like Joseph. She does not want to think about how Jules would react if she opened her eyes and saw Joseph's face. As Arsinoe and Billy escort Cait and Ellis from the hall, she stiffens with sudden realization.

"He doesn't know." She grasps Billy's arm. "Matthew and the Sandrins, they don't know about Joseph. They don't know that he's dead!"

"Dead?" Ellis exclaims as Billy shushes them both.

"I'll tell them," he says. "He was my brother, too, in a way. And I can describe what happened as well as you can."

"Tell them where he's buried," Arsinoe says hurriedly. "Tell them about the headstone, the inscription—"

"I'll tell them everything. Go. Take them to see Jules."

Arsinoe nods and leads them on, almost in a daze. As they make their way up the stairs to the tower, she tries to prepare them for what they will find, telling them as gently as she can what happened: how the legion curse was cut free when Madrigal died and what a violent reaction it sparked in Jules.

"She might not even be awake," she warns. "The tonics I craft to keep her calm sometimes make her sleep during the day."

"The tonics you craft," Cait repeats. "So the rumors are true. Our naturalist queen was only ever a poisoner."

Arsinoe pauses with her hand on the door. "You raised a naturalist, and a naturalist I will always be. Though I do feel better about never being able to grow anything."

To her surprise, Cait chuckles. "True. But we never schooled you in poisons, Arsinoe, as we didn't know. Is it safe, what you're doing?"

Arsinoe swallows. Safe? Nothing about the ingredients she must use feels safe. If she is not extremely careful in her measurements, Jules could simply stop breathing. But in Arsinoe's use of it, she has discovered that there is an instinctual aspect to the poisoner gift. Her hands are always sure. She blends the tonics as if in a trance. But that would be difficult to explain to a naturalist. "There's a healer here who fills in the gaps that my gift doesn't."

She opens the door of the outer chamber, and they go inside. At the sight of Cait and Ellis, Camden rises on her three good legs and grunts softly.

"You're happy to see us at least," says Ellis as he goes to her and strokes her soft, golden fur. "Shouldn't she be with Jules?"

"It isn't always safe. Camden is violent when Jules is unwell. And Jules . . . hurt her when the curse was cut free." Cait and Ellis frown; for a naturalist, there are few crimes worse than the abuse of a familiar. So Arsinoe clears her throat and brightens her tone. "But when she's quiet, Camden's basically fine. Her old self. If Jules is resting, she can go in with you."

She unbars the door. Inside, Jules lies on the pile of straw, pillows, and blankets that Arsinoe and Emilia arranged for her. Her hands and feet are chained. Ellis frees Camden from the wall, and the cougar trots quickly into the room. She circles Jules twice before lying down and resting her head in the hollow of Jules's shoulder.

Without a word, Cait kneels in the straw and gathers her granddaughter into her lap. Ellis places his hand on her shoulder. It is harder to watch than Arsinoe expected, and her throat tightens.

"I'm so sorry, Grandma Cait."

Cait takes Jules's hand, so dug into the links of the chain that she has to pry it loose. "Don't say that. It wasn't your fault. None of this is your fault."

"If not mine, then whose?"

"No one's," Ellis says.

"They say she tried to save her," Arsinoe whispers, her voice choked. "She tried to save Madrigal."

"Of course she did," Cait says. "That was always her way. Saving you, protecting you, trying to keep you out of trouble. And before you, there was Joseph. Our Jules was born a guardian, just as she was born a naturalist, and a warrior. Just as she was born cursed."

After Cait and Ellis leave Jules and drift away to rest, Arsinoe remains. She stays in the tower of the castle with Camden, idly scratching between her ears and looking down on the city. There is much activity below. So many goods and supplies coming in that the gate is rarely closed. So many weapons being forged and horses being shod that the fires at the smithy are always burning. Sunpool, not so long ago a failing ruin, has come alive again with war.

When she hears footsteps on the stairs, she expects that it is Billy, but instead, a man knocks and enters, wearing the yellow-and-gray tunic of the seers.

"You're not supposed to be here," she says, glancing at Jules's barred door.

"Forgive the intrusion, but I need to know where to house the new naturalists. The newcomers from Wolf Spring."

Arsinoe rubs at her brow. The tower with Jules had become her hideaway, and his intrusion is an intrusion indeed.

"There's no need to house them anywhere. They'll not be with us long. And they're naturalists. Perfectly happy in tents by the sea."

"Surely some will want to stay?" he asks.

"I wouldn't count on it."

"What is he asking you for, anyway?"

Arsinoe does not bother to stifle her groan when Emilia walks into the room, with no warning or announcement. The warrior's footsteps are only heard when she wants them to be. She grasps the man harshly by the shoulder and spins him away from Jules's door.

"You are not to be here. And you are not to ask her anything."

"I only thought . . . in the absence of the Legion Queen—"

"In the absence of the Legion Queen, I will handle all arrangements," Emilia growls.

"Good Goddess," Arsinoe says as the poor fellow hunches low and tries to sidle from view. "He only asked me because I am a naturalist and I am from Wolf Spring."

"Naturalist, poisoner . . . ," Emilia grumbles. "You wear whatever hat suits you at the moment."

Arsinoe sighs. "They'll be fine on their own. They'll figure it out," she says, and the man nods.

"No," says Emilia. "Place them in the vacant wing of the Lermont estate and whoever does not fit in the empty servants' quarters adjacent. We need them rested and comfortable if they are to fight."

"They aren't to fight," Arsinoe whispers.

"Some will fight. More than you think." Emilia gestures with her chin, and the man bows to her and leaves to see it done. Arsinoe waits for her to leave as well, but to her extreme displeasure, Emilia does not.

"Is there anything else?"

Emilia looks past her to the partially open door where Jules lies. She has not told anyone besides Mathilde about Mirabella's defection, and Arsinoe knows why. Emilia does not want the rebellion shaken. Not before their Legion Queen is well again.

It is something to be thankful for, she supposes, and then immediately hates herself for thinking it. She looks at Emilia with a softer expression and tries to remember the hours the warrior has spent by Jules's side.

"Emilia, I—"

Emilia's eyes flash to hers, full of contention, setting Arsinoe's teeth back on edge immediately. But before either can hurl another insult, a large, brown hound comes bursting through the door, followed by Jules's Aunt Caragh, with a baby slung around her middle.

"I had a feeling you two wouldn't get on," says Caragh as her brown hound sniffs happily at Arsinoe and goes to whuffle around Camden.

"Caragh," Emilia says, and embraces her. She wiggles a finger before the baby's face. "And little Fenn. Welcome."

"Caragh," Arsinoe breathes. She banishes the flicker of

annoyance that Emilia greeted her first and hugs her heartily, careful to keep from jostling Jules's little brother. "What are you doing here?"

"I missed my sister's burning." Her voice drops. "But I won't be kept from Jules. And I had to bring Fennbirn Milone here to meet his father."

"Yes," Arsinoe says. "Matthew is here."

"I've seen him. And I've seen my mother. And convinced her to give you this."

Caragh reaches into her coat and produces a glass jar with a length of blood-soaked cord inside. It is the color of rust, and beside it rests a yellowed, folded piece of paper.

Arsinoe recognizes the cord and the blood. It is a low-magic spell.

"It's all Madrigal left us about the binding. She never was much of a writer." Caragh taps the glass. "Only a page and a half, but it's all there. All she knew." She pushes them farther into Arsinoe's hands. "And now I'm giving them to you."

"Cait wasn't going to give them to me?"

"Maybe she was angry. Maybe she was blaming you. But if she was, she is over it now." Caragh bounces the baby on her hip. "And she was wrong to."

"What might that do?" Emilia asks, peering into the jar.

"Maybe nothing," Caragh replies for her. "Maybe it's too late. Or maybe you can still find something in there to help."

THE VOLROY

Mirabella wanders through the king-consort's apartment with a morbid fascination. Nicolas Martel died before he could spend even one night inside, but the rooms still feel like his tomb. She runs her hands over the bright brocade of the chairs, and reaches out to touch fresh lace that drapes across a small table. The rugs are soft and new. All of these furnishings, selected by Katharine for her dead husband.

It is a sad thought, made sadder by the silence, though as she looks around the walls, she sees nothing that seems personal or particularly sentimental, no portraits or remembrances of Nicolas Martel. That is no real wonder, she supposes. Such a tragic beginning would have been hastily brushed aside in any reign. The faster forgotten, the better. Still, she wonders how Katharine feels. Everyone knows that she has been in an affair with Pietyr Renard, and long before meeting Nicolas Martel.

But for a queen to lose her chosen partner so soon . . . It must have caused her pain, whether she loved him or not.

Or perhaps not pain, Mirabella thinks, remembering the sight of Katharine and Nicolas together, how darkly and coldly they shone. *Perhaps only disappointment.*

The door opens, and Mirabella straightens. Katharine has not sent the clothes that she promised, and she is still wearing her stained, blue mainlander dress with the ragged, hanging lace.

The woman who enters is one of the loveliest people Mirabella has ever seen. Her light blond hair is streaked with gold, and the violet of her eyes brings life to her otherwise statuesque face. Even beautiful Bree, who comes in behind her, is somehow less impressive by comparison.

"Bree!" Mirabella brushes past the woman to embrace her friend, who is practically vibrating with excitement.

"You are here," Bree exclaims. "You are really here!"

"I am." She touches Bree's cheek, as if to test Bree's realness as well. "Forgive us," she says to the woman behind them. "We have not seen each other . . . often."

"Of course, Mirabella," she replies. "Take all the time you need."

Her dismissive tone drives the friends apart. "I think you mean *Queen* Mirabella," Bree says.

"I am fairly certain that I do not. I am Genevieve Arron, head of the Arron family of poisoners," she says, and cocks her head in a decidedly sarcastic bow.

"Genevieve Arron. I almost did not recognize you outside of Natalia's shadow. Allow me to express my sympathy in regard to her passing. Losing a sister is never easy."

"So it would seem." Genevieve snaps her fingers, and Bree makes a sour face. "See to her quickly." She looks disdainfully upon Mirabella's clothing. "And make sure she is presentable."

As she turns to leave, a black-and-white tufted woodpecker flies past her cheek, making her swat at the air. "Disgusting birds everywhere," she hisses, and when she is gone, Elizabeth slips inside, her white hooded robe making the blush in her ruddy cheeks stand out all the more. As soon as they are alone, she, Mirabella, and Bree fall into one another's arms.

"I'm sorry that Pepper came in so suddenly," says Elizabeth. "I couldn't stop him!"

"No need to apologize," says Bree. "He was perfect. He ruined Genevieve's dignified exit." She turns to Mirabella with wide eyes. "Did you see the way she snapped her fingers at me? Like I was her scullery maid!"

Mirabella steps back to get a better look at her friends. Bree with her quick eyes and colorful clothes. And Elizabeth, a grin from ear to ear, her dark hair wound in a braid that sticks out of her hood, and a curled hand of silver shining from inside her left sleeve. Pepper perches on Mirabella's shoulder and pokes at her ear, intrepidly trying to find a way to burrow into her hair. She strokes his head and his little wings.

"So," she says, and sighs. "What are they saying?"

Bree leans close. "You are not a prisoner. Not exactly. You are free to roam the castle and the entirety of the fortress grounds. But you are not to leave it without the queen's express permission. The guards—there for your 'protection'—have been recently armed with poison."

"Poison to kill or merely sedate?"

Bree and Elizabeth trade a glance. Not even they can say for sure.

"Katharine said she would send you and Elizabeth to me for comfort. But then she sent you with Genevieve Arron. Another show of power? Another hint of control?"

Bree purses her lips. "Welcome to life at the Volroy."

There is a knock at the door, and servants enter, carrying trunk after trunk of clothes and jewels. Elizabeth helps them to the table and directs the rest to the floor.

"Thank you," she says. "We'll see to the queen— We'll see to Mirabella ourselves." The servants curtsy and leave, and Elizabeth begins riffling through the trunks.

"There is not much," Bree says. "No gowns of yours; there was no time to send for them from Rolanth. But the shops here are very good, and I had some of your jewels with me here." She searches through cases until she finds a dark walnut box and hands it to Mirabella.

It is a necklace: three large fire-colored stones hanging from a short silver chain. Even in the box, without light, the stones appear to burn.

Mirabella runs her fingers over them. "These— I would have worn them the night of the Quickening. Had things not gone so terribly wrong."

"So you will wear them now. For luck."

Elizabeth pulls a black velvet gown from one of the trunks and spreads it out. It is relatively simple, without much embroidery. "How about this one? Something comfortable after such a long journey?"

"It is perfect. But I care nothing about these dresses. I want to hear about you. How have you fared? Elizabeth, how are you allowed to keep Pepper even in your priestess bracelets?" She looks at Bree. "How have you come to be on the Black Council?"

"One answer for two questions," says Elizabeth. "The High Priestess sought to make amends with Bree for betraying you, so she offered her a place on the council."

"And in order for me to play nice," Bree says, "I demanded that Elizabeth be allowed to recall Pepper."

Mirabella grins at the bird, who clutches on to the back of Elizabeth's robes. "And how is the new council, Bree? And its mix of elementals, priestesses, and poisoners?"

"We were at each other's throats. And we will be again once the business with the rebellion is settled."

Mirabella would like to ask more. But it is plain that Bree and Elizabeth would rather she did not. They want this one evening to be themselves and to pretend like they are still back in Rolanth gossiping together at the Westwood house. One evening before everything begins. So Mirabella smiles and prods Bree in the shoulder.

"And?" she asks. "Who are you tumbling with these days? Some handsome queensguard soldier? Or perhaps another merchant's apprentice from the city?"

"Who has she not tumbled with?" Elizabeth asks, and Bree throws a glove at her. "Since the moment she arrived in Indrid Down, boys have fallen over themselves to get into her path. Just last month, two from the kitchens nearly fought a duel."

"A duel?" Mirabella laughs. "And who won? Which did you choose? The breadmaker? Or the cheese monger?"

"Neither!" Bree throws the other glove at Mirabella. "Though perhaps later I will choose both." She raises her eyebrow as Mirabella and Elizabeth chuckle, but then she sighs. "In truth, there has been no time for any of that. When I arrived, I thought I would seduce Pietyr Arron—"

"Pietyr Arron? You mean Pietyr Renard?"

"Yes, but no one calls him that anymore. He shed his mother's name like one of their snakes sheds its skin. He might as well be Natalia Arron's own son for the reverence he gets around here."

"You said you thought you would seduce him. So you did not?"

"I *could* not. He clings to Queen Katharine as tightly as he clings to his seat on the Black Council. Perhaps for the same reason."

"That is not true," Elizabeth says. "He loves the queen. He may not love anything else, but he does love her."

"Good," Mirabella says softly. "Even though she is wicked, I am glad that she is loved." Her mind flashes back to Arsinoe and Billy—good, kind Billy, who certainly loves Arsinoe as much as anyone has ever loved a queen of Fennbirn.

"In any case," Bree says, "he would have been the one to watch out for. He would have never trusted you. But it does not matter now."

"Why?"

Bree and Elizabeth stare at her in surprise.

"You have not heard?" Bree asks.

"I have only just arrived. I have heard nothing."

"Pietyr Arron was struck down. He was found in a pool of blood nearly two weeks ago."

"He is dead?"

"Not dead. But he will not wake."

A pool of blood. Mirabella blinks. "Was he stabbed?"

"There wasn't a mark on him," Elizabeth says quietly. "That's the mystery. No one knows what could have caused it, a poisoner with a gift as strong as his. It seems impossible that he could be harmed by anything other than an arrow or a blade."

"Queen Katharine has the best healers in the capital, and one from Prynn, tending to him. Trying to determine what happened. But none can say."

"The poor queen," Elizabeth says. "Him all covered in blood in her old rooms at Greavesdrake Manor, and she was the one who found him!"

Mirabella looks out the window, toward the grand house nestled in the hills. "And she was the one who found him."

Katharine calls Mirabella for supper later than expected. As Bree and Elizabeth escort her up the stairs to the queen's apartments, even the guards five steps ahead must be able to hear the rumbling of Mirabella's stomach.

"It is a good thing Arsinoe is not here," Mirabella murmurs. "She would have eaten half the furniture by now."

Bree glances at her curiously. "What are you going to do about Arsinoe? Will you ask for mercy? Negotiate her pardon?"

Mirabella nods to the guards, and Bree quiets. There are too many ears in the Volroy and too many corridors that carry sound to corners she does not know.

They reach the heavy wooden door, and Bree and Elizabeth embrace Mirabella quickly.

"We will see you soon," says Bree.

"Don't be afraid," says Elizabeth. "She is kind."

They go, and Mirabella straightens her shoulders. "Maybe to you," she grumbles, and reaches out to knock. The door opens. She is surprised to see not a servant answer but Katharine.

"Sister," she says. "Come in."

Mirabella steps into the warm, low-lit space, careful not to make the fire flare when she passes it. She seats herself across from Katharine. The table is round and small. Intimate.

"I like your jewels," Katharine says. "And your gown. You look much better. Perhaps too much better. Perhaps I should make you wear mainland clothes so my people will not love you on sight."

Katharine sits, pretty but restrained in a long-sleeved dress of black muslin, her hands hidden in black gloves. "I hope I did not keep you waiting. I had a special menu prepared." She smiles with dark red lips. "And I wanted you hungry enough not to refuse it." She lays her napkin in her lap and gestures to the covered dishes. "We will have to serve ourselves, I am afraid. I sent the servants away to have you all to myself."

Mirabella uncovers her plate. The food underneath—a small hen stuffed with bread crumbs and herbs, roasted root vegetables shining with butter, and a slice of onion tart—looks perfectly ordinary and smells like a savory dream. But she has never in her life been so afraid of a chicken. *Not even when Billy cooked it*, she thinks, and chuckles.

"Is something wrong?"

"Nothing," Mirabella replies. "Only that you extend an invitation of allyship and I arrive to threats and insults. I sit down to a meal that I am clearly supposed to be too frightened to eat. Is it because of the way you were raised?" She picks up her silver and cuts a sliver of onion tart. "Would Natalia Arron be proud?"

"It is what she would do," Katharine says.

"Perhaps she would not do it in so heavy-handed a fashion." Mirabella takes a bite of hen. "Natalia Arron was a woman of singular power. And those who are truly strong do not need to demonstrate it every five minutes. This is delicious, Queen Katharine. Thank you."

Katharine leans back, and Mirabella forces herself to keep on eating, forces her gift down deep beneath her skin so Katharine will not detect any hint of nerves, no flickering candles, no gusts of wind. She very much doubts that the food is poisoned, even slightly poisoned only to make her ill. But she has not forgotten that her little sister is deadly, and that could change with the very next meal or even during this one, with a sleight of hand and something slipped into her drink.

Katharine looks down at her plate and spins the rings on her gloved fingers before picking up her fork. "Perhaps you should take my demeanor as a compliment. I know you were raised to play this game. The game of reigning. Of politics and favors. I was only raised to win. And then to be moved about like a puppet on a string."

"Have you not met High Priestess Luca?" Mirabella smiles wryly. "The Arrons are not the only ones who are skilled in the art of puppetry. All queens would be made puppets. If they are not careful."

For a moment, Katharine's eyes soften. Then she laughs. "Am I to sympathize? How hard it must have been to be so gifted and such a favorite. Shall we compare scars, then? Did the cruel priestesses give you daily lashings to make your gift rise?"

"It is not a competition. And your own gift seems strong enough."

"Yes. But my gifts took time. Sacrifice. Yours simply . . . was."

Mirabella sits quietly, hoping Katharine will say more. But she returns to her meal with a sigh.

"Why have you come here, Mirabella?"

"Because you asked me to."

Katharine scoffs.

"You asked me," Mirabella goes on, "and it was made to seem I would be welcome. Was that not so? If you were pressured into this alliance or if you have changed your mind, you have only to say so, and I will go."

"You think it would be so easy to leave?"

Mirabella narrows her eyes. She lets her gift loose, and the flame in the fireplace blazes. "I think you will never again take me alive down to those cells."

Katharine stares at the fire, but she is less afraid than Mirabella expected. The way her gaze drifts along the flickers of red and orange seems almost curious. Almost eager, as if she would try to push back.

"I apologize," Katharine says finally. "I do not know why I . . . I did not mean for our meeting to be this way. When I extended the invitation for you to come to Indrid Down, I meant it. I meant to welcome you. Perhaps contention between us cannot be helped. Perhaps it is in our nature. Like the legends say."

"It was not so with Arsinoe and me. It was not so between any of us, once."

"Yet you betray her now."

"I do not betray her," says Mirabella. "Ask me to harm our sister and I will refuse. Ask me to help you as you harm her and I will refuse." She chooses her words with care and keeps firm control of her tone. "This is not about Arsinoe. It is not even really about you."

"Then what is it about? What made you change sides from

the rebellion to the crown? Was it that old ingrained loyalty to tradition? To the ways of the island?" Katharine leans forward, so Mirabella can better see the band of black marked forever into her forehead. "Or was it something else? Perhaps something you saw at Innisfuil that day when I killed Juillenne Milone's mother and cut loose her legion curse."

"Yes," Mirabella says truthfully. She remembers well Madrigal's last words to her. *She is full of them. Full of dead.* And she does not think she was referring to her daughter. The puzzle of those words drove Mirabella here as much as any urging from Luca. "It was Madrigal Milone. That is why I am here."

"No." Katharine slides out of her chair, her movements fast as a striking snake. She grasps Mirabella by the wrist and hauls her up with surprising strength.

"Where are you taking me?" Mirabella asks as Katharine pulls her through one room and then another, until she flings the shutters wide and pushes Mirabella flush to the open-air window so her hair is blown back by the bite of wind off Bardon Harbor.

"Look," Katharine says as she holds her fast, and Mirabella stares out across the water rippling with moonlight. Not far past the northern outcropping of cliffs, not nearly out far enough, lies the mist, thick and constant as a wall. The sight of it makes Mirabella's stomach drop into her shoes.

"The mist," she breathes.

"Yes," says Katharine. "It comes and goes as it pleases. But I saw you fight it back in the valley that day. And I know you fought your way through it to escape after the Queens' Duel. The Legion Queen's rebellion is a problem. But a problem that I can solve." She shoves Mirabella forward again. "But *that*. That is why you are here." She lets go, and Mirabella grasps the edge of the window, hands trembling.

"My Black Council is assembling below. Make yourself ready. You are to go before them."

"Go before them to do what?"

"To plead your cause. To convince them that you are worth keeping alive."

Within minutes, Mirabella finds herself standing in the Black Council chamber. She was placed at the end of the long table, and her hands are clasped before her like a prisoner brought up from the cells to hear her sentence read. Even the faces of those she would call allies—Luca, Bree, to some extent Rho Murtra—are unreadable as stone.

At the head of the table, Katharine crosses her arms. "I do not need to ask where the lines are drawn." She gestures to the High Priestess, Rho Murtra, and Bree. "You three will be for allowing Mirabella to stay. You others"—she waves a hand to indicate the rest—"will be against her. The only question is who of those against her are willing to see if she can help."

"Help," Lucian Arron scoffs. "What was this bargain that brought her to us in the first place? It was not disclosed to us, and though it seems that they know"—he points to Luca, Rho, and Bree—"we cannot wring it out of them."

"Oh, what does it matter?" Bree interjects. "Once the people know that Mirabella has joined with the crown it will only strengthen the queen's position." She looks to Katharine. "When will you make the announcement? Indrid Down should see you both, side by side."

"They should not see her," Antonin Arron hisses. "She should have been dropped by a poisoned arrow the moment she set foot in the city."

The lamps in the room flare, but not from Mirabella, and she casts a look of warning at Bree. Her fire has always gotten the better of her.

"No," says Katharine. "I invited my sister here under a banner of peace. And I will keep my word so long as she meets her end of the bargain."

"What bargain?" Lucian Arron asks again. He and the other Arrons are becoming more and more frustrated. Mirabella would find their wild-eyed expressions amusing were they not currently deciding whether or not to let her live.

"You were not at the battle, Lucian. You did not see her at Innisfuil fighting back the mist. She is the only weapon that we have against it, and until we find a better one, give me real reasons why I should not keep her close. Real reasons," Katharine adds when Antonin opens his mouth.

"On top of her . . . skill with the mist," Luca says slowly, "her presence assures us the allegiance of Rolanth in our growing civil war. Indrid Down and Prynn cannot stand alone against everyone else." She looks at Mirabella and nods, and Mirabella shifts her weight. It will be difficult to be so near Luca again. Difficult to keep her guard up when all she wants is to forget that Luca sided with the Arrons and ordered her execution.

Antonin and Lucian Arron look at each other. They seem miserable. Old. Exhausted. "It goes against tradition," Antonin says.

"That is not enough of a reason," says Katharine.

"And are we just supposed to take her at her word?" Genevieve asks. "That she is to be trusted?"

Katharine's eyes flicker to Mirabella's as Genevieve goes on.

"And you, my queen, have seen her fight the mist. But not all of us have. Who is to say she can do it again?"

That, at least, seems to get Katharine's attention. "What are you suggesting, Genevieve?"

"Test her gift. Send her out into the mist and see if she can banish it."

"And if she cannot?"

Genevieve cocks her head. "Then the mist will take her, and our argument will be solved. And we will really be no worse off than we are now."

"You cannot be serious," Bree says when Katharine appears to consider it. "Using her as defense against the mist is one thing, but to send her into it—"

"We ought to send other elementals along with her." Rho's deep voice cuts through the space and every head turns toward her in surprise. Especially Luca's. "Who is to say that one elemental gift is better than another? Why not test several?

Perhaps we have not needed her from the start."

Katharine drums her fingers on the tabletop. "I feel we are being very rude. Sending my sister out as a sheep to slaughter. Surely, we ought to ask for her consent to this test."

"I consent," Mirabella says.

"Good." Katharine knocks twice on the wood and rises. "Renata, send summons for the five strongest elementals from Rolanth, gifted in wind and storms. And when they arrive, sister"—she smiles—"you will face the mist."

The meeting over, the guards return Mirabella to the king-consort's apartment, with assurances they will stay posted directly outside for her "protection."

Mirabella closes her eyes, and the face she sees is Katharine's. But not the cold, pale-cheeked queen who sat across from her all night. Instead she sees the beautiful little girl who rarely frowned and loved to have her hair brushed.

When she opens her eyes, she sees the mist, still settled over the sea. The same mist she watched creep over the land at Innisfuil and overcome the queensguard soldiers, tearing them apart like strips of cloth.

"Arsinoe," she whispers, and wishes more than anything to be back in Sunpool, where she was no longer a queen but a sister and friend. "It should be you here with your cleverness. I do not know if I can do this."

After the Black Council has disbanded, Katharine lingers in the halls before the chamber. She will never get to sleep tonight. With Mirabella in the capital, her blood is up, and the dead queens are swirling through it like a school of rotting fish. She is so distracted by the sensation, and by her own thoughts, that she does not notice she is not alone until Genevieve says her name.

"Katharine."

Katharine glances at her, annoyed. "Genevieve. What are you doing here?"

"It is late. I thought I might spend the night here rather than taking the carriage back to Greavesdrake." She joins Katharine near the wall. "Will you walk with me a little? You are not the only one left unsettled."

"I am not unsettled." Katharine raises an eyebrow and starts walking. "I am apprehensive. I am undecided."

"Two very unsettling feelings." Genevieve throws a cloak around Katharine's shoulders. "Come. Let us take some air."

They walk out of the castle and into the night, alone except for the constant shadow of queensguard soldiers. At a look from Genevieve, the queensguard fans out and secures the entrances, effectively giving them their privacy.

"I know you wish Natalia was here," Genevieve says. "That even Pietyr was here, rather than me."

"Do not sound so pitiable. Why would I wish for you? Of all the Arrons . . . I like you the least."

To Katharine's surprise, Genevieve does not pout. Instead, she smiles.

"Why should you like me at all?" she asks. "When I was

cruel. When I was ashamed of you, and resented you, as the weak queen we were left with. From the moment you set foot inside Greavesdrake, I knew you would be nothing but an embarrassment. But I was wrong.

"You are a good queen, Kat. All those times I thought you were cowering, you were actually listening. Learning. I was wrong about you, and I am sorry."

Katharine stops. She studies Genevieve suspiciously in the dark, the courtyard lit only by small lamps and the torches of the queensguard. "I half expect that now you will throw a bag of angry snakes at me."

Genevieve shows her hands. Empty.

"Then what are you after?"

"Only a word. I know you never listen to me. That you have no reason to value my advice. But I would caution you against allowing Mirabella to fight back the mist. She is already a legend to the people, and such an act is queenly. They will love her more."

Katharine frowns. "You think I have not thought of that? She is too beautiful, too strong." She balls her hands into fists. The dead queens raise their heads to sniff like hunting hounds at the mere mention of Mirabella. Even they . . . even they would choose her were they given the chance. "But what else am I to do?"

"I do not know. The mist must be dealt with; the port must reopen. I only know that Mirabella will steal the island even if she does not steal the crown."

Genevieve dips her head and says good night. The queensguard moves aside to let her pass back into the castle.

Alone again, Katharine paces the length of the courtyard. Genevieve's caution did nothing to ease her unrest, and her feet carry her through the dark, off the castle grounds. She does not really know where she is going until she smells the salt air rising from the harbor.

Now the queens scurry through her veins for another reason. They fear the mist and so fear the water—with every step closer that she takes, they pull against her skin. She takes a torch from one of the queensguard and motions for them to stay back. They do not need to be told twice.

"Stop," she says to the dead queens as her heels echo against the wooden dock. "What do you have to fear? And why does she not fear it at all? What is so great within Mirabella that is not also great within you? Or within me?" She reaches the end of the dock and holds out the torch. The flame illuminates only a few paces in every direction, but the moon over the water is still mostly full and shows the mist clearly as it stretches toward her.

It curls around the dock, so thick she could use her dagger to slice it into sections. On the shore, the queensguard shifts like nervous horses.

"You are no use to me afraid," she says to the queens, and they, obedient wraiths for once, slip to the surface. They rise to stand with her, and she feels them layering upon her skin like armor. Wisps and tendrils of mist surround the dock on all sides. It is horrifying up close—much worse than it was in the clearing at Innisfuil. It is as if she can see ghosts of shapes inside it. And sometimes, when it thickens, she would swear she senses a solid form.

"You see? It is like it was in the valley. It does not touch us. We are all of the blood. Even you. The old blood."

She reaches out with a gloved hand, expecting the mist to shrink back. Instead, her hand disappears inside it. At first all she feels is mild surprise. A dull ache, as if from cold. And a sudden sense of sadness. Then she starts to scream.

Inside the mist, her hand is torn apart. She hears the snap of her index finger—the sharp pop as her thumb comes out of its joint. At the sound of her cries, the queensguard charges the dock.

"Stay back!"

She bares her teeth, gritting them. She calls to the dead queens, "Help me, stop it," but they do nothing but screech. The sensation of them weakens as if they are leaking out of her with every fat drop of blood that splashes against the wood and falls into the water. Finally, she grasps her arm at the elbow and wrenches herself free, then runs toward shore as fast as her legs will carry her, where her queensguard waits just long enough to swallow her up before running alongside. Only when they reach the top of the hill does she dare look back, and sees the mist still gathered around the dock, still churning and searching for her, and in the dark, she hears splashes, like fish feeding in the water.

"Queen Katharine!"

The soldiers stare openmouthed. Their torches put the injuries to her hand in plain view, the broken, misshapen fingers, the red flesh mixed together with the black fabric of the glove. Blood soaks her to the elbow. It looks like she has been gnawed upon.

Katharine's chest heaves as she pulls her injury close, cradling it.

"Say nothing of this," she orders. "And find me a healer. A discreet one."

SUNPOOL

Arsinoe wakes with a start and strikes out with her fists.

"What—what is it?" Billy asks groggily, jerking awake himself.

Arsinoe exhales and rubs her hands roughly across her face. "Nothing. Just a nightmare."

"A Daphne nightmare?"

"Yes, but it was only a nightmare. It wasn't one of the dreams she sends. Contrary to what you and Mira think, I can tell the difference." She squints up at the windows; the light streaming through suggests it is already late morning. And they are on the floor. All they have are pillows and the small blanket that Arsinoe has kicked up against the wall. "What are you doing here?" she asks. "Why aren't you in our room?"

"Because you're not in our room. I found you here already asleep with your face against the wood. So I fetched these pillows and a blanket." He sits up and stretches his back, wincing.

"I'm sorry," she says, and squeezes his arm.

"It's all right. Have you found anything?"

Arsinoe drags herself toward her work space: knives and bottles and half the inventory from the apothecary shop lay scattered on the solitary table as well as the floor. The jar that contained Madrigal's binding sits open, the letter out and five blood-soaked cords still inside.

"I'm going to try this one." She holds up a vial of rust-colored liquid. "It's the regular tonic, but I stirred in one of Madrigal's blood-soaked cords."

"Well, that's disgusting," says Billy. "So much for breakfast."

Arsinoe rubs her face. She is sick to death of this room, and it is a mess. She is not a careful poisoner and leaves drippings of her concoctions running down the table legs and pooling on the floor.

"Look at this." She gets to her feet and takes up spilled bottles, angrily righting them, then grabs for a cloth and wipes at the spills, even though some have dried into sticky stains. "I never learn." She throws down the cloth and lifts her fist. It takes everything she has not to shove every last bottle and blade onto the floor.

Billy stands behind her and puts his hands on her shoulders. "Hey, it's all right."

"It's not. And don't touch anything!" She slaps him away. "You shouldn't be anywhere near this. Do you want to end up like those two suitors I killed?"

"That was an accident."

"It doesn't matter. They're still dead."

"Listen." Billy reaches out and tugs her away from the table. "I know enough not to lick the spills. And if you're being careless, it's because you're working too hard. How much sleep have you gotten? How much blood have you lost, cutting into yourself?"

She flexes her fingers. Drops of blood have been squeezed from every tip. And her arms are a battlefield of scabs. She thought her days of low magic were finished. Instead, she is into it deeper than ever, deeper than Madrigal, perhaps deeper than any practitioner that came before her.

"I'm not even her daughter, yet I am so like her."

"Like Madrigal," Billy says. "And will you wind up like her?" He gestures to the jars, the knives, and the cloths spotted with red. "There's always a price, isn't that what you said? Low magic always has a price. But you never know what it costs until it collects."

Arsinoe gestures to her weary face. "I think the cost is these big black circles underneath my eyes."

"I don't think you know the cost. Just like Madrigal didn't know that hers would be a knife stuck through her throat."

Billy's eyes are so serious, he hardly looks like himself. Madrigal's death might have been a turn of luck. Murder at Katharine's hands. Or it might have been the low magic. There is simply no way to tell.

"Are you asking me to stop?"

"But I can't ask that, can I? Not when you're doing it for Jules."

"It's not because I want to," she says, but even she hears the lie. Low magic is dangerous, true, but it is potent, and thanks to her queensblood, hers is more potent than most. How can she stop now, in the middle of a war, when she is full-up with one of their best weapons racing right beneath her skin?

"But it will have a price," Billy says. "There's no way around that. No . . . loophole in the contract."

"Maybe it's different for queens."

"Maybe it is," Billy says quietly. "Maybe they pay through the people they love."

Arsinoe swallows hard. The people she loves. Joseph, dead. Jules, out of her mind. Billy takes her by the arms.

"I didn't mean that. I shouldn't have said it. I only thought it because I almost hope that it's true."

"How can you hope that it's true?"

"Because I'm selfish. And it would be better for me if it happened to me or Jules. Just not to you." He chuckles without much humor. "Maybe you should start intensely caring about Emilia."

"That's not funny," Arsinoe says. "And besides, I don't think it would work."

She takes his hand and kicks at the sad blanket crumpled up on the floor. "Let's go find something to eat. And get some fresh air."

"Let's go to the great hall," Billy suggests. "There's bound to be stew. There's always stew. And we'll probably find Luke, and Matthew and Caragh if the baby is sleeping. They found Braddock; did Luke tell you? Someone reported seeing him down the beach, and there he was, picking for shellfish during the low tide."

"They didn't bring him inside?" Arsinoe asks with alarm.

"No. Caragh caught some fish for him, and they let him be. Warned the people here to give him plenty of space. They said that with you so distracted by the rebellion he might be close to wild."

Poor Braddock. He should be off somewhere in a warm den. Instead, the scent of her blood kept him pinned to Sunpool.

They leave her small workroom and walk through the courtyard, where Arsinoe spots Emilia in her bright red cloak. She is standing at the center of a cluster of people, and they are agitated, with crossed arms and broad stances. Poor Emilia. The success of the rebellion hinged upon the strength and the legend of Jules. In the city, work continues: laborers fortify the wall using picks and pulleys and harnessed horses to reclaim stone that has rolled away. Food stores are loaded into the granaries as more people arrive in Sunpool and must be fed. So much being done and so much still to do, but no matter how defiant Emilia is, or how determined, it is not for her that the people come, and it is not her they will follow.

Arsinoe and Billy turn down a quiet alley, in no rush to join the discussion.

"Do you think the rebels are asking about Jules? Or Mirabella?" Arsinoe wonders.

"Probably both. They're growing unsatisfied with Emilia's tales. She's losing her hold on it. On all of it. I wouldn't expect her to keep quiet about Mirabella for much longer."

"I was sure Mirabella would send word by now. To tell us what she's doing. What her plan is."

"Maybe she can't."

"Or maybe there is no plan," Emilia says, stepping out from around the next turn. "And she has abandoned you both to ally with the queen."

Billy shudders and takes a step back. "Gad, how did you get here? Are there two of you?"

"Good Goddess, don't let there be two of her," Arsinoe says, and Emilia cocks an eyebrow.

"I saw you slip away when you spotted the crowd, so I followed you. You ought to be careful, talking in these corridors. The sound carries from one end to the other."

"What was happening out there?" Arsinoe asks. "It seemed tense."

"They want answers. They want their queen." Emilia sighs. "Some of our soldiers are losing faith. If we tell them we face not one but two queens, without a single queen of our own . . ."

"Hey," says Arsinoe, "I'm a queen."

"Of course you are. Forgive me. It is so easy to forget. You have still not gone back to wearing the blacks, and your hair is always full of filth." Emilia reaches out and picks at it. "Is it black? Is it gray?" She pulls out a long piece of yellow straw. "Is it blond?"

Arsinoe swats the straw out of her hand. "Soldiers, you say. Don't you mean farmers and laborers?"

Emilia sighs. "How is Jules?"

"Unchanged."

"Unchanged? But you have been locked up with your poisons and her mother's low-magic curse for days. What is taking so long?"

"It's a binding, not a curse," Arsinoe says, and shoves her aside this time. "And it's not like following a recipe."

"Gather the Milones and meet me in the keep. I want to know everything that you know about the binding." Then she turns on her heel and is gone.

"Grab the Milones and meet me," Arsinoe grumbles through her stew in the great hall. "Like she's the commander of the whole rebellion or something."

"Well, she sort of is," says Billy, grabbing a torn piece of bread from a table as they pass and spreading butter onto it.

Despite Arsinoe's grumbling, they do as they were bid and take Cait, Ellis, and Caragh to meet Emilia in the room outside Jules's chamber in the castle keep.

Mathilde greets them at the door and shows them inside.

"You won't be able to use this room for much longer," Arsinoe says. "Soon, you'll need a space the size of the Black Council chamber."

"Soon we will *have* the Black Council chamber." Emilia smiles. She motions for Cait to sit, but it is Ellis who takes the chair. Cait always prefers to stand, so much so that Arsinoe suspects that when she dies, they will have to erect a special pyre that will allow them to burn her upright.

"I have asked you here because I wish to know what Arsinoe has discovered regarding the legion curse. It has been several days since she was given the low-magic spell and the letter, and I hoped to hear of some progress."

For a moment, Cait stares at Emilia as if she, too, is annoyed by the summons, and Arsinoe hopes she will give Emilia an earful. Even Emilia, a warrior and so full of bluster that she nearly blows herself over, would shrink in the face of stern words from Cait Milone.

"I admit," says Cait, "that I am curious about that as well." She looks at Arsinoe, and Arsinoe swallows. "What have you found, shuttered away in that room of yours?"

Several times Arsinoe opens and closes her mouth before she can find the words to speak. "Not as much as I'd like." Every eye in the room drops with disappointment, and she reaches into her pocket for the vial of blood-infused tonic. "But maybe this."

Emilia unbolts Jules's door, and the Milones and Billy stand outside, necks craned as Arsinoe administers it. She lifts Jules's head and uses her sleeve to dab at the tonic that spills from the side of her mouth. Jules closes her eyes, and they wait. But aside from a shaky sigh, there is no change.

"Nothing," Caragh whispers.

Arsinoe clenches her fists. She knows their disappointment is only because they love Jules so much, but she cannot help wondering what sort of miracle they expected her to perform with some of Madrigal's blood and a piece of paper.

"Did you read the letter, Cait?" she asks.

"I did."

"Then you know what's in it. Or rather, what's not in it. All Madrigal wrote down were the details of the binding spell and instructions for how to remove it if she died. Not much help now, considering it was removed when she was killed."

"But there must be something," Emilia says.

"If you're so sure, why don't you try looking."

"Wait," says Billy. "I'm no expert, but . . . you have the binding spell that Madrigal used. Couldn't you just do the same spell again? Rebind the curse?"

"No," Arsinoe says. "When Madrigal first performed the binding, Jules was a baby. Neither of her gifts had taken root yet. Trying to bind her war gift now would be like trying to stuff an oak back inside an acorn. But—"

"But what?"

She pauses and glances at Jules. Her heartbeat pounds in her ears and sends blood throbbing into her pricked fingertips.

"But maybe it could be tethered."

"Tethered?"

"Tamed, tied down as a loose sail flapping in the wind. Perhaps it could be bound if it were tied to another person."

Arsinoe's thoughts race ahead. It would not be a binding but a sharing. Whoever did it would help Jules to shoulder the load.

"Tethered to someone so that they could be the keeper of the curse?" asks Cait. "Like Madrigal was?"

"No. Not exactly. The curse would be . . . shared. And before you ask, I have no idea what that would mean for the other person. They could lose themselves to the curse as well, over time."

Emilia pounds her fist on the table. "When can you do it?"

"I don't even know if I should. It would be massive. Not like charming a false-familiar bear or even reaching out to old gifts. It's bigger than anything I've ever tried."

Emilia turns to Mathilde. "Do you have any particular feeling about this?"

"Nothing yet," says the seer. "I have seen nothing about Jules's fate. The thread has gone dark. I will keep listening. Keep reading the smoke for visions." That is the only aspect of the gift she possesses, Arsinoe has learned. Visions and momentary flashes. The oracles say it is the stronger side of the sight, but Arsinoe does not know why. It would be much more useful to be able to cast the bones and have an answer when you need one.

"Could it harm Jules?" Ellis asks softly.

"It could harm everything," Arsinoe replies. "It could all go wrong."

"Arsinoe."

At the sound of Jules's creaking whisper, they turn. Jules

lies on her bed of straw, but her eyes are fixed on them, her throat straining to speak. Arsinoe and Emilia nearly dive to her side. It is so good to hear her voice.

"Jules, Jules," Arsinoe says. "You're back."

Emilia smoothes Jules's hair away from her forehead. "I knew you would be."

They fall silent as Jules's lips struggle to form words.

"You have to do it. You have to bind it. I can't . . ." She squeezes her eyes shut and braces against a wave of pain.

"All right," Arsinoe says. "All right, I'll do it."

Arsinoe lays supplies out across the small desk that has become an apothecary table. Bundles of herbs for burning. Candles to burn them with. Two thin, delicately made white scarves, a knife and bandages. Always bandages.

When Madrigal performed the first binding, she bled herself nearly to death and Jules, too. Innocent, tiny, newborn Jules. Arsinoe was not there, just a newborn herself at that time, but she can still imagine the baby's fading, exhausted screams. She squeezes her eyes shut. At least Jules is not a baby anymore.

Across the room, Jules's door opens and Emilia emerges. She looks wrung out, as she always does when she leaves Jules.

"I do not mean to disturb you," the warrior says, leaning down to hug Camden roughly and offer her a strip of dried meat. "Is it . . . going well?"

"The original binding was cast in Wolf Spring, not far from the Milone property beneath the bent-over tree, and if I had a choice, that's where I would attempt this." She looks up at Emilia regretfully. Wolf Spring is too far, and too watched. Innisfuil Valley and the Breccia Domain are out, too, for much the same reasons. "But otherwise . . . all is going according to plan."

"And what," Emilia asks, "is that plan? Who are you going to tether? Who will carry the curse with Jules?"

Arsinoe's brow furrows. That answer was obvious the moment the plan was hatched. "I will, of course."

"You will." Emilia's mouth crooks. "A queen and our one low-magic practitioner. Brilliant. If the tether goes wrong and the curse takes you both, I cannot think of a worse person to have out of control. You might be even more dangerous than she is." She walks to the table and sweeps her hand over the top of it like she would dash the ingredients to the floor. "And of course it would be you. So that Jules could be tied again to your fate. Hers with a queen's."

"How about because it's dangerous and I would rather risk myself than anyone else?" Arsinoe looks away from her and continues working. "Besides, it can't be just anyone. There has to be a bond there."

"How do you know? What do you really know about low magic? Are you a master of it?"

"I'm not," says Arsinoe. "It had a master; she is dead. But I learned from her. When Madrigal bound Jules's curse, she did it out of love and desperation. *A lot* of love and desperation. That's probably why it worked. Low magic is like a prayer, Emilia. A pleading, foolish, costly prayer." She stares at the knife on the table and feels the scar of every cut, every thin, pink line that mars her arms.

"And what will it do to you?" Emilia asks. "Tethering a naturalist-and-war-gifted legion curse when you are already a poisoner?"

Arsinoe narrows her eyes at the warrior as the realization dawns. "You think I should tether it to you."

Emilia stands taller. "I think you should. Why not?"

"A hundred reasons why not."

"It might go easier with me, as I already carry the war gift. I may not even notice the extra burden. And then you could maintain your strength; you would not have to bleed yourself so much during the spell."

Arsinoe turns away and selects a piece of amber to burn, for clarity. "Is that what you're after? A stronger gift for yourself? Maybe even a legion curse of your own so you won't have any need of Jules as your queen. But that's probably not what's—"

Arsinoe gasps as Emilia shoves her into the wall, hard enough to take her breath away, and harder than Emilia could have done with only her hands in such close quarters. That was the war gift. Arsinoe shoves back and Emilia lets go.

"Do not ever say anything like that to me again," Emilia says.

"Fine. Ow."

Emilia holds a hand out to help her off the wall. "I am sorry. Are you all right?"

"Yes."

"You are not the only one who loves her, you know."

"I've known Jules for my entire memorable life. You've known her less than a year. How can you already love her so much?"

Emilia lowers her eyes. It is the first time Arsinoe has ever seen her blush, and blush furiously. "Because I love her in a different way. A way that doesn't take so long."

Arsinoe blinks at the warrior's reddened cheeks. "Oh."

"How long did it take you to realize what you felt for Billy? Not your whole life."

"Billy," Arsinoe says. "Oh!"

"You keep saying, 'Oh.'"

"I know. I'm sorry." She watches as Emilia's cheeks gradually regain their normal deep shade. "Does . . . Jules know? Does she feel the same?"

"No, and I don't know," Emilia says, and flashes her most confident smile. "But she will, if we can make her well enough to consider it." She steps close to Arsinoe and takes her by the arm. "Let me carry the tether. I won't fail her. I promise."

INDRID DOWN

Mirabella stands at a window in the king-consort's apartment, fingers drumming against the sill as she looks over the city. Indrid Down is ugly in winter. Dark and gray and full of smoke. And it smells. Stale almost, as if it does not get enough wind off Bardon Harbor to clear it out. It is nothing like Rolanth, where the winds smell of evergreen and the thin ice that forms along railings and on the white stone is crisp and clear as crystal.

It is almost sunset. She is to face the mist tonight, in the dark, with Katharine and the Black Council watching from a safe distance at the top of the hill. The port at Bardon Harbor will be cleared of people. So no one but the Queen Crowned and her council would know whether Mirabella succeeded or failed.

That morning, she watched from that same window as a line of carriages brought the elementals Katharine had summoned from Rolanth. Her brave "volunteers" who have the gift of wind and weather. Katharine will launch them on the same barge as Mirabella. Challengers, she calls them, when they are truly more like sacrifices.

"Come," says Bree from behind her. "It is nearly time. We should get you into your gown."

"Why dress me at all? Only to push me out into the dark before nothing and no one?" She turns and lets Bree do what she will. But she holds her hand up at the corset. "For this, I will need to breathe."

Bree nods. "A poisoner contraption, anyway," she says as she tosses it back into the trunk. "Though it does do nice things for the breasts."

Mirabella smiles despite her dark mood. At least Bree will be there. One friendly face upon the shore.

She raises her arms as Bree slips the simple black dress over her head. It is light and unadorned, no fancy embroidery or lace, and the cloak she layers on top of it is similarly plain. Nothing expensive, in case she is dragged to the bottom of the harbor in it.

Outside the door, the guards announce that the queen is coming, and Bree steps aside. Katharine sweeps into the room, followed by two servants carrying trays of tea.

"Good. You are nearly ready." Katharine stands before her with her gloved hands clasped demurely at her waist. She gestures to the tea. "Something to settle your nerves?"

"No thank you."

"A little something in the stomach can sometimes help. I have brought tarts. Made with dried fruit and preserves, which we must all get used to if you cannot banish the mist by the summer."

"That is very kind of you."

"I wanted you to have something worthy, in case it is the last thing you ever eat." She smiles sweetly, and behind her, the lamps flare so hot that they char the surface of the glass. "Now, now." Katharine wags a finger. Mirabella's eyes narrow. There is something odd about the way she is using her hands. Only one of them moves. Like there is something wrong with the other. "Save your gift for the mist."

"I am." Mirabella smiles, equally sweetly. "That fire was from Bree."

Bree clears her throat and leaves. "I did not expect to be tattled upon," she whispers as she passes, and Mirabella chuckles.

"I would have rathered it be Elizabeth here with you," Katharine says after Bree is gone. "I am fond of her little woodpecker. I brought a small loaf of nut bread for him."

"That is very kind."

"Do not sound so surprised. I am kind. When I can be."

The tone of Katharine's voice makes Mirabella wither. Youngest triplet or not, the crown has settled upon Katharine and made her more substantial, and cast Mirabella and Arsinoe off as ghosts.

"For what it is worth," Katharine says, "I was reluctant to agree to Rho's suggestion of other elementals."

"It is worth nothing," says Mirabella, "if they die."

"Do not make it seem simple. Being the Queen Crowned is not as easy as right or wrong. What would you do if you were to face what I face? I have spoken to the priestesses since the Ascension, Mirabella. You have done your share of sacrificing."

Mirabella's stomach twists, remembering the priestess she buried beneath the rocks in practice for the Quickening.

"The elementals you summoned . . . are they willing at least?"

"Of course. They have been promised rich rewards simply for making the attempt." Katharine reaches for a tart, again with the same hand. "To be honest, they are not even afraid. Not with you there."

"And you resent me for that. That they think I am so strong. But who knows how strong I really am? You were there at Innisfuil; you saw how the mist tore through your soldiers and all of the people I could not save."

Katharine nods. "Pressure," she says thoughtfully. "True, there is always pressure. But just once, I would like to be given the benefit of belief rather than the expectation that I will fail. Perhaps we are worrying for nothing. Perhaps with you there, the mist will not even rise."

"You do not really think that."

"No," Katharine says. "The mist has risen for every ship that tries to leave the port. But nor do I hope that you fail." She rubs at the black band tattooed across her forehead, perhaps unconsciously, her other hand dangling near her waist.

"They want me to kill you, you know. The Black Council. If the elementals are successful and we do not need you to fight the mist. Since no one really knows you are here, it will be an easy enough thing to hide. They say you are another queen, and it is the natural solution. But do not worry. Once again, the High Priestess saved you. 'You cannot kill her,' she said. 'For even if you find elementals who are strong enough to face the mist, their gifts grow stronger with an elemental queen.'"

"That is a very fine imitation of Luca."

Katharine chuckles. "Good old Luca. Forever at your back. Even finding a way to attribute the entire elemental gift to you. But it worked. Not even Lucian could say a word. So I suppose I get to keep you, at least until both wars are over."

"Luca is not always at my back. She would have overseen my execution. In the end, I failed her, and she chose you." Mirabella swallows. She hates the thickness that comes into her voice at the mention of Luca's betrayal. She is still too soft-hearted.

"If it makes you feel better, she did not really choose me," says Katharine. "She chose the one she always chooses."

"The Goddess," says Mirabella. "The island. Like we all do."

"Like we all do." Katharine casts a look to the window, all shadows now, the only points of light in the city from fires and lamps. "Are you ready?" she asks without looking at Mirabella. "It is time."

* * *

Bardon Harbor is eerily quiet as Mirabella and the elementals are loaded onto the barge. Even though it would naturally be subdued, the fishers and dockworkers gone home and the sea-birds back in their nests, the silence hangs like a pall. There is not a soul out tonight, and no faces peek from the windows. There are only the queensguard and the Black Council and Queen Katharine herself upon the shore.

Beneath Mirabella's feet, the barge rocks gently back and forth. Normally, she finds waves soothing, but these only make her sick to her stomach.

The elementals who responded to the summons line up on her left and right. Before they boarded the barge, Katharine draped a medallion around each of their necks: a silver circle, like a coin, bearing the queen's seal. A mark of favor, from Katharine the Undead, hung from a length of braided black cord.

"It is heavy," says the boy next to her as he cups it in his hands. "I know she meant it as a blessing, but just now it feels like—"

"An anchor," says a woman on her left, and they laugh.

They are afraid. Whether or not they chose to come does not change that. Mirabella looks at each of them in the torch-light. She has seen them all before—their faces glowing in the lit candles of the temple or receiving blessings on a festival day—but she does not know them well. The boy on her right is even a Westwood, one of the cousins who would sometimes visit the house with his sisters. She should have expected to see a Westwood there. Their gifts are among the strongest in the city. She remembers the boy's name: Eamon Westwood. He had a fierce gift of wind. But she never saw him call a storm.

At a nod from Katharine, they send the barge out into the bay. They must propel themselves, using their gifts to control the currents, as not a single member of the queensguard could be compelled to row. As they go farther and farther from shore, their nerves start to betray them: gusts of wind come in sudden blusters, uncalled for and uncontrolled. When they arrived, they looked so sadly hopeful, dressed in their best as if they expected a grand ceremony.

"The queen tells me you have come of your own free will," Mirabella says.

"We have," says Eamon. "We were there when the mist rose in Rolanth. When it devoured the Midsummer Festival. We should have done more then, but . . ." He lowers his eyes, shakes his head.

They have seen what the mist can do. They know what to expect. That should make her feel better, but it does not.

Do not hate the mist, Luca whispered to her before they set off. *It is still our protector. We still have need of it. We must only hold it at bay. Discover what will appease it.*

Appease it, Mirabella thinks. *Train it, like a dog.*

She has always thought of the mist as an embodiment of the Goddess. An extension of her, just as the blood that runs through her own veins.

We can try to know the Goddess's will, she thinks as if she were speaking to Luca. *We can fumble about and try to please her. Or we can fight.*

In Mirabella's experience, fighting has worked better.

They are close now, close enough to see it in the distance: a barrier of fog, stretched out in both directions and straight into the sky, much farther than their torchlight can show. The barge beneath them slows as a few of their gifts slacken and hesitate. But it is too late now to turn back.

"In Moorgate Park, I saw it reach down a girl's throat and tear out her insides," Eamon says.

Mirabella nods. "At Innisfuil, I saw the same."

"What are we doing? Are we mad?"

"Do not think about that now!" shouts the woman to Mirabella's left. "Call your wind. Push it back!"

Mirabella takes a breath and feels her gift rise alongside the others'. Their courage makes her proud. As does their strength. The wind they call must be felt all the way back onshore. It must tear through the tents of the marketplace. The waves that rise will send the moored boats crashing against their docks.

But they were not fast enough. In the space of a blink, the mist has surrounded the barge. Thick arms of it creep over the side, moving so slowly and gently that not even Mirabella tries to evade it. Which is, of course, what it wants.

"Call your storms," Mirabella says. But she does not know if she is heard. The mist has swamped the barge. She can no longer see the rear of it, and the light from the torches has been swallowed, rendering the air a sickening shade of orange. In mute horror, she watches as the mist slips over the first elemental like a shroud. When it draws back, the space where the girl stood only a breath before is empty.

"Where did she go?" Eamon screams.

"I don't know!"

They search, turning in all directions, their wind whipping around them like a tornado.

"Oh, Goddess," the woman to Mirabella's left moans. "The blood."

Where the elemental girl had stood, the deck is splashed with bright red blood, as if someone had thrown out a butcher's bucket.

"Storms!" Mirabella shouts as they start to panic. "Stay together!" Her own storm rises, but it is fractured; she is distracted by the noise and the sight of what remains of the girl. The woman to her left wanders toward the blood, and the mist flows over her. One second she is there, and the next all is white, and a sickening scream rings out, cutting off abruptly at the sound of popping, as a hand of clenched knuckles. Worse still is the ripping noise that follows.

"I can't . . . ," Eamon sputters. He falls to the deck and grabs hold of Mirabella's skirt. "I can't!"

"You can! Focus!" She calls her storm again, eyes to the sky where thunderheads gather beside the moon. Crackles of lightning give them their eyes back, showing the strange shadows that move through the mist. "Wind," she whispers. And the wind obeys. The elementals who remain still fight beside her;

she feels their push added to her own. Their wind cuts through the gray, the diseased whiteness that surrounds them. But it is not enough. It flows through the mist like a sieve, and the mist keeps advancing.

Has it grown stronger since she last faced it? Has it taken her measure and learned new tricks?

"Ah! Help me!"

She looks down and sees Eamon half swallowed. She grasps his arm and pulls him closer as he screams.

She cannot save them. She will watch them all torn apart, turned inside out, one by one.

"Into the water!" She drags Eamon to the side and throws him overboard. "Dive! Swim for shore!"

Above, the storm bears down upon the mist. She grits her teeth, sends it coursing through the center of the blemished gray whorl. She sends lightning to crack it from the inside. Gusts to churn the waves and force the mist back to sea. Her blood sings with the rage of the weather, rage this time, not joy or freedom; she is not running on the cliffs of Shannon's Blackway or singing a sailor safe. Her rage is blacker than the clouds that pummel the mist, louder than the wind that screams in her ears. And before it, the mist recoils. It comes apart. It turns tail and runs.

Mirabella holds the storm high long after she could let it rest. She holds it until the last weak wisps of white disappear back into the darkness.

* * *

Katharine and the Black Council watch the battle from the safety of shore, gathered before their torches, dark clothing and cloaks giving them the appearance of a murder of crows. When the elementals had cast themselves out to sea, it had taken so long for the barge to reach its destination that Cousin Lucian and Paola Vend had grown bored and started to idly complain about the state of the docks. But since the mist rose, Katharine has heard nothing aside from faint, fast breaths.

She sees them in her periphery, watching, their sight extended by spyglasses. Katharine does not bother with one. The mist is vast. She sees it swallow the barge easily enough. And her sister's storm is impossible to miss booming out over the water.

They feel it, too: as the wind flaps through their clothing, and the rain, stinging cold and miserable, sticks their cloaks to their bodies.

"They are ditching into the water," Antonin says. "They have failed."

"How many are left?" asks Rho. "We should have had launches ready to retrieve any who made their escape." She turns and barks to the queensguard, giving orders without waiting for Katharine to agree. But that is all right. She would have agreed, anyway.

"There's blood," Bree says, and gasps. "So much blood, on the deck."

"Come on, sister," Katharine whispers. "Save them."

And as if she heard, Mirabella's storm twists down upon the

mist, joining the battle like lines of fresh cavalry. It batters the white down into the water and tears bits of it off to disappear. Just below her skin, Katharine feels the dead queens stretching toward Mirabella in awe. She cannot blame them. More than once she has wished that she were born the elemental. A storm like that would be a very useful pet to have. She watches the lightning strike and crackle across the sky in bright veins. She can see just when Mirabella tells it to attack and just what she asks it to do.

When the storm weakens, the torches on the barge relight, signaling that it is over, and that the elementals live.

"Launch the boats, Rho, like you said." She turns to the stunned queensguard and claps her hands at them. "Now! Hurry! Make sure that they have aid!"

They go, and Rho goes with them. Katharine faces the rest of her Black Council. Bree looks so relieved that she may weep, and Luca's lips curl in a small pleased smile. The others bow their heads, shivering in the winter wet.

"I do not need you to say that I was right to bring her here," Katharine says. "But are you satisfied?" She cranes her neck to the men at the rear. "Lucian? Antonin? Are you satisfied?"

"Yes, Queen Katharine," they mumble, and nod contritely.

She turns back toward the water. They will be safe now. Her port, and her people, will have nothing to fear. If she has to send Mirabella out as an escort to every fleet of ships, if she has to lash her to the prow like a living figurehead—then so be it. She will gift her sister jewels and the finest gowns. People say that she is small and vindictive, but they are wrong. She is willing to bury the past as long as the island is safe.

"But it is only a temporary solution," Antonin adds. "Only a stalemate. And perhaps not even that. There is only one of her; she cannot protect the entire island."

"A stalemate is still preferable to the nothing you have suggested," Katharine says, and grits her teeth.

The barge returns, escorted by Rho and the queensguard boats. Mirabella steps onto the dock. Three elementals have survived and join her. Two appear uninjured, but the third, a young man not much older than the queens themselves, holds an arm that is bleeding and mangled to the shoulder. Seeing him, Katharine's heart is heavy. Perhaps she should have refused Rho's suggestion to test the other elementals. Yet it is a small price to pay, in order to know. Now no other elemental will be asked to do the same.

Mirabella walks to Katharine with her chin held high. She is soaked, and her cloak hangs askew. The simple dress they put her in has been stretched and torn, and her black hair is slicked down her back. But she is still beautiful.

"You are pleased?" Mirabella asks.

"Of course I am pleased. You did it. You are everything that you promised. I could almost embrace you."

"I lost two. And Eamon requires a healer."

"He will have the best of them. Let us return to the Volroy to celebrate."

"And to keep your council from turning blue," Mirabella

says, with a worried look at Luca. "But you are not shivering."

"How could I after the exhilaration of what I just witnessed?" Katharine uses her unhurt arm to draw her cloak more tightly around her. She has grown careless these past months, showing the gifts she borrows from the dead. The dead elemental queens have made sure that tonight she feels no chill.

She gestures for Mirabella to walk ahead to the waiting carriages and feels the dead queens surge toward her, like a wave. They rise so forcefully that she feels them in her throat, as she did the day they escaped from her and entered Pietyr, and the thought of them taking over Mirabella fills her with dread. Mirabella is far too strong a vessel. In her their wickedness would be unleashed and unstoppable. She had thought, perhaps, that her sister could in time help her shoulder the burden of the dead queens. To help her control them, or find the strength to banish them back to the Breccia Domain for good. But she sees now that is impossible. She must find another way.

The dead queens stretch their necks toward her sister and she snaps them back.

"No," she says, and clenches her teeth together. "You cannot have her."

SUNPOOL

The morning that they are to perform the tethering spell, Arsinoe leaves the city and goes to look for her bear. Inside the gates, there are too many faces and questions that she has no answers to. So as soon as she can get away, she stuffs a small sack with dried apples and swipes a few of the larger fish from the kitchen before heading out to the woods.

Thanks to the low magic that ties them together, Braddock knows that she is coming, and it is not long before the shrubbery rustles and he bursts through to stand up before her on his hind legs.

"Come down, boy," Arsinoe squeaks. She holds out a dried bit of apple, and his big lips take it from her fingers, gentle as a baby. He shoves his head into her chest and she hugs him, burying her nose in his fur until she feels him rooting around her sack for more apples and the fish.

"Hold on, hold on. Let's find us a nice rock to picnic on." They walk together toward the beach, and the flat black stones that line the northern edge. There they hunker down in the long dune grass, almost thick enough to obscure her completely, though there is only so much that can be done to conceal the rump of a great brown bear.

Arsinoe rubs Braddock's head as he eats, and steals a bit of dried apple. But even with him beside her, she has never felt more alone. No one inside the city walls wants to know about the low magic. None of those who know of it wish to see it performed. Not even Billy, who would stop her if he could. And Mirabella is gone.

Arsinoe hopes that she is all right, and that she knows what she is doing. She hopes that she will come back soon.

"She was always the most levelheaded of the three of us," she says to the bear. "Well . . . except when she's really angry."

Braddock sniffs the air, full of fish now and happy to let her lean against him. They look across the beach out at the cold northern sea. There is no sign of mist. There has not been a single mist attack off the coast of Sunpool, despite consistent reports of continued attacks on the capital. Emilia often fixates on that fact, as further evidence that their side is right.

"This spell today," she says to the bear. "It won't be that different from the way you and I were bound. And it didn't hurt you, did it?"

He turns his cheek, a request for a good scratch. But she is lying, of course. The tethering spell will be much harder.

Much bloodier. And the link it creates between Jules and Emilia will be—

"Unbreakable," she says softly.

"How are we feeling today?" Arsinoe asks as she tucks Jules's blankets up tighter around her throat. The tonic she infused with Madrigal's blood has worn off, so she keeps her fingers well away from Jules's teeth, and does not look her in the eye. She cannot stand to see the bright red blood streaked through the whites or the sickly yellow as vessels that have burst attempt to heal. But even though she does not look, she can feel Jules's eye on her. Tracking her, without a drop of kindness. It feels like being hunted, and when Camden growls, Arsinoe flinches away.

"I can't wait until this is over and you're back to your old selves," she says. Camden growls once more and then settles on top of Jules's legs.

The small room at the top of the tower feels stuffier than usual today, full of new scents forced into the stale air. Amber resin and hot wax blend with herbs and oils and the lingering aromas of sickness and cougar. And it is too quiet. No sounds besides her own breath and the scrape of her shoes against the floor. No one in the room with her since Billy, who accompanied her and helped to assemble the ingredients for the spell.

"Are we bringing her out?" Emilia asks, and Arsinoe spins. The warrior leans over the desk and picks up the piece of amber. She sniffs it and makes a face.

"No. It'll be easier to go in to her. And I wish you'd stop sneaking around like that. Can't you scuff your heel on the stones? Or clear your throat when you arrive?"

"I'm sorry."

Arsinoe sighs. Emilia is not sorry, not really. She is pleased that Arsinoe finds her warrior ways unsettling. Arsinoe joins her beside the desk and makes one last check of her supplies. She leaves the door to Jules's chamber open and stiffens when Jules groans.

"How long has it been since she had any tonic?" Emilia asks.

"A day. I don't want to give her more in case it interferes with the tethering."

Emilia studies Jules through the open door. "That's all right. Her chains will hold. Though maybe we ought to chain Camden."

"You're welcome to try." She takes up her knife and tests the edge against her forefinger. "I've been thinking."

"Oh?"

"Maybe we should both hold the tether. Like, you and I."

Emilia frowns.

"Is that how it works? Spread the legion curse like butter across a piece of bread? Why do we not bring Caragh, then, and give her a bit, too? Why not your Billy and"—she gestures back toward the door with a jerk of her head—"the cat?"

"I'm just saying—"

"You're saying you do not trust me with her on my own."

"I don't trust you with her on your own," Arsinoe says, and her eyes flash. "But that's not what I meant. I'm saying it might ease the burden on you."

Emilia looks down at the desk, perhaps a little guiltily. "Forgive me. I should not have been so sharp. But I think . . . I will be fine."

"Maybe you're right. Maybe with your war gift you won't feel the curse at all."

"But we are not only binding the war gift," Emilia says. "We are binding the legion curse. She will still be war-gifted?"

"We're making Jules well by any means necessary. I don't really know what will happen. Maybe nothing. Maybe it will drive us all mad."

"It did not drive Madrigal mad," Emilia says. "And is it not the same spell? You aren't changing much."

"I'm changing the intent. And it's the intent that matters."

Emilia exhales and looks to the ceiling, as if for patience. She does not understand the intricacies of low magic, its strength and its sinister nature. She seems nearly as skeptical as Billy when he first heard of it, and Arsinoe is possessed suddenly by the urge to prove it to her before they start, to slice through her skin and let her feel the rush of the magic.

"It's nearly time," Emilia says. "Will you tell me what it entails?"

Arsinoe stares into the light of a flickering candle. Days are so short in the winter, and the light coming into the keep has already begun to slant and turn gold. "Madrigal bled herself into a cord, and bound Jules tightly with it, round and round. Then she bled Jules into a cloth and tied that cloth up in bloody cord. The cloth knot she buried beneath the bent-over tree. The rest of the cord she kept, and that is what Cait brought to me."

"That sounds like a lot of blood and many cuts. I am going to tie the cat." Emilia goes to the wall and unfurls the rope that is attached to it.

"She should be near. Jules might need her."

"Aye, she might need her to rip our throats out."

"I can't explain it, Emilia. But her familiar should be at hand."

"Very well." Emilia stalks to her and snatches her knife, then uses it to cut the rope free from the wall. "I will hold her, then, while you make the cuts to Jules. And I will hope for your sake that she doesn't get away."

In the room, on Jules's legs, Camden has begun to hunch her back, sensing their intent. She hisses as Emilia tosses the loop of rope around her neck and digs her claws into the floor as she is dragged away from Jules.

"It is not for long," Emilia says to her through her teeth. But Camden keeps on hissing and spitting just the same.

With Camden secured, Arsinoe brings her supplies into the room and spreads them out on the floor. A small sharp knife, whose blade glows orange in the light. Two lengths of thin white scarf. The herbs. The oil, for anointing Jules and Emilia, to be mixed with Arsinoe's queensblood. It will be her link to them, as she is not a part of the tether.

"Not even cut yet and my hands are shaking," she whispers.

"You are not the only one," Emilia says as she keeps the cougar's rope taut. "I have never before seen low magic cast. I am wondering about the price. They say that there always is one."

"Yes. And it's usually more than you want to pay."

"Jules's mother practiced this magic often. Do you think she paid with her death?"

"Maybe."

"It would seem an unfair price," Emilia says, "when the collection of it undid the low magic it was purchasing. But then again . . . for seventeen years of her daughter well . . . and I think she would say it was a bargain."

"You didn't know Madrigal very long, did you?" Arsinoe asks, and Emilia laughs.

"Maybe it was not the price at all," Emilia says. "Perhaps our price will be something we will never know. A man from some small village falling off the other side of the mountain. Some girl in the capital run over by a carriage."

"Is that better?"

"It is less painful, since we would never know." Emilia's eyes harden. "And it doesn't matter. There is no other way. What price in the world would be too high? What cost would keep you from trying to save her?"

Arsinoe looks down at Jules. At her bloodshot eyes watching her with nothing but hatred.

"Those scars you have," Emilia says, "that you would hide

behind a mask. They are the finest part of you. Now let us earn a few more."

Arsinoe takes up her knife. With the first cut across the back of her hand, the air in the room changes. It becomes charged, fresher, as if the keep itself is inhaling. Her queensblood drips into the bowl of oil, and the hairs on the back of her neck prickle as she dips her finger and bends to smear the blend across Jules's forehead. Jules—whose lips had drawn back to show the tips of her teeth—relaxes. Her eyes lose their predatory edge. She does not so much as blink when a little of the blood runs down the bridge of her nose to pool in the corner of her lid.

As Emilia tightens her grip on Camden, Arsinoe pauses. "Wait. Bring her here." She marks the cat between the ears, red painting her fur and turning it spiky. Camden sits down.

"What . . . is that doing?" Emilia asks as she drops the rope and comes to kneel before Arsinoe when she beckons. Arsinoe places the queensblood on her, and she shivers.

"It is preparing the way."

"I did not really believe," Emilia murmurs, her voice odd and faraway. "Even as I hoped it would work, I did not really believe."

Arsinoe does not respond. The low magic has its hold on her now, too. She feels her heartbeat in rhythm with the island, her whole body thrumming. The pain in her hand is a spark as more blood leaks with every pulse.

She lights a bundle of herbs with the candle flame and

blows the bundle out to breathe in the cloud of fragrant smoke, the scent sending her even further into the spell. Her thoughts rise from her head and float. She has to blink hard to bring her mind back into her body and focus.

Intent is everything.

She takes up a length of the scarf and holds Jules's arm. Quickly, she makes the cuts, working around the chains: three shallow slashes and the blood runs forth. She wraps the cuts around and around with the scarf and the white soaks red.

"Emilia, give me your arm."

The warrior does not hesitate. She is no stranger to pain, and when Arsinoe makes cuts to mirror the ones she made in Jules, Emilia seems to relish it even as she grimaces. She watches the blood run through the scarf that Arsinoe wraps her in and stares as her blood pools on the ground. "You are wasting it."

Arsinoe looks down. She is right. The small puddle of Emilia's blood is joined and blended with a small puddle of Jules's. Blindly, Arsinoe reaches behind her for a piece of cloth or rope or ribbon, but what she finds is a scrap of bread. She shoves it into the mingled blood and lets it soak before placing it into her mouth and biting down.

The blood touches her tongue and she rocks back, the taste and sickening thickness enough to make her gag. She is barely aware of her movements as she joins Jules's and Emilia's hands, making more cuts into her palms and thumbs, joining their scarves with knots. She squeezes her fist and turns it over, lets her queensblood drip into her opposite hand. Then she grasps the joined knots.

Jules and Emilia jerk as the queensblood meets theirs, and the candle flares, hot enough to burn it down to a nub.

"How much more?" Emilia moans as their blood spreads across the floor. There is more blood than there should be for such shallow cuts.

"As much as you can bear to lose," Arsinoe replies.

A gust of wind blasts through the room, and she and Emilia duck as their hair whips into their eyes.

"Don't let go," Arsinoe calls as the wind rages. "Hold on!"

With gritted teeth, she shields her face with her knife-wielding arm and cracks an eye open. Camden has collapsed. Her paw has drifted into the pooled blood, and Arsinoe tries to nudge it back with her foot. But crouched as she is and fighting the wind, it nearly makes her fall over.

Jules's and Emilia's fingers start to loosen inside her grip. Jules's eyes roll back. Emilia's head droops.

Arsinoe squeezes more blood from her hand and soaks the ends of the scarves. Then she knots them again. Three more knots, adding more queensblood each time, until her head begins to swim and the sound of the wind is far away.

That is it. That is all. She slips the blade of the knife beneath the scarf and cuts it away from Jules. Then from Emilia. Their arms fall, and Emilia slides onto her side, fingers feebly reaching to apply pressure to her wounds.

Arsinoe looks down. Her hands are coated and sticky with

red, already drying. She uses her knife to cut the long, dangling lengths of scarf, separating the pieces from the knots, and rolls them carefully into the jar beside the last of Madrigal's blood-soaked cord.

The knots that joined Jules and Emilia together are soaked through. There is so much of their blood and her blood that holding them in her hands is like holding a freshly harvested heart. She drops the mess into a small burlap sack.

On the floor, Jules and Emilia lie motionless, still bleeding. She hurries to her desk and retrieves bandages to pack and bind their cuts. Now that the spell is finished, the wounds are not so bad. They are not deep and will leave only thin scars. In a few years, they may fade completely.

"Arsinoe."

At first she does not hear Jules speak. She is too distracted by her task.

"It worked," Emilia cries. "Arsinoe! She is here!" She fumbles with the chains. "Get these off her!"

"Wait." Arsinoe holds her breath, watching Jules. And then Camden nuzzles Jules's cheek and purrs.

"All right," Arsinoe says, and takes the key to the chains out of her pocket.

Billy and Mathilde look down from the castle upon the deserters leaving through the city gate. The Legion Queen has finally been gone too long from view, and the rebellion has begun to leave in earnest. They have no doubt heard, too, the rumor that is circulating: that Queen Mirabella has left them and gone to fight at Queen Katharine's side.

"It's not your fault, you know," Billy says to Mathilde. "We both tried to convince them to stay. I used every charming trick I know on these deserting rats." He had even thought he had changed a few minds, only to wake the next morning and find they had snuck out in the night. "They're just tired. It's not easy being uprooted from home and living in strange, makeshift spaces."

"You must be tired as well," Mathilde says. "You, too, are far from home in a strange place. You must care for your exiled queen a great deal."

"Yes. A great deal."

Down below, a cart of young rebels leaves, five of them packed in behind the driver and clutching their small sacks of belongings.

"Oh, would you look at that," Billy says, and throws up a hand. "They're taking one of the best mules!"

Mathilde smiles. "It was probably their mule to begin with." But her eyes follow the cart sadly. "Let a few of them go. The true-hearted will stay, and it will cause the crown to underestimate us when their spies report how easily we fall apart."

"Spies?"

She nods, and Billy looks around as if he might see one right there in the empty room with them.

"How many? How long have you known?"

"So far we have identified three. There are undoubtedly

more. It is not unexpected."

"What will you do with them?" he asks warily.

"Better to know your spies than to kill them and have to search for new ones sent to take their place." She nods toward the gate. "Another mule leaving."

"Another mule?" Billy leans out the window. "Go on, then," he half shouts. "Go on with the lot of you! Who needs you, anyway?" He turns his back on them and crosses his arms until he hears shouts as both mules and both carts come clattering back through the gate. "What, they're coming back?"

"No," Mathilde says as they crowd the sill together. "*She* is back." She points to the crowd quickly gathering in the square below. At the people racing through the streets to join it. And at the head of them all, Camden leaps through the air and swats with her good paw. She roars and hisses and lashes her tail back and forth. Behind her stands Jules, flanked by Arsinoe and Emilia.

Emilia places an arm around each and raises her voice to the people.

"Our two queens return," she declares, triumphant. "Queen Jules! The Legion Queen! Queen Arsinoe!" It does not take long for the crowd to take up the chant.

"Our two queens," says Billy, looking down. "As in, against their two queens." He shakes his head. "Emilia is so clever."

"She is," says Mathilde. "And she is determined to win this, one way or another."

THE FOUR QUEENS

THE VOLROY

Up on the topmost battlements of the West Tower, Mirabella takes some air with Bree and Elizabeth.

"Not even Pepper likes to be up this high," Elizabeth says. Inside her hood, the woodpecker chirps with agreement, and she edges away from the cutout in the stone.

"He flies across mountains to ferry messages," says Bree, "yet he is afraid of the height of the tower?"

"He flies across mountains, true, but never so far from the ground!"

Mirabella smiles as her friends talk. She leans back, lets the wind ruffle her black dress and whip through her hair. This is her favorite place in the capital by far. Or at least her favorite of what she has seen. She has been allowed only in the Volroy and the most secluded of its gardens, always flanked by armed queensguard soldiers. Up here on the battlements, though, the soldiers wait on the stairs just inside. Perhaps they do not care for heights either.

"Come here." She holds her left hand out for Elizabeth to take. "I will not let you fly away."

"But will you let me?" Bree asks, spinning, her elemental gift also delighting in the cold gusts and clouds. "You could call a gale to carry me out to sea and back again! Then set me down gently in the courtyard."

"Could I?" Mirabella laughs.

"It is so good to have you back again, Mira," says Elizabeth, grasping her hand tightly. "And I'm sure that the queen will allow you more freedom as soon as she declares your allegiance before the city." She sidles closer and Mirabella wraps her in her billowing black cloak. "The people will be so happy; even in the temple, there are rumblings of approval."

"That is surprising," says Mirabella. "Two queens together . . . two queens alive after an Ascension . . . It is not allowed to be."

"So perhaps now you see the truth of the temple," Bree says to Elizabeth. "It is not tradition but the word of the High Priestess that determines their course."

"Do not be so hard on them, Bree," Mirabella says when Elizabeth frowns. "They have seen things that no other generation has seen. The mist rising. A legion-cursed girl who is strong as a queen. Two traitor queens disappeared into the mist only to show up again alive and well. The temple does not know what to do. So they listen to Luca, because she is the Goddess's voice to the people."

In the whip of the wind, she cannot hear Bree's muttered

reply. But she sees the bitter twist of her lips, and it fills her with regret. When they were children, Bree was always so pious. Wild, of course, always wild, but she prayed at the temple every night with her eyes squeezed shut. Unlike Elizabeth, who has always understood the flaws and shortcomings of the priestesses, Bree's faith was fragile. She held it up too high. And now she has lost it, unable to accept the temple's human failings.

Bree wraps Elizabeth in her cloak from the other side. "When Queen Katharine announces your allegiance, she will want to present you to the people. When she does, you must make sure that you do not outshine her, Mira; even now that she is queen, she still feels so uncared for."

"Uncared for?"

"She said something to me once. That she had never had friends like you and Arsinoe had. She only had the Arrons."

"And they are a cold lot, to be sure," Elizabeth adds.

Mirabella looks at them quietly. "She has won you over by degrees. Even though she murdered a boy right before your eyes. Even though she cut Madrigal Milone's throat."

Bree's mouth tightens guiltily, but she does not deny it. What else can they do? The Queen Crowned is the Queen Crowned. And no matter which queen they wanted to see on the throne, eventually the island comes to love the one they have.

"We would never choose her over you," Bree says. "We would never let her hurt you. Maybe in bringing you here, she has begun to show the better part of herself."

Mirabella nods. Part of her cannot help but feel betrayed,

even though she left her friends behind to make her way in another place. It is not fair to be hurt that they have done the best that they can. They are still her Bree and her Elizabeth. They always will be.

"Besides," says Elizabeth, "you're here now. You've turned away from the rebellion and made peace with the crown. So why should we not be fond of the queen?"

Mirabella looks to the northwest. From this height, it seems she can see all the way across the island straight to Sunpool, and to Arsinoe. Or at least she could if the blasted peak of Mount Horn did not rise up directly in between.

"I am no more for the crown than I am for the rebellion," Mirabella corrects her. "I fought my way free of that once, and I'll not be dragged back in again. Not by a Legion Queen, nor by my baby sister."

"Then why have you come?" Elizabeth asks cautiously.

Mirabella sighs. Their lives have changed so much since Rolanth. It feels wrong to ask them to split their loyalties. When she brought them up to the battlements, she intended to tell them everything. But now she knows that she cannot. Whatever Katharine is hiding, it is something she will have to discover for herself, without confidants.

"I came for the island," she says, and at least that is not a lie. "And I came for you. We should go back down. Katharine may have returned from Greavesdrake Manor, and I do not want her to search for me."

Elizabeth grins and shivers, and the woodpecker beak

inside her hood clicks open and shut. "You do not have to tell me twice. Let's go down to the kitchens and find something warm to eat."

They go, but Mirabella lingers a moment. She steps to the edge and wraps her fingers around the cold stone, then calls up one last gust to whisk away her words.

"I did not want to leave you, Arsinoe. But I had to. I had to come here to find what is wrong with our sister, because she is the darkness the mist reaches for."

On the way down to the kitchens, they cross paths with Katharine.

"Queen Katharine." Elizabeth curtsies. "You have been at Greavesdrake? How is your Pietyr?"

"My Pietyr is unchanged," Katharine replies, and her mouth tightens. "But thank you for asking. There are many here in the Volroy who would no doubt prefer to see him lie in that bed forever. Some even within his own family."

"Because they disapprove of his appointment to the council?" asks Mirabella.

"And of his closeness to me." Katharine cocks her head. "Of course, you would never have done something so controversial."

Mirabella shrugs. "I have no boy to appoint." She steels herself, waiting for Katharine to say something cruel about Joseph, but she does not. "And besides, it would be my Black Council, as it is yours. Their disapproval . . . they will get over it."

Katharine's brows rise. "I hope you are right."

"If you will excuse us," Bree says, and she and Elizabeth take their leave.

"That was abrupt," Katharine says. "I would not expect them to leave you so readily. Especially in my company."

"They want us to be friends." Mirabella watches them go, heads bent together. "You would think they were leaving me alone with a suitor, rather than my little sister. I am surprised they did not break out in a fit of giggles."

Katharine looks after them thoughtfully. "I was going to dismiss them anyway. I am taking you on a tour of the capital. Of course we will have to take a covered carriage, and you must wear a veil to hide your face. A white veil. I trust that will not bother you?"

"They are only colors, Katharine."

"Not here they are not."

Outside, Katharine has ordered a black carriage drawn by two high-stepping black horses, their heads adorned with black plumes.

"I thought you wanted us to be disguised," Mirabella says.

"I wanted *you* to be disguised." Katharine hands her a veil, and they climb into the carriage. The driver snaps the reins, and the horses take off, clip-clopping across the cobblestones. Soon enough, they have left the Volroy grounds and made their way through the city streets to the heart of Indrid Down. Mirabella presses to the window, gazing up at the buildings as they go by. They pass Indrid Down Temple, so dark and near to the Volroy that it is like a second shadow, and she twists her head to look up at the spitting, winged gargoyles.

"Are there stairs to go closer?"

"To the gargoyles?"

"Of course." Mirabella grins. "Willa used to show us drawings of them; do you not remember? Delicate sketchings of charcoal and ink. We had names for every one. Moondragon, she was the largest, with wings outstretched. There." Mirabella points back as the carriage continues on. "And she was my favorite. Arsinoe preferred the ones with their tongues sticking out."

"And what about me?"

"You liked a fat one with a porcine nose. You named him Herbert. He rests in a cluster with three of Arsinoe's favorites, set into the southern wall. If we go around, I can point him out."

Katharine stares at her.

"I do not remember any of that. Why do you remember those things when I do not?"

"I do not know. Perhaps because from the moment I could speak, Willa treated me like the oldest. To learn and be serious. To grow up. You and Arsinoe, she let be little children. Me, she only allowed to be a little queen."

Katharine adjusts her hands in her lap. One of them is stiff and nearly immobile. Mirabella nods to it.

"Your arm is hurt. What is wrong with it?"

Katharine does not reply.

"You tried to face the mist."

"How did you know?" Katharine asks.

"I have noticed you favoring it," Mirabella replies. "And then, when I saw how Eamon cradled his injured arm . . . I just knew."

Gingerly and with a grim smile, Katharine strips off her glove. The hand that is revealed is a dark, angry scab, stitched through with black thread. There are so many cuts, it is a wonder any healer was able to put the skin back together. Two of her fingers are splinted and bruised. Two more are missing their fingernails, but those injuries appear to be much older.

"It is healing well," Katharine says. "I always heal well."

"What happened to your fingernails?"

"That? That is from the night of the Quickening at the Beltane Festival. When I was lost and stumbling through the dark woods." She holds the fingers up to her face. "I thought they would grow back. But oh well. I do not feel it."

The Beltane Festival directly preceded Katharine's miraculous return. And shortly after that was when they began to call her the Undead Queen.

Mirabella stares at the missing nails as Katharine lays her hand back in her lap. Katharine looks out the window and nods. "Down that street is the best confectionery in the city. They specialize in poison sweets but have untainted offerings as well. I shall send a box to the king-consort's apartment. You must have been missing the finer things in the rebellion's wreck of a camp."

"We were not with the rebellion long."

"Ah," Katharine says. "I thought not. And where were you before that?"

They are seated directly across one another, close enough that their skirts touch. Katharine is much more frightening in small spaces. She could slice Mirabella across the cheeks with a poisoned blade before she saw the flash of the steel. "We were on the mainland, with Billy Chatworth's family."

Katharine's eyes go dark. "His father murdered Natalia, you know. He strangled her. Right inside the Volroy. It was probably happening as you and Arsinoe were escaping. When the guards were distracted and she had no one to call to for help."

Though she is sorry for that, Mirabella remains carefully silent. Katharine's pretty, angled face has turned sharp.

"What happened to Billy's father?" she asks finally.

Katharine's teeth stop clenching. "Rho Murtra carved him up. Slipped her serrated blade between his ribs and sawed right through the bone, through lungs and heart. He outlived Natalia by mere moments." She looks down ruefully. "Even if High Priestess Luca had not chosen Rho for a Black Council seat, I should have given her one just for that."

Mirabella's brow knits. Poor Billy, waiting so long for a father who was dead the moment they left.

"You are pale," Katharine says. "Are you really so sympathetic to mainlanders?"

"I am not sad for Billy's father. But I am sorry for Billy."

Katharine scoffs. "One day, I will do something similar to him and his whole family. Genevieve and I will cross the sea and poison them until their eyes bleed."

"You should not do that. Billy is not like his father. And his mother and sister . . . they do not deserve to be poisoned."

"If they are so beloved, then why did you return? What brought you and Arsinoe back to the island after you so recently escaped it?"

"If you are searching for information about the rebellion, you can stop right now. But I suppose it cannot hurt to tell you: it was Arsinoe. She was having dreams. Strange dreams of the Blue Queen. They seemed to indicate we should return. That we were needed."

"And so you are." Katharine leans back, and Mirabella breathes a little easier. She wishes Katharine would put the glove back on. Looking at her hand on her lap, like a mangled piece of meat, has begun to make Mirabella sick to her stomach.

"Queen Illiann," Katharine says.

"You know her."

"Of course. I would be a foolish queen indeed if the mist rose and I did not at least look into the history of its creator. I ordered Genevieve to research Queen Illiann and the mist as soon as it began to rise unbidden. Arsinoe's dreams—what did they tell her? What does she know?"

"That is what we returned to find out," Mirabella replies. "But if she has discovered anything, she did not tell me. And perhaps that is for the best. For if she had, I would have to tell you."

Katharine chuckles. "So you would." She points out the window at a pretty town house of red brick, where Bree and Elizabeth stay. "It is odd, is it not? The mist rises and Arsinoe dreams of its creator. Dreams that send you home. Mirabella Mistbane, the only one on the island who is strong enough to banish it."

"Mirabella Mistbane?"

"It is what I am calling you. Mirabella Mistbane and the Undead Queen. We are legends already. But it is strange. I feel the working of something larger, moving us about."

"Perhaps bringing us together. To fight."

"Or to die. But I am not alone in this, am I? You do feel it?"

"I do," Mirabella admits. "The moment I stepped back onto the island I felt the hand of the Goddess casting about me like a net. I do not know why, yet. But I intend to find out."

Katharine inhales deeply. "I am giving you more freedom to move about the capital. So long as you remain hidden from public view and in disguise until we announce our allegiance."

"Thank you, Katharine." She bows her head respectfully, and to hide her smile. If she is free to move, she is free to try and solve Madrigal's puzzle.

"Do not thank me yet. When we meet Arsinoe and Juillenne Milone in battle, I will have to kill them. And Billy, whom you are so fond of. He may not have murdered Natalia, but he has committed his own crimes. He is a rebel now. And he backs the wrong queen."

Katharine puts her glove back on and leans forward to look out the window. "We are here."

"Where?" Mirabella asks as the carriage slows to a halt. The door opens, and she follows Katharine outside. The city lies behind them now, and before them, Bardon Harbor, stretched as far as the eye can see. "We are on the northern cliffs."

"Very good. Now come!" She reaches for Mirabella's hand. Mirabella flinches, and Katharine's expression falters. For just a moment, her large eyes are the eyes of the little girl Mirabella once knew.

"I thought you would like it. I know you have places like this in Rolanth."

Mirabella thinks of the dark basalt cliffs of Shannon's Blackway. This place is a little like that, a similar cut to the rock. Not white like the cliffs of Sunpool but pale and brown like sand. "Yes, Bree and I used to race across them."

"Then what is the matter?" Katharine holds her hand out again, and Mirabella steels herself and takes it.

Katharine leads her closer to the edge, so close that they can lean over and look upon the beach and see the waves striking the rocks. "According to Genevieve, these very cliffs are where the mist was created. This is where the Blue Queen cast her spell and called it to us, and all the years since, it has preserved our way of life. Protected us from the outside world." Katharine snorts. "Well, until recently."

Mirabella stares at the ground where they stand. Did Queen Illiann once stand in the same place? Queen Illiann, the Blue Queen, who Mirabella feels like she almost knows, thanks to Arsinoe's account of her dreams as Daphne, Illiann's lost sister.

"Look," Katharine says, and points out over the water, where the mist has risen to swirl angrily, darting closer as if it would crash against the sides of the cliffs.

“What does it mean?” Mirabella asks, unsure whether she is asking Katharine or Arsinoe or even Illiann, so long ago.

“I think it means it does not like you standing here. I think it means it is afraid.” Together they watch the mist recede. “I used to be so jealous of you. Jealous of everything you are. Maybe I am jealous still, that you remember what we used to be.”

“Arsinoe started to remember. Maybe you will as well now that we are together.”

Katharine looks down, perhaps regretfully.

“I am not like you,” she acknowledges. “I can be cruel. As I can be kind. And I am a better queen than you would have been because of it. It is time for us to return. So you may enjoy your new freedom! And I can announce our allegiance. And begin preparing for the parade.”

SUNPOOL

The morning after Jules's reawakening, Arsinoe finds herself once again crowded inside the rebellion's makeshift council chamber.

"Can this not wait?" Arsinoe asks, looking from Billy to the Milones for support. "She's barely had a moment to breathe."

"I know it is not the best time," Emilia says. "But the matter of Mirabella's defection must be addressed."

Arsinoe shakes her head. But no one disagrees. Not Mathilde, nor even Cait or Caragh. And Jules, though calm, seems weak and deflated despite a long night of sleep.

"It must be made known that Mirabella has gone over to Katharine," Emilia says.

Arsinoe's jaw clenches.

"We don't know that's what's happened. She might have been taken. The note might have been staged."

"She wasn't taken. I know everything that happens in this

city. Down to the routes that the rats take to feed."

"Well, that's probably overstating things," Billy says quietly, but Emilia pretends he is not even there. Arsinoe opens her mouth to argue, but Mathilde steps in between them.

The seer has a calming way about her. Arsinoe has seen her silence a room by simply walking through it. Now she uses that stillness to shush Emilia and fixes Arsinoe with her steady gaze.

"All of her things are gone. And Mirabella would not have been taken easily. Can you think of a reason that Mirabella would go?"

"No," Arsinoe says. She crosses her arms over her chest. Mirabella never supported the Legion Queen. But neither had she, not really. And that was certainly no reason to go to Katharine. "But—" She looks at Billy. "Did she overhear us talking about the cave?"

"No," he says. "I don't know."

"Did you tell her?"

"No!" He opens his eyes wide. "Of course not!"

"The cave?" Emilia asks, and even the Milones step closer. Only Jules hangs back warily as Billy holds his hands out to keep Emilia and Mathilde at bay, their attention fixed on him like wolves who have just noticed that a deer is limping. "Why"—he lowers his voice to a loud whisper—"why on earth would I tell her?"

"Tell her what?" Emilia asks. "What happened at the cave?"

Arsinoe faces them. She looks at Cait and Caragh and

Ellis and considers for a long moment what to say. Jules trusts Mathilde and Emilia. But Jules's trust is sometimes misplaced.

"It's a long story." Arsinoe's eyes lose focus, remembering the memory pressed into her head by Daphne's long-dead fingers. Daphne and Queen Illiann standing atop the cliffs at Bardon Harbor, watching the ships of the enemy defy even the Blue Queen's elemental storms. The argument and then Illiann plummeting to her death. Arsinoe squeezes her eyes shut. Maybe it was an accident. A fall. Maybe Daphne was not truly a murderer.

Or maybe the island's will always wins. Sister killing sister was nothing new on Fennbirn, after all.

"It was revealed to me that there may be a way to stop the mist."

"What?" Cait asks, and she and Mathilde step closer. "How?"

"The mist was created by killing a powerful elemental queen. The Blue Queen, Illiann. And so it may be unmade by killing another." She looks at Jules, who as always, immediately knows what she means.

For a long time, Emilia and Mathilde say nothing. Then Emilia throws up her hands. "And you let her get away! We had the key to eliminating the mist—here, right under our noses—and you let her run."

"What do you mean 'let her run'?" Arsinoe shouts. "Even if she were here, you wouldn't touch her!"

"Stop!" Billy and Mathilde exclaim, and look at each other

with the understanding that only reasonable people must feel.

"In any case," Billy says, "it doesn't matter. Mirabella's not here. She's out of danger and out of reach."

"I wouldn't necessarily say that being at the Undead Queen's court is out of danger," notes Caragh.

"And we will get her back," says Emilia. "And when we do—"

"You will do nothing," Arsinoe growls. "And we don't even know if it would work. Why take the word of a centuries-dead murderer? Mirabella is my sister!"

"She is one life. And how many will the mist take if it cannot be stopped? Our rebellion seeks to bring peace to the island. And safety. We cannot just ignore—"

"Yes, we can," Jules says quietly. She looks at Arsinoe, her expression somber.

"Jules," Emilia objects.

"No. It's out of the question."

"But—"

Jules presses her fingers to her forehead, and Cait moves to disband the meeting.

"You heard my granddaughter," she says. "She is the Legion Queen, and she will decide. Now let's leave her to her rest."

They all file out, even Billy. Emilia's eyes flash indignantly at Arsinoe as she goes, but not even she will speak against Cait. When they are gone, Arsinoe lingers with her hand on the door.

"Do you need anything? Water? Wine? A haunch of something for Cam?"

"Just you," Jules says. "Stay." She walks to the hearth and warms her hands. Arsinoe steps back inside.

"How are you feeling? Are you sleeping? I could craft you a sleeping draught."

"I'm fine, Arsinoe. I'm well. You saved me again."

"Does that make us even?" Arsinoe asks, burying her fingers in the cougar's scruff. "Or do I need to save you one more time?"

Jules smiles wanly. Her brown hair hangs in unkempt waves to her chin, and they fall into her eyes as she picks at her bandaged wrist.

"I feel like I've been asleep for a hundred years."

"It's not easy to step right back into things. Emilia pushes too hard."

"It's not Emilia's fault," Jules says. "I just don't trust myself. I remember what I did."

"You weren't you."

"Then who was I?" She looks down at her bandages, and at her bad leg, weakened and made painful by the poison she ate, poison that helped Arsinoe discover her true gift. "I'm broken in body," she says. "And broken in mind."

"Is that what you see when you look at yourself?" Arsinoe asks. "Because it's not what I see."

"It doesn't matter what I see. No one should follow me. What I've done . . . I'm no leader. But Mirabella is."

Arsinoe looks at her in surprise.

"I know I had my reasons to dislike her," says Jules. "But

she was the one. So strong. Strong enough to end us all, yet not a killer. You're not a killer either, Arsinoe. I'm sorry that I tried so long to make you one."

"It's okay," Arsinoe whispers, not knowing what else to say. "And you know . . . that Mirabella doesn't want to be the Queen Crowned."

"But you know her, don't you?" Jules asks. "If she's needed, she'll do it anyway."

INDRID DOWN TEMPLE

The initiate priestess leads Mirabella, disguised in a hood and veil, through the austere interior of Indrid Down Temple, past the rows and rows of pews in carefully preserved oiled walnut, and past the Goddess Stone that winks to her from behind its barrier of ropes. She leads her behind the altar and through the cloister and up, up, up the stairs that lead to the room Luca has taken for herself. Or rather, that she has taken back. Her old quarters from the time before she came to know Mirabella and before she abandoned the capital and the semblance of neutrality to live with her in Rolanth.

Mirabella inhales and smells cold stone. There are so many stairs that her legs have begun to burn. They must be high enough to lean out a window and pat the heads of Arsinoe's favorite gargoyles.

"I hope you will forgive the distance," says the priestess ahead of her, carrying a torch to light the path. "Many were surprised when the High Priestess elected to reclaim her old rooms. We had thought to prepare some more comfortable space on the ground floor."

The ground floor. Luca would never submit to that. She would force them to carry her up and down on their backs first.

They reach Luca's door, and the initiate bobs a curtsy and takes her leave, a little careless with her torch as she passes it near Mirabella's face. Perhaps the girl had the gift of fire before she came to the temple and has not yet learned to be mindful of it.

Mirabella knocks once and enters Luca's chamber. What she sees inside is so familiar that for a moment she is transported across the island to those afternoons in Rolanth when she would race up to the High Priestess's quarters for tea.

"Look at you," Luca says, bent over her desk and pouring a steaming cup. "Out and about, with no escort."

"The queensguard is waiting below with the carriage," Mirabella says. She pushes back her hood and removes her veil, walking to one of Luca's couches piled always with too many soft pillows. She unfastens her cloak and slings it across the arm. Then she nods to the tea. "Honey and lemon?"

"Honey and preserved lemon," Luca replies. "Fresh fruit will become a distant memory if the problem of the mist is not resolved soon. None of the importers from the mainland have been able to make it through. Or none of them have dared return once they heard what was happening."

"The naturalists will look after the island when the spring comes."

"Not even they grow lemons and oranges. We simply do not have the climate." She sets the tray of tea on the table between the couches and hands Mirabella her cup. "The way you speak. 'The naturalists will look after the island.' The island. Not 'us.' As if you are not a part of it. What wonders there must be on the mainland to claim you after so little time."

"Yet I am here. Serving the island. Doing my duty, as you said." Mirabella sets her cup down without drinking. Neither sit, and Luca manages to make standing look very comfortable, sipping her tea with her eyebrows raised, back straight and shoulders loose as if her old bones have never felt a single ache. "You seem younger here than you did in Rolanth, High Priestess. The air off Bardon Harbor must agree with you."

Luca smiles.

"Why did you want to see me?" Mirabella asks.

"Because I finally could! Now that you have found your way into the queen's favor, I need not avoid you any longer. You must have realized that my not coming to see you was not without cause."

"I am sure you never do anything without cause."

Luca picks up a plate of biscuits and offers them: meringues topped with custard and a bright spot of jam. Mirabella's favorite. She takes one off the plate.

"How are you enjoying the capital now, with your newfound freedom? How are you finding your time with your younger sister?"

Mirabella frowns, looking down at the meringue. She is very hungry. And though she would prefer to snub everything Luca offers, Arsinoe would not want her to waste food.

"She is calling me Mirabella Mistbane," Mirabella says, and Luca chuckles. "She has ordered special armor to be made for us both. Silver breastplates engraved with clouds and lightning for me and skulls and snakes for her. She wants to parade me beside her through the city." She glances at Luca. "Are her moods always so changeable?"

"Queen Katharine is quick to hate," Luca replies. "But she will forgive you anything the moment you show her the smallest kindness. You and she share many traits, though they manifest in different ways. You are both softhearted. And you are both lethal."

"Lethal." Mirabella looks Luca square in the face. "How is Katharine able to ingest so much poison?"

"Her poison gift is strong."

"She has no poison gift," says Mirabella. "Arsinoe is the poisoner."

"Perhaps there were two."

"Not according to Willa." Mirabella's eyes narrow. "Yet I have seen Katharine swallow poison after poison as if every meal is a *Gave Noir*. How? What low magic did you and Natalia Arron work on her to turn her into such a . . . talented queen?"

Luca scoffs. "There was no low magic. No tricks. I was not working in secret with the Arrons. Up until the last, I was working in secret for you. Which is why I know you so well." She lowers her voice. "I know it was not truly my words that swayed you to the crown. What are you doing here, really? What are you up to?"

"Only what you told me to do. I am protecting the island, and trying to solve the puzzle that is my sister."

"And what will you do when you solve it? Whatever secrets she keeps do not matter. She is crowned."

"So much loyalty," Mirabella says bitterly.

"You learn to love the queen you have. You know this. Had you won the throne, you would have found Arrons lining up to become your allies. It is no different."

Except it feels different. Mirabella would have expected that the Arrons would quickly change their colors. Arrons are changeable and lack conviction. But it was a shock to come to the capital and find that Katharine had won over her two best friends.

"Perhaps I am being silly," she says, and to her surprise, Luca steps forward and embraces her, patting her lightly on the shoulder.

"It is not silly, Mira. It is natural. As subjects, we must love our queen. But we have always loved you. And we are all glad that you have come home to us."

Mirabella takes the old woman's hand. That familiar, wrinkled hand with its practical, short-clipped fingernails, the knuckles slightly swollen with age. She lowers her head and kisses it, and smells the almond oil that Luca massages into her skin.

"Are you truly glad?" she asks. "Do you really still love me?"

"Mira." Luca's brow knits. "What is the matter?"

"I should not say," Mirabella says, her eyes fixed upon Luca's hands. "For I do not know if I can trust you. But I am going to ask you anyway, because I am lost here and without a confidant. And because you did love me, once . . ." She looks up at the High Priestess and finds her soft blue irises trembling.

"Before Madrigal Milone died, she told me something about Katharine. 'She is full of the dead.' That is what Madrigal Milone said, just before her life ran out into the snow at Innisfuil. What did she mean?"

Mirabella waits, and Luca pulls her hand free.

"I have no idea. She was dying. Perhaps she was rambling. Perhaps you misheard."

Mirabella studies the High Priestess carefully. Her expression is haunted but not confused. "I did not mishear. You know something. You want to tell me."

"What do you mean I want to tell you?" Luca brushes her away and turns, walking to her desk to open drawers and move papers without purpose.

"You have lied to me many times, Luca, and I have never been able to tell. So if I can tell now, it is because in your heart you want me to know." She follows the High Priestess to her desk and grasps her by the arms.

"'She is full of the dead,'" Luca whispers.

"Yes. What did she mean?"

"A thought forms in my mind. . . ."

Mirabella waits as Luca thinks, her eyes distant. "Tell me."

But Luca jerks herself loose. "It is not certain yet. And I will not speak against the queen."

"Not even if that queen is a danger?"

"A danger to who?"

Mirabella sighs hard through her nose. She picks up her cloak to leave and moves for the door. She will find no answers here. The best she can hope for is that Luca will not go running straight to Katharine to advise Mirabella be executed by poison in the square. But as she reaches for the doorknob, Luca speaks.

"I will not speak against the queen," she says again. "It is not my place. But if someone were to speak"—she looks at Mirabella meaningfully—"that someone would be Pietyr Renard."

Pietyr Renard. And just how was she supposed to get to Pietyr Renard? By all accounts, he was unconscious, at Greavesdrake. And Katharine would be sure to keep her beloved under heavy guard. Besides, if she ran directly to him the moment she had the slightest freedom, Katharine would guess her true intentions.

Mirabella presses her lips together in frustration as she fumbles with the tangle of her veil. Back in Sunpool, the rebellion is still gathering, and Emilia will lead them to attack in the spring. By then she must know all there is to know about Katharine, if she is to find a way to bring peace back to the island.

"And then Arsinoe and I will leave," she says out loud. She says it out loud, because with each passing day, she believes it less and less. Dangerous as her presence in Indrid Down is, she feels more at home in the capital than she ever did on the mainland. The mainland is strange rules and limitations, imposed traditions to keep things orderly. But this—this is what she was raised for: intrigue and political movements.

Veil still crumpled in her hands, she steps into the corridor directly beside the initiate priestess, who gasps when she sees who she has escorted up the stairs.

"Oh!" Mirabella's eyes widen. She pretends to try to hide herself. "I was not expecting you to be waiting!"

The initiate, flustered, tries to look everywhere else but at Mirabella's face.

"It is all right," Mirabella whispers when she has put her disguise back on. "The Queen Crowned knows I am here, though my presence must remain a secret."

"I won't speak a word!"

"Good. I thank you." She squeezes the girl's hands, and the initiate sinks into a fast, low curtsy. Mirabella quickly tugs her back up. Her respectfulness will get them caught. "But, as long as I am here, might you be able to sneak me into the temple library? Hidden away in the Volroy, I am afraid I am dreadfully bored. I would enjoy exploring the temple collection, if only for a few hours. I would require somewhere private."

"I know just the place." She leads Mirabella deep into the temple, down to the library on the lower level. It is smaller than Mirabella expected and poorly lit, with only a few windows. She squints, and the initiate hurries to light the lamps. Mirabella notes the way they flare. It is true then; the girl was an elemental before joining the temple, and it makes Mirabella feel more at ease, even though she knows it should not.

"You'll not be bothered," the initiate promises. "Few come to the library at this time of day, and I will do what I can to keep the area clear. Shall I fetch you . . . at dusk? If you do not find me first? My name is Dennie."

"Dennie?"

"Well, Deianeira. But who wants to say all that?"

Mirabella chuckles. "It is a queenly name. As much of a mouthful as Mirabella. Dennie, it is. And if you like, you may call me Mira."

Dennie's eyes widen, and she shakes her head vigorously as she turns to leave. "No, I could never!"

Alone amidst the books, Mirabella removes her veil. The room has such a lonely feel that she can believe no one else has been there in the last month. But it is very clean and does not smell of dust or mold. The books appear to be well preserved and no doubt carefully organized. And even though it is a modest collection, she does not know where to start.

She wanders the rows and runs her finger across the leather-bound spines. So much of the island's history sits resting here. Kept and recorded, and hidden away. Effectively buried. And it is not only books, but ledgers, journals, artwork, and tapestries, relics from time and reigns gone by. She had come to the library to snoop for only a little while, but she really could linger happily until sundown.

After a few minutes of wandering in aimless wonder, she

begins selecting volumes and pulling them from the shelves, taking them back to her small table by the armful. Then she sits down and begins to read.

Within the crisp, seldom-turned pages, accounts of past queens are easy to find. There are several volumes devoted solely to the tales of the Ascensions, and in them she reads the familiar stories of Queen Shannon and Queen Elo, the strong elementals whose murals grace the walls of Rolanth Temple and whose stories she knows nearly as well as her own. Beside them are the Ascensions of Queen Elsabet the mad, and Queen Bernadine, the naturalist champion of Wolf Spring. Bernadine's Ascension is depicted in paint, a small illustration of faded red blood and a fierce black wolf. They are grand tales, romanticized. Descriptions of triumph. Mentions of the queens who were killed—and who also vied fiercely for that same crown—are sparse and rarely congratulatory. In reading of the Ascension of Queen Theodora—a naturalist whose familiar was a horse—her fallen sister is simply described in terms of her condition after the horse had trampled her into the road.

Mirabella flips more pages, her eyes moving quickly. So many queens who have come before. Each faced her own challenges, both before and after the crown. But only one has returned and recently made her presence known. Queen Illiann. The Blue Queen. Creator of the mist. There should be volume upon volume about her. Yet after more than an hour of searching, Mirabella has found nothing. She finds tales of Queen Andira, the White-Handed naturalist whose sisters were both born oracles and drowned. She finds reference to Queen Caedan, the first Blue Queen, born over a thousand years ago. But nothing of Illiann.

She closes the book she had been perusing and stands, looking over the shelves and the many trunks. There are no holes in the stacks, no suspicious spaces. But whatever there was must have been taken.

"Hello?" The initiate, Dennie, pokes her head out from the entrance and then steps inside to curtsy. "Mmmm . . . Mirrr . . . m'lady?"

Mirabella rolls her eyes and laughs. M'lady will have to do. "Yes?"

"Is there anything you need? Tea? Some food?"

"No, I—" Mirabella pauses, her focus still on the shelves. "I am reading the histories of past queens, and I find that I cannot . . . That is, there does not seem to be anything here about the last Blue Queen. Queen Illiann. Does the temple really house nothing here?"

"We do," Dennie says. "But all that we had was taken recently to Greavesdrake Manor, at the request of Genevieve Arron."

"Of course it was." Mirabella sighs. "Queen Katharine told me that she had set Genevieve to look into it." She leans her head back and stares at the ceiling as if she can see right through it, all the way up to Luca. Maybe if she grabbed her by the shoulders and shook, all of the answers would simply fall out of her. "Goddess. Now I am thinking like Arsinoe."

"What did you say?"

"Nothing. The Arrons—do they often make demands upon the temple? Is it easy for the priestesses to function here, so close to the crown and the council?"

"It can be difficult," Dennie admits. "Though perhaps the greatest difficulty lies in simply being acknowledged. Sometimes I think that the Black Council has forgotten the reason that the capital city was founded here in the first place."

"And what was that?"

"It was the site of the first temple, of course."

"This"—Mirabella gestures around them—"this was the very first temple?"

"No. This is a monument to the Volroy. Completed before it but made to match. The first temple has been lost to time. Like so many things. But you mustn't worry about us. It has been much better since the High Priestess returned."

"The High Priestess . . . does she know about the first temple?"

"Yes, but perhaps no more than I do."

If only it still existed. The answers it must hold. Mirabella picks up a book and runs her hand across the cover.

"I have been reading about the other queens. But I can find no mention of any before Queen Bethel the Pious. Are there other, older volumes kept elsewhere?"

Dennie's brow knits in thought. "Perhaps in other temples. Perhaps pilfered away to the Volroy. Or even to Greavesdrake Manor. Or perhaps, those ancient queens have also been lost to time."

"As long as there has been the island, there have been the

island's queens," Mirabella says absently, and the initiate nods. Everyone on Fennbirn knows that. And they know the first, though she has no name. The first queen, known only through myth and legend. Bearer of the first triplets. Some say she was the Goddess herself, that she bestowed the gifts upon the early people and ruled for a hundred years. Mirabella has seen her in many paintings: a dark beauty with shadowed eyes, always depicted with her arms extended above the island and three dark stars beneath her.

But those are only artists' renderings. Nothing ancient remains from her time. No accounts. No relics. Not even her name.

"The Goddess herself," Mira muses quietly. "And what would that make us?"

"My lady?"

"Nothing. I was only wondering about those queens who have come before. Those ancient ones who are lost to us. What wisdom might they have? What secrets would they share? Was it easier in their times?" She rubs her hands roughly across her face and her tired eyes.

"It's a shame no one knows where the ruins of the first temple lie. And it is a shame to have lost such a sacred site."

"It is a shame," Mirabella says. "Perhaps some queen someday will find it."

GREAVESDRAKE MANOR

Whenever she can get away from the castle, Katharine goes to Greavesdrake to tend to Pietyr herself. Lately, it has not been easy. With Mirabella in the city, the whole of the Black Council is as jumpy as cats in a thunderstorm. The members want their Queen Crowned close at hand. They want to be sure that she is watching, and ready, like they are, should Mirabella prove to be less than trustworthy.

"I am sorry I am late," she whispers to Pietyr as he lies resting peacefully in her old bedroom. There has been no more bleeding, and Edmund has told her that occasionally there are twitches of reflex in Pietyr's legs or movement behind his eyelids. She knows that he will wake soon. She can feel it. And then he will be back with her, where he belongs.

"And when you wake, we will be even. Truly even. You threw me down into the Breccia Domain, and I . . ."

As she looks at him, the dead queens rise, fascinated by

him as he lies there. As if not even they can believe what they have done.

"No," Katharine whispers. "Stay away from him. When we are in this room, you will not be here."

The dead queens ignore her. Instead, they grasp for control of her hand and reach for his cheek, as if they might feel for warmth, and peel open his eyes to gaze inside them. It is indecent. Monstrous.

"Get out," she orders.

They crowd inside her body, and her skin crawls with their soothing touches, their whispered apologies. So many excuses. So many cold embraces in the hopes that she will forgive them. But behind the comfort there is always the threat: *Without us, sweet queen, you are a weak child. Without us, you will lose your crown, and then your head.*

"If you do not recede to the deepest, darkest corner of me," Katharine shouts, "so help me, I will cut you out and put you back into the stones myself!"

At her words, the dead sisters constrict in her blood so fast that it feels like a punch to the gut. She takes a deep, shaky breath. She must be more careful. Controlling her temper is better to manage them. But in the room with Pietyr, she only wanted them gone.

Katharine runs a hand across Pietyr's forehead. It is dry, not clammy or feverish. She brushes his ice-blond hair back from his eyes. She is tired. The dead sisters, Mirabella, and the Black Council have left her weary, and she allows herself a moment to climb onto the bed with him. To snuggle down into the warm crook of his shoulder and listen to him breathe.

"Please wake up," she whispers. She presses her lips to his and tries to will him to stir for a moment, she imagines that she feels his lips open against hers. But it is only pretend. She kisses him again and again, harder, on his mouth and cheeks and collarbone.

"Queen Katharine."

She jumps and turns to see Genevieve standing in the doorway.

"Genevieve." Katharine extricates herself from the bed and straightens her apron. "What do you want?"

"To look in on my nephew," she says. "And to look in on you."

"You were never so concerned with his well-being before." Katharine returns to the tray of food. It is soft, near liquid. Edmund has added warm milk to help it go down easier. In his unconscious state, Pietyr must be fed through a long, flexible tube.

Genevieve comes to Pietyr and leans down to kiss him on the head. Her long, blond braid falls from her shoulder and thumps against his cheek. She picks a bit of lint off her dark brown trousers before glancing at the bowl of cooling food. "Shall I help you?"

"No, I will do it," Katharine says, and takes up the tubing in her hand.

"Look how you are trembling. Let me do it. I am very deft, I promise."

Reluctantly, Katharine gives it over, and Genevieve lubricates the tube with oil. She tilts Pietyr's head back, and Katharine holds her breath as Genevieve guides it smoothly down his throat. He does not fight it much before the reflex swallows it down.

"The funnel."

Katharine hands it to her, and she affixes it to the end of the tube.

"How are you faring with Mirabella, Katharine?" Genevieve asks as she spoons the vegetable mash. "You say she is here by your invitation, but I know you. I am surprised you have not killed her already."

"Perhaps you do not know me as well as you think. I am not so bloodthirsty as to place my own vengeance above the interests of my island."

"And what if your bloodthirst is at the very heart of the island's interests?"

"What are you talking about?" Genevieve knows something. Her lilac eyes are narrowed with contentment.

"There," she says as the last of the mash goes down the tube. She reaches for the goblet of water and sniffs. It has been infused with hemlock.

"It is Pietyr's favorite."

"A nice addition. It is important to nurture his poison gift as he recovers." Genevieve pours it slowly, flushing the last of the food down into Pietyr's stomach. Then she carefully removes the tube and wipes his mouth.

"I have received an interesting report from my spies in Sunpool. It seems the rebellion has found a solution for the problem of the attacking mist."

"What solution?"

"The death of an elemental queen."

Katharine scoffs. "What are you talking about?"

"I would not have believed it either, had I not also previously discovered this during my research into the Blue Queen." She reaches into her pocket and pulls out pages of ancient-looking parchment. She hands them to Katharine. "But the call for the death of an elemental queen, when put together with this, makes the puzzle complete."

Katharine unfolds the pages. They appear to be from a journal of some kind. "This is from the journal of Henry Redville," she says. "Queen Illiann's king-consort."

"I know," Genevieve muses. "It is a lucky thing they were even kept. For who preserves the thoughts of a king-consort?"

Katharine reads on. What follows in the pages is a largely rambling account of a man wracked with guilt, and quite possibly in his cups. It is a confession of sorts. Written to Queen Illiann as if she was not there and had been gone for many years.

"Why would the death of an elemental queen stop the mist?" Katharine asks.

"Because according to Henry Redville, the death of an elemental queen was what formed it in the first place." Genevieve gestures to the pages. "Read on."

Katharine's eyes move feverishly across the scrawling hand of the king-consort. It is a muddled composition, so full of apologies that Katharine wants to slap him, though he is long, long dead. "'Please forgive Daphne, who has continued to love you as her sister,'" Katharine reads aloud. "'Please forgive me, who was not strong enough to repel the Selkan attack. Your death upon the cliffs that night haunts us both, and we have often been unable to enjoy our happiness, as it came at the loss of you. Sometimes I wonder if this is truly what you would have wanted, but they insisted that the line of queens must go on, and Daphne was still a queen . . .'" Katharine stops. "What is he speaking of? Her death? The Blue Queen reigned in peace after the creation of the mist for another forty years!"

"Did she? Not according to that. No, Queen Illiann was killed, by who he does not say, and after her body created the mist, this . . . Daphne . . . was put on the throne to rule in her place."

"But the Blue Queen's sisters were all to have been put to death, days after birth. Could this Daphne have really been a queen?"

"Enough of a queen to fool the populace for another forty years. Enough of a queen to bear the sacred triplets." Genevieve looks at the yellowed papers. "I cannot say for sure—there is no record of a triplet born under the name Daphne—but I think she is actually the other elemental born: Roxane. It would have been the only way for their deception to work."

"Queen Illiann replaced by another queen." A Queen Crowned replaced so easily.

Genevieve stands and takes the pages back, folding them and returning them to her pocket. "I have done as you asked. Become your eyes and ears. So now we know why Mirabella truly fled the rebellion. Because they planned to kill her to put an end to the mist."

Katharine looks at her. "And now you would have me do the same. When I have given her my word she would be safe."

"Her safety or the safety of the island," Genevieve says, weighing them on her hands.

"She has already secured the safety of the island. She fought the mist and won."

"She fought the mist, yes, but she did not win. Not for good. It will return. We should kill her now, and put an end to one threat at least."

"No." Katharine shakes her head. "Not yet."

"Why not?"

"I do not know. I only sense that I need her." For what? Not even she can say for sure. To help her rid herself of the dead queens? But how? She cannot allow the dead queens to set one foot inside her powerful sister.

"Katharine, you are being unreasonable."

"I cannot bear the triplets, have you forgotten that?" Katharine snaps. And once it is past her lips, it is like she has known all along. "I need another queen. A trusted one. One who loves me enough to bear them for me in secret!"

Genevieve's mouth drops open. Then it closes, and she nods. She even seems impressed.

"If you can secure that kind of loyalty, you would be an

Arron queen indeed. Very well. We will wait and see." She turns to leave.

"Where are you going?"

"Back to the Volroy. To be your eyes and ears." She pauses at the door and looks at Pietyr one more time. "You have lost Natalia, and Pietyr is asleep. You have few people left whom you trust, and few who remain to give you advice. But I will give you a caution now, so that later I will not feel that I failed in my duty. Do not be quick to trust Mirabella. No matter how she might help or what she might say." She steps out into the hall. "A queen should never trust a queen."

SUNPOOL

In the tavern off the square, Arsinoe and Billy sit at a table by the windows and watch Jules. She has been well now for nearly a week, and still she is mobbed wherever she goes. Cait, Ellis, or Caragh are always in her shadow. And Camden has not strayed more than a few feet since the two left the castle keep together.

"It's so good to see them without ropes and chains," Arsinoe says. She laughs when one of the rebels gets too close and Camden swats him with her good paw.

"Always something for the Legion Queen to do," Billy muses. "Somewhere to be seen, someone she must speak to. And you're getting annoyed by it, aren't you? You haven't had enough time with her."

Arsinoe does not bother denying it. Not to Billy, who seems to be able to read her mind. "My days of having Jules all to myself are over. All of those simpler times are over."

A frown flickers across Billy's face, and he hides it behind a mouthful of fried fish. "At least she's well."

"Or seems to be."

"Do you have doubts about the spell?" He watches Jules carefully through the glass. "She doesn't seem at all volatile."

No, she does not. She seems like she has since the tether woke her up. A little deflated. A little ashamed. And underneath that, a little angry.

"All the more suspicious, then," says Arsinoe. "Jules was always a little volatile."

The tavern keeper arrives with fresh mugs of ale, and grimaces at the scabbed cuts on Arsinoe's hand and forearm. The look on his face says he would throw her out if she were not the exiled queen.

"Don't pay any attention," Billy says as Arsinoe tugs her sleeves lower. "They don't know that it's those cuts that gave them their Legion Queen back. If they did, they'd be asking to kiss them."

"Then I guess I'm glad they don't," she says, and Billy pulls her hand close and kisses it anyway.

In the square, the crowd begins to jostle and murmur like spooked sheep. Before Arsinoe can spot the source of their unease, Billy's eyes bug nearly out of his head.

"She's got Braddock!"

Arsinoe jumps to her feet and races out of the tavern. The great brown bear is up on two legs, his large lips extended in a low roar, just outside the gate. And just inside of it is Emilia, dangling a strip of meat to try to entice him inside. "Emilia, you idiot!" Arsinoe gets to them as fast as she can, sharp elbows making an easy path through the people. "What are you doing?"

She holds her hands out to Braddock and he comes back onto all fours. His big dark eyes are frightened until Jules arrives with Caragh, and use their naturalist gifts to calm him.

"I was bringing him to you," Emilia explains. "For what is a bear queen without a bear?"

"A bear queen who leaves her bear in the wild outside the city, where he belongs!"

"But he must be seen occasionally," Emilia says. "And I wanted to test my new bit of naturalist gift."

Jules shakes her head, but it is not a true admonishment. To Arsinoe's horror, Jules seems merely amused. "Why would you think you're suddenly a naturalist?"

"The spell. Arsinoe said it might . . ." She trails off and shrugs. "And it must be true. For the bear is here, and I am alive."

"You could have chosen a better way to test it," Arsinoe says, her arm slung protectively around Braddock's large head. "I'm taking him back out to the woods." Inside the walls, there are too many people. And even outside has become dangerous, with the soldiers' training grounds spilling into the dunes and hills. So many noisy swords clashing and stray arrows shot by rebels who have never held a bow before.

"I'll come with you," says Billy.

"And so will I," says Caragh.

They walk together back through the gate, past the open mouths of those gathered. Perhaps Emilia was right, and seeing the bear will make them look upon Arsinoe more fondly. Arsinoe purses her lips. What need does she have to garner favor with the rebellion?

When they reach the trees, Billy digs in his pockets for a little strip of dried meat and offers it to Braddock as one last treat.

"Though I'll miss him," Arsinoe says, "I have to ask you to take him back to the Black Cottage." She turns to Caragh. "When do you think you'll return?"

To her surprise, Caragh lifts her chin. "I don't intend to return. And I am not going to Wolf Spring."

"What do you mean?"

"I'm going to remain here, with the rebellion. So is Luke. And my parents. And many of the people who came with them." She exhales. "But not Matthew. I am sending Matthew and the baby home. If Sunpool falls, it'll be safer there. And though she won't say it, I think it would be better for Jules if he wasn't here. He looks too much like Joseph would have looked."

"You should go back with them," says Arsinoe. "Help them to hide. Matthew might be safe from Katharine, but the Legion Queen's little brother?"

"You think she would target a baby?" Billy asks, aghast.

"I think she would target anyone if there were an advantage to be gained. She's at war. I can't even blame her."

"They're departing this afternoon," Caragh says. "Sailing back to Wolf Spring with the rest of the Sandrins. Come to the beach with us and say goodbye to them."

That afternoon, when the sun starts to tilt, Arsinoe makes her way across the cold, stiff sand to join the others at the water's edge. Aside from the Milones, Billy and Luke have come, as well as Mathilde, who feels her link to the baby as she was at the Black Cottage the night he was born.

Poor little Fenn. Bundled in blanket upon blanket against the chilly sea wind and passed from person to person like a jug of ale around the fire. When he comes to Arsinoe, she holds him out in front of her to look into his eyes.

"Jules's little brother," she says. It is such a strange thing to say—a brother in a family full of sisters. So small and his mother already gone.

"Pull him close," Matthew says, and laughs. "Give him a kiss."

Arsinoe makes a fondly disgusted face. "I think he's covered in enough kisses already." But before she gives him back, she whispers to him to take care. Beside her, Caragh's stoic eyes are wet, though she hides her tears well. Her brown hound sits beside Matthew miserably, pressed against his side.

"Joseph was his uncle," Billy says as he prods the baby in the tummy. "And I was foster brother to Joseph. So does that mean I can claim him as my foster nephew?"

"No need to carry on with the 'foster' bit," Matthew replies.

"And you're always welcome at the Sandrin house."

"Give him to me," Mathilde says, and holds out her arms. The baby reaches for her and gurgles. "I was near when your light came into the world, and I will always sense when it is near."

"Strange folk, oracles," Luke comments.

"Says the man with the rooster on his shoulder," Billy notes. "And speaking of chickens, Luke, how is my Harriet?"

"She's overfed, and a distraction to Hank," he replies, and his rooster clucks sheepishly.

Billy pokes at the baby in Mathilde's arms.

"Will he be a naturalist, do you think? Is that how it goes? Even if one of the parents is giftless?"

"I charm fish," Matthew objects, reaching for his son.

"You charm everyone in equal measure," Billy assures him. "But really, is that how it works?"

Cait studies the baby with a stern expression. "Every Milone born has the naturalist gift. That is how it works. And his gift is sure to be a strong one."

"Cursebreaker," Mathilde says suddenly. Then she blinks. "Forgive me. I do not know why I said that."

Cait and Ellis trade a glance. "It's all right," Ellis says. "We know why."

"Why?" asks Billy.

"For as many generations as can be recalled, Milone women have been born in twos. Two girls: one who goes on to have two girls of her own and the other who goes on to have none. Leave it to my Madrigal to go changing the rules."

Billy offers the baby a finger to grab, but it seems the excitement has finally been too much. Fenn is fast asleep. "A little naturalist. I wonder if he'll bring home another cougar one day. The house has to feel rather empty without one."

"No," Cait says, and for once her face cracks into a smile. "He will have a good familiar but not one like Camden. More likely a dog or a bird. We would be happy with a hawk, perhaps."

"He will have a fox," Mathilde declares, loudly enough to snap the baby's eyes back open. "A red fox. With a bright white chest and a dark tail." She swallows and shakes her head a little before wiping at her eyes.

"Well," says Matthew, grinning. "So much for surprises."

"A fox," Caragh whispers sadly. "His mother would have loved that."

Matthew lets her have one last look at the baby. "We'd better go."

"Take good care of that little man," Billy says. "And my chicken."

Matthew bounces Fenn in his arms and raises his small hand to wave. After a moment of hesitation, he cups Caragh's cheek and kisses her, hard. Then he turns, and he and the baby board the boat.

Arsinoe calls farewell and nods to the other Sandrins. Jonah, the younger brother, smiles at her. But Joseph's mother's glare catches her off-guard. She had not realized that Joseph's mother would hate her and blame her for all of this.

As the boat casts off and grows smaller in the harbor, Caragh follows it along the shore, and Arsinoe frowns.

"What's the matter?" Luke asks.

"Nothing."

Luke's eyes narrow, and the rooster on his shoulder peers at her with a slightly open beak. "You can't lie to me, Queen Arsinoe."

Arsinoe smiles grudgingly. She does not know, quite, what is bothering her. It was something about the way Matthew looked beside Caragh just now. Something about the way he looked at her. "I guess it seems unfair. Madrigal is dead; I know that, but . . ."

Billy slips a hand up the back of her neck and squeezes.

"The Sandrin boys and the Milone girls," Luke says, and Arsinoe wonders whether she really cannot lie to him. "They're doomed from the moment they set eyes on each other."

"Looking at it another way," says Billy, "Sandrin hearts are true. Distractible, certainly, given the right mix of tragedy and low magic. But they always return to their first love."

If Matthew and Caragh can overcome the barrier of grief, that will be true enough. But where will that leave Madrigal in Matthew's memory? Where was Mirabella left in Joseph's? Cast aside, and somehow that seemed an unworthy ending for them both.

Slowly, their small gathering breaks apart to return to the city. Arsinoe is about to follow Billy when Jules calls to her.

"Stay by the water with me for a while, will you?" she asks.

"Sure." Arsinoe goes back, and they walk a few paces, side by side. And though Arsinoe yearned for this time alone, she finds she does not know what to say. "I'm glad I can finally look you in the eye again," she blurts. "Without all the exploded blood vessels."

"Aye." Jules laughs. "Those really hurt." She holds her hand up and studies the fingers. "Think my nails will ever grow back? Look at that one." She pushes her middle finger into Arsinoe's face. "Torn off all the way down."

"Yeesh," Arsinoe says, and dodges it. "I'll make you some salve."

Jules takes a deep breath. "I'm glad I was awake to see my baby brother again. Though seeing him off so soon wasn't easy. I can't believe Caragh actually cried."

"Did you see Luke and Ellis? They're going to need new handkerchiefs."

They walk together, and as the silence stretches out, so does Arsinoe's unease.

"Now that Caragh's joined the rebellion, does that mean the Black Cottage has declared against the crown?" Arsinoe asks.

Jules shakes her head.

"No. Caragh says that no matter what happens, Willa won't go against the crown. She won't go against her Katharine."

"*Her* Katharine. What about me? I'm the one she's seen the most. And one of the two who aren't deranged." Arsinoe flinches when Jules's face falls. "I didn't mean that. I didn't mean deranged—"

"It's all right."

"Well . . . how are you feeling? Anything unusual?"

"What do you mean?"

"I don't know. Anger? Disorientation? Paranoia?"

"All three." Jules picks up a small stone and throws it into the waves. "But I don't think that counts as unusual, given the situation."

"I suppose not."

Jules takes a deep breath. "I have to shake it off soon. Emilia and the others . . . they'll need me to fight."

"So you mean to keep on. You mean to be the Legion Queen, then?"

Jules looks down, and a shadow crosses her features. "I mean to remove the Undead Queen from her throne. She put a knife to my mother's throat, Arsinoe. And she kills her own people. After that . . ." She raises her head, and Camden rushes past, intent on the wet sand and the chill of the waves.

"And how do your gifts feel? Have you tested them, since the tether?"

"They're both still with me," Jules says, and makes a fist. "Still strong. You don't like it, though, do you? You'd rather the war gift stayed bound. You want me to stay a naturalist."

Arsinoe shrugs. "You'd rather I'd been a naturalist. And you don't really like me working with poisons. Nobody likes change, Jules." She sighs. "And after all this, maybe you really are the island's champion."

"The island's champion. Or its doom. I've heard it both ways."

She means it as half a joke, but Arsinoe does not laugh. "Which do you think it is?"

"I think I should have been drowned as a baby. Or left in the woods. I think my family murdered an oracle because they didn't have the stomach to do what they should have."

Arsinoe swallows. That poor, murdered oracle hangs over them like a cloud. She cannot believe that it was Cait and Ellis who did it. Cait, who taught her how to build a fence. Ellis, who sang to them. She cannot believe that Caragh stood by as it happened.

"I would've done the same thing," Arsinoe says. "I'd do it now if anyone tried to hurt you."

"Even if I deserved it?"

Jules looks out, sending her naturalist gift into the sea. A dark shape crests in the waves, visible even through the shaded blue of the water.

"What is that?" Arsinoe asks just as the shark's dorsal fin slices up. It throws itself onto the beach, tail thrashing, until it lies gasping upon the sand. It is beautiful, with shining, black eyes and a bright white belly, and terrible to see dying, its mouth open as if in a mix of confusion and regret. When Camden leaps upon its back and begins tearing into it with her teeth and claws, shredding the slick, gray skin, Arsinoe wants to clap her hands and shoo her off. But Camden is no tabby. Ears back and teeth red with shark's blood, she would only snarl and dig her claws in deeper.

Jules pulls a knife from her belt and walks to the edge of the surf. With one fast motion, she stabs forward through the back of the head, and the shark goes still. "It's good meat," she says, and lays her hand on the creature gently. "Boil down the bones for broth. Even the fins are good eating. We need all of it that we can get."

It is true enough. And Arsinoe has seen Jules use her gift to hunt before. It is part of what the naturalist gift is meant for. But somehow this time it seems like war.

"I still am a naturalist, Arsinoe. And I'm still your guardian. Part of me will always be doing this for you. To kill Katharine. To make sure you're safe. But you're right. I'm not the same. And by the time this is over, none of us ever will be again."

When Arsinoe and Jules return to the city together, they are immediately approached by a messenger with word that they are to meet Emilia at the rear of the castle's west stable.

"She likes to give orders, doesn't she?" Arsinoe grumbles as they hurry to comply.

They find the stable predictably deserted, except for the horses who reside in the stalls. As she and Jules walk down the corridor, the horses sense Jules's gift and stick their heads out to say hello. It would be comical were the mood not so cautious and the corridor not so eerily quiet. As they near the end, Jules reaches out to pat the nose of her own horse, the tall black gelding she stole from Katharine. She must be relieved, Arsinoe thinks, to know that she did not accidentally kill him during the battle at Innisfuil.

"Emilia?" Jules calls. "Are you here?"

"I am here." Emilia steps out from the last stall.

"Well, you could have said something sooner," Arsinoe mutters. "What's going on?"

"We have a visitor."

Arsinoe shifts her weight nervously as the cloaked figure steps out. Whoever it is, they are tall, and hulking with armor. At a nod from Emilia, they lower their hood, and Arsinoe gasps.

"Margaret Beaulin! What is she doing here? What are you—"

Jules puts an arm across Arsinoe's chest.

"She's come to pledge the whole of Bastian City and its warriors to our cause." Emilia hands Jules a rolled paper, which Jules unrolls and Arsinoe reads over her shoulder. It is a treaty. A written treaty outlining the allegiance between Sunpool, the rebellion, and Bastian City. It carries the signatures of all the great houses of war.

"The Vatros clan," Jules says. "Emilia, your father signed."

"That does not surprise me."

"Didn't we already have the allegiance of the warriors?" Arsinoe asks, confused. "What does this matter?"

"You had those warriors loyal to the Vatroses," Margaret says. "But you did not have all. Now you do."

"Now we do." Jules's eyes narrow. "And we should trust this? Trust you?"

"That is up to you. It is why I came myself, rather than sending a messenger. I knew Emilia would not believe me unless she could look me in the eye."

"And you believe her?" Jules asks.

Emilia glances sidelong at Margaret, and the hairs on the back of Arsinoe's neck begin to prickle. She has never seen Emilia look unsure or vulnerable. Now she appears to be both.

"Margaret Beaulin has been a bootlicker to the poisoners for a long time," Emilia says. "But perhaps she is not anymore. If we can trust this, it would be useful. One of the war-gifted is worth twenty regular rebel soldiers."

"Regular rebel soldiers," Arsinoe says. "What about the elemental fighters with their lightning and fire? What about the naturalists with fierce dogs and cavalry?"

"With Bastian City, we can lay siege to Indrid Down," Emilia goes on. "Our forces can cut their access to the harbor from the north—"

"And mine can cut off their path to the river, from the south and east." Margaret nods. "And if somehow the Undead Queen should rout us, all forces can fall back to Bastian and make a stand behind the city walls, which have stood longer than even the Volroy."

"But only if we trust you," says Jules.

"Would it be easier to believe me if I demanded a seat on your new Black Council in return?" Margaret raises her eyebrows. "I considered it."

"If that isn't your demand, then why?" Jules asks.

"For Emilia," Margaret replies. "Because I failed her and I owe her a debt. And because I failed her mother," she adds quietly. "Whom I loved."

Arsinoe glances between Emilia and Margaret, each in pain merely by being in the other's presence. Whatever happened between them was not kind.

"Bastian City is proud, but you can't deny it's a city in decline," Jules says, and rolls up the treaty. "How well fortified is it presently?"

"Very well fortified."

"Then send us a supply of weapons. Spears, crossbow bolts, swords, and shields. Whatever you can spare. Send us that, and we will consider you allies."

THE VOLROY

In the Black Council chamber, Katharine sits at the head of the long table of dark wood. She is restless and troubled, and her patience for another meeting of arguments is stretched thin. The High Priestess had the gall to suggest that Mirabella be allowed to sit in on the council meetings, but the notion was quickly silenced. And even had the opposition been less vocal, Katharine would have forbidden it herself.

The dead queens, in their eagerness for Mirabella, have forced Katharine to remain distant from her sister. Every time they see her, they rush to Katharine's surface with such force that her head spins. And soon, they will find a way to take what they desire.

Unless Katharine finds a way to distract them.

"Has there been any word about Jules Milone?" Katharine asks.

"The Legion Queen has not been seen since the battle at Innisfuil," says Genevieve. "Though her forces still rally to Sunpool. And it seems we have lost Wolf Spring."

"To lose something," says Cousin Lucian, "we must first have had it."

"Had them or not," Genevieve says mildly, "we hoped they would remain out of play. The island over knows that the naturalists do not take sides. That they have involved themselves in the conflict may seem to some like a tipping point."

Katharine looks to Rho Murtra, her Commander of Queensguard. "Has the entirety of Wolf Spring emptied? Or only those tied to the Milones?"

"Our spies say the group was large," Rho replies. "But it was by no means the whole city. Genevieve is, as usual, overstating the situation."

"And what word of Arsinoe?"

"What last we heard, she did not believe that Mirabella had defected. She ordered search parties into the hills and along the cliffs, as if Mirabella had simply fallen out of a window."

Around the table, the Black Council snickers.

"Stop that," Katharine snaps. "Before my sister hears you and sets you on fire." She glances at Bree, who winks.

"Arsinoe's denial is good evidence that Mirabella can be trusted." High Priestess Luca sets her hand on the table, her expression serene.

"I do not like it."

Everyone on the Black Council turns to Rho. She is the last

person expected to speak against anything the High Priestess says.

"What do you mean," Luca asks, "you do not like it? What do you not like?"

"It seems too easy. Like that day at Innisfuil seemed too easy." Rho turns to Katharine, her white hood down inside the council chamber, her hair, red as blood, falling over her shoulder.

"Too easy," says Genevieve. "Have you forgotten how many queensguard we lost? How many—"

"The Legion Queen is not dead," Rho replies. "And Arsinoe now has a strong adviser in Cait Milone."

"So what do we do?" asks Lucian.

"Nothing," says Antonin. "We wait, and see if they will fray. And we cannot march on them anyway until spring."

High Priestess Luca leans forward. "The parade for Mirabella will ease these concerns. Flaunting her will show the rebels there are two queens to fear, and her usefulness against the mist will increase your popularity."

"This is a mistake." Lucian Arron shakes his head.

"Cousin Lucian. Lucian," Katharine corrects herself, since there are no longer two Lucians on the council and it is unnecessary to give him the fondness of the familial title. "We have had spies and soldiers in her shadow since the moment she arrived. She has made no attempt to contact the rebels and no attempt to flee. And even if she were to go, what would it matter? She knows nothing now that she did not before. And we would be no worse off."

She turns to Bree. "Bree Westwood. What is your

opinion? What are your observations of your old friend since she arrived?"

Bree presses her lips together. Whenever the council business has turned to Mirabella, she has remained quiet. Usually with her eyes fixed on her lap, careful to appear neutral.

"She still has love for Arsinoe," says Bree. "She always will. But she was raised a queen. Her loyalty is to the people and to the crown." Bree looks at Katharine and arches her eyebrow. "And she is more than a little afraid of you."

"Flattery," Lucian mutters.

"Truth," Bree snaps.

"Enough." Katharine raises her hand. "If you do not want me to show Mirabella to the people, then what would you have me do with her? House her and feed her in secret in exchange for nothing? What if the mist moves against the city? Should she be kept hidden away until then, so she can come charging out like an unexpected savior?" The corners of her mouth twist down. "Surely, that would do nothing to make the people remember how . . . popular she was."

"There is something else." Renata Hargrove clears her throat and demurely places her hand upon the table.

"Renata," says Katharine. "And what is that?"

"As Genevieve has maintained spies within the rebellion, I have maintained spies elsewhere. Including within Bastian City."

Genevieve crosses her arms and leans back, eyes narrowed. "You have been in contact with Margaret Beaulin."

"Until recently, I believed her loyal, despite her dismissal from the Black Council."

"But that is no longer so?"

"She insists that she is still with us," says Renata. "But that is not what my spies say. They say she left for Sunpool, with a signed treaty, to declare the city for the rebellion."

"A signed treaty? Who signed it?"

"The head of every major family of war-gifted."

Katharine sits, overcome. "How has this happened? How has the crown lost Wolf Spring and Bastian City? At least Mirabella may help us keep Rolanth!"

Rho Murtra slides her palms eagerly across the wood. "We might also march on Bastian."

"Now?"

"There are no mountains between us. No reason to wait for a spring thaw."

"No," Antonin objects. "We should hold our resources until the spring."

"When the rebels can march from the north and Bastian can flank us with warriors," Rho says, and lazily reclines. "It is clear that poisoners have led few battles."

"Because respect for us has kept anyone from rising in the first place," Antonin hisses, "for the last hundred years!"

"Enough." Katharine stands, signaling the meeting's end. "You have all been heard. And now I will consider the options."

After the Black Council disbands, Katharine retires to the privacy of her rooms in the West Tower.

"Is there anything you need, Queen Katharine?" her maid asks.

"No, Giselle," she replies. "Not just now. And when you go, please bar the door."

The loss of Bastian City and the betrayal of Margaret Beaulin are regrettable. But Katharine cannot help but be pleased. She could not have asked for a better solution to fall into her lap.

"Dead sisters," she whispers to her reflection in her dressing mirror. "Our reign is once again threatened. I would have a word."

She steps closer as the dead queens rise. Had someone else been watching, they might not have detected the change—a subtle shift in her facial muscles, a tremor in her iris, a small collection of tics belonging to many different queens—but she can see when they have drifted out of her blood and into her skin.

What word? they ask, and hiss. *What threat?*

"The war-gifted move against us. They would turn from the crown and join the rebellion."

The rage of the dead queens ripples across her face.

They must not. They cannot.

"They will unless we stop them."

Yes. Stop them. Kill them.

"But I cannot go. I am needed here."

We must ride. Ride with the army.

"Yes," Katharine says carefully. "But you must go alone."

We cannot go alone. We have no body and no blood. You are our vessel.

"What if I gave you another one?"

Mirabella . . .

Katharine's voice hardens. "No. Not Mirabella. Never my sister," she says, and clenches her teeth as the dead queens continue to whisper Mirabella's name. "Someone else. Can you move into someone else?"

Not permanent. A lasting vessel must be of the blood.

Of the blood. Queensblood.

"Temporarily, then. How is it done?"

They fall silent. Katharine tenses.

They must be willing. Or they must be weakened.

"Weakened? Like I was when I fell down the Breccia Domain." They say nothing. She hears only the multitude of their breaths. "No. I cannot do that. The temporary vessel must be willing. And you will still obey me when you are with them?"

You are our permanent vessel. You are a queen. Of our blood. Queen Katharine. Beloved.

"Good," Katharine says. "I have the perfect soldier in mind."

SUNPOOL

A few days after the Sandrins depart with baby Fenn, Arsinoe and Billy are roused from their room by a sight-gifted girl in a yellow cloak.

"Queen Arsinoe, Master Chatworth, please come with me."

"Why?" Arsinoe asks, swinging her legs out of bed. "And why so early?"

"Um, Arsinoe," Billy says, buttoning his shirt and looking down at the square from their window. "We'd better go. Everyone's down there already—Jules, Emilia, Mathilde, even Cait and Caragh Milone. As my mother would say, something's afoot."

Curious, they ready themselves and go down to the square. They follow Jules and her entourage through the courtyard, past the now-working fountain with its statue of leaping fish. Parts of Sunpool have come alive again, cleaned and refurbished after the influx of new, skilled labor. Yet as they pass a few of the scattered oracles in yellow cloaks, Arsinoe feels a pang of guilt. The oracles were ghosts before as their numbers dwindled. And they are still ghosts now, their quiet and stillness overrun, pushed aside to make way for the war.

"Isn't it strange?" Arsinoe says quietly to Billy. "They invite the rebellion here, yet they don't seem to want a say in it."

"Maybe it's because they already know what's going to happen," he replies. "But it is odd. Since we've been here, I've only seen Mathilde speaking with Jules and Emilia. But Mathilde isn't even a Lermont. The Lermonts are like the Arrons of this city, right?"

"She has Lermont blood," Caragh says, overhearing. "Through her father's side. I asked her about this very same thing just after I arrived. They let her take the lead because of all the oracles she is the most warlike. It's sad. The sight-gifted have been made to feel so weak and unwelcome for so long that not even they always trust themselves anymore."

"Somehow I think they trust themselves today." Arsinoe and the others stop behind Jules as two oracles step out from behind the pillars of the colonnade. The cloister that they stand in and its rows of pillars are called the sight garden, a place within the castle walls for seers to commune and practice their gift in quiet. Arsinoe finds it both pretty—with its green grass and rows of flowering shrubs—and strange. It is full of scrying bowls filled with water or sometimes wine, and the pillars in the center of the green space support nothing, each with two stone benches at their base.

Arsinoe elbows her way to the front.

"Josephine, Gilbert," Jules says, nodding to each of the seers. "Is Mathilde on her way?"

"I am here." Mathilde approaches through the garden and embraces both oracles: one a tall, blond woman who looks a little like Mathilde and another an older man with hair nearly the same sandy shade as Billy's. "I already know what they have seen."

"Well?" Emilia asks. "What is it?"

The woman, Josephine, speaks. "We have seen a battle in Indrid Down. Forces swarming even to the base of the Volroy."

Emilia smiles. "Good. When?"

"There was no snow. Beyond that, I cannot say. But I have also seen something else: Mirabella, on horseback beside the queen and clad in silver armor."

"Her lightning could lay low whole fields of us," Emilia says, glaring at Arsinoe. "And you thought she would never turn."

"She hasn't," Arsinoe snaps. "She won't."

"There is more," says Josephine. "An opportunity will arise to reclaim Mirabella. If you take that opportunity, she will not be at that battle. This is what the bones say."

The bones. It does not sound like much to go on, to Arsinoe's ears, but the only words that matter are "reclaim Mirabella."

"When? When can we go get her?"

The oracle called Gilbert takes a deep breath. He walks to an empty scrying bowl and grasps the bottle resting against its base, uncorking it with a twist. Then he pours the deep red liquid into the shallow marble basin. Arsinoe swallows. She would rather he used water. The wine looks too much like blood.

Once the bottle is empty, the wine stills, faster than is natural, and the seer breaks the surface with the tip of his finger, moving in one circular swirl. His gift is strong. For a moment, Arsinoe swears she can see Mirabella's face and flowing hair, and the glint of a silver breastplate.

"The Undead Queen means to hold a public parade through the capital," Gilbert says. "To formally announce the allegiance between the two sisters. It will take place in six days."

"Six days," Jules repeats. "Not much time."

"The entire route will be heavily guarded," says Mathilde. "She will have archers in the windows of every building and cavalry on the streets."

Emilia puts her hands on her hips. "We cannot hope to escape with her. Not without an entire army chasing us back to Sunpool."

"Perhaps we could lose them," Jules suggests. "We could lay traps outside the city. Ambushes to slow them down as we make our way to cover."

"A good suggestion. But 'we' are not doing anything. No matter what we decide, you will stay back. Out of danger."

"A fight is the only thing I'm good for. You can't hold me from it."

The oracle Josephine clears her throat. "That is not all. We have seen that, if you take this opportunity, then Mirabella will not be part of the battle at the Volroy."

"And?" Jules prods.

"But neither will you be."

Arsinoe looks at Jules in shock. "What does that mean?"

"Speak, oracle!" Emilia advances on her angrily, but Mathilde steps in between them.

"If there were more to say, then she would have said it," she says quietly.

Jules puts a hand on Emilia's arm, and the warrior stands down. Jules nods to the seers. "Thank you. I need to speak to my friends. I would appreciate it if you said nothing of this until we have decided."

They return to Jules's private quarters, and Arsinoe, Emilia, Cait, and Mathilde accompany Jules inside to gather around the hearth. Billy, Luke, and even Caragh, she asked to wait outside.

"Friends," Emilia teases. "You are a queen now. You must say 'advisers.' Or 'counselors.' Or 'generals.'"

"If I'm a queen," says Jules, "can't I say whatever I want?"

She stands at her table and pours a cup of wine, but stares into it for a long time instead of drinking.

"You're nervous," Arsinoe says, and runs Camden's tail through her hand. "I can tell because the cat won't sit. What are you thinking?"

"I'm thinking that I wish visions were clearer."

"We all wish that," Mathilde says, and smiles.

Jules sets down her cup and studies the table as if looking at a map. Her fingertip traces imaginary routes between Sunpool and Indrid Down, so quickly and precisely that Arsinoe has to check to make sure a map has not actually been carved into the surface.

"I don't know how to do it, Arsinoe. I know you want me to save her—"

"Who says she wants to be saved?" Emilia asks. "Nothing is more complicated than rescuing someone who has no wish to be rescued. Though we will know precisely where she is." Emilia's hand drifts to the dagger at her belt. "Even if we can't get her out, it would be possible to slip in and—"

"If you say one more word," Arsinoe growls, "I am going to get my bear."

"I do not say it to be cruel. Or even because I want her dead, despite the fact that she is a faithless, troublemaking traitor."

Arsinoe's fists clench, but Emilia's voice is light and in jest. Almost gentle.

"But you know her, Arsinoe. You know how strong she is. And that she is *too* strong." She sighs. "And beyond that. You know what the dead queen Daphne told you. What Mirabella's death might mean. For an end to the mist, it would be worth it."

"Emilia," Jules says, still leaning over the table, "that's already been decided. We won't pursue Mirabella's death." She stands up. "And without her, we lose the whole of Rolanth."

"Perhaps you shouldn't be entertaining this at all," Cait says. "If what the oracles saw is true, what will it mean for you, Jules? Perhaps you should leave it alone. Let the moment pass."

Jules rests her hands on the table, and beneath her hands, the wood begins to shake.

"Jules?" Arsinoe says, and Jules steps back.

"I'm fine." She swallows and then she moves her wine cup with her war gift just to prove it, hopping it across the table like a rabbit as her grandmother watches with a stern expression.

"You've been practicing."

"I had to be sure that both gifts were safe," Jules says, sounding slightly ashamed.

Arsinoe looks at Emilia. The warrior is cradling her arm, the one with the low-magic cuts. When she sees Arsinoe looking, she quickly lets go. But Arsinoe knows she felt something when the table began to rattle. When Jules's war gift flared, the tether between them was pulled taut.

"We will let it go," Jules says. "We'll wait for another chance. Another vision."

"There might be no other chance," Emilia says. "I am afraid for you, too. But the opportunity to remove Mirabella from the field of battle—"

"I'm not afraid for me. That I'm not at the battle of the Volroy could mean anything. But I won't risk anyone else. Not on something with such poor odds. I won't have a repeat of what happened to my mother!"

She steps back again as the table shakes and her wine cup spills red across it. Camden leans against her good leg. Cait catches Arsinoe's eye and shakes her head once, sternly. She is worried. Afraid that Jules is not ready for this.

Arsinoe stares down at the table, an invisible version of the Volroy forming across it as if she too had the war-gifted's talent for maps. "What if there was a way to get Mirabella out without anyone needing to do anything?"

"What way is that?" Jules asks warily.

"I will sneak into the Volroy and find her. I'll tell her we're there. We can lay a distraction somewhere along the parade route where she can break free and escape. We'll arrange a meeting point, and Emilia and the warriors can get us all out of the city."

"How will you sneak into the Volroy unnoticed?" Emilia asks. "You are not exactly easy to miss when you are either scarred or have a scarf wrapped around your face."

"I know the back ways through the fortress. All the hidden passageways. Even the ones in the Queen's Tower."

"How do you know those?" asks Jules.

Arsinoe shrugs. "Because I dreamed them through Daphne's eyes."

Jules and Emilia look at each other, Jules's expression doubtful.

From outside the door, there comes a loud squawk that gradually turns into a crowing: Hank, Luke's black-and-green rooster. Such a great sound from such a small beak. It practically shakes the wood.

"There's Hank," Arsinoe says. "Luke must be getting impatient. So what do you say, Jules? And bear in mind that if you say no, I'm probably just going to do it anyway."

THE VOLROY

In the capital, preparations for the parade take up most of Katharine's time.

"A deeper blue for the cape," Genevieve says to the attendants as they show her the garments that the elementals will wear. She touches a jacket with silver buttons and caresses the collar. "And more silver thread. Here. I want every elemental in black and blue and silver, just like she is. I want them recognized, these dutiful subjects of the crown."

Those elementals who survived the encounter with the mist in Bardon Harbor will ride at the head, out in front of the queens. Genevieve has also spread word that every elemental is invited to wear the colors, to show their gift with pride. The survivors will look very fine, outfitted in black wool and capes of deep blue, daggers at their hips each with a polished silver handle and capped with a fat river pearl. Mirabella will also wear mostly blue, to show that she is different from the queen, and the custom silver breastplate that Katharine has ordered. Katharine will of course be in all black, except for a breastplate of gold and skulls.

"You are very good at this, Genevieve," Katharine says as Genevieve runs her hands over the beaded skirt she has had designed for Bree, the official elemental of the Black Council.

"I am glad you see the use in the talent," she says, eyes on her work. "Others might call it a waste. But there is power in the show of power. The way you are presented . . . it matters."

"It does. I ought to put you in charge of every formal function."

Genevieve glances at her from the side of her eye. "You ought to put me at the head of your council."

Katharine smiles kindly. Genevieve has struggled to find her place in Natalia's absence, attempting to be many different things: the kind leader; the cunning, cutting Arron matriarch. She could tell Genevieve that she does not need to be her sister. But somehow she thinks that is something that will have to be learned on her own.

"Yet Rho Murtra is overseeing the soldiers," Genevieve goes on, "and Antonin and the High Priestess oversee the accounts."

"Is it not enough that you are my master of spies?"

"Co-master. A title I must share with giftless Renata Hargrove, of all people."

"Renata," Katharine says. "Renata is nothing but eyes, and she knows where and when to place her ears to the ground. But it is you I trust the most, Genevieve."

Genevieve turns toward her, dismissing the servants with a flap of her hand. "You trust me the most?"

"I do."

"Because our goals are aligned?"

"Because our goals are aligned," Katharine says. "And because you are Natalia's sister. Do not worry, Genevieve. It is not because I think you care."

Genevieve wraps a measuring tape around her hand like a rope. "I do care. I care very much, now." She tugs the tape tight until it digs into her skin. "You know the Legion Queen rides always with an oracle. Even though the sight gift is fickle and weak, I worry about the things it may tell her. What she may know before we do."

"I would perhaps be more inclined to fear that the Legion Queen rides with Arsinoe and that bear."

Katharine and Genevieve spin.

"High Priestess," Katharine says. "We did not hear you."

"Few do. It is the robes, I think. The material of them. I know that Renata has a fair number of spies outfitted in temple garb." The old woman steps closer, and Genevieve quickly takes her leave. Like her sister before her, there is no love lost between Genevieve and the High Priestess.

"The parade preparations are going well?" Luca asks. She walks close to the tables where the elemental garments have been laid out. "I know that Rho is barely sleeping, mapping and remapping the city, identifying holes and possible places of trouble."

"Yes. I have seen her riding out with the soldiers morning and night."

"And Genevieve has ordered banners made and flags?"

"All that remains are fittings," Katharine says. "And the food. And the wine. And—"

Luca chuckles. "Do not worry so much. The people of the capital have more than enough experience putting on a show. Nothing will go wrong."

When she, Bree, and Elizabeth are summoned to the throne room to help with the parade preparations, Mirabella hides a frown. Another dress fitting and another choice of lace are not high on her list of priorities. She must still find a way to get to Pietyr Renard. And find a way to wake him.

She is full of the dead.

Madrigal's final words swirl through her head, as do thoughts of Daphne and Queen Illiann. The volumes about the Blue Queen in the Indrid Down Temple library were taken for researching the mist. But why had they not been returned? Is there something more? Something to hide?

"Mira?" Elizabeth asks. "Don't you want Bree to try on her gown?"

"Yes, of course. I am sorry. I am having a hard time concentrating."

"Is something wrong?" asks Bree.

"Everything is fine," she lies.

Arsinoe. How I wish you were here. Even if your counsel

would prove rash and terrible.

Mirabella follows Bree and Elizabeth down the stairs as if in a dream. When they arrive in the throne room, she watches with a frozen smile as they excitedly direct the tailors. Ribbons and pearls fall to the floor in streams and seem to bounce toward her with molasses-like slowness.

"Are you all right, sister?" Katharine asks, and Mirabella jerks back alert. "Or perhaps this bores you. You have had many days like this: playing with dresses and laughing with friends." Katharine leans back against the edge of a table, with a serenely happy expression. "For me, it is still a novelty."

Mirabella reaches for a pretty silver pendant. "Forgive me. Such days should always be appreciated." Across the room, Luca laughs as Bree shows off her beaded skirt. For the briefest of moments, the High Priestess's eyes meet Mirabella's. *What are you waiting for?* her old eyes ask. *Do you think you will have forever to find your answers?*

"Katharine. How fares your Pietyr?"

Katharine clears her throat.

"He is well. As well as he has been. Why do you ask?"

"I know it must weigh heavily on your mind. And . . . I would like to see him."

"See him?"

"Visit him," Mirabella amends. "And I would like also to see Greavesdrake Manor, where you were raised."

Katharine studies her curiously, but Mirabella's expression does not waver.

"Of course. I will arrange it."

Bree comes to show off her skirt, and Mirabella admires the beadwork. She steps up to the table and runs her hand over the handles of the ornamental daggers. Such finery. It is hard to imagine that Jules Milone would wear it someday. Hard to imagine that she would command the queensguard army in a crown and a gown. Or that Luca would ever bow to her.

Mirabella had meant it when she told Bree and Elizabeth that she had no allegiance to either Katharine or the rebellion. But for there to be no queen of the line within the West Tower . . . She would be lying if she said it did not feel unnatural.

She goes to the window and looks down; from there, she can see the inner ward of the Volroy grounds, where Rho sits astride a large white horse directing rows and rows of queensguard soldiers through their drills. Even if she cannot make out the words, she hears Rho's booming bark and watches the soldiers respond with crisp precision.

"She is very good," Katharine says, joining her at the window. "A great asset to the Black Council. As I am sure she was to you in Rolanth."

"Rho's first loyalty was to the Goddess," Mirabella replies. "And it seems, to the line of succession."

"She will be of much use against the rebellion."

"I am sure she will be." Below, Rho has shed her white hood, and her red hair blazes down her back. She is the Commander of the Queensguard now. Hardly a priestess at all.

INDRID DOWN

Arsinoe and Billy slip through the early-morning streets of the capital dressed in warm gray cloaks. He carries a basket, as if on his way to the marketplace. She carries nothing. Before they parted ways with Emilia and Mathilde outside the city, she asked them to dress her up to look like someone else. Nothing too fancy to draw the eye. She wanted the clothes of a merchant or a bookkeeper. So they left her in her soft brown trousers, and Mathilde lent her a vest of goldenrod to button over a clean white shirt. Then they twisted her short hair into a pair of loose low buns, a few strands tugged free to slightly obscure her scars. She does not know whether she looks like a bookkeeper, but she certainly does not look like herself.

"Good Goddess," Arsinoe mutters as they walk along the side streets, doing their best to keep their feet out of slushy, wet pockets in the pavement. "I'd hoped I'd never see this place again." She sniffs. "But at least in the winter it doesn't smell." They have nearly reached their destination now; the towers of the Volroy are clearly visible, blotting out the sky as they pass between buildings.

"I don't like this," Billy says. "You shouldn't go alone."

"Alone is safer. And I won't have to be dragging someone along behind me who doesn't know the ways."

They hurry to the end of an alley and stop short. Another few cross streets and they will be at the Volroy. Arsinoe puts her hands on Billy's shoulders. "You should stay here."

"Why? I'm dressed like a Fennbirnian. No one will notice if I go onto the grounds with you and leave alone." He glares up at the towers. "How are you going to reach the secret passageways, anyhow? Is there some other entrance? Something underground?"

"If there is, I don't know it. I've just got to go in with the other folk who seek governance. I'll slip into the passageways once I find one."

Billy looks at her, aghast. "You never said—! You'll be recognized!"

"Maybe not. If I'm only glimpsed by queensguard and no one from the actual council, I doubt they'll realize who I am. Not dressed like this and when it's so unexpected."

Billy cannot manage words. He just stares at her with his mouth open.

"We knew there were going to be risks," she says.

"You never told me there was no secret way in. You

shouldn't do this. We should smuggle you in through the servant's entrances or the kitchen."

"That's a whole lot of interaction in a city full of unfriendly traitors."

"I thought we were the traitors."

Arsinoe frowns. "Anyone who sides with Katharine is a traitor to their own conscience. Now I'm going in. Kiss me for luck."

Billy hesitates, but in the end, he does as he is bid and does it well, pulling her close, his fingers cradling the back of her neck.

"Arsinoe, are you ever going to listen to me?"

"Yes. Absolutely."

"When?"

"When you're right. Look, I'm the one who ought to be afraid for you! All I need to do is slip in, tell Mirabella what to do, and slip out." Billy's part in the plan is much more dangerous. He is to hide with the warriors along the parade route and provide a distraction so Mirabella can escape.

"Be safe," he says, and she leaves him in the shadowy alley.

She crosses the last few streets to the Volroy grounds, her breath fast, white puffs in the chill air. With every step she takes, her knees want to lock up and turn around. There are no good memories here. She shivers as she passes the spot where Katharine kept Braddock caged prior to the Queens' Duel.

But Mirabella needs her. She is there, somewhere, in who-knows-how-much danger inside the hulking, black stone monster of the towers. And Arsinoe will not leave her.

"Not even if you got yourself into this mess," she whispers as she rounds the path toward the entry gate.

Ahead, people have gathered to see the queen. From the looks of them, they are mostly merchants, with bolts of fabric beneath their arms: black and many shades of blue. When she gets closer, she sees they are not actually raw bolts of fabric but completed banners and flags. At the front, a woman stands holding something large and draped in black cloth. She has an air of nervous pride. Whatever she holds, it must be important.

Arsinoe walks alongside the waiting carriages, blending in with the apprentices. Too soon she finds herself blocked in, in the middle of the waiting group, with queensguard soldiers making inspections. The soldiers begin to bark instructions, and the crowd around her jostles itself into a line.

She does her best to look like she has been here before. But when she stands up on tiptoe and sees the queensguard searching and questioning every person, her heart jumps into her throat.

"When did they start doing this?" she hears a man ask irritably.

"Ever since the Legion Queen rose in the north," someone replies.

Arsinoe wants to turn tail and walk out of there on fast legs until she can dive behind a shrub to panic properly. But if she does that, she will never have the nerve to try again. And she will probably be caught.

She thinks quickly and worms her way through the line, ignoring every cry of "Hey!" and "Where do you think you're going?" until she manages to get directly in front of the woman holding the item draped in cloth. Now that she is closer, she can make out the faint outline of the item's shape. It looks to be armor. Custom armor.

The line moves fast. The last few ahead of her answer questions with downcast eyes and hold their arms out to be searched.

"Surrender all personal weaponry," one of the soldiers calls down the line. "It will be returned to you as you leave."

Arsinoe reaches for her belt and unbuckles the leather sheath that holds her small sharp dagger.

"Next, step up."

She goes forward and turns over the knife, trying to keep her fingers from lingering. She has had that dagger for a long time. It survived the Ascension. It went with her to the mainland and back again. Now it is lost.

She holds out her arms, and a soldier runs her hands over them, flattening her sleeves and patting every inch of her vest before turning her attention to Arsinoe's trouser-clad legs.

"What business do you have here at the Volroy?"

"Consultation," Arsinoe answers quickly. The soldier's brow furrows, and she starts to really look at Arsinoe's face. Arsinoe turns her scarred cheek slightly away. "I'm an associate of one of the other merchants. I lost her in the line. She's already come through." None of it sounds any good. But before the guard's suspicions can be raised any further, another soldier pulls Arsinoe along to clear the path for the woman behind her.

"That's the armorer," he says. "They've been waiting on her. Get her through." He nods to Arsinoe. "Get on."

Arsinoe walks through the raised gate and into the interior of the castle, falling into step with the rest of the line as they meander through the corridors. She takes a deep breath. She feels safer now in the shadows of the torchlit hallways. But she has to find an entrance to the passageways soon or a discreet staircase to slip up or down. If she does not, she will wind up nose to nose with her little sister, and a pair of buns is not a good enough disguise for that.

The good news is the queensguard escort seems to pay little attention to the merchants now that they are in the Volroy proper. So when they turn a corner, it is all too easy for Arsinoe to slip out of line and dash quickly around the next corner, moving so smoothly up a staircase of the West Tower that it is like it was meant to be. From there, it takes only a few moments to find the right ancient tapestry and open the right stone, allowing her into the walls to move about undetected.

All of that time she spent living Daphne's life in the Volroy, dreaming those long-ago dreams, has finally come in handy.

Far up in the hills, the rest of the rebel party lies in wait, blended into the trees and snow-covered stones. They will wait there undetected until Arsinoe returns from the city, and then they will wait longer, until the parade is under way and Billy's party springs the diversion.

"Do you think you kept me far enough back?" Jules asks sarcastically. From there in the hills, Indrid Down looks like a play city made of blocks. Something for a child to build and knock down on a whim.

There are not many there, tucked into their cloaks behind the rocks, sharing plates of bacon and barley mush. A small faction of soldiers, totaling twenty-five, not counting those six who went with Billy to hide for the night along the parade route. They are mostly warriors, but a few naturalists and giftless as well.

Jules growls deep in her throat. "We're too far away."

"We will move closer on the day of the parade," Emilia says. "There is no reason to endanger you yet. You *should* have listened to me and not come at all."

"Arsinoe and I never listen to anyone. Didn't we tell you?" Jules pats the neck of her own mount, who is actually Katharine's old gelding, and the horse flinches. Since Jules's return, he has been shy of her, and only her naturalist gift allows her to come close enough to mount. She must have given him such a fright that day when she lost control at Innisfuil Valley.

Emilia pokes Jules hard between the eyebrows.

"Does all of Wolf Spring raise its children to be so stupid? You must fight smart, Jules. Fight to survive the war."

"But it won't really matter, will it? The memory of the Legion Queen is enough to unite the cities and the new council. You won't need me."

Emilia's chestnut horse stomps closer at her urging, to bump against Jules's gelding. "We won't. But I will."

Jules looks away, back toward the city. Thinking of Arsinoe alone in the Volroy makes her stomach clench in knots.

"I don't like this plan of hers."

"It is not a plan at all."

Jules smirks. "That's what all of Arsinoe's plans are like."

Emilia laughs. "Someday I must explain to you naturalists the difference between recklessness and calculated sacrifice."

Emilia's dark eyes sparkle. She referred to Arsinoe as a naturalist. Not a queen or a hated poisoner. The moment is warm, and Jules reaches out to touch Emilia's cheek.

"Don't be afraid." Emilia covers her hand with her own. "You and I are tethered now. And I will never let you fall back into darkness."

Jules takes her hand back.

"If I'd been fully myself, I never would have let you do that. To take on this burden."

"You are not a burden."

Emilia looks over her shoulder, back to their makeshift camp and Mathilde, who has polished a piece of ice to blow smoke across for visions. "We always knew it would not be easy. But it will be worth it."

THE VOLROY

Katharine catches Rho as she is returning from her morning rounds in the soldiers' barracks. The tall priestess is so focused on her task that Katharine must call out to her twice.

"Yes? What is it, Queen Katharine?"

"I would speak with you a moment. If you would follow me?"

Rho nods. She does not hesitate when Katharine brings her through the entrance to the Volroy cells. Nor does she hesitate when they go down stair after stair, deep into the belly of the fortress. Why would she? She has nothing to fear, the great warrior priestess, not from Katharine, who is only a pale and sickly poisoner and small for her age to boot. Katharine leads Rho down to the lowest floor, to the cells that have long stood empty and are rarely checked, except for rats. She brings her to the last cell and steps inside.

"What are we doing here, Queen Katharine?"

Rho inhales through her nose. Though she is not afraid, she is on alert. Her broad shoulders and neck give her the look of a bull about to charge.

Katharine hesitates. To make this request of Rho is to tell her all. And if she refuses . . . She looks down, gravely, her fingers dancing across the poisoned blades she keeps ever at her hip.

"In the time you have served on the Black Council, I have come to trust your advice. But I must ask. You are a priestess of the temple. Where do your loyalties lie?"

"With you," Rho says, surprised. "And with the Goddess."

"All gifts come from the Goddess," says Katharine. "And the queens are of the Goddess's line. Descended from her. We are the Goddess, on earth."

"Yes. That is known."

"So what if I could make your gift stronger? Do not mistake me. It is strong already. But what if I could make it . . . invincible?"

"What do you mean?"

"I was not a poisoner born, Rho." Katharine walks around her, cutting off her exit. "I expect Luca has told you that already."

The priestess lowers her eyes, as much of an admission as she is going to get.

"I was not a warrior born either," Katharine continues. "Yet I can throw knives with perfect aim. The people say that when I came back from the Quickening at the Beltane Festival, I came back changed. And they were right." As she speaks, the dead sisters slip to the surface, listening. They look at Rho through Katharine's eyes and sense the strength of her gift.

"Changed how?"

"For the better," Katharine says, and Rho gasps. The dead queens have begun to show through. Black rot rises on Katharine's cheeks; she feels the softening of the skin across her forehead.

"What are you?"

"Do not be afraid. I am the keeper of the Goddess's other daughters. She has sent them to me, to look after her island. And I would share them with you. If you are willing." The vessel must be willing. Or it must be weakened. Katharine's hand again trails along her blades. "I need your help now, Rho. Genevieve and Renata tell me that their spies have indicated that the Legion Queen has left Sunpool. I fear that she may be here. That she may seek to sabotage the parade or worse, assassinate my sister." Katharine waits as Rho studies the rot on her cheeks, and the sickly shadows swimming under her skin. Either Rho will draw her sword and try to run her through, or she will ask another question and Katharine will know she has her.

"What do you mean, share them with me?" Rho asks.

"There is only one way for you to truly know." Katharine reaches up and touches Rho's shoulder. "Kneel. Kneel, and receive them."

Mirabella returns to the king-consort's apartment with a throbbing headache. She had forgotten how much she dislikes dress fittings. All of the endless dress fittings she underwent at

Westwood House, being made to stand this way or that way, to raise her arms and square her shoulders. To hold very still and avoid the pins. But what really bothered her was having the armor put on. Seeing herself in the mirror outfitted in shining silver, the breastplate etched with thunderheads and veins of grooved lightning, standing there as Mirabella Mistbane, ally of the Queen Crowned.

She walks through the room to the bedchamber. Perhaps if she lies down for a little while and gets some rest. If only she can keep from dreaming of Madrigal Milone choking on a mouthful of blood.

She spins at an odd sound of grinding and calls fire to her fingertips as someone steps out from behind the tapestry of the interior wall.

"Arsinoe!"

She shakes the fire out and runs to her sister, embracing her before the vision can dissolve. But Arsinoe holds firm. If indeed it is really Arsinoe; she hardly looks like herself in a bright yellow vest and her hair twisted prettily onto the back of her head.

"Thank the Goddess, you're still breathing!" Arsinoe says, and pushes her away. "I half expected to arrive and find parts missing."

"How?" Mirabella asks, and peers at the tapestry. "Where did you come from?"

"Remember I told you I know the hidden passageways in the Volroy?" Arsinoe taps her temple. "Daphne's dreams."

"But what are you doing here? You're in danger every moment." Mirabella's stomach sinks. There could be an army of rebels hiding in the southern woods along the river. "She will know you have come. I have heard she has spies in Sunpool."

"We know about the spies. They've been handled. Is that why you came? To be our spy? I've been trying to figure it out since we discovered you gone. And I can't." Arsinoe waits. The frustration in her eyes grows by the second. "Never mind. What matters is we're here now, and we've got a way to get you out."

"No. You cannot."

"Of course I can. Grab some kind of disguise, and let's get out of here! I can get us close to the servants' entrance, almost all the way outside!"

"Arsinoe, the guards check my room constantly. More often if they do not hear me. We will be caught, and you will be killed!"

Undeterred, Arsinoe reaches out with pursed lips and tries to drag her. But Mirabella digs in her heels.

"If you don't come with me now," Arsinoe growls, "Billy's going to create a diversion along the parade route. Just past the marketplace. When you see it, bolt for the market. Make it to the north end of the city on the main road toward Prynn. When you reach the old gate, Jules and Emilia will join you. And then you disappear."

She shakes her head. "You have to stop him. I am to have my own detail of queensguard."

"You're telling me you can't blow back a couple of queens-guard?"

"Arsinoe . . . I left the note for you to find so you would not follow me!"

"Well, you should've known that wouldn't work!"

Mirabella looks at her sister sadly. She should have known. She could have left a dozen notes from the capital scattered around her room. She could have written a goodbye letter in her own hand. It would not have mattered.

"What I said to Emilia before I left, the argument we had about Jules—"

"You didn't mean it!"

"I didn't mean it as much as I made it seem. But I did mean it. A little."

Arsinoe steps back. "All right. Fine. But it's time to stop messing about now. I can't stay for much longer."

Mirabella smiles. She has wanted to see Arsinoe for so long; she refuses to waste time arguing. "You are shivering." She pulls a blanket off her bed and wraps it around Arsinoe's rather dusty shoulders. "Those passageways must be freezing."

"They are, in places. And they're dark. I was sure I was going to get lost and die and Billy would have to tear this whole place down searching for my corpse."

"How did you find your way?"

"I told you: I knew the way. And when I was in doubt . . . I just followed the rats. Them and me, we're the only ones who know about the hidden passageways anymore."

Mirabella glances at the tapestry hanging on the wall. It is old but not so old as the Blue Queen. Lucky that it was there for Arsinoe to hide behind.

"Brr," Arsinoe says. "It doesn't feel any warmer in here than it did in the walls. Don't you like fire? Why isn't there one burning?"

"Too much fire at my disposal makes the guards nervous." But they have left her one log. One, lonely log. She turns her attention to it, and immediately it begins to smoke and then catches with a whoosh, flames licking hungrily up all sides.

"That's better." Arsinoe shrugs out of the blanket and goes to warm her fingers. "I suppose they don't think you can freeze. You never shiver."

"I never shiver," Mirabella repeats. Then she stops. Katharine has visited her many times, and she does not shiver either. Bree is an elemental and almost equally resistant to the cold, but the guards are always in heavy cloaks, and poor little Elizabeth huddles inside her hood. But how could Katharine, a naturalist born and perhaps a forced poisoner, have any touch of the elemental gift?

"Will you tell me what you're doing here at least?" Arsinoe asks. "Because I know you haven't joined the crown."

"Oh? How can you be so sure?"

"Because even if you didn't want to fight for Jules, you would never fight against me. Katharine is dangerous, Mira. Deadly. You saw her put that bolt through my back. You watched her dump poison down my throat, as if that could do anything—"

"She is not like that now. The Ascension is over."

"Is it?" Arsinoe says skeptically. "I've never heard of an Ascension ending with more than one queen alive."

"Except that you have. Illiann's. Queen Illiann lived side by side with her sister. Happily. And if there was a way for her, then perhaps . . ."

At Mirabella's words, Arsinoe looks away, out the window as the sky begins to drop small snowflakes. December nears its end.

"It is almost our birthday," Mirabella murmurs.

Arsinoe looks at the snow and snorts. "I guess it is. If the Ascension weren't over, like you say, I guess they'd be getting ready to lock us up in—" She eyes the room. "Well, in here."

"They would not lock us in the tower until after Beltane."

But even so, she and Arsinoe eye the walls uncomfortably.

"It is unsettling, though, isn't it? They've locked queens up in these very rooms. To kill each other. One might have died right there." Arsinoe points. "Or there." She points again. "Or over there."

"Arsinoe, stop that."

"Mathilde says that sometimes with the sight gift she can feel the place where someone died. That it lingers, like a stain. And Katharine *lives* here now."

"So would you, and so would I, if we had won."

Arsinoe shrugs. "I would've stayed in Wolf Spring. But her? The Undead Queen? I suppose it suits her."

"She is not like that. It was—"

"The Ascension, right. I heard you. Except what about that boy she killed? The one who stood against her and had his head ripped clean off?"

Mirabella closes her eyes. The Katharine she has come to know does not seem like she could ever have been so brutal. She cannot reconcile this Katharine with the stories she has heard. Yet she saw it herself at Innisfuil when she ran the long-bladed knife through Madrigal's neck.

"She is a danger, but she is my puzzle to solve."

"She isn't a puzzle at all. This isn't a game."

"It is almost like she is two different people," Mirabella says softly, and something about the words sticks. Katharine never shivers. There is some secret, that perhaps only Pietyr Arron knew, and that Madrigal somehow found out. She turns the pieces over in her mind. There are places where they almost fit. But there is something she is still missing.

"Two different people," Arsinoe says. "Or she just grew up." Her eyes lose focus, and she half laughs, remembering something. "I loved her, too, once, you know. That day they came for us at the Black Cottage, after you were gone, I scratched Natalia Arron's face when she tried to take her. Camden would've been proud. But that was a long time ago. Now I'd throw her at Natalia Arron."

Before she can reply, Mirabella hears movement from the hall: the guards shuffling position and telltale footsteps approaching in the corridor. She grasps Arsinoe by the arm and pulls her back toward the tapestry.

"You have to go!"

Arsinoe lifts the fabric and stops. "Not until you tell me you understand the plan for tomorrow."

"There is no plan for tomorrow. Call it off. Get out of the city while you still can!"

"Mira, I won't just leave you here!"

"You have to!" She shoves her sister a little harder, wishing she knew which stone to push or which to slide or kick to get the passageway to open. "I have made my choice, and I am safe here."

"Have you gone daft? How can you be safe here when we're going to war?"

Arsinoe opens the passageway, too quickly for Mirabella to know how she did it, and Mirabella prods her inside. Before she lets the tapestry fall, she reaches for Arsinoe and kisses her hard on the head. Then the fabric drops, and her sister is gone. But before she hears the wall grind shut, she hears Arsinoe whisper.

"You cannot always be the peacemaker."

"Mirabella!"

Mirabella spins around just as Katharine is admitted into the room. She cranes her thin neck this way and that until she spies Mirabella in the bedchamber.

"There is a fire in the fireplace," Katharine says. "Is everything all right?"

"Yes. Only nerves. It helps, to play with the flames."

Katharine looks back at the fire. But she does not move to

it or hold her hands out to warm them. Perhaps she is warmed enough by the excitement of the coming parade. Her pale cheeks are even slightly flushed.

"Is everything all right, Queen Katharine? Was there something you needed?"

"Only to get away from the whispers of the Black Council in my ear. That the parade is a mistake. That to display you to the capital like this will somehow raise you up as queen."

"And what do you say?" Mirabella asks.

Katharine cocks her head. "I say that the people can wish for you all they want; it will not make it so. And besides. They do not know . . . what plans I have for you."

"Plans? What plans?" Mirabella steps away from the wall, sensing Arsinoe is still there. She has not fled down the passageway as she should. Instead, she is just behind the stone, listening.

"Soon," Katharine promises. "Soon I will tell you everything."

INDRID DOWN

Getting out of the castle is easier than getting in, and Arsinoe makes her way back through the city and into the hills, to Jules and Emilia, without any trouble. She slips off the road and into the sparse cover of winter trees and brush to the clearing where they wait.

"Arsinoe!" Jules and Camden stand, slipping out from underneath their fur blanket beside Emilia's small fire. "Thank the Goddess."

"Don't sound so surprised. I told you I knew what I was doing."

"Did you see her?" Emilia glances at her from beneath her brow. She kneels beside the fire, skinning a rabbit to roast. "Will she be ready?"

"Well?" Jules asks when Arsinoe does not reply.

"I don't know."

Emilia tips her head back and throws her knife down to

sink in the snow. "What do you mean you don't know? Did you speak to her or not?"

"She's up to something."

Jules and the warrior trade a frown. They have come a long way and risked much. For what?

"So she won't come," Jules says quietly.

"I don't know." Arsinoe clenches her fists and presses them against the sides of her head. The rush of sneaking into the castle, of being so near both of her sisters, has begun to wear off and leave her shaky. "I was right there, Jules. So close I could have reached out and cut her throat. That's why I should have come. To end Katharine. To put an end to all of this."

"That is the poisoner in you," Emilia says. She takes up her knife again and stands, wiping the blade on her trousers. "The assassin. We will have need of your skills yet, in the coming battle. But do not be too hard on yourself. Though you were born a queen—born to be a killer—Jules is right: you are not one."

Arsinoe looks at her, surprised. She nudges Jules. "Are you telling everyone now?"

"So what do we do?" Emilia asks them both.

"Burn the black smoke," Jules says. "Call Billy and the others back. We'll leave Mirabella here, to do what she will." She turns to Arsinoe. "I hope you're right, and she really is up to something."

After leaving Arsinoe outside the Volroy, Billy successfully joined the six warriors from the rebellion. Using the oracles' visions as a guide, they secured lodging at a livery stable not far from the parade route and prepared to wait out the night.

As night falls, Billy sits with his shoulder against the east window of the hayloft. Three of the warriors are in the loft with him, and three more are below in the stables with the horses. Outside, the city is quieting, and torches and gaslights illuminate the streets. The small torches outside of the livery they sleep in cast a circle across the cobblestones and part of the fenced-in pen where a dozen horses doze or lazily munch hay. The flag hanging over the door is white and bears the face of a fox in gold and black paint.

"Here." One of the warriors hands him a steaming mug. She is called Bea, and is one of Emilia's most trusted fighters. To Billy she seems not fierce at all. She even looks a little like his sister, Jane, with soft cheeks and a small mouth. But he has no doubt she would not hesitate to put a knife right through his eye.

"Thank you." He takes it and sniffs. Tea. No wine or ale. They must all be clearheaded for tomorrow, when they will turn loose the horses and set fire to the stable. They will rain down flaming arrows into the lead queensguard and scatter them. They will cause chaos.

He hopes Arsinoe is all right. He can tell by the looks the warriors give him that they see him as a burden. A boy to babysit. But he could not let Arsinoe attempt this alone. He had to be close in case something went wrong.

He hears footfalls in the straw behind him and looks over his shoulder. The warriors have gathered at the west window and whisper to each other. Bea nods and hurries back to his side.

"What?" he asks when she hauls him up by the arm. "What's happening?"

"Black smoke. It has been called off. Get your things. Hurry."

"What do you mean it's been called off?" He looks about the floor of the hayloft. He has no things, except for a borrowed blanket and the cup of hot tea. But he supposes those should not be left and reaches for them. When he bends, he catches a glimpse out the window.

"Bea. Wait. Is that normal?" The horses in the adjacent pens are riled. They stomp and mill about.

Bea bends down beside him, just in time to see the flash of silver. "Queensguard armor. They know we are here."

"How?" Seeing the soldier, Billy freezes with fear. He reaches for the hilt of his sword. A sword. Ridiculous. He has never had cause to use one before. All his life he has settled his rows with words and fists.

"They are inside," says Bea. She shoves him to the window. "The roof. Go."

"What?" he asks as he slings a leg over the sill. There is nothing to hold on to and the ledge is not a ledge but a slim bit of timbering. He looks down. He may be all right if he falls, as long as he aims for a pile of straw.

The door of the hayloft is kicked in and a lit lamp heaved through the opening. The flames catch instantly, lighting up the space and showing warriors arming themselves. Bea pulls a crossbow from her shoulder as a barrage of bolts follows the lamp. The warrior near the window manages to deflect many, until one sinks into her gut. The hit makes her gift falter, and she is taken down by the next volley, so many bolts stuck into her that she looks like a pincushion.

"Anne!" Bea shouts, and fires as the first of the queensguard comes through the door. She drops him with one bolt, right to the head. "Go!" She shoves Billy farther out the window and coughs. The smoke inside is already thick.

"What about you?" he asks, but she shoves him again, so hard he nearly loses his grip and falls to the cobblestones. As he climbs, desperately finding one foothold after another, one fingerhold after the next, he hears someone begin to fight the fire inside. What has become of the warriors inside? Were any able to make it out? He reaches the side of the building, throws his arm over the roof and starts to drag himself up.

The bolt catches him in the ankle, and he reaches back without thinking, losing his grip on the roof. He falls. When he comes to, he is facedown on cold, wet straw, staring at a set of boots. Before he can so much as shake his head, he is lifted until his feet dangle, like a newborn puppy picked up by his scruff.

"Let go!" he shouts. Then he looks into her eyes and stops speaking. Even in the dark, he can see that they are black, like the queens' eyes. But they bleed that blackness in veins down the cheeks, and in wetness, like tears.

"What are you?" he asks, just before she knocks him unconscious.

THE VOLROY

When Rho comes to Katharine's chamber to inform her of the rebels' capture, she knows it before she arrives. The dead queens still inside Katharine sense the return of their dead sisters, lent to Rho in the cells beneath the Volroy.

Katharine lights a lamp.

Inside Rho, the dead queens have made themselves right at home. Though Katharine had not given many, their blackness spills from the tall priestess's eyes like tears. And though Rho speaks in a gentle voice, she cannot seem to stop baring her teeth.

When Rho has finished telling her that two rebel warriors and the suitor William Chatworth Junior have been captured within the capital, Katharine extends her hand.

"Give them back."

Rho shrinks.

"I know," Katharine says. "But you must. You are not a true

vessel. You are not a queen. I will give them to you again, when they are needed."

Rho nods, and Katharine cups her cheeks almost like a kiss. The dead queens slide out of Rho's mouth and into her own, down her throat like trout released into a stream.

With the boost to her gift gone, Rho collapses to one knee. She wipes her face, breath heavy.

"Are you all right?"

"Yes, Queen Katharine."

"Then take me to the prisoners."

Rho leads her down, through the gate that leads below, the cold, stale air blanketing them even against the warmth of their torch.

"I feel strange," Rho says quietly.

"That is to be expected." Katharine watches the priestess as they go. The more steps they take, the more Rho seems to return to herself. The warrior is strong. It is why Katharine chose her. She is strong enough perhaps to satisfy the dead sisters and keep their minds off Mirabella. At least for now.

The prisoners are housed on the first level beneath the castle. Two warriors, one with a crossbow bolt sticking out of her shoulder and another whose back and side have been badly burned. The smell of burned flesh wrinkles Katharine's nose before she sees the extent of it: one whole arm of the warrior is charred, her clothing fused with her skin. Half of her hair is gone as well, and the scalp is bright red and weeping.

"Have the healers mix a salve," she says to the guard. "And

get someone to remove the bolt. Rebels they may be, but they are still our subjects and will receive treatment."

"What about me?"

Katharine turns.

"I'm not your subject."

"Indeed, you are not." She looks into the eyes of William Chatworth Junior, the first suitor she kissed. He has been wounded as well, and favors his leg. "So it really is you. I admit I am surprised. I thought my commander might have caught a decoy."

"Your commander," he says, and shudders. "What is she? What's wrong with her?"

"Nothing." Katharine gestures to Rho, who looks completely well again, red hair shining beneath her white hood.

"When she took me, there was something. . . ."

"You must have been mistaken. Moonlight plays tricks on the eye. As does panic." She looks over the faces of her queensguard, and sees how they avoid Rho's gaze. The furtive glances they send her way. Katharine will have to speak with them. Assure them that their commander is nothing to fear.

"What were you doing here?" Katharine asks.

"Touring the capital," he spits.

Katharine laughs. "You are brave. We will see for how long. Whatever you were planning, it will not happen now. And my foster family, the Arrons, will be most pleased to discover that we have captured the son of the man who murdered Natalia."

"My father? He murdered—"

"Yes. He strangled her. Perhaps to aid your escape."

Katharine narrows her eyes. He seems so bewildered. Disbelieving.

"If he . . ." He hesitates as if unable to even utter the words. "He didn't do it for me. Where is he now?"

"Where is he now?" Katharine turns on her heel and stalks back down the corridor. She gestures to Rho as she passes. "She killed him."

THE PARADE

Only five queensguard soldiers were lost in the capture of the rebels. With the dead queens' help, Rho had foiled whatever plan the rebellion had hatched, and now Katharine has Arsinoe's boy. But the fact that the rebellion had a plan at all. . . .

"The black pearls, my queen?" Her maid Giselle holds them up against her neck. "Perhaps the black pearl choker?"

"Not now," Katharine says, and pushes free. "Send me my Commander of Queensguard."

"Yes," Giselle replies, and hurries to the door.

"Wait." Katharine takes a breath. Giselle has been her maid since Greavesdrake. She has always been kind. Almost a friend. "I did not mean to be brusque. Do not worry about the pearls. I wear no jewels today. Only armor."

The maid dips her head, and Katharine knows she is forgiven.

Not long after, the guards at her door announce Rho's arrival, and the tall priestess strides into the room.

"The prisoners remain silent," she says before Katharine can ask.

"Yes. I expected them to."

"But if the Chatworth boy is here, you can be sure that the Bear Queen is here as well."

"Do not call her that," Katharine snaps. "Double the queensguard presence at the parade. Nothing must go wrong. Have you"—she hesitates—"have you any reason to suspect Mirabella's involvement in this plot?"

Rho takes a moment to consider. "No. And I have been monitoring her closely. Even down to the woodpecker."

"Good." Katharine sighs and walks to her bed, where a black embroidered gown has been laid out to wear beneath her gold breastplate. "For I am surprised to discover that I actually trust her."

"She is a powerful ally to have."

"As are you," Katharine says. "I want to thank you, Rho, for your loyalty. And for your discretion." She lifts the strap of the gown. "Will you send my maid back in, please?"

Rho nods and leaves. The moment the door closes behind her the dead queens begin to chatter.

Mirabella, Mirabella, they murmur until Katharine wants to tear her hair out.

Mirabella is not to be trusted. Not until she is ours.

* * *

Bree and Elizabeth arrive early to dress and arm Mirabella. Elizabeth wears her finest robes and an adornment of blue ribbon, the splash of color permitted in celebration of the Mistbane and the heroic elementals. Bree wears the custom gown Katharine ordered made, and the blue and silver beads of the skirt sparkle as she moves, giving her the impression of a shining, swimming fish.

"It's not as heavy as I thought it would be," Elizabeth says, holding the breastplate in place with her right hand as Bree buckles it. The smooth, silver panel shines across Mirabella's chest. She will have to be careful not to look down at it if the day proves sunny. She might blind herself.

Bree runs her fingers across the engraving of clouds and lightning, so expertly worked into the metal, the veins of the bolts spidering down to the edge of the armor. "It is beautiful. Even Luca was raving about it. I think she wishes we had made you something like this for the Ascension."

"Does she think that would have helped?" Mirabella looks down at herself, then over her shoulder, toward the hanging tapestry and the secret door. She knows that Arsinoe is gone; after Katharine left her alone, she fiddled and tapped at the wall for what felt like forever, unable to get the passage to open. If Arsinoe had still been there, she would not have been able to disguise her laughter.

"Are you all right, Mira?" Elizabeth asks. "You seem very nervous for a simple parade."

"You will not have to fight the mist today, after all," Bree adds. “Well, unless it decides to rise . . .”

“That is very helpful!” Mirabella forces a grin. “But I am fine. And as usual, Bree, you will outshine me.” She gestures to the beaded gown, and Bree twirls.

“It is glorious! But heavier than your breastplate. I feel sorry for my horse.”

“They’ll have to put you on a nice, heavy draught horse, then,” says Elizabeth.

“Good Elizabeth. Always thinking of the animals. Perhaps a charger. I do not think Queen Katharine will allow any plow horses into her parade.”

Mirabella squares her shoulders. Arsinoe will not have given up on trying to get her out of the capital, no matter how foolish and impossible the task. Will she be there, somewhere? Will Mirabella have to see her face in the crowd, and the betrayal in her eyes when she does not use the distraction to run?

“Mira, do you want to wear any jewels? I do not know how they will go with this armor. . . .”

Anything could happen today. Something could go wrong. People could be killed. And there is no way to avoid it. She is utterly powerless to stop her sisters as they gnash their teeth at either end of her outstretched hands.

“No jewels,” she hears herself say. “Just the blue cape.”

“We should go, then,” says Bree. “They will want us in the council chamber. The soldiers will have already lined up.”

Mirabella follows Bree and Elizabeth down the stairs and listens to the sounds of the city at every window. It is louder than usual. Excited. The marketplace is alive, and vendors have taken up places along the parade route to sell hot hand pies and skewers of roasted meat. People will crowd along the streets ten or twenty deep.

When they enter the Black Council chamber, no one bows. They only nod, and after a quick glance, their eyes slide by to linger on Bree. Only Katharine remains fixed on her, whispering to Rho from the corner of her mouth and beckoning Mirabella closer.

"Sister," Katharine says. "Are you ready?"

"I am. You look very fine in your armor." Katharine's gold breastplate, engraved with a skull and snakes, gleams against the black of her sleeves and cape. Everything on her is black and gold, from the hilt of her ceremonial sword to the dusting of gold across her painted lips.

"Thank you," Katharine says. "To the horses, then."

The sight of the parade assembled in the inner ward makes Mirabella's knees go weak. So many queensguard soldiers. So many silver buckles, on them and on the horses. Flags of blue, white, silver, and black flap softly in the breeze. But there is no sun. The sky is overcast with low gray clouds. So at least she will not have to worry about blinding herself with her own chest.

"How well you look," Luca says as she appears at Mirabella's elbow. "How well you both look."

"Are you sure you will not ride with us, High Priestess?" Katharine asks. "I would have the people see a strong showing from the temple."

Luca nods to Rho, already mounted on a tall, white mare whose mane and tail have been braided with blue and silver streamers. "One of my priestesses leads your guard. That ought to be strong enough."

Mirabella says nothing. It is not her place to weigh in on matters of the crown, and even if it were, she could not have managed a word. How could Arsinoe have thought she could escape? She will be held fast in the center of a sea of bodies. Soldiers, mounted and on foot. The waving elementals whose lives she saved in Bardon Harbor. And half of the Black Council: Genevieve and Antonin, Bree. Paola Vend. Even if she would have run, she would never have made it.

"Your mount, Mist-breaker." A soldier approaches, leading an enormous gray horse. An odd gray, and Mirabella wonders whether he has been dyed to resemble the mist. That would be a silly amount of detail, but given the scope of the parade, she is not surprised when she strokes his shoulder and her hand comes away coated in gray powder.

"I hope that Mist-breaker is the horse's name," Mirabella says after she is helped into the saddle, "and not something new that they are calling me. 'Mirabella Mistbane' is grand enough." Katharine rides close on her black stallion, and the gray gelding stomps his feet. "And I hope that he is steady. I should have told you: I am not much of a rider."

"That cannot be true," Katharine says, a little coldly.

"I am afraid that it is. I spent most of my time in carriages. I can ride and at any pace. But if he shies or startles, I might need you to take hold of his bit."

Katharine's brow knits. She stares at Mirabella quietly before finally nodding. "I will take hold of him if anything happens."

At a signal of trumpets, the first soldiers begin to march out, leading the procession out of the Volroy and into the streets of Indrid Down. When they come upon the start of the crowd, Mirabella waves beside Katharine. The cheers of the people are loud in her ears, their reactions to every part of the processional like announcements of who is passing: for the brave elementals they cheer, and for the queensguard they respectfully clap. Gasps and exclamations for the Black Council, which is no doubt due to Bree's gown. Then the queens arrive, and they explode.

"See how they love you?" Katharine shouts into her ear. "Are you worthy of it?"

"I hope so!" Mirabella shouts back.

"Good. I would hate for them to be disappointed."

Mirabella glances at her. It is on odd thing to say. There is an edge to Katharine that Mirabella has not felt since first coming to the capital, and it makes her nervous.

They make another turn, heading for the marketplace before the parade winds around to end in the square. Mirabella takes a deep breath and continues to wave. She hopes that the smile on her face looks true as her eyes dart over every stack of crates, every slumping canopy, anywhere that Billy and the war-gifted might be crouched down to hide. In moments, something will happen. And she will ask Katharine to take hold of her horse.

They come upon the market, and the hand upon her reins begins to tremble. At any moment, any second, someone will start to shout. Something will burst or burn. Except that they ride on, and it does not.

"Are you well, sister?" Katharine asks. "You seem nervous."

Mirabella sighs and smiles. "No. I think I am fine."

INDRID DOWN

"Something's wrong." After staring for a long time on tiptoe, Jules has climbed up to stand on the haunches of her black gelding, peering toward the city with her hands shaded over her eyes. "Why haven't they returned?"

"Maybe they thought it best to wait for the crowds to clear," Arsinoe says.

"They must have seen the smoke," Emilia says. "We sent the signal up as long as we dared."

Camden leaps onto the gelding's back beside Jules, her claws digging into the saddle leather. The horse snorts, and Arsinoe pats his nose fondly. He may have chased her down so Katharine could shoot a bolt into her back, but he was also the one who carried her and Jules to safety afterward.

Jules looks to the city, then back to Mathilde, as if the seer might have new answers.

"I should be there. I should have gone with them."

"But you are not there, and you are not going." Emilia slaps at Jules's ankle. "Get down."

After a moment, Jules relents, and slides down the gelding's flank.

Down in the capital, tendrils of smoke rise from chimneys, and the hated towers of the Volroy obscure the sky. As she stares at the city, Arsinoe wills Billy and the others to ride out of it, to emerge over the sloping hill.

"I'll go," Arsinoe says. "Jules always has bad feelings about things, and she always thinks she should be there, but this time she's right. I'm going to get Billy and the others out."

"No." Emilia's fingers dig into her arm. "Not you. These are my warriors. My friends. You've put them in danger as you've put Jules in danger, and you are a fool to think you will be any use in rescuing them."

"Your warriors," Arsinoe says. "Don't you mean the rebellion's? Don't you mean the Legion Queen's?"

Emilia raises her fist, but Jules takes her hand and pulls it down.

"Enough of this," Jules says. "Neither of you is going anywhere. We'll give them until nightfall." She looks between Arsinoe and Emilia, clearly more angry at one than the other, but in the end, it is Emilia whose shoulder she touches. "Go back to the others and tell them we're waiting."

Emilia goes, eyes flashing as she passes Arsinoe.

"They will return," says Mathilde, and Arsinoe and Jules turn to see the oracle crouched in the crusted snow. She has lit a bundle of herbs and blown it out to scry through the smoke. "They will return," she says again, in a voice that is not exactly hers but the voice of the visions. "They will. But not all."

THE VOLROY

That evening, Katharine sits with Genevieve in her room, trying to relax with a glass of Natalia's tainted brandy and Pietyr's favorite hemlock biscuits.

"Today was a resounding success. Everyone has said so. Even Cousin Lucian. Turnout was higher than expected, and barely a scrap was left over from the feast. We had not hoped to see the capital so happy again until after the rebellion was over. I cannot wait for word of the alliance to reach Sunpool. The trickle of deserters will strengthen to a stream. Katharine, are you listening?"

Genevieve prods her in the arm.

"I was not," Katharine admits. She takes a bite of the baked hemlock biscuit she has been holding in her fingers and wipes at the corner of her mouth with her napkin.

"I thought you would be pleased. There were even some children seen, playing near the shore. Having Mirabella here has soothed their fears. Is that not what you wanted?"

"It is."

"But?"

Katharine stands and worries the biscuit between her fingers until crumbs cascade down the front of her dress. "I was ready to hate her. Even though she came as an ally. You know this."

"Yes. I know this."

"But she is so steady! She has a . . . certain quality. Almost like Natalia had, and since she has been here, I feel less alone."

Genevieve leans back on her elbow. "What of the suitor in the cells? Was he here to rescue her? To contact her for information?"

"I do not know. And even if he was, there is no way to know whether she was involved in the plot."

"You want her to be innocent." Genevieve sets down her pen. She comes to Katharine's side and cocks her head sympathetically. "You want to trust her for the sake of the triplets."

And perhaps, for the love of a sister. But Katharine does not dare say so. Genevieve would scorn her, and the dead queens lie inside, coiled and listening.

"But can she be trusted?" Genevieve asks. "And if she cannot, is there a better use for her, like the old king-consort said? Killed to quiet the mist."

"Those pages you showed me could be the rambling of a drunkard on his deathbed." Katharine shakes her head. "No. I will keep my word. And I believe that she will keep hers."

"Very well. But what will you tell Mirabella about the suitor? He is her friend. She will not be pleased with what you have planned for him."

"I know. But she will understand. We are at war. And his family's crime against us was personal."

By the time Mirabella learns about the rebellion prisoners, Billy is already out of the cells. Katharine has ordered him trussed and shackled, and made to serve.

"Where is he?" she demands when Bree cuts her off in the hall.

"Mira, it is at Queen Katharine's pleasure."

"Where is he?" she asks louder, and skirts around Bree's raised hands. Through the open doors of the throne room, she hears snickering and laughter. Shouted commands. Bree grasps her arm as lightning crackles across her knuckles.

"Mira, it could have been worse."

Mirabella pulls free and bursts into the throne room. The sight before her makes her instantly furious. So furious that every torch in the room blazes, hot enough to scorch the walls.

Katharine lies reclined, her leg slung over the arm of the throne. She eats a pastry off a tray resting upon Billy's back. He is bent over, his arms tied behind him painfully, elbows used to secure the platter. At his wrists are soft leather manacles. His feet are connected by a short length of chain. And he has been gagged.

Mirabella storms up the aisle, passing Arrons and members

of the Black Council as they laugh and nibble pastries of their own. She reaches into the first lamp she passes and draws the fire into her hand until it is a roiling ball. Then she casts it at the floor before Katharine's feet.

Everyone in the room gasps and recoils at the scorched stone. Guards rush to the aisle and cross their spears before her, protecting the queen.

Mirabella dares not look into Billy's face. If she sees the way they make him suffer, the last of her restraint will fail.

"What is the meaning of this?"

"What do you mean, sister?" Katharine asks, righting herself to sit up straight.

"This." Mirabella gestures to Billy, his brow wet with sweat, his face straining against the cloth gag as he struggles to keep from spilling the tray. "What are you doing to him?"

"Well, I have not killed him yet."

Around the throne room, the Black Council laughs. All but Luca and Rho.

"Mirabella," Luca says softly. "This former suitor was arrested along with two war-gifted rebels last night. It is thought they were here to disrupt the parade. Perhaps even to kidnap you."

Mirabella's eyes flicker to Billy's. Two rebels and the suitor. But not Arsinoe. They do not have Arsinoe.

She takes a breath. Collects herself. Looks sideways at each of the guards.

"Get your spears out of my path."

The guards obey, in no hurry to be scorch-marked like the floor, and Mirabella walks to Billy. She kneels and pulls the gag from his mouth.

"Are you all right?"

"He is fine," Katharine answers.

"He is not fine." Where the gag rested against his skin, angry, red blisters have begun to rise. At his wrists, too, where they touch the leather of his bonds, deep red welts have formed. It has all been tainted with some kind of poison.

"It is not lethal," Katharine says.

"At least not yet," Genevieve adds.

"They killed my father," Billy growls. He fixes his eyes on Rho, across the room. "She killed my father!" He struggles up and charges at her, sending the tray and all its contents crashing to the floor. Rho does not so much as flinch. He barely makes it three strides before the guards are on him, shoving the blunt ends of their spears into his gut and striking him across the shins.

"Stop it!" Mirabella cries.

"Where is he?" Billy shouts from on his knees. "Where is my father?"

"He is here somewhere," Genevieve says, and chuckles. "Or at least his bones are. Somewhere in the river."

Mirabella watches with pity as Billy's expression crumples. There are so many bruises on his face that he is almost unrecognizable.

"From what I understand," Katharine says. "Rho nearly carved him in two. From lung to heart. Perhaps if you ask her nicely, she will take you to the place by the shore where she ordered him dumped."

"Perhaps if you dive, you might find him still in the rug we rolled him in," Genevieve adds. "Or at least what the fish have left behind."

"Enough," says the High Priestess. "He is only a boy. He does not need to be told so cruelly."

"You have to let him go," says Mirabella.

"The only thing I have to do is question you." Katharine removes her leg from the arm of the throne and leans forward in it, resting on her elbows. She snaps her fingers to the guards at the rear. "Have the prisoners brought up."

"What about Billy? You know he is my friend. You know I cannot support this."

"You will support what your Queen Crowned supports," Antonin Arron hisses, but Mirabella ignores him.

"Please, Katharine. Release him. Release him into my care, at least."

"No. You are far too kind. Honestly, sister, I do not know why you are so upset. None of the poison is lethal, as I said. It will not even leave a scar!"

"Katharine, you must see," Mirabella starts. But then she remembers that Katharine was raised a poisoner. Striped with painful poisons since she was a child, over and over, with poisons that did leave a mark. She glances about the room at the Arrons and Paola Vend, who watch Mirabella and cast judgment. They think her foolish. They think she is weak and overreacting. Perhaps she is, when they no doubt encouraged Katharine to order his death.

"For how long must he serve?" Mirabella says finally.

Katharine exhales. "Until he is contrite. And until we are satisfied. His father murdered Natalia and paid too light and swift a price. So we must exact our vengeance upon his son."

"How is that fair?"

"How is it not?" Katharine gestures again to the guards, and they haul Billy up by his bound elbows until he shouts from the pain.

"Don't expect anything different, Mira," he says. "Not from this pack of murderers."

"The son of a murderer criticizing us!" Lucian Arron scoffs, and spits upon the charred floor. Billy must be careful of what he says. Genevieve looks angry enough to cut his throat, right there, before everyone.

"Wait." Rho steps forward from her place on the wall. She seems tired, with dark rings beneath her eyes, and the luster gone from her long, red hair. "Let the boy say to me what he would say."

The guards loosen their grip and allow Billy to stand on his own.

"You do not care for me," Rho says. "Nor I for you. Not even when we were in Rolanth, when you served as Mirabella's taster and we were on the same side. But I was the last person to be with your father. So if you would know anything, you may ask."

"And that is supposed to make it better? Make us even?"

"I do not seek to make us even. I do not know who my father was. So there is no 'even.'"

Billy glares at her impassive face. Rho might as well be made of stone. Only someone who has known her as long as Mirabella has, or Luca has, could see the markers of weariness, and perhaps of compassion, on her features.

"What . . . ," Billy starts, and swallows. "What happened?"

"I came upon him in one of the rooms in the East Tower. A room Natalia used as a study. She was on the ground, and he was choking her to death."

Billy looks away, his expression disgusted. "Go on. Tell me everything."

"When he stood up, I put my knife into his ribs. He had not seen me coming. But I was too late, and Natalia was already dead."

"Did he . . . say anything?"

"He wheezed. A little blood came out. I cannot say whether he was trying to speak or to scream."

"You," Billy gasps. "You murdering—"

"He was a murderer," Rho interrupts, and her voice booms through the throne room. "Afterward, I had him wrapped in a rug and thrown into the river. No one has found him or at least not that I have heard."

"And that's it."

"Yes. That is all."

Mirabella bows her head as Billy bares his teeth, as he strains against the guards. He has never been quick to anger.

Seeing it transform him so is ugly to behold.

"I'm going to kill you when I get out of here," he says.

"It is easy to make threats when you are in shackles and under the queen's protection. I killed a murderer, and I do not regret it, though I do regret that you suffer. What you feel is up to you, but your father did not strike me as someone to be mourned heavily."

They are silenced by the throne room doors being thrown open and the other two prisoners marched inside. The guards bring them nearly to Mirabella's feet in the aisle and force them to their knees before the queen.

"Well?" Katharine asks.

"Well, what?" asks Mirabella.

"Do you know them?"

She looks down, and the guards jerk the prisoners' heads up and to the right so that Mirabella can better see their faces.

"I do not."

"How is that possible? You were in the rebel city for weeks."

"I was. But the rebels were many and varied. New war-gifted arrived from Bastian City every day."

Katharine studies her quietly. Then she exhales and reclines again upon her throne. "They will have to be questioned."

Mirabella swallows. Everyone on the island knows what is meant when a poisoner says that someone must be "questioned."

"Genevieve will do it; she is the best." Katharine waves her wrist. "Start right away."

"No." Mirabella squares her shoulders. "They were here to free me."

"Free you? And why would you need to be freed?"

"It was a misguided attempt. They thought—I was being kept here against my will."

"Did you not leave a note?" Genevieve asks sarcastically.

Mirabella ignores her. "They would have disrupted the parade and used the distraction to facilitate my escape. I told them not to do it. That is why I seemed nervous before the parade began."

"Because you thought they would help you escape," Katharine says softly.

"Because I feared they would try to make me. That is why I asked you to take hold of my horse's rein."

Luca sighs. "Why did you not say something?"

"I hoped I would not have to."

"But there were rebels in the city. And you knew."

"Yes," says Mirabella. "And Billy Chatworth is my friend. I make no secret of that." Finally, given the excuse, she looks at Billy again. But his expression is unreadable.

"How did you communicate with them?" Katharine asks, and Mirabella looks back at her. "You said you told them not to. How did they get word to you? How did you respond?"

"By bird," Mirabella lies. She cocks her head at Genevieve. "I trust you will not 'question' every sparrow that makes her nest upon the Volroy."

Genevieve narrows her eyes, and they wait. Katharine has gone still. Such stillness does not seem as dangerous to

Mirabella as it once did, when all she knew of her youngest sister was that she was a snake and likely to strike. But there are no easy answers for what to do with the rebels. Or with Billy.

"The secret of these prisoners has been kept already for a night and a day. But we cannot keep it for much longer."

"All of Indrid Down should know about their capture," says Genevieve. "It will be the most festive month on record. A parade and a public execution."

"Or perhaps they should not know," suggests Luca. "It may make the people uneasy, that rebels were so near. We do not want to shake their confidence in the crown right after we have bolstered it."

"I think you should let them go," Mirabella says.

Genevieve throws up her hands. "Of course you would."

"I think you should not be the queen that people fear." She raises her eyes and looks into Katharine's. "You are the Queen Crowned of Fennbirn Island. The rebels are nothing. Not even led by a true queen. Show them how little they mean. Send the war-gifted back, with a warning never to return."

"And what of him?" Katharine asks, nodding with her chin toward Billy.

Mirabella swallows. That question is only a test.

"Billy Chatworth, the former suitor, should not be released. He is leverage. I know Arsinoe. She will do nothing against you as long as you have him."

"Mira," Billy says. She looks at him but does not waver. "What are you doing?"

Katharine waits for what feels like an age before speaking.

"I am glad to hear you say that, Mirabella. Because it is true; I could never let the suitor go." She nods to the guards at the back of the room. "Release the war-gifted. Take them to the road toward Prynn. Give them mounts and set them free."

INDRID DOWN

Genevieve goes with Rho to oversee the release of the war-gifted at the ruins of the old city wall. She rides behind them in the dark as Rho rides before, their way lit by fewer and fewer streetlamps.

Let them go, Mirabella said, and Katharine did, as if Mirabella had enchanted her. As if she were the Queen Crowned instead.

"This is far enough." Rho halts the prisoners and moves her horse out of the way. It will be just that easy. They will return to the rebellion alive and well, free to fight another day.

"Wait." Genevieve draws long strips of fabric from the pocket of her coat. "I would have them return gagged. We do not need them raising the alarm for any possible counterattack."

Rho arches her brow but says nothing as Genevieve stuffs the cloth between the warriors' teeth and ties each tight behind their heads. Through it all, they barely acknowledge that they are being touched, their swollen and blackened eyes trained on the road ahead. After she is finished, she nods, and they nudge their horses with their heels. They ride away at a trot, straight down the road they were brought to, relying on their horses' eyes to take them through the night.

"They will turn off the road as soon as we can no longer see them," says Rho. "Lose themselves in the woods."

"Do you think there is a support party waiting for them outside the city?"

"I do. Though not in great enough a number to mount any sort of 'counterattack,'" Rho snorts.

"I hope they are not too far away."

Rho turns in the saddle, and her eyes fill with understanding. "What was on those gags?" she asks.

"Just a little something," says Genevieve, "to rectify the queen's mistake."

At the makeshift camp outside the city, nestled in a clearing in the trees, Jules puts on a show of trying to sleep in the hopes that Arsinoe will follow her lead. So far it has not worked. Arsinoe sits at the edge of the camp, where she has been for hours, no doubt staring down the hill at the road, though it is far too dark to see anyone coming. If Jules strains, she can hear her whispering. *Come back. Come back now.*

But Billy and the others have not returned, and the thought that they never will sits heavy as a stone in Jules's gut. Below, to the east, the capital lies quiet: no strange sounds and no hint of upset. Nothing out of the ordinary after the celebratory noise of the parade had subsided. She wants to go to Arsinoe and sit up with her, but instead she stays on her side next to Emilia, getting rest in case they have to fight, or run. She has not mentioned the solid weight in her stomach. Emilia would only tell her that it is what being a queen feels like.

Jules snakes a hand out to ruffle Camden's shoulder fur. The cat is not sleeping either; her head is up, gaze fixed on the spot where Arsinoe must be.

Jules sighs and adjusts her position on the cold ground. The leather bedroll does not do much against the bumpy, uneven snow.

"Just go," Emilia says groggily.

"What?"

"Just go to her. But leave me the cougar at least if you refuse to keep me warm."

Jules smiles in the dark and squeezes Emilia's shoulder. After she leaves the small tent, she hears Camden circling and circling inside before thudding down and making Emilia grunt.

"That you, Jules?" Arsinoe asks as Jules makes her way through the snow.

"Of course it is. Nobody else likes you well enough to stay up with you." She sits down to share the pile of sticks that Arsinoe is using as a chair. "Anything?"

"I thought I saw something . . . a while ago. But nothing on the road below."

"They might not take the road below. They might leave

from another direction, double back. They might pop out of the trees from anywhere." She speaks lightly, trying to comfort her friend. She has warriors posted in all directions; they will know when Billy and the others return long before they can "pop out of the trees." But so far, none of the lookouts has made a sound.

"What if they don't come back tonight?"

"If they're not back by dawn, we'll go in after them."

"Who will?"

"You and me."

Arsinoe snorts. "Emilia won't like that." She snorts again and goes back to watching the road. "Emilia doesn't like much."

"She likes me," Jules teases.

"Aye. She definitely likes you." She shifts her weight around on the sticks. "Do you . . . ?" she asks after a moment.

"Do I what?"

"Nothing."

Nothing, indeed. But Jules knows what she wants to ask. It is the same thing that Emilia wants to ask. And it is another question that Jules is not ready to answer.

"I think Joseph would like her," Arsinoe ventures finally. "If that helps."

"Why would that help?"

"I don't know!" Arsinoe shrugs away. "I'm just saying."

Jules pulls her back. "I know what you're saying." Thoughts of Joseph still hurt. Maybe they always will, though the pain is less sharp, and it no longer keeps her from smiling. When she first arrived in Bastian City, she thought there would never be space in her for anything like that again. But there will be someday. She just does not know whether that space will be filled by Emilia or by someone new.

Before either of them can say anything more, Jules feels a tug from Camden and looks back. Emilia is up and out of the tent, and Camden is trotting toward them. The small camp is suddenly lit by a flicker of a match and then illuminated by the light of a small lantern.

"What is it?" Arsinoe asks, and scrambles up.

"Horses," says Emilia. "Coming this way from the south."

Arsinoe dashes off through the southern tree line before Jules can even reach for her.

"Arsinoe!" Jules hisses, and plunges in after, the light of the lantern following as Emilia and the warriors come quietly along. Mathilde catches up and falls in beside Jules, graceful as a ghost. When they hear the hoofbeats coming up the hill, Jules cannot help but hear the memory of Mathilde's vision. They will return. But not all.

"Where are the rest of you?" Arsinoe asks as the two horses come to a stop. "Where is he?"

Two. Only two. And neither of them Billy.

"Get them down," Emilia orders. "Free their hands. Remove the gags."

"What happened?" Jules asks.

"We were found out." Bea speaks through split and swollen lips. Even in the dark, Jules can see that her arm is a ruin of burns, and the smell of the blackened flesh lingers. Emilia offers her a skin of water, but she shakes her head. "They came for us at the stable, the night before the parade. Queensguard and the priestess who leads the Undead Queen's army."

"Where are the others?"

"Dead. Killed in the stable. Except for the two of us and Billy."

Arsinoe nearly collapses, and Jules steadies her. "Bea, where is he?"

"They have him." Her eyes flicker regretfully toward Arsinoe. "They are torturing him."

"I'll kill her!" Arsinoe shouts, and Emilia glances at her, irritated by the volume.

"How did you get away?"

"We didn't. She let us go."

"Queen Katharine?" Jules asks. "She let you go?"

"Yes. Queen Katharine. She let us—" Bea lurches forward and vomits. In the light of the lantern, Jules can see the snow, slicked red.

Emilia and the other warriors descend as both of the survivors drop to the ground, spitting blood.

"Poisoner!" Emilia calls to Arsinoe, but she is already there, holding Bea's head still to pull back her eyelids and open her mouth.

"Did she give you anything?" Arsinoe asks. "Did you eat anything or drink?"

"No." Bea's eyes roll to her friend as the girl stops breathing. "The gags. It was the gags."

"No," Jules echoes as Bea falls silent. It happened so fast. They had returned. They were speaking.

"Get them onto the horses." Emilia stands, and her voice is harsh. "Get the Legion Queen out of here."

"We're not leaving," Arsinoe exclaims. "We can't leave without him!" She starts to back away, and Jules jumps for her and wraps her tight in her arms. "Let me go! They're torturing him!"

"Hush, Arsinoe." Arsinoe struggles hard, but despite being smaller, Jules has always been the stronger. With Arsinoe's arms pinned, it is easy enough to hold her fast. Harder is hanging on through the sound of her shouts. Hearing the miserable terror in her voice.

"If you make me leave him, I'll never forgive you, Jules! I'll come right back the moment you let go, the moment you sleep—"

She stops talking when Emilia takes her face between her hands.

"You and Jules will return to Sunpool," Emilia says, and draws her short-bladed sword. "You will go. And we will follow after."

"Where are you going?" Jules asks. "What are you up to?"

"I am going . . . to get one of theirs." Emilia bares her teeth in the lamplight. The look in her eyes leaves no room for argument.

With a nod, Jules loads Arsinoe onto the back of the black gelding. She climbs up behind her and rides away, back to Sunpool in defeat.

THE VOLROY

After the prisoners are released, Katharine leaves the Black Council in the throne room to continue their revelry and torture of the former suitor, and slips away to her rooms. Once there, she sits before a table full of food brought by the servants, who assumed she would be ravenous after the long day. But the soft, rich bread spread with oleander butter and the yew-smoked fish go untouched. Alone, she takes a deep breath and listens as she lets it out. There will be no visitors tonight; Bree and Elizabeth, who are sometimes kind, do not really approve of her treatment of the boy. And Mirabella—if Mirabella were to visit her, it would be to blow the door open and burn her up in a ball of fire.

Give her to us, the dead queens whisper. *In her skin, we could defeat the mist.*

"The mist," Katharine murmurs. Even now she feels it, as if its eye is always upon her even through the thick walls of the Volroy.

With Mirabella, the dead queens could hold the mist in check forever. Perhaps they could even banish it for good and return the island to the world. An end to isolation.

An end to safety, Natalia would say.

Katharine makes a fist as the dead poisoners writhe in her stomach, their blackened tongues urging her toward the bowl of soft pennyroyal cheese.

She knows that Genevieve would have her act upon the information she uncovered, the journal pages written by the Blue Queen's king-consort. Queen Illiann's killing created the mist. Mirabella's could destroy it. Except the more that Katharine thinks upon those pages, the more she doubts them. Illiann was in the company of this secret, long-lost sister for years. The very suitor she wed was at that sister's recommendation. They had seemed to be . . . friends. Family amongst queens. Unthinkable, yet it had happened between Mirabella and Arsinoe. And despite her caution, it was happening between Mirabella and Katharine.

Katharine frowns. Maybe no one murdered Queen Illiann at all. If she is anything like Mirabella, she more likely sacrificed herself and jumped.

Give her to us. Weaken her. Give her to us.

"Weaken her. Shall I throw her into the Breccia Domain, as was done to me? No. I will not."

Inside her skin, the dead queens are displeased, and she feels the shadow spread up her neck like a moving bruise. The skin of her wounded wrist and hand softens, as though it has suddenly shifted its course from healing to rot.

"You cannot have her," Katharine says, and hears their hiss

deep in her ears. "I have other plans for her."

Other plans?

"Yes. I need her for more than just the mist. And I need her to remain . . . untainted."

Inside they roil, their dead coils shifting like sea serpents beneath the waves. Katharine inhales sharply. It is not pleasant to share her skin with them. To have them in her blood. It is even less pleasant when they are angry.

"You are mine," she whispers gently, though she wishes nothing more than to have them gone forever. "And with me you will stay. But I will let you out to play."

Mirabella waits until the castle is asleep before sneaking into the throne room to see Billy. She brings a bowl of warm water and clean cloths to wash his wounds. She thinks she is prepared, but when she finds him, on his knees and tied to the arm of the throne, his head hanging and his whole face dark with blood, she knows she was wrong.

"I am no healer," she says, voice shaking. "But I will do my best."

She sets her lamp on the floor and dips an end of a cloth into the warm water, and starts to sponge his face.

"Mirabella." He jerks away. His eyes are cold. "You left us."

"Billy . . . you must know . . . how much I did not want to."

"But you did. And you broke her heart. I'd hate you for that already, even if you hadn't also broken part of mine."

Mirabella goes on sponging his wounds, though the words cut. She takes special care around his bonds, not only because the poison on them has raised blisters as delicate as bubbles in honey, but because if she touches them, she will be blistered as well. And then Katharine will know for certain that she has been there.

"So many times I have thought of Arsinoe. And of you. How I wished you were safe. How I wished we were not apart."

"Then why did you go?" He grimaces when he moves. He has been in the contorted position for so long. She slips her arms beneath his chest and helps him to lift his weight, to get his legs into a more comfortable position. "Ah. That's better." He leans back, rests his head against the edge of the throne. "So why did you go?"

"Billy . . . I was no use there. No use to Arsinoe or anyone, hidden away by Emilia and Mathilde."

"You were of use to me. And as for Arsinoe, you can't pretend that you don't know how much she needs you."

"I miss my sister very much." Mirabella presses her lips together. "But I had another sister. Here."

"So that's it, then?" he asks. "You really have turned against us."

Mirabella closes her eyes. She wishes she could tell him everything. That there is something wrong with Katharine. That she must discover it and why the mist reaches for her. But if he knew, it would only become more information to torture him for.

"I can only tell you that I will never be against Arsinoe. And that I am still your friend."

He looks at her hopefully through eyes that are nearly

swollen shut, from poison or from the kicks of the guards.

"So you'll get me out of here? You'll let me loose?"

"I wish I could. But I cannot. Not yet. Please understand," she says when his head hangs. "I wish this was not happening to you. I wish you had not come."

"But it is. And I did." To her surprise, and through all of his bruises, he smiles. "I suppose I missed you."

At his unexpected kindness, Mirabella bursts out crying.

"I would have much preferred meeting you somewhere else, though," he adds, and her tears change to laughter.

"I missed you, too."

"Did you see Arsinoe?" he asks softly.

Mirabella peers over her shoulder for listening ears. There are no guards visible, but they must take care so their voices do not carry down the corridor.

"I have never been so happy to see anyone as I was when she popped out from behind that tapestry."

"I can't believe she did that," Billy says. "I should've known. She can do just about anything."

"Whether she ought to or not." Mirabella takes up the wet cloth and wipes the dried blood from his jaw; she presses it against the swelling on his cheek. "I am sorry about your father. They told me what happened, when I first arrived."

He nods.

"I hated him," he says. "But I still thought he was immortal. Mira, if I don't get out of here, will you write to my mother and Jane?"

"Of course I will."

"Their lives will be so changed with both my father and me gone." Tears slip from the corners of his eyes, and she wipes them away as quickly as they come. "You have to get me out of here, Mira. I don't belong here."

She kisses his cheeks and his clammy forehead. "You will see Arsinoe again. You will see her even before I do. And when you do, you will tell her how much I love her. And how I never betrayed her."

"Mira, please!"

She kisses him again, as hard as she dares. And then she slips away.

THE VOLROY

Sometime in the night, a rebel warrior sacks Greavesdrake Manor. Edmund, Natalia's loyal butler, says the warrior slipped out of the shadows like she was a shadow herself and slipped back into them just as easily. What staff members were not sleeping quickly found themselves tied to chairs or barred inside their rooms. Pietyr's caretaker she knocked out with a blow to the back of the head. When the poor girl came to, she could not recall a moment of what had happened. But the bed in Katharine's room was empty. Pietyr Renard was gone.

"How is this possible?" Katharine asks. "How did she dare?" She sits stunned at the head of her Black Council table. She has summoned them all to the chamber. Even Mirabella. Even old Luca from her quarters in the temple, and now the wise High Priestess sits, just as useless as the rest of her advisers, looking like she was shaken from a very deep sleep.

Katharine runs her hand over the grooved wood of the table

in an effort to remain calm. But she would very much like to remove her glove and dig gouges into the surface until what fingernails she has left are split and bloody. Inside her, the dead queens boil. Pietyr was theirs, they whisper. And no one had the right to take him.

"Shut your mouth!"

Everyone startles as Katharine pounds her fist.

"My queen," Cousin Lucian ventures meekly, "no one has spoken."

"No one has spoken," Katharine says. "Because no one ever speaks when I need them to." She takes a deep breath as they blink at her. Renata, Paola, Bree, and Lucian seem afraid. Genevieve and Antonin wearily apprehensive. Of all the people in the room, the only one who conveys any sympathy is Mirabella. Mirabella, who caused this, in a way.

"Did you know," Katharine asks, turning to her sister, "that Arsinoe was capable of this? I thought you said she was good-hearted? I thought you said she was not devious."

"I never said she was not devious," Mirabella says, and Katharine does not know whether to listen or throttle her. "Though I doubt that she or anyone would have tried something like this had you not taken Billy captive. And even so, it does not seem like her. It seems too . . ."

"Tactical," says Rho. "She has at once tied your hands and brought you to the bargaining table. This was not the idea of the upstart naturalist. This was the war gift. This was the plan of the Legion Queen."

"The war gift," Katharine whispers. "I want the army mustered. Now."

"How many soldiers?" Antonin asks.

"All of them. I want my army ready to march."

No one moves to obey. They glance between each other.

"The journey around the mountain would take us several weeks," Rho says. "Perhaps longer, in the deep snow of the northern valleys. By the time we reached them, we would be fatigued and cold. Frostbitten and low on supplies where they will be dug in and fortified. We lack the ships to transport that number of soldiers by water, and no one will dare the seas and the mist, anyway." She gestures to Mirabella. "Not even if we were to strap her to one of the hulls."

"And remember," Genevieve leans forward. "The rebellion will not hurt him. Not as long as we have the suitor. What feels like a loss is actually a stalemate."

Katharine grits her teeth.

"We do not march on Sunpool."

"Then," Luca asks. "Where?"

"We march on Bastian City." Katharine shoves her chair back and stands. "On the city of the warriors. We march on them now. So speaks the Queen Crowned!" she shouts, furious that she must add it.

"Yes, Queen Katharine," Antonin says.

"Get out, all of you." She waves her hand. "Leave me alone with my commander."

One by one they rise and hurry from the chamber. Mirabella

is the last to go, and when she does, she crosses quietly behind.

"She will not hurt him," she says quietly. "I am sure of it, Kat."

Katharine closes her eyes. She almost reaches back and squeezes her sister's hand. Instead, she growls low in her throat.

"You had better be right."

After Mirabella is gone, Rho rises and comes to Katharine's side. She does not need to be told what is to happen. She accepts the gift of dead queens as if accepting a kiss.

Katharine allows more of them to flow out of her than she did before. Yet once inside of Rho, they bleed out of her less. They darken her eyes and add bulk to her shoulders. But except for a slight mottling of black veins in her neck, Rho still looks like Rho.

Until she smiles.

"You are growing used to this," Katharine says.

"Yes."

"Good. Then take my army. Go to Bastian City and raze it to the ground."

When Rho walks out of the Black Council chamber, Luca is waiting for her in the hall.

"She has ordered you to go, and so you must," Luca says, falling in beside her old friend. "But take care. The warriors may have fewer numbers, but no one knows what the war gift is capable of better than you."

"Do not worry, Luca. All will be well."

Luca peers at the tall priestess from the corner of her eye. The war gift is upon her already. It changes her stride and the heft of her shoulders. It makes her voice lower and rough. When she tries to look closer, Rho jerks away.

"Stop and face me," Luca says. "That is not a request."

Reluctantly, Rho obeys and turns toward the High Priestess. What Luca sees in the warrior's eyes fills her with horror. But she will not show it.

"This rebellion has brought out another side of you, Rho. You flourish in it. No queen in the island's history has ever had a finer commander."

"Thank you, Luca."

The High Priestess nods.

"You have climbed far higher in the Queen Crowned's esteem than anyone could have guessed. And the silver armor does not look as out of place atop your priestess robes as I would have thought."

To Luca's displeasure, Rho's lips curl in a sneer. "Speak plain."

"Very well," Luca says. Fast as a striking snake, she grasps one of Rho's wrists and holds it up. "Do you see these black bracelets you wear? They are as permanent as the crown that I placed on her head." She lets go. "And you must not forget that."

Rho lowers her head. She nods. Then she goes, to follow the queen's orders, her steps far too fast for Luca to ever keep up.

SUNPOOL

Arsinoe leaves through the main gate and finds her bear surrounded by townsfolk. While they were away, Caragh used her gift to call him closer, and now he waits outside the walls for easy meals and a few pats from those who are bold enough to try. When the people see her coming, they bow and return to the city, leaving the bear to his queen.

"Shall we go to the woods, boy?" she asks, but Jules and Camden catch them before they can leave the road.

"Can we join you?" Jules asks. She has a huge silver fish in her arms and her cougar trotting beside, looking up at the fish with happy, slitted eyes.

"Fine," says Arsinoe. They walk in silence out into the snow. When they reach the crest of a far-enough hill, Jules tosses the fish onto the ground and lets the bear and the cougar decide who gets which end.

Watching the two of them—Camden crouched, tail twitching,

and Braddock on all fours with his head bobbing like a bird's—Arsinoe almost smiles. But it is no good, being back in Sunpool without Mirabella. It is no good with Billy taken hostage.

"Were you able to get some rest?"

"Some," Arsinoe replies.

"And something to eat?"

"Plenty."

"Are you going to be mad at me for another day?"

"I'm going to be mad at you for as long as I want," Arsinoe snaps. "You don't just get to drag me out of places."

"Sometimes I have to. When you're upset, you don't always think clearly."

"You're the one with the war-gifted legion curse. But *I'm* the one who doesn't think clearly."

"That's not fair."

"Well, what is?" Arsinoe crosses her arms. "I can't stop thinking about what Katharine is doing to him. I should never have come back here."

"I didn't ask you to."

"I know!"

"But I'm glad you are." Jules reaches out to tentatively tug on her sleeve. "I'm sorry about Billy. We'll get him back."

"How?" Arsinoe asks. However they manage it, it will not be soon enough.

Before Jules can answer, a familiar whistle cuts through the air, and Emilia, Mathilde, and the warriors burst up over the hills.

"They're back," Jules says with relief as they hurry to the road. Emilia charges her mount nearly over the top of them before pulling up to rear. Her face is ablaze, dark hair loose and wild for once. Jules puts her hand on the horse's shoulder.

"You're back," she says breathlessly as the horse quiets. "And no others lost. I was worried you would do something stupid."

"Who says she did not?" Mathilde asks, and dismounts to greet Arsinoe, and the bear and the cougar.

Arsinoe does a fast count of the party. All of the warriors except those who fell in the raid or to Katharine's poison are present. But there are three bodies wrapped in blankets and slung over the backs of the horses. Two will be Bea and the other poisoned warrior. The third is draped across the front of Emilia's saddle.

"If you're all here, then who is that?" Arsinoe points at the body. She sees Billy in her mind's eye, lost and poisoned in the dark, falling down beside the road, trying to get back to her.

"See for yourself," Emilia says, and slides the body off.

Jules kneels over it cautiously and draws the blanket back away from the face. "Good Goddess."

"What? Who is it?" Arsinoe rushes to her and grasps Jules's arm. But the body is not Billy. The boy who lies in the snow, wrapped in a blanket, not dead but certainly not conscious, is Pietyr Renard.

"She takes our boy," Emilia says, and grins. "So we take hers. I told you I would make it right."

GREAVESDRAKE MANOR

Mirabella takes a deep breath as she arrives at Greavesdrake Manor. At the queen's request, she took the carriage west from Indrid Down, through the hills to the Arron estate. Though the Arrons are rarely there these days. Not even Genevieve.

Her eyes drift skyward, up the vast face of red brick to the pitched roof of black. Such grandness. Such solid, monumental weight. As she walks to the front steps, she feels the house watching, every empty window a curtain-lidded eye. She nearly tugs down the hood of her cloak to conceal herself.

The door opens before she has a chance to knock. A butler in a smart black jacket and gray vest bows hello. There is a green scorpion clipped to his lapel but not a real semi-live one, thank the Goddess.

"Queen Katharine sent for me."

"Of course." He steps aside, and she walks into the foyer, heels echoing off the marble. "The queen is in her old rooms."

Her old rooms, where Pietyr Renard was kept during his long illness. And now the rooms that he was kidnapped from.

Mirabella stretches her neck to get a better look at the butler's face. The shadow of a fading bruise mars his cheekbone.

"It must have been frightening for you when the warriors attacked."

"'Warriors,'" he says. "I saw only one. And yes, she was fearsome."

She follows him through the foyer and past several open doors. Greavesdrake is almost too much to take in. Her eyes wander up to the molding on the high ceilings and windows, and the wallpaper of textured velvet. She listens to her footsteps change from the marble floor to dark, polished wood. Every table is set as though ready to be committed to canvas: ornate gold candlesticks and shining trays spread with sinister red jewels. No doubt the jewels are replaced by poison berries when poison berries are in season.

"What a beautiful place to grow up," she comments, though she means exactly the opposite. Greavesdrake Manor is opulent and menacing. Much like the poisoners themselves are.

"I could tell you many stories about the young queen. Perhaps after you are dismissed, I may bring you to the library. It was Queen Katharine's favorite place to hide. In the stacks. Behind the curtains. We would lose her there for hours, bricked up behind a fortress of books."

"A fortress of books," Mirabella says. She imagines little Katharine stacking volumes to craft a careful, curving tower. And then reading her way out.

Little Katharine. Gone as Little Mirabella is gone, and how she mourns them. How all women must mourn the loss of those little girls, relegated to shadow as they grow.

He leads Mirabella up a long set of stairs that overlooks the center gallery and great room, and along the hall before stopping at a set of open doors.

"The queen is expecting you," he says, and bows. "I am called Edmund, should you have need of anything."

Mirabella nods and steps into the room. It appears untouched. Nothing upended or rifled through. Emilia—for it must have been Emilia—has left no trace.

She steps farther inside, past fine tables and a chaise of striped silk. The servants have kept the space up nicely. But it still carries a smell. Sour and stale. The smell of a body fallen into disuse. As she reaches the threshold of the bedroom, she sees Katharine standing at the foot of the bed.

"Katharine?"

"Yes, yes, come in."

Katharine seems distracted. Or perhaps merely upset. As Mirabella moves to join her, she cannot help but remember: it was here that Pietyr was discovered after whatever had befallen him. And perhaps whatever that was has left something behind.

She scans the walls and furniture, not knowing what she is looking for. But that is pointless. Luca said that Pietyr would be able to tell her what is wrong with Katharine. But only if he is conscious. And here.

"Thank you for coming."

"Of course," Mirabella says. "Though I do not know how much help I may be. Do you mean to send me back to the rebellion? Try to convince them to release him?"

Katharine glances at her like she is a fool. "Of course not."

"Then what would you have me do?"

"What will I do?" Katharine asks. "The queen in me says I should do nothing. That Pietyr has been as good as dead for months, and his body . . . his shell . . . is not worth any risk."

"But?"

"But I would ride there tonight if I could. Take the fastest horse from the stable and gallop through the frozen pass." She seems exhausted. And smaller, somehow, as if the trappings of the crown have fallen away inside her childhood bedroom. "There were rebels in my city. Warriors, who came here, to the Arron estate, and stole the thing I hold most dear. What sort of Queen Crowned am I, Mirabella, if they would dare that?"

Mirabella frowns. She looks around the floor, into the shadowy corners, searching for some kind of clue. Nothing—until her gaze catches on a bright, ugly rug.

It is not truly an ugly rug. Like everything else in Greavesdrake, it is very fine, spun from eggshell-colored silk. But it does not seem to belong. As if it is new. Or was hastily brought in from another room.

"But he is not lost, Katharine, not yet," Mirabella says, and discreetly walks behind her. She toes the edge of the silk. What could it be hiding? A trap door? A carved rune? As she draws more of it up with her foot, the wood beneath appears darker. Stained.

"Mirabella?"

Mirabella lets the rug fall, but it is too late.

Katharine's eyes narrow.

"Get away from there."

"I was only—"

"I know what you were doing!"

"I find that very hard to believe," Mirabella says, "considering that I do not."

"I came here to ask you . . . and immediately find you searching my room!"

"Ask me? What did you want to ask me?"

"Something that requires trust."

"Then ask." Mirabella opens her hands. "Ask for trust. Earn it. Or can you only demand? After a queen is in her crown, does she lose the ability to ask for anything?"

Katharine's lip twists into a snarl. But it fades as quickly as it came.

I am not afraid of her today, Mirabella realizes.

"Ever since I arrived in the capital," she says, "I have done everything that was expected of me. I faced the mist. I have contacted no one from the rebellion. Not even our sister. And I have not gone against you, though I should have. Your treatment of Billy is a disgrace."

"You have a soft heart for mainlanders. I had such plans for you, Mirabella. Such hopes."

"What plans, Kat? Beyond the mist?"

"You call me 'Kat' sometimes." Katharine nods toward the empty bed. "Like he did. You are too many things, you know. Too charming. Too powerful. Even too beautiful. It would make you easy to mistrust if you were not also too good.

"I think I am remembering you. Like Arsinoe did. Perhaps that is why they keep us apart: to keep us from our memories. To keep us from each other. I would tell you the truth now. But I am afraid to."

"There is a crown forever etched into your head," Mirabella says quietly. "What have you to fear?"

Katharine touches it, the black band, stretched across her brow. "Luca is so shrewd. Even Natalia was impressed. They thought of me as a silly girl. A child, to be controlled. They still think so."

"To rule as queen is to be ruled as well by the interests of the people. Of the island."

"It is in their interest that I speak now," Katharine says. "It is for the island that I will tell you the truth. The night of the Quickening, Pietyr threw me down into the Breccia Domain. I nearly died."

"He threw you? But—does he not love you?"

"Pietyr loves me. He was confused. And it was in a way lucky, because it was in the Breccia Domain that I was found. By the dead queens."

"The dead queens?"

"Those sisters who lost their Ascensions and whose bodies

were cast into the heart of the island. They found me. Healed me. And joined with me so that I could win."

"'She is full of the dead,'" Mirabella whispers.

"An impossible story, I know."

Mirabella thinks of all the strange things she has seen Katharine do. The way she does not shiver. Her uncanny abilities with knives and crossbows. How she devours poison with a naturalist gift. "And they are with you?" she asks. "Now?"

"Not now," Katharine says. "Or, not all. I have sent them out. That is what happened to Pietyr. I sent them into him, by mistake." She gestures to the rug at Mirabella's feet. "That stain there that you are so curious about. He was trying to banish them. And I let them out. I did not even know I could. And now they have a taste for it. They seek out new vessels. They seek out you."

"No." Mirabella's skin tightens at the thought. Her elemental gift rises in defense, and the air crackles with electricity. "If that is what you ask, I will never allow it."

"Nor will I. You are too powerful, as I said. If the dead sisters had control of you, no one would be able to stop them. Not me. Not the mist."

"Then what is your plan for me?" Mirabella asks. "What do you want?"

"I want you to help me be rid of them. I want you to be my big sister. And I need you, to help me to continue the line."

Slowly, Katharine reaches out and takes Mirabella's hand. The touch feels different—her fingers are warm today, even through the gloves—and Mirabella folds them in her own without hesitation.

"What has happened to me," Katharine says, her words halting, and ashamed. " . . . carrying the dead for so long . . . it has made it impossible for me to carry the next triplets. These gloves I wear are not for fashion. They are to keep me from harming people by touch. To keep my skin from poisoning anyone by accident. I am . . . compromised."

"Kat," Mirabella says, and looks down.

"After Nicolas was killed, Pietyr and I feared that my reign would be the last. But the line of queens is not as straight as we are led to believe. There have been other methods to maintain the line. Nontraditional methods. And now that you are here—" Mirabella looks up. Katharine's eyes are wide with hope.

"You want me to bear the triplets," Mirabella says breathlessly.

"Yes," says Katharine. "I need you to ensure that Fennbirn's queens do not end with me."

Katharine watches Mirabella. Her pretty sister has never learned to camouflage her emotions. She is afraid, confused, shocked.

"I do not know what to say."

"Perhaps I have told you too much."

"At least I know now," Mirabella says. "Why the mist has risen. Why it reaches for you."

"You do not know that. It may rise in opposition to Jules Milone, to the legion curse—"

"Katharine!" Mirabella's admonishment is a fevered whisper. "You reign beside the dead!"

"Dead queens," she corrects. "Who had just as much right to the crown—"

"Queens they may have been, but to support them would be no different than supporting the rise of the rebels. They lost. Neither Legion Queen nor undead queens were ever meant to rule."

"So you will not?" Katharine shrinks. She can almost hear the Black Council laughing at her, even Pietyr, for thinking her sister would help.

"I will not ally with them," Mirabella says. "But nor will I turn my back on you. You are not them, Katharine. And you are different when they are quiet. The boy at the pier—Madrigal Milone—"

"Yes. They guided my hand. They grow stronger. Bolder. When they assert themselves, sometimes it is like I am being worn. Like they are wearing my skin."

"And they would wear me?"

Katharine nods. "You are the vessel they want. In you, they would be unstoppable."

"And you . . ." Mirabella squeezes her eyes shut as if she cannot believe it. "You . . . put them . . . in Rho? How does she bear them?"

"She was willing. I did not force her. If I had she would have ended up just like Pietyr. Rho is strong; they may be happy with her, for a time."

"But only for a time," Mirabella says grimly. "To stay, they require a queen." When Mirabella looks at her again, Katharine struggles not to fidget. "*You* were not willing," she says.

"No. I was weakened. The fall. I should have died. That is how they are allowed. The vessel must be willing, or weakened to the point of near death."

"Katharine."

Katharine remembers that tone. She remembers that voice from a long time ago. Even then, Mirabella, the eldest by not even an hour, had perfected that blend of exasperated, disappointed, and sympathetic. It makes Katharine feel as though she has just been caught with her finger in a pie. It makes her feel protected.

"I wish I did not have to ask you, believe me," she says. "To carry the next triplets. I hope it did not make you feel like a broodmare."

Mirabella arches her eyebrow and chuckles lightly. "If I did not before, I do now." She sighs. "I cannot give you an answer, Kat. Not yet."

"There is much to think about, I know."

"It is more than that. So many old queens have returned. To you and to Arsinoe. Perhaps even to me, in the form of the mist. Old queens to new."

"Living queens or dead," Katharine whispers, and Mirabella's eyes flicker to hers.

"Yes," she says thoughtfully. "Living queens or dead."

THE TWO PRISONERS

SUNPOOL

Arsinoe wakes covered in sweat and kicks her blankets away. It has been a long time since she got her facial scars, and they are completely healed. But sweat still makes them itch.

"Bad dream?"

Jules and Camden lie on the floor beside her, Jules on her side, head propped on an elbow, her other hand lazily stroking the cougar's back.

"What are you doing here?"

"Well, I was sleeping." Jules nods toward two more lumps on the floor. "Just like Granddad and Luke."

Arsinoe blinks. Ellis and Luke are asleep, snoring softly under their blankets and familiars: the white spaniel, Jake, curled up between Ellis's feet and Hank, the rooster, clucking peacefully on Luke's chest.

"Don't you remember?"

Arsinoe rubs her eyes. "I remember everyone celebrating in the great hall, and then we came up here and Luke brought more ale."

"A lot more ale," Jules says, and shuts her eyes. "The room is still tilting."

All of Sunpool had celebrated the taking of Pietyr Renard. Mathilde even flexed her barding muscles and sang the tale of his capture. It was a good story. Emilia breaking into Greavesdrake Manor and silently rushing the halls, incapacitating servants with the blunt handle of her dagger. Then pulling Pietyr Renard from the queen's own bed. She just threw him over her shoulder and carried him out. With him unconscious, she said it was a little like kidnapping a rolled-up rug.

"What were you dreaming about?" Jules asks.

Arsinoe frowns. She dreamed that she had received a package from Katharine. But she had been too afraid to open it. It had been prettily wrapped in soft blue paper and tied with a black bow, but she knew that if she opened it, she would find Billy. Dead, folded up or in pieces.

"Nothing. I don't really remember."

"How long have I known you?" Jules asks.

"What?"

"How long?"

Arsinoe sighs. "Since we were six."

"Since we were six," Jules repeats. "And you don't think I know when you're lying?"

Arsinoe gets to her feet. The dream has left her with a chill.

She craves some crispy, fatty bacon and eggs fried in the same pan. "I think you know me so well that it doesn't matter whether I lie or not. You know what I was dreaming about anyway."

Jules purses her lips, but she stands, too, satisfied. Then she doubles back over. "You had far more ale than I did; how are you so spry?"

"Poisoner constitution." Arsinoe pats her belly. "It would take a lot more than that to give me a headache."

"I need more sleep. Go without me."

Arsinoe leaves the room, careful not to disturb the sleeping men, dog, and fowl. She arrives in the great hall and finds it a wreck: upended bottles spill wine and ale across tables to drip puddles on the floor, and half-eaten chunks of bread lie here and there, along with bones from a roasted bird. There are plenty of people, too, who did not make it to their beds and settled for a bench or a tilted-back chair.

"You will have to serve yourself." Emilia is seated at a table alone, in the slanting shadow of early morning.

"I didn't see you there. Is that some unknown warrior trick?"

"Becoming invisible?" Emilia grins. "That would be a very good trick. Here." She pushes her plate of food across the table. Some of it is eaten, but she must have overloaded it in the kitchen, because there is plenty left. "I think we are the only ones awake in this entire city."

"If that's true," Arsinoe says, and picks up a bit of fried potato, "then who cooked the food?"

"Where is Jules?"

"Hungover. She went back to bed."

"She left me for you last night." Emilia smiles ruefully. "As always."

"I didn't ask her to choose." Arsinoe takes up a fork and shovels down egg, still good even if it is cold. "But if I had, she would have chosen me."

"For now."

"For"—Arsinoe pokes her with the fork—"ever."

It feels odd, arguing with Emilia over Jules like this. She does not care for Jules the way that Emilia cares for Jules. She knows that it is different. But she cannot help feeling possessive.

Possessive for who? she wonders. *Am I guarding Jules for myself or for Joseph's ghost? Shouldn't it be for Jules to decide when it is time to let him go?*

It should be. And it will be. And maybe when she does, things between Arsinoe and Emilia will have to change. She squints up at her between bites of food, and Emilia gives her a haughty, know-it-all wink. Maybe not.

"Where's the hostage?"

"At the Lermont house, under the protection and guard of the seers. Mathilde is there with him now."

"The Lermont house?" Arsinoe asks. Long ago, the castle was the Lermont house. But as their numbers dwindled, it was abandoned for a large white manor house in the southwest corner of the city. "Why not put him under guard here?"

"Too many people come and go within the castle. Lermont

House is quiet. More easily watched. Though I do not know what use he will be as a hostage or who would want to take him. He cannot move or speak. We have kidnapped a dead body. Not good protection for your Billy if Katharine comes to terms with that."

Arsinoe stops eating. "Katharine would never . . ."

"You don't think so? She is the queen now. She has no time for foolish first loves. If I were on her Black Council, that is what I would advise."

"So you think she'll kill Billy anyway."

"That is what I fear." She looks at Arsinoe gravely. "But I am sorry, Arsinoe. I did try."

Quickly, Arsinoe eats the rest of the food. She wipes her mouth with the back of her sleeve. Emilia did try. And Arsinoe will not let that effort go to waste.

"Where are you going?" Emilia asks.

"I'm going to wake up Pietyr Renard."

Arsinoe has never been to the Lermont house. She has seen it, though, passing by on her errands in that part of the city. The best butcher is not three blocks away, where she often goes to fetch scraps for Braddock, Camden, and the other familiars. But standing outside the gate, she feels out of place. It is early morning, even to those who did not spend the last night celebrating, and the Lermonts are the first family of Sunpool. Who is she to barge in on their household?

As she works up her nerve to march up the flagstone walk,

the front door opens and a man steps out. She recognizes him as Gilbert, the oracle who foretold the opportunity for Mirabella's rescue. She remembers the way his fingers broke the surface of scrying wine that seemed like blood, and now, after how badly things went in the capital, the sight of him brings a sour taste to her mouth.

"Hello," she says. "Did you foresee me coming?"

"No. But I did see you standing at my gate."

"Of course." She walks up the slate-gray stones to shake his hand, but he keeps them folded and instead bows slightly. Then he steps aside and welcomes her into the house. Once inside, she does her best not to gawk. The oracles have such an enigmatic reputation. But the interior of the Lermont house is like any other. There are no garish runes painted on the walls, no bones or beads strung from the ceiling. The fortune-telling shop she found on the mainland had a stranger feel. The only thing that sets Lermont House apart, so far, is a small marble pedestal set near the window in the sitting room.

"Do you use that to scry out of?" she blurts, then hunches her shoulders apologetically.

"Yes," Gilbert replies. "Though it is easier to use the ones in the sight garden. Here we tend to use a simple bowl of water. Would you like me to take you to him?" He laughs when Arsinoe's eyes widen. "It does not take a seer to know why you have come. It is this way."

He leads her through the first floor of the house and up a set of stairs.

"Are you the only one awake?"

"Except for the guards."

"Guards?"

"You missed them. They knew who you were, of course, and let you pass. Here." He stops beside a window and draws back the drape to point out a guard positioned behind the hedge, armed with a spear. A bow and a quiver of arrows rests beside her in the snow. "And there, the edge of his shoulder." He points across the yard. Arsinoe had not had any hint of the guards when she walked by. "Mathilde has gone to her room to bed, and when she wakes, she will likely return to the castle. I think she is satisfied now that Master Renard is safe with us."

In the hall, he opens the last door on the right and steps back so that she may enter first. Arsinoe walks in and whistles.

"Safe with you and very comfortable." The room where Pietyr rests has to be one of the finest in the house. The drape is floor-to-ceiling lace, all white, and the bed is hung with white curtains. Beneath her feet, the floors shine brightly, and crystal vases, bowls, and candlesticks adorn nearly every flat surface. The air smells of sugared lemons. She hopes they did not oust one of their own just to accommodate an unconscious poisoner.

"Don't worry. This room was unused. It was hastily prepared but well, I think."

"You can read minds?" Arsinoe asks warily.

"Sometimes. Just now it was easy enough. But do not worry. Scrying is the only reliable aspect of my gift."

"I wasn't worried. I mean, maybe a little. But it's impressive."

"I am the strongest one left now that Theodora is gone."

Arsinoe nods and tries very hard not to think about masking her thoughts while simultaneously trying to think quietly. In the bed beside the broad wall of windows, Pietyr Renard lies motionless beneath thick white blankets. Next to the bed is a chair stuffed with gray pillows, a yellow throw slung over the arm. It must have been where Mathilde sat, all night, keeping watch.

"And there has been no change?"

"Nothing," Gilbert replies. "He is now as he was when we laid him down."

Arsinoe frowns. It was what she expected to hear, but just once, could not things be easy? "Maybe if I slap him across the face," she says in a bright, quick voice.

Gilbert snorts. "Somehow I do not think so. But in his state, he will probably not mind if you give it a try."

Arsinoe approaches the bed. She reaches out and touches his hand, folded over his other atop his chest. His skin is warm, his pulse steady if not strong. He looks pale. Though that could be the effect of all of the white, and the intense light blond of his hair.

She touches his face and tilts his head back and forth. He does not stir. No twitches or movement, even beneath his eyelids. And according to every rumor they have heard, he has been this way since returning from the botched trade for Madrigal at Innisfuil.

"I would say he was poisoned," she murmurs. "Except how

do you poison a poisoner?

"Gilbert," she says suddenly. "Can you see? Can you . . . sense anything with your gift? Any thoughts inside his head? Or anything about what was done to him?"

"Perhaps it was only an illness. A natural illness."

"Where my little sister is concerned, I doubt it." She gestures to the bed. "Please."

With a deep breath, Gilbert comes closer and lays his hands on Pietyr: one across his forehead, the other across his eyes.

"Nothing. I'm sorry. There is simply nothing there to read, he—" Gilbert's arms stiffen all the way to the shoulders, and his words cut off so fast that Arsinoe hears his teeth clamp shut. Whatever passes through him leaves him gasping. He sinks onto the chair and wraps himself tight in the yellow blanket.

"Gilbert? What was that?"

"Nothing good," he says, staring at Pietyr's sleeping face. He takes a moment to swallow. "I saw a chasm. And blood. I heard the voices of queens."

"What did they say?"

"I could not tell. It was . . . mutterings. Wails."

Arsinoe leans back, relieved.

"This pleases you?" he asks.

"This pleases me. Because whatever happened to him was decidedly *unnatural*. And unnatural I can work with." She reaches for Pietyr's hand again and pushes the sleeve up his arm to look at the pale skin of his wrist. As she grasps him, she feels something uneven and rough across his palm. She turns it over, and clucks her tongue. "Did you notice this?"

"We did. An old wound. And an ugly one."

"Not that old." Arsinoe leans close to study the scars. There are so many, it is a wonder his hand did not just fall apart. Most of the palm is dark pink scar tissue. But the lines are still there, for someone who knew where to look. His scar is the mess one makes when one is trying to cover over a rune. A low-magic rune.

"Pietyr Renard," she whispers. "You have come to the right place."

As she hurries through the city to the apothecary shop, Arsinoe's mind spins so fast that it forms knots. Pietyr Renard was doing low magic. And she knows who it was who taught it to him.

"Madrigal," she whispers. "You always knew how to make the most of what time you had."

The shop is empty this early in the morning, but she and the shopkeep have a generous understanding: she is free to come and go and take what she needs as she pleases. Quickly, she goes to the shelves and pulls down a mortar and pestle, a bottle of rose oil, and a tightly bound bundle of rosemary. Chunks of resin or amber would be best, but the herbs will have to do. She stuffs a small bag of dried flower petals into the mortar and quickly returns to Lermont House.

The house is awake. And full. Gilbert must have gotten nervous and raised the alarm. Mathilde is back, her hands pressed to Pietyr's forehead and eyes. Emilia stands at his bedside with a drowsy, sick-looking Jules. Even Cait and Caragh have gathered there, with their arms crossed.

"I can't do this with all of you in here."

They turn to Arsinoe. Mathilde removes her hands from Pietyr's face.

"Do?" asks Cait. "And just what is it that you are going to do?" By the way she frowns, it is plain to see that she knows very well.

"If I don't," she says, "he stays how he is." She looks to Jules, who glances at Emilia before nodding.

"Leave her to it," Jules says. And one by one, the others bow their heads and go.

Caragh pauses at her ear. "You turn to this too quickly and too often," she says. "You are too like my sister."

"I don't have a choice," Arsinoe replies.

When the room is empty except for her, Jules, and Camden, she begins laying out her materials.

"Don't listen to her," Jules says. "You're not like my mother."

"Maybe not," Arsinoe mutters. "But Caragh's right. I turn to it. Even though it destroyed you and Joseph. Even though it might have killed him. Even though it scarred my face and gave the cat a limp. I still—" She stops and looks down at her hands and the marks the low magic has left on her. No one else has been able to wield it like she has. And the greater the magic, the greater the cost.

Arsinoe pours oil into the bowl of the mortar and pestle and adds a fat pinch of flower petals. They are deep red, from roses. Rose petals into rose oil. Perhaps she should have chosen a different oil, but she was in a hurry.

"So you're going to try and wake him up."

"That's the idea."

"But haven't the healers in Indrid Down been trying to do that for months?"

"I'm sure they have. But not like this." She nods to his hand. "Turn that over."

Jules winces at the sight it, lips drawn back in a silent hiss.

"I think your mother taught him."

"You think my mother taught him *this*?" Jules holds up his palm. "It's nothing but scars."

"No," Arsinoe says. "It's just been buried. And we're going to dig it back up."

"Why do I not like the sound of that?"

"I don't know," says Arsinoe. "You're very queasy for a warrior."

"Half a warrior," Jules corrects her as Camden sniffs at Pietyr's face.

Arsinoe leans forward and smears rose petal oil in a crescent across Pietyr's forehead. The smell is strong. Strong enough, she hopes, to reach him all the way down wherever he is hiding. She lights one of the short candles by the bedside and uses the flame to ignite the herbs before blowing them out and waving the smoke across his chest. In her own chest, she feels the tug and tickle of the low magic as the oil and smoke open the path. It makes every scar on her arms come alive and her mouth water.

She sits beside Pietyr on the bed, and Jules brings the light close as Arsinoe peers into his hand. A dagger, a new one, to replace the one taken by guards at the Volroy, comes out of the sheath at her waist. It makes a dangerous, almost ringing sound as it does; one would think she was war-gifted herself for how sharp she always keeps it.

"How can you dig anything up out of that?" Jules wonders quietly as they look upon the nest of intermingled scars. So many slashes. So many cuts. It seems someone made a flurry of them in all directions. And Arsinoe senses that it was not Pietyr.

If she looks hard enough, there are a few lines that seem different from the rest. Longer and more deliberate. Some curved, and deeper perhaps, and defined, like they had been cut more than once. Those will be the lines of the original rune, whatever that original rune was. But there is no way to trace it. The new cuts have obscured it almost completely.

Jules tilts the candle away so it will not drip wax onto Pietyr's skin. "What are you thinking?"

"It's not about thinking," Arsinoe says, her voice flat. "It's about feeling. About instinct." She takes up the knife and looks at her own mottled palm of scars. She too has had too many lines, too many runes cut into it. "Palm to palm," she whispers, and stabs deeply into her hand.

"Arsinoe!"

But before she can change her mind, she pulls the blade out of her skin and brings it down hard into Pietyr's. Their blood pools, and she seals their hands together. Their mingling blood releases magic in a jolt; it makes her head spin as whatever remains of what Pietyr did tries to invade her. She feels their hands jerk and feels the skin of his palm burst open wider. His fingers close around hers, and he pulls hard. Their blood smears across the white blankets and sheets. Whispers fill her head like wind, babbling whispers so loud that she drops her knife and plugs her ear with her free finger.

They are seeping into her head. "Jules, get him off me!"

Camden bites gently onto her arm to pull, but when she tastes Arsinoe's blood, she leaps off the bed and cowers in a corner. With a grimace, Jules grasps on to their joined hands. She pries on their fingers. It should be easy to part hands that are so slick with blood. But they do not release until Jules wraps both arms around Arsinoe's waist and heaves her away.

When the connection breaks, Pietyr Renard wakes with a shout. He grips his wrist and stares down at the deep, broken open wound in his hand. Then he peers around the room, at the cougar and at Arsinoe and Jules. Despite being in pain, startled, and unconscious for months, it takes him no more than two blinks to recognize the naturalist pretender and the Legion Queen.

"How did I get here?" he asks.

"Do you know where 'here' is?" asks Jules.

"I could make an educated guess."

"And . . . do you know who you are?"

His eyes flicker, the slightest movement, as he considers whether or not to lie. "I am Pietyr Arron," he says flatly.

"Good," Arsinoe says, and sighs. "Because that makes you someone worth keeping."

THE VOLROY

In the throne room, the suitor is facedown on the floor. His eyes are open but blank, his sand-colored hair dark and stringy with sweat. The only sign of life he gives at Katharine's approach is a small puff of breath that fogs the dark marble. The Black Council has been having too much fun with him. They have broken him down too fast, and spoiled their own game.

Katharine draws one of her poisoned daggers and slices through the rope that binds him to the throne. He moans gratefully as his arms fall free.

"Behave yourself," she cautions as he eyes the guards near the door. "I could slide this knife between your ribs faster than they could reach you with a spear."

"Is that any way to treat the boy to whom you gave your first kiss?" he asks, and winces as the feeling returns to his fingers.

"My first kiss. Is that what I conspired to have you believe or simply what you assumed with your inflated mainland ego?"

He glares at her, stretching his stiff shoulders and gingerly touching the angry red blisters at his wrists.

"The poison has a bite, does it not?" She motions for a tray of tea and biscuits to be brought to the table nearby. "But you will get no sympathy from me. I have been made to endure much worse. And I endured it better. Fetch the biscuits."

He climbs to his feet and shuffles to the table. "Ah yes. The abuse you suffered at the hands of the Arrons. Is that how you enticed Mira to come to you? By playing the wounded girl?"

"My sister is a queen. She comes to her queen's aid."

"Mirabella is good. Not like you."

"Who says I am not good? I take no joy in seeing you this way. Filthy and scarred. Scarred like your Arsinoe."

"Shut your mouth."

She draws back. She nearly apologizes. Since the dead queens have been gone, she has felt no real malice toward Arsinoe, though she is a fool and a traitor to ally with Jules Milone. It is the dead sisters who keep all her rage and all her morbid indulgences. Every gift Katharine borrows from them has been corrupted by their endless hunger for more blood, more pain, more flesh torn apart. But just now they are far away, with Rho, and she is free to be merciful.

"You should not speak so to the Queen Crowned, Master Chatworth."

"You're no real queen."

"I am the only true queen of Fennbirn."

"Then why have people been trying to snatch the crown off your head from the minute they put it there? Do you think they'd have done the same to Mirabella? Or Arsinoe?"

"My sisters did not want it. They chose to flee. Do you still dream of how it would be had the Ascension gone another way? Do you imagine yourself in the king-consort's apartment? Do you see your father wandering the fortress, barking orders?"

"If Arsinoe or Mira had won, there would be no rebellion. No Legion Queen, no rising mist. Your precious Natalia would still be alive. You were the worst queen that anyone could have hoped for."

At the mention of Natalia, Katharine's fingers dig hard into the arms of the throne. "The only reason you live is because to kill you would sadden my sister."

"And because Arsinoe and Jules have your boy," he says. "People talk. I've heard plenty about your tantrums, stomping around because they came and stole him right from under your nose. Sending that murderess, Rho, to attack the people of Bastian City in retaliation. How do you think Mirabella is going to react to that?"

"She heard me give the order. She is a queen. She knows what it is to be at war." But would she truly understand? When she knew the extent of it and the havoc that Rho would wreak, infested as she was by dead queens . . . Mirabella would look at her like she is a monster. And perhaps she is.

Katharine backs away. She will not let a mainland boy, a

former suitor, get into her head. It will all be different after the rebellion is over. And after the dead queens are gone for good.

"I think you will find that Mirabella and I understand each other completely," she says. "Before long I think you will see we are allied in ways that not even she imagined."

"She will never turn against Arsinoe."

"Then why has she not once asked me to let you go?" Katharine asks. She snaps her fingers to the guards near the door. "Tie him up again. I have lost my appetite."

"Mirabella." Luca greets her at the door of her chamber and kisses her on both cheeks. "It is nice to see you here. And not hidden behind a veil." She leads Mirabella inside to a tray of tea and savories and the meringue cookies she likes. "How are Bree and Elizabeth?"

Mirabella walks the edge of the room, looking out the windows down upon the capital from all directions. They are high in the temple; the only things higher are the Volroy towers.

"Elizabeth yearns for spring. She is worried that one of the bee colonies in the apiary has not wintered well. And as for Bree . . ." She reaches out and opens a window, letting chill air rush in, sending Luca's papers flying up from her desk.

"Troublemaker." Luca laughs as she snatches rolling parchment out of the breeze. Her hands are still fast. And not the least bit stiff.

"As for Bree, you would know better than I would, since you are on the Black Council together."

Luca presses the last of the papers to her desk and weights them with a stone. "Bree has become a fine politician. Fair, and she sees things from interesting angles. She still needs help controlling her temper. She singed Paola Vend last week over a disagreement about import tax."

"Paola Vend could do with some singeing."

"Indeed," Luca says as Mirabella takes up a meringue. "But what brings you here, Mira? Though I wish it were not so, our afternoons spent in the pleasure of each other's company are over."

"You are not happy to see me?"

"I am always happy to see you. I regret that our goals have . . . estranged us." The High Priestess sighs. "But what use are regrets? We learn our lessons, and we do our best."

Mirabella nods. The meringue breaks apart in her fingers, and she sets it down upon a saucer.

"What I tell you now," she says, "I tell you as the High Priestess, as well as my old mentor and friend. It was told to me in the queen's confidence, and I am entrusting you with it. Because I feel that you want her reign to succeed, and to preserve the line of queens."

"Yes. Of course I do."

"And I am telling you"—Mirabella looks at her levelly—"because I suspect that you already know."

Luca's steady eyes lose focus for less than a blink before she inhales and nods resignedly.

"The dead queens. She showed you."

"She told me," Mirabella amends. "I do not think I would like to be shown."

"It is difficult to believe, isn't it?" Luca runs her fingertips across the seam of a blue silk pillow. Her quarters are always furnished with wide chairs and sofas piled high with soft pillows and blankets. Yet Mirabella has rarely seen her sit upon them. "Even after I watched and suspected, I would not have believed. Had I not seen the way the mist circled her at Innisfuil. And had I not followed Pietyr Renard to the Breccia Domain and watched him strip stones from inside it.

"The dead queens. Who would have thought they would be lying there in wait? Who could have imagined the force that was being created every time another was thrown into the pit?"

"Who can imagine anything about the power of queens?" Mirabella murmurs. "We do not even know it ourselves, what we are capable of. Not until we are needed."

"And what will you do now?" Luca asks. "Now that you know?"

"She wants me to carry the triplets. She wants me to continue the line." She looks at Luca. Is she surprised? Horrified? Hopeful that Mirabella will say yes? She cannot tell. The High Priestess is impossible to read. "But no matter what is to be done, the dead queens and the mist must be dealt with first."

"They are headed for a confrontation," Luca agrees. "And I cannot guess the outcome."

"The mist will overtake the dead queens. The mist is our protector."

"You are certain?"

Mirabella shakes her head. "How can one be certain of anything? I only know that we—my sisters and I—are at the heart of this conflict. And if we come together, I believe we can put an end to it. I would write to Arsinoe."

Luca turns away. She waves her hand and walks behind her desk.

"Arsinoe is a rogue. She has chosen the side of the Legion Queen. If she sets foot in Indrid Down, she will be executed immediately. And besides, what could she do? What use is she? A bear? Against the dead?"

"I have seen Arsinoe do things with low magic that you could not even dream of. And do not," Mirabella adds when Luca's eyes widen, "come at me with temple rhetoric about low magic. Arsinoe can oust the dead queens from Katharine and serve them up to the mist on a platter."

She waits as Luca imagines it. As she rolls the possibilities in her mind.

"And then what?" Luca asks. "If the dead queens are vanquished and the mist is quiet? What will we do then?"

"Then Katharine will rule. The true Katharine. My little sister, as good a Queen Crowned as I ever would have been."

Luca stares down at her desk and at her hands, hands which have shaped the course of the island for many years. Mirabella hopes that she will agree. But she did not come to ask the High Priestess's permission.

"You think that Arsinoe will come?"

"I know she will."

"Then write your letter. Send it with Pepper. But you must tell Katharine that you are doing it."

"Of course. I know." Mirabella smiles. She relaxes her shoulders. Every bone in her body feels like it has been over-cooked, like she has danced with lightning for hours.

"There is one more thing I would ask of you," she says, and Luca smirks.

"I am almost afraid to hear it."

"What do you know of the original temple? The first temple that was built here in Indrid Down, before the capital was the capital?"

"I do not know much," Luca replies, surprised. "Why do you seek it?"

"It is just a sense I have," Mirabella says. "So many old queens return. Old queens and old tales brought to light. If we are to face them, I would know as much of our history as I can."

"Very well," says Luca. "I will see what I can find."

SUNPOOL

Arsinoe watches as Jules's ax comes down in a graceful arc and cleaves the log in two. A clean, fast cut through a fallen trunk as thick as Braddock's back leg. It should have taken many more swings than that. It would have taken Arsinoe the better part of the morning. But the strength in Jules's ax does not come from her arms. It comes from her war gift. She did not really even need the ax at all.

Arsinoe goes to the pile and takes a log in her arms to load onto the cart. They have come fairly far into the forest to cut wood, so far that Braddock got bored and stopped following. But she hears him, off somewhere not far away, rustling through brush for old frozen berries or other things to eat. She smiles. The bear may not be her true familiar, but they are still quite alike.

"Trusting yourself around an ax again, eh?" Arsinoe asks. She means it as a joke, but Jules loses concentration and the blade buries itself only a few inches into the wood.

"Aye," Jules says, and grunts as she pulls the blade free. When she uses the war gift, Jules's edges are sharper. Her glances cut, and Camden's claws are quicker to come out. But the tether is holding, and that is what matters.

"And what about Emilia? With your gifts tied together, is she a full naturalist yet?"

"No." Jules pauses midswing. "But she has grown very involved with her horse."

Arsinoe laughs.

"She wants me to be queen so badly. The Legion Queen. But you and I both know I'm not suited for it. With this curse or without. I'm a soldier. A warrior."

"A guardian," says Arsinoe, and Jules smiles.

"A guardian."

"You're as much of a queen as I am," Arsinoe says.

Jules looks at her.

"No. I'm not."

And it is true. After all that has happened, Arsinoe could rule if she had to. Sometimes she even feels the pull to lead the rebellion, which could explain why she and Emilia always butt heads.

Camden grunts and hops on top of the log pile, sniffing the air. A few moments later, Emilia and Mathilde ride into the clearing. Mathilde with Pietyr Renard on the back of her saddle.

"And what do we do with *Master Renard*?" Arsinoe asks, exaggerating his name.

Jules shrugs, eyes narrowed as she watches them approach.

"Emilia says the spies will report back to Katharine that he's awake. My bet is that she'll decide for us."

"I hope they tell her that I woke him up when she couldn't." Arsinoe smirks. "That ought to stick in her craw."

Jules sinks the ax deep into a chunk of wood and wipes her hands. The horses stop at a respectful distance, and Mathilde lets Pietyr slide to the ground.

"What's this?" Jules asks. "Afternoon exercise?"

Emilia nods to Pietyr.

"The prisoner has asked to see the queen."

"Not that queen," Pietyr says, looking at Jules with a curled lip.

Emilia dismounts and shoves him hard. "She is the only queen we have. So speak if you will."

"You brought him all the way out here?" Arsinoe asks.

"We have eyes on the roads. Birds in the sky. The forest is secure."

Jules looks at Arsinoe and sighs, then crosses her arms. With Camden seated beside her, the cougar's head nearly reaching her waist, she gestures for Pietyr to come closer.

"What do you want, Master Renard?"

He frowns, like his name on her lips hurts his ears. "To thank you, I suppose. For making me well again."

"You're welcome. Though it's not me you should be thanking but Arsinoe. It was her low magic that did it."

"I know." He frowns again. "I can feel it like mold growing across my skin."

Arsinoe snorts. "That's some thank-you."

"I . . . apologize. I should not complain. Since it was low magic that got me into this mess in the first place."

"You?" Emilia asks. "An Arron was practicing low magic? For what purpose?"

Pietyr glances between Jules and Arsinoe. "Should we not have this conversation someplace more private?"

"Say what you would say." Jules lifts her chin. "Emilia and Mathilde are leaders in this cause. We have no secrets."

"Very well." His hands have begun to tremble, and he stuffs them into his pockets. They have put him in a thick gray coat, but he wears no scarf, and the skin of his neck and chest are exposed at the open collar. The healer in Arsinoe resists the urge to wrap him in a cloak. He is still weak and should be in front of a cozy fire with a hot bowl of soup.

"How is it that I have come to be here?" he asks. "I gather that I was stolen from the capital."

Emilia shoves him again. "You are here to give information, not get it."

"Emilia." Jules shakes her head, then returns her attention to Pietyr. "You were stolen from your sickbed in Greavesdrake Manor. From what we have heard, you had been there for a long time."

"You don't remember anything?" asks Arsinoe.

"Have you ever been unconscious, Queen Arsinoe?"

"Yes."

"Then you should know that is a stupid question."

She frowns. In her mind, she takes away his bowl of soup.

"I was performing low magic in order to help the queen," Pietyr says, looking back at Jules. "Needless to say, it did not work."

"Help her to do what?"

"Help her to rid herself of the dead queens who have inhabited her since the night of the Quickening Ceremony. When she fell into the Breccia Domain. The rumors are true, you see. 'Undead' is not just an honorary epithet."

Dead queens. Katharine is possessed by dead queens. To the credit of those assembled beside the wood cart, no one cries out or falls over into the snow. They only go very quiet. The shock and disbelief are as plain on their faces as Pietyr's enjoyment watching them.

"That is why she seems so strong," Mathilde says. "And at times, so monstrous. That is how she survived."

"Yes," says Pietyr. "And I was trying to get them out. Using low magic taught to me by Madrigal Milone."

"Is that why Katharine killed her?" Jules asks. "Because she was helping you?"

"No. Katharine did not know."

"But it did not work, you said." Emilia's face is still as stone. "You could not get them out."

"She did not want them out. She said she did—she thought she did—but in the end, she used them to . . . Well, you saw the state I was in. She was not trying to kill me, but—"

Jules snorts. "You don't think she was trying to kill you?"

"If she was or they were, I would be dead. The boy murdered on the docks, your mother—those were not Katharine. It was them. They have taken her over more and more. I thought if they were gone she would go back to being my Katharine. I was a fool."

Despite his effort to remain cold, he sounds miserable. And still in love. Even Emilia seems to soften, like she might reach out and give him a bracing punch in the shoulder. Their sympathy makes Arsinoe want to scream.

"Who cares about your romantic foibles? The Queen Crowned is full of the dead! That's why the mist is rising! Why everything is going wrong! And Mirabella doesn't know!"

"She does not know?" Pietyr smiles. "I thought perhaps that was why she went. Abandoning the weaker queen for the stronger."

"How did you know she was even there?" Mathilde asks. "If you were asleep for all that time?"

"I have not been asleep for the last day. And no one in the Lermont house seems concerned about what I might overhear."

Mathilde looks ashamed. But she is not responsible for the voices of every oracle. Nor can the oracles really be blamed, when they are unused to keeping prisoners.

"Could that be why she left?" asks Emilia. "She ran to the stronger queen?"

"No," Arsinoe says. "She wouldn't."

"It doesn't matter," says Jules. "All that matters now is what do we do about it." She looks around the circle. Not even Emilia has a ready answer. How do they attack a queen who is not only one but dozens?

"I've dealt with dead queens before," Arsinoe mutters. "Believe me, they're even more dangerous than live ones."

"This is a fine Black Council you have assembled," Pietyr says after watching their silence. "An oracle, a warrior, and an exiled queen, all in service to a legion-cursed naturalist." He looks to each in turn, and even Arsinoe shivers beneath the weight of his ice-blue eyes. "But you are still missing something." They raise their eyes, and he grins. "A poisoner."

Arsinoe's mouth drops open. "What? You?"

"I would make the perfect addition. Katharine would tell you I am an excellent adviser. She would have made me the head one day."

"If she hadn't nearly killed you."

"Is that why you've given us this information so freely?" asks Jules. "Because you hope to trade it for a position within the rebellion?"

"No," he says, and looks at her squarely. "I am telling you because I do not want to go back."

Jules looks down, watching Camden's thoughtful, twitching tail.

"Don't worry, then. We have no immediate plans to send you back."

"What are you talking about?" Arsinoe tugs her sleeve. "We have to trade him. For Billy!"

Before Jules can respond, a hawk descends sharply through

the tree canopy. It dives to Jules with a piercing cry, spooking the horses and Pietyr Renard. Jules winces as it lands on her bad side, putting weight on her bad leg. She quickly reads the message it carries, and her face goes pale.

"What?" Arsinoe asks. "What is it?"

"Bastian City has been attacked. The queensguard has marched upon them."

Emilia leaps onto her horse's back.

"Wait!" Jules takes the reins of Mathilde's mount from her and jumps into the saddle. "I'm coming with you. We'll need supplies."

"We will get them along the way," Emilia growls, and before Arsinoe can say another word, she and Jules put heels to their mounts and race out of the clearing with Camden running behind.

THE VOLROY

Bree and Elizabeth sit with her as Mirabella writes her letter to Arsinoe. Normally, she would be glad of their company. But today she craves quiet. She must get her words just right. And the way Bree and Elizabeth watch her . . . it has begun to make her uncomfortable.

"Stop staring at my belly, Bree. There are no triplets in there yet. Perhaps not ever."

Bree smiles guiltily, and Elizabeth blushes from chin to eyebrows. But they still both look like they want to come and press their hands against her stomach.

It was not Mirabella who told them this secret plan. It was Katharine. Perhaps to further sway Mirabella's decision. To show her she would not be alone. Or perhaps without the dead queens to put their hands over her mouth, Katharine was simply a girl who was eager to confide in her newfound friends.

"Forgive us," Bree says after a moment. "It is just that we are excited."

"It may never happen. The Goddess may never choose to send the triplets to me, a queen who is not crowned. Besides, it could be twenty years before we know or begin to doubt. Twenty years is a long time to foster excitement."

"She will send them," says Elizabeth. "She must. And then the Goddess will have what she has always wanted anyway: triplets from her favorite."

Mirabella's mouth twists wryly and goes back to writing. "And the Goddess always gets what she wants," she murmurs.

"Queen Katharine has been in a good mood of late," Bree says, peering over Mirabella's shoulder at the letter. "But I still cannot believe she agreed to an alliance with Arsinoe."

"She agreed, because she trusts me. And because she knows that I can bring them together."

"But can you be so sure?" Elizabeth asks. "There is so much hatred between them."

"No more than there was between Katharine and me when I first arrived." Mirabella sees them look at each other; they are not so sure. "Katharine knows that we need Arsinoe. We need her low magic."

Elizabeth's face constricts. The priestess does not approve, and Mirabella wishes she could tell her everything, about the dead queens and what Arsinoe can do. But those secrets are not hers to tell.

"I will understand, Elizabeth, if you do not wish to send Pepper with this letter."

Across the room, stuck to the rough stone of the fireplace, the woodpecker cocks his small tufted head. Then he flies to

Mirabella and sits on her shoulder.

"Pepper is always happy to serve his queen." Elizabeth smiles. "Though he would appreciate an extra worm and seed cake upon his return."

"A worm and seed cake. I will see what I can do." Mirabella reads through what she has written. Then she reads it again. She does not know why she is so afraid to send it. With a deep breath, she rolls it up and seals it, and little Pepper sticks out his leg to receive the message.

"Fly fast, you good bird," she whispers, and the woodpecker flits to Elizabeth and then out Mirabella's open window, on his way to Sunpool.

SUNPOOL

Arsinoe is in the apothecary, restocking shelves, when Pietyr Renard finds her.

"Where's your guard?" she asks, watching him wander the shop, touching this jar and then that, sometimes impressed, sometimes disdainful.

"Outside."

She looks through the window. One warrior, armed with a sword, stands before the entrance.

"One guard. This really is a shoddy rebellion."

"You are not wrong," Pietyr says. "When your Legion Queen and her commander race off alone, without advice of counsel or any preparation. The war gift. It is so impulsive."

"They care about each other, if that's what you want to consider impulsive," Arsinoe snaps defensively, even though had he been anyone but Pietyr Renard, she would have agreed. "And they'll be back soon. So don't get any ideas."

"Soon. If they return at all." He pulls a jar of hemlock off a shelf, removes the cap and inhales deeply. Then he replaces the cap, and Arsinoe watches the jar disappear down his sleeve as if it never was.

"Aren't you usually supposed to wait until no one is looking?"

"I thought you might indulge me. You know, poisoner to poisoner?"

Arsinoe narrows her eyes. He has his color back, whatever color an Arron can be said to have. And he is as handsome as ever in his haughty, deceptive, murderous way.

"The guard outside," he says, and nods to her, "she thinks me soft. That I would not make it far in these wilds if I tried to run. She thinks I do not need much guarding."

"And is she right?"

"That I do not need much guarding, yes."

"Oh, really?" Arsinoe finishes tying a bundle of herbs and drops it into a drawer. "So you don't intend to run back to Katharine as soon as you spot the chance?"

"I will not deny that I want to see Katharine very badly. Almost as badly as I do *not* want to see her."

There is more than fear in his voice. There is dread, and Arsinoe is surprised to find that she believes him.

"What is she?" she asks. "What can she do?"

"I do not know. Perhaps not even she knows. When she sent the dead queens into me, I think it was by accident. A reflex." He smiles weakly. "Or perhaps I do not want to admit that she would try to kill me."

"She sent the dead queens into you, so she can send them into anyone?"

"I do not know."

"You don't know, or you won't say?"

He rounds on her, eyes burning.

"I do not know. But I think you should assume that she can."

He leans against the shelves. He is awake but not fully recovered. Perhaps he never will be.

"It's odd to see you so dejected," Arsinoe says, and he lifts his head. "I always thought of the Arrons as such a hard people. Driven, if a little lacking in passion. Yet here you are. And your broken heart is plain to anyone looking."

"Broken-hearted and a fool. I should have known what she was becoming. I should have always been afraid of her. Yet how could I be when she was not a monster to me? Take care, Queen Arsinoe. I thought I was safe. But no one is."

BASTIAN CITY

Jules and Emilia ride hard from Sunpool, pushing their horses to the limit with Jules's naturalist gift and trading them for new mounts when they can go no farther. When they stop at night, Camden hunts for them, and Emilia builds fires. They speak little and keep moving. It is when they skirt south past the capital that they know they are too late.

The path of the army is impossible to miss. A great number of mounted cavalry rode out toward Bastian City in haste. And a great number had already returned.

Emilia studies the tracks. She looks ahead, to the east. No smoke rises from where Bastian lies. Or at least not enough to see from such a distance.

"The horses are tired," Jules says.

"Push them again. One more time. Please, Jules."

They ride on. The closer they get, the more uneasy Jules becomes. They have passed no bands of wounded. No fleeing survivors.

"Perhaps the wall held," she says, "and the army couldn't make headway."

Emilia says nothing. She nudges her horse with her heels.

Bastian City is visible for a long time as they ride, and they stare at it, searching for movement. As they near the wall, they see the holes, the places where it has been breached by catapult. There is still no smoke, and all is quiet. As if the city has been abandoned.

They tie their horses outside of the wall, and Emilia runs inside, sword drawn.

"Emilia, wait!"

But she need not have worried. They are far too late. Inside the city, Emilia stands amidst a carpet of bobbing heads and shifting wings. Carrion birds and seagulls arguing over the feast of dead. There are so many of them that the ground seems to seethe.

"Emilia—"

"Get them out!"

Jules hesitates. The birds are terrible, but the sight of what they hide could be much worse.

"Get rid of them!" Emilia kicks at the gulls and slices black feathers from the tails of crows.

Jules takes a breath.

"Go."

The birds lift their heads as if waking from a dream. At once, they take wing, stirring the foul air and revealing the fallen that they fed upon.

"We should hurry," Jules says, watching them fly high

above the city. "Someone may have seen that."

Emilia does not respond. She stands with arms at her sides, surveying the dead. There are so many. Piles before the breaches in the wall, warriors who stepped onto the backs of their friends to fight. This is not the city that Jules remembers, the people who took her into hiding and protected her. Bastian was red clay tiles and clean, bright banners. It was a warm breeze off the sea. It was not these stones splashed with rotting blood. Nor these streets clogged with bloated bodies.

"There are no queensguard soldiers."

Jules looks up. Emilia has wiped her eyes and is picking her way through the battleground, kneeling to study wounds and scrutinize the edges of swords in the hands of the dead.

There are no queensguard soldiers. Not one amidst all of the fallen near the wall. Nor those strewn farther back through the streets.

"It is impossible," Emilia says. "These are warriors!"

"Maybe they gathered their dead," Jules suggests. "They must have."

Beside her, Camden grunts. The cougar is no stranger to a bad kill, but she does not like this. Her ears flick nervously, and when Jules offers no comfort, she lopes ahead, away from the worst of the carnage. Jules kneels beside a woman whose legs have been severed. And not only severed but shorn off, as if by one stroke.

"These wounds," Jules murmurs. "I don't know what could have made them."

Every wound is terrible. Every sword-strike deep and brutal, almost enough to cleave a torso in two. Other warriors lie broken against the sides of buildings, as if they were thrown like dolls. When Jules sees a head caved in, crushed flat as if by the stomp of a boot, she stands up and takes a deep breath.

"The queensguard couldn't do this. Emilia, have you seen—?" She turns up the street. They have wandered among the carnage for so long, they are nearly at the temple steps. When Emilia sees what lies upon them, she screams.

"Margaret!"

Margaret Beaulin is strewn in pieces across the steps of the temple. Emilia stumbles up, scrambling. She crawls to her and falls upon her chest.

"Emilia!" Jules follows, but even her stomach turns at the sight of what was done. She cannot bring herself to go closer as Emilia gathers the severed parts.

"She was my mother's blade-woman," the warrior cries. "She would not have fallen like this! What could have done this to her?"

"I don't know." Margaret's hand still grips her sword. The echo of a grimace still warps her face. Margaret Beaulin was fierce. One of the strongest war-gifted on the island. She would not have gone down easily. Yet the edge of her sword is clean.

Jules looks back through the streets. Bastian City is a city of the dead.

"What could have done any of this?"

From some distance, Camden screams.

"Camden!"

The big cat is not hurt; Jules can sense that. But she is

agitated. Afraid. They find her in an alley, scratching at the door that leads to the Bronze Whistle, the underground pub where Emilia raised the rebellion. Emilia quickly kicks down the door and runs inside. Jules grits her teeth; the warrior is as rash and impulsive as Arsinoe sometimes. But before she can catch up, Emilia's sword clatters to the ground.

"Emilia!"

Jules runs in and finds her on her knees, embracing two small boys. Jules quickly lowers her sword and urges Camden back as the children shrink away from her. There are at least twenty children crowded into the Bronze Whistle. Survivors. Little warriors with short daggers in their hands and wide, ready eyes.

"Hush, hush, it is all right now," Emilia says, and draws as many close as she can. "Now you are safe."

They waste no time getting the children out of the city. They find more horses in the stables and load the little ones into carts, set the older ones to driving.

"We'll pass by Indrid Down in the night," Jules says. "We won't be seen. And then we'll take them on, home to Sunpool."

"No. Not Sunpool." Emilia glances at the faces of the children. "The rebel city is not safe, and they have seen enough. We will take them to Wolf Spring." It is an order but said with hope.

"Yes," Jules says. "Wolf Spring. They'll be looked after."

As they mount their horses, Jules looks back at the broken city. Bastian had fallen completely. One whole arm of the rebellion snuffed out as quick as a candle. And it had been Emilia's home. Jules cannot begin to imagine what she would feel if she had ridden into Wolf Spring and found it the same.

"Are you going to be all right?"

"Yes." Emilia wipes her eyes dry. She looks at the children, and the tears return, so she wipes them again. "Beneath my sadness, I am angry. Soon the anger will rise to the top." She takes up her reins. "Are you all right? You must be angry as well. Is the . . . tether holding?"

Jules nods. She does not, in fact, feel angry. All she feels is grief. And dread.

THE FIRST TEMPLE

Mirabella and Katharine ride their horses down the cliffs on the northwest shore of Bardon Harbor, dark hoods pulled down against the wind. High Priestess Luca follows behind on a steady white mare.

"Can you not ease this wind?" she calls out.

"I could," Mirabella replies. "But it adds to the sensation of adventure!"

Ahead, riding in the lead on her black stallion, Katharine turns and smiles. The cliff path is not terribly steep, but it is narrow in places. Mirabella's mount is the same gray charger she rode in the parade. Despite his high step and good looks, he has proven to be sweet and reliable, even for a poor rider like her.

They reach the beach, and the horses dance in the sand, happy as Mirabella is to be back on even ground. The day is cold and slate colored, and the beach is deserted except for a few small birds racing back and forth before the surf.

"The northern cliffs are wild," Katharine says. "Even before the mist rose, they were often empty. You probably did not need to wear that brown cloak as a disguise, High Priestess."

"Perhaps not, Queen Katharine." Luca dismounts and tugs the cloak tighter around her. "But an overabundance of caution has saved my old skin more than once." She nods ahead. "There it is."

Mirabella follows her gaze. The opening of the cave is not wide, though perhaps long ago, it was wider. When Luca said she had discovered the location of the first temple, Mirabella had not imagined a cave. She had thought they would follow the river, perhaps, and find an old circle of stones, or a crumbled foundation. A place to dig. Not to descend into.

"And just what, sister, do you expect to find?" Katharine asks, voice raised against the wind and the waves lapping at the rocks.

"I do not know."

"Maybe nothing," says Luca. "Maybe I am wrong, and it is only a cave."

But looking into the dark, Mirabella's queensblood begins to sing. Whatever remains of the first temple, they will find it inside.

"If you will not soften the wind, you can at least light us a torch," Luca says, and holds out three. Mirabella lights them with a cupped hand as Katharine watches with wonder.

"Surely you have seen Bree light torches before."

"Yes," says Katharine. "But not even she makes it look so easy."

They each take one and go, with Luca leading the way.

"Watch your footing," the High Priestess cautions. "Do not slip."

"She says that as though we are the ones with swollen knees," Katharine whispers, and Mirabella smiles, shushing her with a glance. Inside the cave smells of salt and other minerals. And faintly of sea life. It sits above the tides, but the high tide must barely kiss it, leaving behind small pools and wet stones. Past the entrance, the ground rises and becomes drier, and the ceiling opens up to a small dome. The walls are smooth, worked by long-ago currents and perhaps by hands.

"Do you feel that?" Katharine asks.

"Feel what?" asks Mirabella, though the hum in her blood is almost as loud as the ocean.

"That sensation. It feels like I have been here many times before. Many times . . . yet—"

She does not finish her sentence, but Mirabella knows what she means. As they follow Luca, her eyes study every crack, every curve of dark, dripping stone. Soon enough, the flat path gives way to stone steps, down and curving deeper into the cliffs.

"Luca, how did you find this place?" she asks.

"Vague references in old writing."

"Old writing?"

Luca waves her hand to end the questions, though that has never stopped her before. But then they reach the end of the path, and all of Mirabella's words are forgotten.

The interior of the first temple is magnificent. The domed walls have been carved into ancient sculptures, etched with ancient stories. And at the heart of it sits a shrine inlaid with gold.

"Look at it," Katharine says breathlessly, and hurries to the walls, her torch close as she touches the carvings. Some of the figures and scenes have been reduced to vague shapes by dripping and seeping water. Others are so well-preserved that they could have been carved yesterday. Even some of the ancient pigments have survived in blues and reds and yellows. "What must it have been like when it was new?"

"What was the world like when it was new?" Luca asks, her eyes wide. "How many have come before to worship? And how long has it been since anyone has walked this room? Breathed this air?"

Mirabella carries her torch above her head, urging the flame a little higher to better view the ceiling. She sees depictions of sun and stars, water and waves. Dogs and deer. She sees figures racing through forests of trees, telling stories she has never heard. She sees the shrine.

The gold is so bright in the light of the torch that it hurts her eyes. Upon the floor, plates of ancient bronze still sit, corroded green by minerals. Once, they must have held the offerings of the people or the burning herbs of priestesses. She looks up at the image behind the shrine, depicted in jewels and black tiles.

The first queen of Fennbirn.

"Katharine. Come here."

Katharine comes to her side, and they look upon her, their ancestor. The origin of the line. Above her head is a crown in gold and below her feet, three dark stars: the first triplet sisters.

"Do you see her?" Mirabella asks as Katharine takes her hand.

"I see her."

The first queen of Fennbirn is shown with five arms. Upon each of her hands rests each of the gifts. Fire in a clenched fist. An apple in an open palm. A clutched dagger. An open eye, faced out. And a snake twisting through her fingers. The first queen was a Legion Queen.

Mirabella reaches out toward the image, the lightest of brushes against her ancient cheek. When her fingertips touch, the picture in her mind comes fast. Strong enough to rock her back on her heels, and to ripple into Katharine through their joined hands.

Jules Milone. She knows from the stricken expression on Katharine's face that she saw her, too. It was unmistakable.

"What?" Luca asks. "What did you see?" The High Priestess edges closer.

Mirabella turns to her sister. She draws her nearer and rubs the tattoo of Katharine's crown gently with her thumb.

"The beginning of the line," Mirabella whispers. "And the end. The dead queens rise and the Goddess has chosen her champion."

"But why her?" Katharine asks. "Why not us? We are of her. Descended from her!"

"I do not know, Kat. Maybe *because* we are of that line. And that line has gone too far in the wrong direction." She lowers her head. "Maybe there is no reason at all. But you saw her. We cannot deny it."

"So what do we do? Are we not queens anymore?"

"We will always be queens," Mirabella says, her hands on her smaller sister's shoulders. "So we will fight the dead. And we will fight the mist. We will help her."

She turns away from the shrine and feels the jeweled and painted eyes of the first queen on her back.

"Let us go back to the horses, Luca. We have much to consider."

Mirabella gathers her skirts and prepares to make the long climb out of the temple. But before she can, a foul wind whips into the space, and all of their torches are extinguished.

"Strong wind," the High Priestess says. "The tide must be coming in. Mira, relight them."

She does, first her own and then Luca's, and the cave is illuminated again. Katharine has crumpled onto the floor.

"Queen Katharine!"

They hurry to her and kneel. She has gone cold. And too late, Mirabella knows why.

"The dead queens," Mirabella whispers as the dagger stabs into her stomach.

She shoves Katharine away and staggers back, hand pressed against the blood that soaks through the black of her gown.

"What have you done?" Luca shouts.

"No, it was not me!" Katharine grips her head with both

hands, the bloody blade dragging across her cheek. "It was them!"

The dead queens had found her in the temple. They had returned somehow and found her in this sacred place.

"They would wear your skin," Katharine cries. "Run, Mira. You have to run!"

Mirabella turns and races up the damp stone steps, through the narrow passageway with her torch thrust before her. She ignores the wet warmth that sticks her gown to her legs, her breath loud in the cavern as her footsteps ring off the rock. When she hears the dead queens scream with Katharine's voice, she wants to cry.

She bursts out of the mouth of the cave and stumbles in the sand. Somehow, she reaches her horse and climbs onto his back.

"Go, go," she moans, and he obeys, galloping up the cliff path. She can see the summit. She can see her way to Sunpool. To the rebels and to Arsinoe. The horse is good, strong and steady. He can run for half a day, well past the shadow of Indrid Down. He can carry her to safety. He leaps the last strides up onto the cliffs.

And Mirabella loses her grip and tumbles from the saddle.

Dazed, she rolls onto her stomach and grimaces, fist pressed to her belly. She is bleeding badly. Weakening. But what she sees when she looks back makes her claw and shove against the ground to get away. Katharine has come up the path. Only it is not Katharine. This is what she meant when she said the dead queens wore her like clothing. The rotting skin mottling her cheeks. The milky eyes. The blackness seeping from her and rising like smoke.

"Katharine!"

The dead queens shake their head. When they smile, dark wetness shows between their teeth, as if their mouth is watering.

Mirabella calls her storm; she has no choice. She gathers her lightning as the queens lift her up by the arms, but her gift slips through her fingers like so much blood. They have done it. Weakened her, and made her a ready vessel.

"Katharine," she cries, and touches her sister's face. "You can't let them have me!"

The dead queens recoil. The eyes close, and when they open, they are Katharine's again, clear and black and suffering. Afraid.

"Little sister." Mirabella smiles. "Do not let them have me."

"I am so sorry, Mira."

Katharine starts to cry, and Mirabella exhales. The blade against her throat is only a sting, and then Katharine shoves her clear, over the side of the cliff face. The wind at her back as she falls is like the wind atop Shannon's Blackway. When she strikes the rocks below, it only hurts for a moment.

Katharine rides back to the Volroy alone. She could not remain on the beach, watching Luca weep and hover over Mirabella's body, looking this way and that, back to the cave, up the path to the cliffs, as if there were something to be done. Nor could she stay and listen to the dead queens snapping their jaws, muttering bitter nonsense as they stared down at their broken vessel on the rocks.

As she storms into the Volroy, one of her guards bows and hurries forward to meet her.

"Queen Katharine. We found the commander this afternoon unconscious—"

"Get away from me!" Katharine bellows. "Leave me alone!"

Except she is never alone. Not in the empty halls, not when she presses her hands to the sides of her head so hard she thinks she will crack her skull. Nor when she slams the door of her rooms closed behind her and listens to her breathing in the quiet.

She tried to rid herself of the dead queens. To distance herself from them. Appease them. She has tried to control them and lull them into silence. They had won her a crown. But they had cost her Pietyr. And they had made her murder her sister.

We are you now, they whisper as they twist themselves back into her veins.

Do not fight us, anymore.

In the quiet shadows of the throne room, Billy lies on his stomach, hands bound behind his back. His feet are bound to his hands. He has stopped being able to feel either set hours ago.

He turns his head to the side, which makes it easier to breathe. He is not sure what poisons they gave him today. Perhaps they did not give him any. But every time food or drink passes his lips he imagines for hours that he can feel the effects: his throat closing, his stomach and chest tightening. At night, he weeps with silent panic, alone and tied and hating that it is only his imagination making him suffer.

But it is not all in his head. The Black Council has been inventive in his torture. Renata Hargrove is a master of knots and continues to find new ways to twist and truss him. Paola Vend prefers setting him to impossible tasks and laughing and kicking him when he fails. She challenged him to find a sewing needle in a bowl of grain using only his tongue. She made him try for an entire day. When he failed, Antonin Arron dipped the needle in wasp venom and stuck it in each of his fingers, and the swelling made it much more difficult to serve the bastards their tea.

Mirabella has not visited him since the first night. And he has had to admit that Arsinoe is not coming either. He is glad of that. He would never have her risk herself. But at night, in the dark, fearing his tongue is beginning to thicken, he stares at the tapestry behind the throne and wishes and wishes that she would step out from behind it.

When he hears shuffling feet near the door, he thinks it is only a changing of guard. He pays no attention to it at all until someone gives a muffled cry and a body thumps to the rug.

He twists his head. All he can make out are whispering white robes. At once, he is surrounded by them and feels his feet and hands cut free.

"Luca?" He flexes his fingers and tries to push himself up.

"Help him," the High Priestess whispers, and he is hauled up by the arms.

"What's happening?"

"What do you think is happening?" Luca slides her knife back into the sheath at her belt. "I am getting you out. Would you rather stay?"

He does not argue. He hobbles quietly along with the priestesses out of the throne room, and through the dark castle to the kitchen entrance. Outside, a priestess holds a saddled horse, with something large and dark thrown over the front of the saddle.

"Quickly, quickly." Luca takes his arm and helps him to mount. He feels what the shape is at once and tenses.

"What is this?" he asks. "Who?"

"It is"—her mouth tightens—"it is Queen Mirabella."

Billy's heart seems to stop. It cannot be Mirabella, this cold, stiff shape rolled into a blanket. But from the look on the High Priestess's face, he knows it is.

"I am sending her home with you. I could not protect her. Tell her sister that it was Katharine and the dead queens who did it. Tell her to come and fight. The temple and the High Priestess will not get in her way."

Billy adjusts Mirabella carefully in his arms. "I can't believe—"

"Nor can I. But there is no time. The path through the rear gate is clear. I know you are a mainlander, but you will have to find your way from there. We can offer you no more help."

He takes up the reins. The blood has returned to his fingers and lower extremities, but they are still sore and clumsy.

"Why are you doing this?" he asks.

"For Mira," she says. "And perhaps for me. Now go!"

Billy turns the horse and rides through the gate. When he is safely out, he turns back and sees Luca with her hand raised in farewell. He raises his in return. After all, Katharine will know she was the one who freed him, and he doubts that he will ever see her alive again.

SUNPOOL

For Jules and Emilia, the ride back to Sunpool is grave and filled with silences. After seeing the surviving children from Bastian City safely to Wolf Spring, where they were welcomed with gruff embraces, as Jules knew they would be, they traded for fresh horses and, after a brief reunion with Matthew and little Fenn, returned to the road. Emilia did not want to talk about Margaret. Neither of them wanted to speak about what they saw at Bastian City and what could have done it. But as Sunpool draws ever nearer, they will have to soon enough.

The road from the south winds near to the sea, and when the rebel city comes into view, so does the western shore. Only a season ago, Arsinoe and Mirabella came aground there. Jules can almost see them, sputtering and cold, stumbling onto the dunes.

Ahead in the city, lookouts will see them coming. The gates

will open. Arsinoe will run out. She will leap at the horses, relieved they have returned. She will tell them how stupid they were for going in the first place.

But she'll understand, Jules thinks. *After she hears what we have to say.*

"They are opening the gates," Emilia says. "And there is a rider."

Jules looks. She sees no one coming from the city.

"No. On the road. There." Emilia juts her chin. A lone figure on horseback appears from where they had been hidden behind the rise of a hill.

Camden raises her head, and with a grunt, leaps off the back of Jules's horse to race ahead to them.

"Who could that be?" Emilia asks.

Jules watches her cat's happy, flailing tail. She nudges her horse into a canter.

"I don't believe it. It's Billy!"

Together, she and Emilia race to meet him. She is astounded that he is alive, let alone free. But when Camden recoils, crouching low, she and Emilia slow their horses.

"How did he get free?" Emilia wonders. "And what is that he's carrying?"

He pulls up when he sees them, far short of the open gate and the gathering onlookers. He looks pale and ill. Filthy.

"Billy Chatworth," Jules says when they reach him. Then she stops. She does not know what else to say.

"They let me go," he says quietly. "Luca let me go. She sent me, with a message for Arsinoe."

"What kind of message?" Emilia asks, her eyes on the rolled blanket.

Billy's face constricts. He lets go of his horse's reins and adjusts the blanket in his arms. Then he uncovers Mirabella's face.

Jules cannot believe what she is looking at. It does not seem possible.

"Jules!"

Arsinoe bursts through the gate, racing for them like Jules knew she would. Jules's heart pounds. She maneuvers her horse in front of Billy's.

"Don't let her see, do you hear me?" She knows it is a ridiculous command. Something like this cannot be hidden.

Arsinoe reaches them and clasps her leg. "You were gone too long," she says. "I didn't know— Billy?"

Jules looks between them as Arsinoe half smiles.

"But how did you—how did you get him?" She pushes through the horses, and her smile disappears.

"Arsinoe," he says softly. "I'm so sorry."

"No." She grabs at Mirabella's body, trying to pull it to the ground. "No. What happened to her? What happened to my sister?"

"Arsinoe—" Billy leans back, struggling to control his horse, and Jules quickly dismounts. She grasps Arsinoe around the waist.

"Let go of me!" she shouts, and strikes Jules in the head. "How did you find them? You were supposed to be in Bastian

City! I don't understand!" Her voice is high. Strained, as Jules holds on tight. She does not know what happened, only that Mirabella is dead. And that for the rest of her life, she will never forget the sound of Arsinoe's voice screaming that she does not understand.

In the room that they share in the castle, Arsinoe watches Billy put on a fresh shirt. It is quiet there; the whole city is quiet, in the wake of Mirabella's death. Almost like they cared.

"Here, let me." She stands up and helps him with the buttons. There are so many blisters on his fingers that a new one pops every time he makes a fist. She took a long time cleaning them, gently, with warm water and soothing herbs. Knowing they came from poison filled her with disgust. But even as she looked upon the welts and the cuts and the ligature marks at his wrists and ankles, the anger she felt was muted compared to what she felt when she thought of Mirabella.

They had murdered her. Impossible as that seemed, when she was so powerfully gifted. When she was the one who could battle the mist and win. Yet she was dead.

Before Jules dragged Arsinoe away, she had seen the clean cut across Mirabella's throat like a second smile. She had seen the mess they had made of the back of her skull when they dashed it against something solid.

"Is the horse all right?" Billy asks quietly. "I rode him too hard from Indrid Down. I should have stopped, but I was afraid."

"He's fine," Arsinoe says. She does not really know. But

there are plenty of naturalists in the rebellion to look after him.

Billy turns to her and slips his injured hands up onto her neck. He rubs his thumb along her cheek, and she lets him press his forehead to hers for just a moment. Billy's touch would make her soft. She would curl into it and cry, use him to forget where they are and what has happened.

"You should eat." She turns away and gestures to an untouched plate. Some bread and cheese and one of the cakes Luke has started to bake after commandeering the ovens.

"We should eat," Billy corrects her. "And we should sleep. But I don't want to do either."

She would be surprised if he could sleep at all, with the amount of pain he must be in. His right eye is so swollen, it is almost closed, the entire socket a deep and sinister purple. Someone without the poisoner gift would assume he had been struck. But she knows he was stung with something. Injected with some venom.

"I'll brew you some willow bark tea," she says. "Make you some salve." She clenches her hands into angry fists. But Billy takes them and tugs them open.

"She didn't betray you," he says. "I accused her of it, but I believe her. She loved you, Arsinoe. Maybe she loved you both and just couldn't see what Katharine was."

"They'll say she was stupid. Or a traitor. A stupid, gullible fool or a turncoat. And that's all they'll ever say. No one here really knew her. Only me and you."

"So we'll set them straight."

"She would have been a better Queen Crowned than any one of us still living," Arsinoe whispers. She pulls her hands free. "I should have stopped her. I should have stopped myself."

"Yourself?"

"Every cut I made into my arm. Every favor I asked for from whatever the low magic is. I knew the whole time it wasn't free. And I did it anyway!"

"Arsinoe—"

"You warned me. You told me to stop. You said it was the people around me who would bear the cost."

"That wasn't what I meant. This . . . it wasn't what I meant at all."

He looks away, and a silence grows between them. There in the room with Billy, something is slipping away. And if she would just reach out and take his hand, she could catch it and keep it from disappearing.

"My father's dead," he says dully. "They murdered him, too. Punishment for murdering Natalia Arron."

Arsinoe looks up.

"I'm going to have to go home and look after Mother and Jane. They deserve to know what's happened."

"You're going now?"

"No. I won't go now." He pauses. "Maybe I'll come and find you after they're settled. We can go away together like we talked about."

It was not so long ago that they made that pact, to start over together someplace new.

"The people who said that," she whispers, "were from another world. Now there's only this one." *This one*, she thinks, and shuts her eyes bitterly. Where war presses in against the walls and will force them to battlefields soon enough. Where in the morning, she will have to burn the body of her sister.

"I think we had our chance, Junior. And I think we missed it."

"I think so, too," he says through clenched teeth. He walks to the door and pauses with his hand on it. "Luca gave me a message for you. She told you to come and fight. That the temple wouldn't stand in your way."

Arsinoe nods. "Good. Then that's just what I'll do."

INDRID DOWN

After Mirabella was killed, Luca made no attempt to hide what she had done. She confessed to freeing the suitor and sending Mirabella's body with him home to the rebellion. She gave Katharine no choice but to summon the guards and have the High Priestess escorted to her rooms in Indrid Down Temple to await her sentence.

Rho, meanwhile, recovered from the sudden abandonment of the dead queens, regaining consciousness after a day and a night. Though she is not entirely the same. Her eyes, at times, seem to be missing something. But only Katharine herself knows what that could be.

With Genevieve in her shadow, Katharine walks atop the battlements between the Volroy's indomitable towers, where the wind is strong enough to nearly knock her down. The Black Council refuses to meet. After the arrest of Luca, Bree is terrified she will be next, and as for Antonin, Cousin Lucian, and the rest . . . When first they were reluctant to have Mirabella in the capital at all, now they are more than happy to blame Katharine for the loss of their champion against the mist.

Katharine looks out across the harbor to the place below the cliffs where her sister died. The presence of the dead queens rests heavy and cold in her belly, as if she had swallowed a sphere of ice. After she stole Mirabella from them, they had stormed through her blood, cutting like razors, rotting her flesh from the inside out. But she is all they have, and soon enough, they quieted.

Katharine cannot be quiet. She feels only hate. Hate and impotent anger. But at least she had spared her sister the experience of sharing her skin with the dead.

"The mist still hangs there," Genevieve says, leaning against the stone of the battlements and looking out at the bay. "Like it is waiting for something. But for what?" She shivers and then cocks an eyebrow. "So much for the promises of a dead king-consort."

"Have you told anyone else what you found in those pages? That Mirabella's death might have vanquished the mist?"

"No. Only you. Though perhaps we should. We could say you had to try, based on what we learned. That you sacrificed her in an attempt to save the island. Even if it failed, no one could fault you for that."

"No. I do not want to make excuses." Katharine glares out at the mist. "Mirabella wanted to bring Arsinoe here. She would have brought Jules Milone. She would have had us fight beside them, had me stand aside and put the crown on the Legion Queen's head. Perhaps that is still what I should do."

Genevieve studies her carefully.

"Do not worry," Katharine says. "I would only be that brave if she were still here. Now I will be a coward and let them bite and claw and scratch until there is nothing left."

"Kat," Genevieve says, but Katharine turns away. "Very well. What, then, do we do with the High Priestess? I never thought I would plead for mercy, but . . . seeing Luca's eyes as she confessed . . . Her heart has broken, and her influence wanes. I think this was the last disappointment her old heart can bear."

"Let the High Priestess remain in her rooms under guard. Let her stay there until it is over."

"Over?"

"If you do not think that Arsinoe will come for me now, you are a fool. She will come. And the mist will come. And the Legion Queen will come. And then there will be an ending."

SUNPOOL

Jules and Billy try to keep Arsinoe from preparing Mirabella's body herself. But who else could do it? Who else knows the way she liked to wear her hair or which perfumed oils she preferred? Only Arsinoe. So the morning of the funeral, she stands before her sister's broken body and tries to work up the courage for that first touch.

She will be cold. A shell. And the bits of dried pink matted into her hair make Arsinoe's stomach wobble. No one else should see her like this.

She places her hands atop Mirabella's shoulders.

"There," she whispers, as if it is done, but despite herself, she is disappointed that Mirabella does not sit up and tell her it was all a ruse.

"Do you do this alone?" Pietyr Renard asks from the shadows behind her.

"Get out."

"I only thought to share the load."

"I don't care what you thought. No one else can see her this way. Especially not you."

"I can help you reset the bones. Help you to restore her."

"There is no restoring her," Arsinoe half shouts, and Pietyr, with typical Arron boldness, walks closer, uninvited. As he looks upon Mirabella's wounds, all Arsinoe wants to do is give him wounds to match. Cave in his skull. Break his ribs and legs. Cut his throat and send him back to Katharine wrapped in a blanket. And then he touches Mirabella's face so tenderly that Arsinoe's tears pause in surprise.

"She was so lovely," he says. "And so strong. How we feared her."

"Then how did this happen?" Arsinoe asks.

Pietyr's finger hovers over the dark red cut across her throat. "Perhaps the same way it nearly happened to me." He glances at Arsinoe as if ashamed. "Or perhaps not. I cannot pretend to have any answers or to know the truth." With slow hands, he moves Mirabella's arm so it lies bent, her hand atop her stomach. He moves her shattered leg beneath her gown so that it looks straight and strong again.

Without a word, Arsinoe joins him, and they reset every broken bone. They clean every bit of redness out of her hair. She wraps the wound at Mirabella's throat with a blue silk scarf, and Pietyr drapes her in a fine embroidered blanket of black. When they are finished, Mirabella is beautiful again.

"I will not say she looks like she is sleeping," Pietyr

whispers. "I have always hated that lie."

"Not sleeping," Arsinoe agrees. "But better. Almost like I remember her."

He nods and turns away to go.

"Renard."

"Yes?"

"You know we are going to kill your queen."

"Yes."

"And you won't try and save her?"

"I already tried," he says quietly. "I failed."

After the body has burned, Jules and Emilia stand in the dunes of brown-green winter grass and look down on the beach at the remains of Mirabella's funeral. It had not been, perhaps, fit for a queen, but the people of the rebellion had worn what crimson they had, even if that was only a bright red scarf wetted dark. They left offerings to Mirabella in the waves: paper lanterns painted with thunderheads, braided ribbon soaked in scented oil. The elementals called the wind and moved the currents to carry them out to sea. After Arsinoe had lit the fire, Camden walked the edge of the surf, pausing now and then to call through the smoke, making the sound that mother mountain cats make when they call to their hidden cubs. Even Cait's crow, Eva, flew out over the sea, her caws strange and high, like the cries of a seabird.

"You should go down to her," Emilia says, and leans against Jules's shoulder. But Jules had been there all through the burning and the releasing of gifts. She had been there, with Billy, and Cait and Ellis. Aunt Caragh and Luke. Emilia and Mathilde. Even Pietyr Renard, though he did not dare to speak to any of them.

As the crowd dwindled with the sunset and the day turned colder, Jules retreated up the beach in the hopes that Arsinoe would follow. But Arsinoe remained with the embers. The only ones with her now are Camden, seated on the sand, and Billy. Luke has lingered a few steps away, shivering and holding his rooster.

"I'm not really welcome," Jules says. "Mirabella and I . . . we never . . ."

"That doesn't matter now." Emilia gives her a light shove. "Go. Help her to mourn."

Jules drags her feet. "I'm of no use. I know how to send an arrow through an eye. I know how to fight. I don't know how to do this. Besides, she needs time. Distance."

"And she will have it, until the snow melts."

The snow would melt in a few weeks' time. And then the rebellion would march on Indrid Down. This time with Arsinoe riding beside her at the head of it.

Jules takes a breath and goes back down to the beach, her feet cold from seawater soaked through the leather, her short, brown hair whipping into her eyes. She nods to Billy and to Luke, who bow their heads and turn, shivering, back toward the city. Arsinoe does not move. She holds her diminishing torch and stares out at the darkening sea.

"Arsinoe. You should come away."

Jules reaches out to tug on her sleeve. She expects to be shrugged off or yelled at. But Arsinoe only rocks backward with the pull, and then forward again.

"I don't know what to say," Jules says.

"You don't have to say anything." Arsinoe's voice is thick. "I left you here with this. I left you alone with this same thing, when Joseph died."

"That was different. Joseph was different." Joseph was killed in an escape, by some soldier doing a duty. Looking back, she feels no hatred, almost like he died in an accident. "And besides, I left you, remember?" She nudges Arsinoe softly. "I know I'm not your real sister, but—"

"Be glad of that." Arsinoe clenches her teeth and looks at her with dead black eyes. "I only have one left. And not for long." She turns back to the water, and Jules looks out to sea as well. When the mist appears, hanging in the distance like a swirling, white curtain, she grabs Arsinoe by the arm. But Arsinoe smiles.

"Don't be afraid. It won't hurt us."

"How do you know?"

"Because she's a part of it now," Arsinoe whispers. "And she's only here to say goodbye."

THE QUEENS' WAR

INDRID DOWN TEMPLE

Bree and Elizabeth make their way up the many stairs that lead to Luca's rooms atop Indrid Down Temple. Elizabeth goes first, carrying bowls and a pitcher of hot soup. Bree follows with a loaf of bread and nearly drops it when Elizabeth stumbles.

"Take care; the stairs are steep." She grimaces as Elizabeth sets down the pitcher and shakes spilled soup off her scalded hand. "Are you all right?"

"I'm fine." The priestess sucks on her reddened thumb. "The heat feels good, really."

Bree smiles. "Our Elizabeth. Able to find a bright spot in anything, even a burned finger."

"Almost anything," Elizabeth says softly.

They reach the door to Luca's rooms, and Bree directs the guards to let them in. The guards have not been too much trouble. At least some in the queen's service still revere the temple, and the High Priestess, regardless of the charge.

"You girls have to stop coming here," Luca says when they are inside. She embraces them both and squeezes Bree so hard that she nearly crushes the bread.

"You say that every time." Elizabeth takes the bread from Bree and busily sets the table, wiping the surface with the sleeve of her robe and pulling the High Priestess's chair out.

"I know," says Luca, sitting. "But I do not expect you to listen. When have you girls ever done anything that I have asked?"

"Here." Elizabeth pours a bowl of soup and tears off a chunk of bread. "It's chicken and carrot, with a little cream. I made it this morning."

"I made the bread," says Bree, sitting down and tearing off her own piece.

Luca snorts. "You did not."

Bree smiles at her.

"Of course she didn't," Elizabeth says. "Bree is no use in a kitchen."

"I am of no use anywhere," she says. "Except as a queen's companion. It is what I was raised for. And now . . ."

Luca dips her spoon into the soup.

"Blow on it first," Elizabeth cautions. "We have to keep it near to boiling for it to stay warm up in these rooms. I don't know why you prefer them. So high and drafty."

"I liked them because I could see," Luca says. "But I could not see enough."

Bree watches the High Priestess quietly. Bree had been so

angry when Luca crowned Katharine. When she pronounced Mirabella's execution. But those feelings seem far away. She and Luca and Elizabeth, they are all who remain, the only ones who can truly remember Mirabella from that time before the Ascension.

Bree dips her bread into her bowl and takes a warm bite. Spring has come to the capital. The passes through the mountains are opening. New shoots of grass have begun to sprout. It is just taking longer for the air up here to realize it.

"What word is there from the Black Council?" Luca asks, and Bree clucks her tongue.

"You know I cannot tell you. The guards outside your door might be kind, but they are still always listening."

Luca chuckles. She seems much the same, but if Bree looks closely, she can see that the edges of her pristine white robes are marred by dust. Her silver hair is clean and combed, but it has thinned, and the pink of her scalp has started to show. Once, Bree and Mirabella had sworn that Luca had been born old and therefore would never grow older.

"She will keep me here until I am dead," Luca says, and Bree gives a start, worried that her face was too readable. "Or they will execute me. Those are my outcomes, and the only thing to be determined is the method of my downfall. Shamed publicly in the square? Or killed quietly and my body burned among the priestesses of Indrid Down Temple?"

"Those are not the only ways," says Elizabeth, but her bright voice is unconvincing. She reaches into her hood for Pepper, like she always does when she is afraid or uncomfortable. But

Pepper is not there. He is somewhere between the capital and Sunpool, on a pointless errand for a fallen queen. Perhaps he beat Billy's horse and delivered the letter before Arsinoe knew Mirabella was dead. Bree hopes so. Delivering it now seems too unkind.

"Maybe the rebellion will win," says Bree. "Maybe the Legion Queen will rule and let you go."

"Katharine will send someone here to kill me if it looks like things are going badly. I can assure you of that." Luca grabs Bree's hand and lowers her voice to a whisper. "And do not speak so unless you want to find yourself in the Volroy cells!"

Bree's eyes burn. She focuses hard to keep her gift from affecting the torches and scorching the walls.

"I believed her when she spoke of the truce. I had even come to like her."

"So had Mirabella," Luca says. "So had we all."

"She murdered my best friend!"

"Bree." Elizabeth eyes the closed door.

"I do not care." Bree waves her hand; she sets every candle in the room alight, every lamp. She wants Katharine to appear before her so she can burn her alive. Except even as angry as she is, she would not have the nerve. No one has the nerve to stand against the Queen Crowned. No matter what kind of mess she has gotten them into.

"Soon enough, the rebellion will come. They will march their army through the mountains and down through the valleys and fields of Prynn." Luca looks out the window, at the Volroy's enormous towers. "They will come with the support of Rolanth and the temple."

"And they will still lose! You know what Katharine is. You know there is something . . . about her, some power she wields."

"Arsinoe will know it, too. She will receive Mirabella's letter."

Bree looks down. "How has it come to this?" she asks. "That we should welcome the rebellion and the end of queens?"

"I do not know," says Luca, and wipes her mouth with a cloth. "But you girls had best not tarry." She gets up, and Elizabeth reluctantly gathers the bowls and pitcher. Before she can leave, Luca takes Bree by the arm.

"We have come far, you and I," Luca says. "A great distance and many years from Rolanth. Back when you loved me. Whatever happens at the end of my life, I am glad that I will leave it with you loving me again."

Bree frowns. Her feelings for the High Priestess are not so simple as love and hate. But it is true that she has never really stopped caring for her.

"Did Mira love you again, at the end?"

"I think so," Luca replies. "But I did not deserve it."

"She wasn't right, was she, Bree?" Elizabeth asks as they return to the Volroy. "When she said she would die there or they would kill her? There has to be some way that Luca can survive."

"She usually manages to find one," Bree says. "But this time I am not so sure."

SUNPOOL

There is not enough room around the table in Jules's chamber for everyone to sit. Mathilde, Billy, and Gilbert Lermont stand in a semicircle starting behind Arsinoe's left shoulder, an imaginary extension of this "new council." For this is how it will be, if the rebellion succeeds and topples the crown. Jules and Emilia seated at the heads of the table with Caragh in between. Pietyr Renard somehow managing to sit across from them.

"Don't worry," Emilia says as they jostle. "The Black Council chamber will be much larger."

A few in the party chuckle. But not Arsinoe. "Aren't you getting ahead of yourselves?"

"Even we must have a council," says Mathilde.

"But will this be who sits upon it? What about someone from Rolanth? Or the temple? Maybe even Renata Hargrove, to unite the old with the new. Or do you intend to roll the army over the top of everyone in Indrid Down?"

The new council members glance amongst themselves.

"Maybe Queen Arsinoe is right," says Jules. "Maybe we'll even take the High Priestess if she survives. She's certainly earned it."

"Does anybody want to tell me what he's doing here?" Billy asks, and juts his chin toward Pietyr.

"Perhaps we should better ask why you are here," Emilia replies. "This is not your fight, mainlander."

"His father was killed by Rho Murtra," says Arsinoe. "And he was taken captive and tortured."

"He's been in this since the moment he jumped between Arsinoe and a bear," Jules agrees. "This has cost him as much as anyone."

Emilia sighs. "Pietyr Renard is here because he knows the capital and the ways of the Undead Queen better than any other."

"So you give him a seat at the table?" Billy asks. "Isn't he a prisoner? Couldn't he provide that information just as easily from the confines of a cell?"

"I was never in a cell," Pietyr says. "I was in a spacious, comfortable room at the Lermont house."

Billy clenches his jaw, and Arsinoe puts an arm out before he can launch himself across the table. "I don't trust him either, but he is the reason we know what Katharine is."

"That she's full of dead queens," Billy says. "That was the secret that Mirabella was after."

"She would never have discovered it. Katharine hides them well." Even after she nearly killed him, Pietyr's voice is full of pride. He is an Arron, after all, and they are a twisted, morbid lot. Arsinoe removes her arm from Billy's path. Let him launch across the table. Let him tackle Pietyr to the floor and wipe that Arron smirk off his face. Truthfully, she would not mind watching them roll around for a while.

"But what does that mean?" Gilbert Lermont leans forward, his long-fingered hands folded atop one another. "'She is full of dead queens.' What is it, really, that we face?"

"More than you think," Jules says darkly. "After what we saw in Bastian City."

"You said she sent the dead queens into you," Mathilde says to Pietyr. "Can she do that often? Is that all she can do?"

"I think she is constantly learning new ways to use them." His blue eyes drop to his lap. "Or that they can use her."

Jules pushes away from the table and gets up to pace.

"Jules," Emilia says. "Do not worry. We have numbers to match hers."

"Numbers to match. But that is not enough."

"Every war-gifted fighter is worth five regular soldiers. Strongly gifted ones, like you and I, are worth twenty."

"And what of the war-gifted who fought to defend Bastian? What of Margaret Beaulin? She was strongly gifted, too, and she was—" Jules stops. She and Emilia have not told many of the carnage they found in an effort not to frighten the soldiers. But even Emilia is afraid. Arsinoe saw it when Jules said Margaret's name.

"Whatever she sent," Jules says quietly, "no army could best it."

"Then what do we do?" Emilia whispers through her teeth, eyes shining. "Do we let her get away with it?"

"No, we don't let her get away with it," Arsinoe growls, and stands. The thought of Katharine continuing to rule, continuing to exist while Mirabella is ashes upon the sea makes Arsinoe's heart twist inward on itself. "The Undead Queen can't be allowed to remain. She has her dead queens—" Arsinoe clenches her fist. She feels every scab and every scar from the low magic stretch and sting. "And we'll have ours."

Billy's mouth falls open.

"What are you saying?"

"I'm saying we use Daphne. I know where to find her." Through the window, the peak of Mount Horn juts into the clouds. "And you could say that, after everything, she owes me a favor."

"Arsinoe, it's too dangerous."

"I'm not afraid."

"I didn't say you were." She expects him to tell her she is being reckless. Or to try and change her mind. Instead, he says no more.

"But even with a dead queen," Caragh says, "what difference does that make? If they are that much more powerful, like you say, then what is one against dozens?" She looks to Jules, who looks to Emilia and Mathilde. They look to Pietyr, but he has no more answers than they do.

"Daphne is stronger," Arsinoe says. "She's not like them."

"What do you mean?" Jules asks. "She was a queen like they were. She is dead like they are."

"Not like they were. She ruled. She wasn't killed. She didn't *lose*."

Her words ripple around the room. It is their best chance. Their only gambit. Arsinoe feels their eyes come to rest on her with cautious hope.

"If you think she'll fight with us," Jules says, "then go get her."

"When the army marches, I'll separate and head to the mountain. I can catch up with you afterward."

"Then let us march."

They quickly depart, talking in hushed tones, Emilia once again at the helm to mobilize the rebels. Before Billy leaves, Arsinoe takes him by the arm.

"I know you don't want me to do this. But I have to."

"I know. Just like you know that I have to fight." He touches her face. "Mirabella would be proud of you. I'm proud of you. And I hope you know what we're riding into."

When Pepper arrives, Arsinoe is alone in her room, watching rebels prepare in the city below. From her window, she has a clear view of the archery practice in the hills, where targets used by the war-gifted stand filled with arrows split by other arrows down the center. Others have arrows sunk into them from every possible angle, like pincushions, or shot into them to form elaborate patterns. She looks down to the square, where wagons are loaded with weapons and naturalist-ripened grain.

The entirety of the rebellion has redoubled its efforts in the wake of Mirabella's death. As if they knew she would be the reason, finally, for their marching.

The little bird flies onto her windowsill. She knows him immediately, even before he greets her with one bright chirp. For a moment, it feels as though he is Mirabella, come back to visit her, before Arsinoe remembers that Mirabella was no naturalist. Only a friend to one.

She holds her hand out, and the black-and-white tufted woodpecker hops into her palm. He is tired, and agitated, the poor little fellow. His wings hang loose and away from his body, and his small sharp beak parts in a pant.

Arsinoe is no naturalist either, but the moment his feet touch her skin, he settles down and fluffs his feathers. She carries him farther inside as his tiny, dark eyes drift shut, and sits down in her chair by the fire.

"No sleeping yet, friend," she whispers, and tickles his belly.

Irritated, Pepper cracks one eye open. Then he thrusts out his leg with the note tied to it, shaking it slightly as if to urge her to hurry so he can get some rest.

Arsinoe removes the note and unrolls it. Her breath catches when she recognizes Mirabella's writing. She sets it in her lap and strokes the bird a moment. She thought it would be from his naturalist, Elizabeth. Or perhaps from Bree Westwood. When had Mirabella written it? When had she sent it? She purses her lips and looks down at the woodpecker. He is asleep already.

She unrolls the parchment and reads.

Please come to the capital. Katharine is not what you have heard. Nor what you have seen. Something has taken hold of her that only you can remedy. We three queens have been steered here by the Goddess for a reason. Me to face down the mist. Katharine to be the vessel. And you to banish them with low magic. I am sorry I left, but please come. Your sisters have need of you. Both of your sisters. With love, M

Arsinoe sits quietly for a moment. Then she crumples the parchment and throws it into the fire.

The morning they are to depart—the rebel army to Indrid Down and Arsinoe to the mountain—Arsinoe and Billy accompany Luke to be fitted for his armor. It is merely a helmet and breastplate. The rebellion has not had time to outfit its fighters in more. But Luke is excited nonetheless. He stands with his arms out and turns back and forth for them as Hank the rooster pecks at the metal to test its toughness.

Luke should be behind the counter at the bookshop. He should be setting his table with biscuits and cakes or sewing handsome panels of embroidery into a gown. Luke is a creator of things, not a destroyer, and it is hard for Arsinoe to smile and nod as he shows her his crossbow and pike.

"It's a pity you can't bring Braddock along," Billy says, watching Hank kick his spurs into Luke's helmet. "What tales they would tell of the battle afterward, of Queen Arsinoe riding into war on her great brown bear. We could have had him some armor made."

"They'll tell those tales anyway," Arsinoe says. "Half of every legend is made-up nonsense. They'll talk about the two of you as well—running into the fray with a pair of armored chickens."

Luke's eyes widen. "Harriet would look beautiful in armor! But she's no familiar. Even Hank, who is as fierce as they come, must stay back from the fighting." He looks at the rooster, who cocks his head defiantly. "Only the dogs and the flying birds will be safe. The larger familiars. Like Camden."

"No one will be safe," Billy whispers, but Luke does not seem to hear.

"Speaking of familiars, or false familiars, I'd better go and find mine. I'm taking him to the mountain with me before depositing him back at the Black Cottage."

In the disarray of travel with an army, in the chaos of battle, she and Luke might never see each other again. Good Luke, who has always believed in her, and who cries at the drop of a hat. But this time it is her eyes that are misting over.

"I'll find you before we march," she promises, and he shakes her hand.

As she and Billy leave the city in search of her bear, the rebels have started to line up, and the square is packed tight with rows and rows of saddled horses. Every street that leads from it is packed as well, with fighters waiting for the order to go. They sit on barrels or on their own packs of supplies, each one at least as afraid as they are determined.

Arsinoe runs her fingers along Billy's wrist to see if he will wince. "How are your injuries? Do I need to change the bandages?"

"No. I don't know what you put in that ointment, but—"

"Magic," she teases. "A little of my blood."

"Arsinoe." He half smiles even as he makes a squeamish face.

"You shouldn't go," she says finally. "You're no fighter. You should stay behind the lines and direct the battle. Or find a ship and get out of here altogether."

"I've been training with the army. And I'm a fair shot with a bow, you know. Archery. My father insisted."

"Keep. To. The. Back."

"I'm a fast learner. I'm just as good now as half of these lads."

"But not near as good as these ladies," Arsinoe says, and swipes him on the back of the head. "Mainlander."

"Arsinoe!"

They turn at the sound of Jules's shout. She and Camden are coming up behind, the cougar's tail swinging lazily back and forth. Billy gives Arsinoe's hand a soft squeeze.

"Go with Jules," he says. "She'll be better at tracking down Braddock anyhow. Find me before we march."

"All right," she says, and he kisses her. Then he jogs back toward the city gate and tips an imaginary hat to Jules and Camden.

"Looking for a bear?" Jules asks. "I think I saw him earlier, searching the vines for early berries."

"Far too early for those."

"I might have ripened him some," Jules says. She points, and they walk along the wall toward the most tenacious of the berry vines. It does not take long to find Braddock; his broad, brown backside is difficult to miss.

"We just came from seeing Luke. He's being fitted for his armor," Arsinoe says. "He doesn't seem to know that it's real. Hank seemed more concerned than he did. I wanted to grab him by the neck and scream at him."

"Scream what?"

"That he doesn't belong in armor. That he doesn't belong in a fight."

"Neither do you," Jules says. "Of all the queens, you're the least likely to come out of this intact. Katharine has become a warrior, thanks to the borrowed gifts of the dead. And Mirabella was—"

"A thunderstorm. A wildfire."

"Yes. But you? Despite your affinity for shoving people, you're no fighter. You fight with your wits. With subterfuge. And magic."

"Like a poisoner," Arsinoe says. "I suppose I was always like one, deep down. We're such a terrible crop of queens, all of us. None of us is what we were supposed to be."

"No," says Jules. "We're all more. And don't call yourselves a 'crop.' You're not a vegetable."

Arsinoe chuckles softly. "Don't say 'crop'; don't say 'whelp. . . .' You have too many rules, Jules."

"I never said you couldn't say 'whelp.'"

Arsinoe's smile fades. "That's right. That was Mirabella."

They watch as Camden swats playfully at Braddock's behind. It is a wonder how well they play together. Camden gnaws on Braddock's leg, and he sends her rolling through the wet moss. She comes up shaking her head, her fur stained dark and sticking up in places, only to go right back to gnawing.

"She needed this," Jules says, her eyes on her cat. "It's lifted her spirits."

"And Braddock's, too." But not theirs. They linger in the comfort of each other's company, but it cannot last.

"Sometimes I just want to run to Grandma Cait and have her take me home."

"So do I," says Arsinoe. "And I'm surprised she sends Caragh to the war meetings. I kind of hoped she would advise us."

"She does advise me. Just not in front of a council."

"What does she say?"

"That we can't win. But that we have to try."

"She's not so great at raising spirits either, then," Arsinoe says, and Jules puts a hand on her shoulder.

"My spirit will rise when the battle is over. And I see you alive on the other side." She pulls Arsinoe into a hug. "Be alive on the other side."

INDRID DOWN

"The rebel army is marching."

Genevieve comes to stand behind Katharine's shoulder as she looks out the window, down at the city. For days, the citizens of Indrid Down have fortified their homes, boarding windows and bringing storage barrels inside.

"Queen Katharine. Did you hear me?"

"I heard you," Katharine says. She and Genevieve watch as an old horse that is more bones than meat is led quickly down the street, perhaps for safekeeping at some farm in the countryside.

"Should we have the outlying farms searched? Conscript more supplies for the siege before the rebels arrive?"

"It will not be a siege. It will be a battle. And a final one."

"Should we relocate those we can who are not fighting?"

Katharine nods to the boarded-up windows.

"They know what is coming. They choose to remain. Half

of them will probably take up arms against me."

Genevieve steps up beside her, hands white and trembling on the stone of the window ledge. She is afraid. They are all afraid. For all of the arrogance and strength on the Black Council, none of them has seen a war.

"Kat, do not give up!" She fixes Katharine with her lilac eyes. "My sister did not raise you to stand aside!"

"Your sister raised me to do what I am told. She raised me to serve. To please." Katharine flexes her hand and feels the dead queens there, just below the surface, taking up more and more space as the days go by. She has certainly served them well. "I loved Natalia. And she loved me, in her way. But she never believed. And now you do not believe either. You think that Arsinoe and Jules Milone march to us with an army of elementals and naturalists and warriors, with oracles to show them our traps and the giftless to rush our cavalry. You think they will overcome us with a flurry of diving hawks and lightning strikes. You have no idea what my army can do."

"Then you are not afraid?" Genevieve asks. "You do not fear we will lose?"

Katharine lowers her eyes sadly.

"No. We will not lose."

MOUNT HORN

The afternoon sun is warm on her back when Arsinoe climbs the trail up the slope of Mount Horn with her bear. Though most of the snow has melted in the lowland meadows, the trail itself is still coated in white.

Behind her in Sunpool, the rebel army leaks from the city gate in a steady stream. She will catch up when she is finished. They will have not gotten far, an army that size and unused to marching. The first night that they make camp, Emilia will scream herself hoarse getting them organized. But Arsinoe must admit, it is impressive how quickly they moved once Jules gave the order.

Arsinoe keeps her pace steady and leans into her bear. She squints her eyes and tries to see Jules riding her black gelding at the head or Emilia on her bright red charger but does not find them. Billy is there, too, somewhere, on a borrowed horse. Carrying borrowed weapons. To fight in a borrowed war.

Before she left for the mountain, Billy asked if he could accompany her.

"It's queens' business," she had said.

"Like you have with Katharine."

"Yes. Like I have with Katharine."

He had not argued, as if even asking had been only an act, a line he was supposed to say. At night, he still held her like he would never let her go. But something had changed. Since his time as Katharine's prisoner, Billy has not been the same.

"There is no future for queens," she murmurs, and Braddock nudges her gently with his head.

When they step inside the cave, the air smells of the stone of the mountain and the thawing earth. She reaches into her pack for wood, to start a fire to warm her chilled hands, and for a piece of dried fish to thank the bear for his company. It takes some time to get the wood lit; her fingers fumble with the matches and she has never been as good at assembling the wood as Jules. But soon enough, the cave is lit by orange light, and she sits down beside Braddock, her eyes on the shadows in the rear, where the cave plummets to the center of the mountain.

She is not afraid, this time. Not wary or even apprehensive. This time, she knows why she has come.

"Don't be shy, Daphne," Arsinoe whispers. "You owe me."

She stares into the blackness at the shape of the stones. Finally, she gets up and stalks into the dark.

"I didn't come all this way to speak to a hole in the ground."

She waits. Any moment, Daphne will appear: a dripping shape, fingers tipped in sharp points and legs that stretch too long and bend in unnatural directions.

Except that she does not. Arsinoe leans over the side of the stones, suspending herself above the abyss. Once, in her dreams, she had thought of Daphne as a friend. Perhaps she had even thought of her as a part of herself. She does not anymore.

"Come out of there!" she shouts, and listens to her voice ring off the depths. "Mirabella is dead! And the mist remains! Did you ever really think it could be quieted? Or did you only want to see another dead elemental queen?" The questions hang in the air and echo back to her unanswered. She sees no movement in the shadows, no drifting bits of smoke. Nor does she sense her hidden behind the stones.

Arsinoe reaches for her small sharp knife. She makes a shallow cut on the side of her hand and smears it against the cave wall. She squeezes her fist and lets her queensblood drip down, down, down to the heart of the island. But the mountain is empty. Daphne is gone and whatever force raised her is once again silent. She will be of no help to them.

They are on their own.

THE REBEL CAMP

"It wasn't easy," Jules says as she and Caragh look down upon the army from Jules's campsite on the knoll. "But we did it." They moved an entire fighting force through the mountains. Below, rebels set up tents and construct temporary paddocks for the horses. Thanks to the naturalists, almost none were lost to lameness despite the uncertain and rocky terrain.

"The rebels are rebels no more," says Caragh. "They're soldiers." She inclines her head toward Jules. "Arsinoe should have caught up with us by now. Maybe she's just lingering with Braddock."

"Maybe you should go back and see." Jules looks at her aunt from the corner of her eye.

"What do you mean?"

"I mean I want you to go back."

"Absolutely not." Caragh shakes her head. "Your mother is

gone. I'm no warrior, but I won't let you go alone."

"I'm not alone."

"But I'm all that—" Caragh stops.

Jules looks at her. Caragh raised her, when Madrigal left. She taught her how to use her gift. And those years she spent away at the Black Cottage were all for her. For Jules. No one makes Jules feel safe like Caragh does. Even now, when she would ask for no more, all Jules wants is for Caragh to stay.

"I need you to go back. For Fenn."

"Fenn has Matthew," Caragh says, but her face falls.

"I need you to go back for the others, to get them to safety if we fail. Every Milone's life will be forfeit if we lose, and I can't let that happen to Grandma Cait and Ellis. I need you in Sunpool to help the others fall back to Wolf Spring. And from there to disappear. Take my little brother. Take Matthew. And don't let Katharine find you."

"Jules," Caragh says. She reaches out and hugs her tightly, like she has not done since Jules was a little girl. Too soon, she turns and walks away. "I'll go," she says over her shoulder. "And if I see Arsinoe, I'll send her in the right direction."

Caragh heads quickly down the hill, and passes Emilia on her way up.

"Caragh?" Emilia calls. "Caragh, where are you going?" She joins Jules at her campsite. "Where is Caragh going?"

"I sent her back."

Emilia stares after her, as if considering the loss of another fighter. But then she nods.

"Good. I'm glad."

"Arsinoe should have caught up with us by now."

"She'll be here," Emilia says, unconcerned.

"We should send a scout back to look for her."

"Mmph," Emilia grunts.

"Is that a yes? I haven't figured out how to interpret all of your noises yet." She nudges the warrior in the shoulder. Emilia swats her away.

"Do not try to disarm me." She glances at Jules, annoyed. "And it was a no. We will not waste scouts. The battle is ahead, not behind."

"You know we need her and Daphne to stand against Katharine and whatever Katharine controls. What she did in Bastian—"

"We only need you," Emilia snaps. "Our Legion Queen. I hope that Arsinoe falls down that hole inside the cave. I hope she and her dead queen leave us in peace."

"You don't mean that, and you don't believe it. You're brave, but you're not stupid." Jules looks down at the army, and stiffens. She cannot forget the things she saw in the warriors' city. The brutality of it. And the utter one-sidedness.

"Are you afraid?" Emilia asks.

"Of course I am. Aren't you?"

"Yes." She grins. "But the war gift . . . I enjoy the fear. I drink it like ale. Do you not feel that?" She turns to Jules and runs a finger along her chin. The touch and the look set off something deep in the pit of Jules's stomach. Something that feels both familiar and completely new. "Do you not like it, even a little bit?" Jules takes a shaky breath, and Emilia steps closer to take her face in her hands.

"It is not long before we fight. Not long before this is settled, one way or another. The fighting will be . . . chaotic. Full of blood and chance. We will lose friends."

She is so close. Her dark eyes glittering.

Jules chuckles awkwardly.

"Is this what passes for war-gifted flirting?" Emilia laughs, and Jules takes her hand. "All this talk of losing each other . . ."

"I will not lose you," Emilia says.

"You don't know that. Unless—" Jules steps back. "Do you mean to keep me out of the fighting? So surrounded by soldiers that I'm completely out of danger? I didn't come this far to do that, Emilia. That's not the kind of warrior queen you made."

"And it is not the kind of queen I want," Emilia says. She pulls Jules close. Just as their lips touch, Jules shakes her head, and Emilia withdraws.

"I'm sorry," Jules says.

"Are you afraid?"

"No."

"Do you not feel it, then?"

"No, I—I don't know. And I know this sounds stupid. I know that Joseph is dead. I know he's not coming back, and he wouldn't mind. I know that we're fighting soon, and we might not have much time. But I—I just don't know."

Emilia drops her eyes, clearly disappointed.

"Are you angry with me?"

"For your loyal heart?" Emilia reaches out and tucks Jules's hair behind her ear. "I would never be angry about that."

Arsinoe creeps into the camp in the middle of the night. The fires are low, but it is still impossible to miss. Even traveling in the dark, she could feel the tracks of the horses and wagons through the soles of her boots. The Legion Queen makes no secret of her intentions. Anyone following the progression of the camp smoke will know that the rebellion is marching on Indrid Down.

"Queen Arsinoe." One of the scouts bows when she sees her.

"Bowing again, are we?" Arsinoe says. This near the battle, everyone has become superstitious. They search for blessings and bargain with their consciences. They beg the oracles for signs that they will survive, and that they fight for the right side. "Never mind. I didn't mean to bark at you. Do you know where to find Billy Chatworth?"

"Camped on the northern ridge." She points. The camp is so large that she has to stop twice more and ask for further directions, but she finally finds him standing outside his tent beside a small cookfire.

"Arsinoe." He reaches her in three strides and takes her in his arms. "You took so long; I was worried."

"I'm sorry. It took longer than I thought to leave Braddock with Willa at the Black Cottage."

"He didn't want to be left?"

"She didn't want to take him on."

"She's not a naturalist," Billy says, "so I guess I can't blame her."

"Aye, she's not. But she knows him. I left her with a sackful of smoked fish to keep him in line. He'll likely wander off into the woods anyway when he sees that Caragh isn't there."

Billy nods. He does not look the same without his smile and without the mainland sparkle in his eyes.

"You've changed so much," she says softly. "Since turning up on this island and telling Jules you had a deaf cat with two-colored eyes like hers."

He laughs. "My god. Did I really say that? How did you put up with me?"

"With the patience of a queen," she says, and they chuckle until something inside Billy's tent shifts and starts to grumble.

"Keep it down out there, will you! Some of us are trying to get some sleep before we commit outright treason."

Arsinoe blinks. "Who's in your tent?"

"Pietyr Renard." Billy frowns. "I drew the short straw."

Arsinoe peers in through the slit in the tent flap and sees a sliver of him on his side, his arms crossed tensely over his chest.

"I'm surprised they brought him at all," Billy says. "He can't be trusted."

"Trusted, no. But Katharine did try to kill him. She left him unconscious for months. I believe he's afraid of her if I don't believe anything else."

"Hmpf. He may be a poisoner, but his real power is in

persuasion. Oh!" Billy raises his eyebrows. "I saved some food for you." He wraps the handle of a pot in a cloth and turns the contents out onto a plate. She smells carrot and onion and meaty gravy.

Of course he would know to keep a pot full of food for her. He knows her so well. But when she takes the plate, she finds that she is not hungry. Or at least not for food.

"Are you saying we have to share a tent with an Arron all night long?" She takes his hand and rubs her thumb along the inside of his palm.

"Would be rude to turn him out." He pulls her close. "But I'm sure we can find some cozy place."

Neither needs convincing. They hurry away from the camp, huddled close together.

"It's so blasted dark," he says. "Be careful. I think we passed a small lean-to not far back. Looked deserted, except for a few goats."

"A lean-to, a barn, a sturdy tree, for all I care," she says, and Billy laughs.

Somehow, they find their way to it and climb through the fence. They lay down a layer of fresh straw and a blanket, and Billy nudges away a few curious goats.

"A shame that lean-tos don't have doors," he says, and she pulls him to her.

"Come here and be quiet."

"Quiet?"

"At least try not to startle the goats."

She hears him laugh. They cannot see each other in the dark, but their hands have had plenty of practice. It is not long before they both forget the goats and the chill in the night air and think of nothing but each other.

Afterward, they lie together quietly.

"I don't want to go back," she whispers.

"Maybe we can keep the sun from rising for a day or two . . ."

"Why not a month."

"A month of sleeping on the cold, hard ground. You really were raised by naturalists." Billy wraps her tighter in his arms and nestles down into the blanket. "I'm glad that Renard had the use of the tent. I like being out here with you, away from everything."

"So do I." She rests her head against his chest. "But poor Pietyr Renard. Knowing Emilia, she's sure to have a use for him."

"I think she only wants him seen. To rattle Katharine and goad her into something foolish."

"It won't work. Katharine may be many things, but foolish isn't one of them."

Billy sighs. "I suppose I don't envy Renard. Standing on opposite sides of a battlefield. I can't imagine what it would be like if it were you. But then, it would never be you."

"It shouldn't be any of us. This isn't how it's supposed to be. All the people who are going to die, none of them would if their queens had done what we were meant to."

"You can't think like that. It *does* have to be. Fennbirn is finished with the old way. Emilia might come off like a swindler, but she's right. Every person we've passed on the march. Every soldier in the rebellion. They're ready for something to change."

"I hope they mean it," Arsinoe says. "Because after this, everything will."

His hand goes still on her skin. Their time is almost over.

"During the battle, we won't be together," he says. "Jules will draw the queensguard attack—"

"And I will go after Katharine."

"What are you going to do?" he asks. "Are you really going to kill her?"

"I'm going to do what Mira asked me to," Arsinoe replies, rubbing the scars in her palm. "I'm going to banish the dead queens. And then yes. I'm going to kill her."

She waits. She cannot see his expression in the dark.

"After the battle is over, I'm not going to stay on Fennbirn," Billy says.

"Because of that?" She sits up.

"No. It's a war, Arsinoe. After it's over, none of our hands will be clean. But . . . I have to go home. I have to take care of things there."

"Then I'll go with you."

"You don't belong there. They need you here. I just wish I belonged here, too."

"You do," she says weakly. But she does not fight too hard. He is right, and she cannot shake the feeling that after the battle is over, none of the queens will remain, living or dead. "You know I tried really hard to not be what I am."

He pushes up on his elbow, and now she is glad he cannot see her face.

"And you know that I loved you, don't you, Junior? You know that I always will."

INDRID DOWN

"The rebels are here."

Katharine turns. The message that Rho delivers is not unexpected.

"What are the numbers?" Katharine asks, without much interest.

"High," Rho replies. "The initial estimates given by your spies were treasonously low."

"What is that supposed to mean?" asks Genevieve. Only she, Rho, and Renata Hargrove have come to her rooms. The rest of the Black Council hides from Katharine's summons. She is not surprised. They are cowards. And besides, she does not need them.

For the last two days, Katharine has felt the Legion Queen approaching. She has felt it in the excited chatter of the dead queens in her blood, tasted it in their craving for her flesh between their teeth. Those twisted and corrupted dead queens, whose names have been forgotten.

"We have more horses," Renata says. "Trained soldiers with full armor and weapons made of steel instead of wood."

Rho opens her mouth to argue, but Katharine quiets her with a look. She knows full well that a disadvantage of numbers will not matter.

"What of the people? Have many fled?"

"Those who could afford it have fled inland—sought refuge in the west at Highgate."

Katharine nods. Those who could not remained and cowered, caught between the battle and the mist.

"We have the provisions," Genevieve says. "They will be safe as long as we can hold the city."

Katharine glares down at the sprawling rooftops. What did the people have to fear? The Legion Queen arrived to liberate them, or so she said. But Katharine will protect them anyway. She will protect them, these people who remain, even if they hold no faith with her. Even if they have turned away from their crown as if it were nothing, rather than the island's entire history. Hundreds of battles fought and won. Illustrious queens of strength and honor, whose gifts turned the island into legend.

"Queen Katharine," Renata asks. "What should we do?"

Katharine steps away from the window and sighs, hands folded over her skirt. "Do we intend for the Legion Queen to simply march through our streets? Muster the queensguard. Set barricades before the main thoroughfares and at the markets.

Fortify the Volroy and arm the gatehouses. And as for me, I will meet them on the battlefield."

Renata and Genevieve wait, looking to Rho.

"I would have a word with my commander. You two will see to this. And pass the message along to the rest of the council who could not be bothered to attend."

They leave quickly, and Rho closes the door.

"They want to flee," Rho says. "And Bree Westwood is nothing but furtive glances of late. She should be watched."

"Let her go. Let them all. If the rebellion breaches the walls of the Volroy, they will receive little mercy in the fever of conquest. They fear the mob of soldiers. They fear being torn to pieces. And they are right to." Katharine looks to the west toward Greavesdrake, though she cannot see it through the walls, settled so proud and alone in the hills. For once, she is glad that Natalia is gone, so she does not have to imagine her there as the rebels come for the manor house with swords and torches.

Rho goes to the table and pours herself a cup of wine. How odd it is, to have found such an ally in her. Katharine used to hate the very sight of Rho, her tight red braid, her jaw always set like it is carved from granite. But that hate was not truly hate. It was resentment, that such a woman stood against her rather than at her side. And now—now when she looks at Rho, all she feels is regret for what she must do.

Rho goes to the window, to look down upon the inner ward as the queensguard begins to assemble.

"It is hard to look into their eyes," Katharine says. "Knowing that I must order them into battle to die. Is it me, after all, that they are fighting for? Do they believe, or do they simply have no choice?"

"You will never know," Rho replies. "That is what it is to be a commander. But you must look them in the eyes anyway."

Katharine steps up beside Rho. The priestess is so much taller than she is, so broad shouldered. She is the embodiment of the war gift.

"What does it feel like," Katharine asks, "when I give the dead queens to you?"

Rho inhales.

"It feels sacred. And it is an honor to fight against the Legion Queen. These rebels hide behind the support of Arsinoe, but they do not love the island or the Goddess. Not like we do. I am grateful for the allegiance of the dead queens. It is as if the Goddess has sent them to us as aid."

Katharine clenches her teeth. Not even Rho, one of the Goddess's finest servants, understands her will. Not like her daughters do.

"Then come closer, Rho."

The dead sisters slither through Katharine's veins. They bolt for the surface so hard that it makes her grimace with the searing, stretching sensation of it. Katharine's hand slips behind the back of the priestess's head. She seals her lips over Rho's mouth. Afterward, Rho kneels, gasping on the rug.

Katharine watches as her veins darken. The dead queens she

sent into Rho were more than ever before. They swell beneath her skin. They turn her eyes to black.

"Ride out," she says, and Rho gets to her feet. "Ride out for the Legion Queen. There is no better death. No larger battle than this one."

THE REBEL CAMP

The call that the Queen Crowned's army has begun to march ripples through the camp like a shudder. It does not matter that the rebels knew it was coming and that the soldiers have been standing ready since daybreak. It does not matter that they were the ones who marched across the entire island to pick this fight. Now it is real, and every woman and every man is afraid.

Billy and Pietyr arm themselves together in the tense quiet of their tent. Arsinoe crept off to Jules just before dawn. Though she ate what was left of their dinner first, and Billy takes that as a good sign.

"Something to eat before we go?" he asks, watching Pietyr struggle with his ill-fitting armor. They have not given him much: a set of leather greaves and shoulder armor, along with a sword and shield. "Though Arsinoe didn't leave a lot."

Pietyr turns his nose up. "How can she swallow that

untainted food? Just the scent of such blandness turns my stomach. She is no poisoner." He fumbles with the straps and curses. "This armor is not worth the beast killed to make it!"

Billy sighs and sets down the spoon of oatmeal and bit of cheese. He wants to point out that his armor is no better but glances at Pietyr's shaking hands and goes to help him instead.

"If I were fighting beside my Katharine, I would be in queensguard armor. Shining silver from helm to heel."

"Would you rather be there, then? Fighting with your Katharine?"

Pietyr frowns as Billy tightens a buckle. "Of course I would. I would be by her side to the end, no matter the odds. But my Katharine no longer exists."

"But she does, doesn't she? Or at least her body. Her face. Maybe you'll change your mind when you see her and try to change sides."

"What is your point?" Pietyr asks, eyes narrowed.

"Only that I'll put a knife in you if you try." He finishes with the shoulder guards and steps back. Then he slaps the front of Pietyr's chest. "Or maybe I'm saying that you're a brave man for fighting in spite of it."

Pietyr tugs on the armor, testing the fit. "You seem to be prattling on this morning. More so than usual. Are you afraid?"

Billy shrugs. He can feel every drop of blood racing inside his skin and every heartbeat that tries to keep up with it. He is afraid. And he knows that Pietyr is as well, no matter how he tries to mask it with disdain.

"I suppose I am," he says, and feels some of that fear drain away with the admission. "But not so much as I'm angry. Today I avenge my father's murder and the murder of my friends. Today my strange time on Fennbirn comes to an end."

"You mean to go up against Rho Murtra," says Pietyr. "You are a fool."

"Maybe. Or maybe she'll be weighed down by all that fancy queensguard armor and I'll land a lucky strike."

Pietyr says nothing. He shakes his head and picks up his sword, and Billy follows him out to the horses.

When Arsinoe gets to Jules's tent, she makes sure to loudly clear her throat and allow plenty of time before entering, in case she is walking into something private. But inside, Jules and Emilia are already awake, seated on the ground with Camden lying in between them. Across the camp, the morning has started to turn blue, showing the capital city to the south and the towers of the Volroy, which Arsinoe could feel staring down at her even through the blackness.

"Thank the Goddess," says Jules, and smiles. "I thought you weren't going to make it."

"You know me." Arsinoe ducks inside. "Always cut it close. Always make an entrance."

"So you've done it," Emilia says. "You have her?" She peers around Arsinoe in the dim.

"Even if I did, she wouldn't be *with* me. Why does everyone always think I have everything in my pocket?" She frowns.

"But I don't. She wasn't there. The cave was empty."

"But that was our best hope," says Jules.

"No it wasn't." Emilia gets to her feet. "It was desperation. A move made out of fear. But we never needed the help of a dead queen. We are not like Katharine."

She sounds certain. She sounds like a leader. Not for the first time, Arsinoe wonders how it is that they have gotten here, laying siege to Indrid Down. It was not so long ago that she and Mirabella were at Billy's brick row house on the mainland or that she was in Wolf Spring, drinking ale at the Lion's Head.

The tent flap opens again; it is Mathilde, come to rouse them.

"Katharine's army is moving."

"Did you see it in a vision?" asks Jules.

"I saw it with my eyes," Mathilde replies.

"Raise the call," Emilia orders. "Form the lines. We will join you at the front."

Mathilde disappears behind the falling tent flap. The sound of the low horns and the responding rush of movement send a chill down Arsinoe's back.

Jules stands and stretches alongside her cougar as Emilia gathers their weapons. Both are already in their armor. Camden will wear armor, too, specially crafted to fit her. Arsinoe wants to throw herself across the cat's lean, furry body at the thought of the arrows and wielded blades.

"Do you think I should have brought Braddock?"

"I think a great brown bear is worth a regiment of cavalry,"

Emilia says. "He would have taken down dozens of queensguard, and drawn their fire. And I think he is your pet, and your friend. And you did the right thing by leaving him."

Arsinoe blinks at her in surprise.

"Focus." She slaps Arsinoe's shoulder as she helps her into light silver armor. "Your whole mind must be in the fight if you are to survive it."

"My whole mind is on Katharine," says Arsinoe. "On where she is and where I'll be."

"She may start the battle at the head. But do not be surprised if they keep her to the back. It may be difficult to reach her."

"I don't care." She feels the armor tightening, the buckles secured. Part of her wants to shrug it off. It will only slow her down.

Jules slips knives into her boots and belt. She straps a sword across her chest. Watching her, Arsinoe cannot help thinking how she and Katharine are both so small, yet both so fearsome. When she faces Arsinoe, Jules's blue and green eyes blaze.

Emilia checks a blade and sheaths it hard. "I have to see to the soldiers. I will find you at the horses."

After she goes, Jules takes up Camden's armor.

"How in the world am I supposed to get her into this?" she asks, and Camden whaps her tail against the ground. "Arsinoe, will you hold her?"

"Oh no." Arsinoe steps back. "She's your familiar; you armor her."

Jules chuckles. "I helped you with your bear."

"That was forever ago. My bear's not here now. And besides, I actually need to go after Emilia. I need to talk to her about something."

"Emilia? What could you and she have to talk about?"

Arsinoe shrugs and steps through the tent flap. "Something. Just something."

Outside, the camp has come alive, everyone moving and in a hurry. From the high ground of Jules's tent, everything is visible, and the rebels appear as a multicolored swarm, disorganized, arguing amongst themselves, but generally moving in the direction of the capital. By contrast, what little bit of Katharine's army is within view is all uniform black and silver, even most of the horses. And they move together like a school of fish.

For a few moments, Arsinoe wanders, unsure which way Emilia went. But then she hears a familiar shout. Emilia is just down the ridge, scolding a group of soldiers around a burned-down cookfire.

When Arsinoe reaches them, the soldiers scatter, seemingly more eager to face the entire queensguard than to stay and face Emilia.

"Is that wise?" Arsinoe asks. "Yelling at them like that so close to a fight?"

"The coming battle is the only reason I did not have them whipped." Emilia holds up a spit bearing what appears to be the well-eaten remains of a roasted lamb. "They stole it from a farm we passed. When I warned all to be sure to pay for anything we took. We march as liberators, not thieves!" She tosses the spit into the ash. "They will make enemies for the new crown before it is even on Jules's forehead."

"Jules's forehead? So you mean to put it on her in ink, like Katharine's?"

Emilia cocks her head. "I don't often agree with a poisoner, but I do like that. A crown etched in blood. A permanent mark. And less clunky than a circlet or some jewel-encrusted hat. What are you doing here? Why aren't you with Jules?"

"I needed to ask you something. I need to ask you to do something."

"What?"

"Do you remember how you said you didn't think Billy should fight?"

Emilia looks away. "I should not have said that. And I did not mean it the way you took it. It is not that I do not think him justified in fighting. But I have seen what the poisoners did to him. I have watched him as he trains and see how his right arm cannot quite stop trembling. Do you want me to hold him back? You should have asked sooner. Now we are preparing to march, and it will not be easy—"

"I don't want you to keep him back." Arsinoe bites her lip. "I want you to look after him."

Emilia blinks like she has misheard.

"Please, Emilia. I'm asking you."

"I cannot. I will be beside my queen."

"Jules doesn't need you. You wanted her to be a warrior . . .

and now she is one. But Billy isn't. And if he faces Rho alone, he's going to get himself killed."

Emilia sighs.

"You know we are all likely to die. Yet you want me to worry about one pitiful mainlander."

"That's exactly what I want. Please."

"All right!" Emilia throws up her hands. "I will try. But there are never any guarantees in battle."

"Thank you." To both of their surprises, Arsinoe leaps forward and hugs her. Briefly.

"Ah well," says Emilia. "It is to be expected, I suppose. Always like a boy, to be in need of protection."

THE BATTLEFIELD

Katharine sits astride her stallion when Genevieve rides up on her black gelding, both Genevieve and the horse outfitted in poisoner purple and skulls over silver armor.

"We have managed to draw the rebels down and to the west," Genevieve says. "They have given up the good ground to the north."

"It wasn't difficult," Paola Vend says as her mount trots up beside her. "They are untrained. Made up of farmers and laborers. Innkeepers. Their numbers are large, but they will prove to be of no use with no one capable of leading them."

Katharine looks out upon her army. They hold formation and perfect position. Across the battlefield, the force they face is nowhere near as polished. Their armor is motley and lacking. Some have only a breastplate and no arm guards. Many have no helmets. The tips of their spears waver in the air instead of holding high and upright. But within that army are naturalists and elementals, oracles and warriors. Over their heads, hawks and crows circle and cry. Dogs growl at their sides, and their horses stamp angrily with no need to be urged forward. Fire flickers across knuckles, and clouds gather above. The warriors' arrows will never miss, and the oracles will know the moves of their opponents before they themselves do.

"They are soldiers of every gift," Katharine says.

"A legion-cursed army for a legion-cursed queen," says Genevieve.

Katharine swallows. Somewhere out there is Juillenne Milone, the Legion Queen returned, sent by the Goddess to exact her vengeance, and who Mirabella would have fought beside. But Mirabella is dead. If she were not, it could all have been different.

Inside Katharine, the only thing that races is her pulse. She sent so many of the dead queens into Rho that she is nearly empty, so she knows that the cowardly sweat that breaks onto her forehead is hers and hers alone. She squeezes the reins hard in her hands.

"Your sister Arsinoe will be out there, somewhere," Paola says. "She turned away from the crown during the Ascension, when she had a right to it. Only to ride on the side of a rebellion and try to steal it from your head."

"If she can take it, she can have it," Katharine says, and Genevieve and Paola look at her in surprise.

In the distance to the right, the queensguard parts before a figure on a hulking black horse. From where they stand, Rho's face is not visible, nor her black eyes or the black veins stretched across her like spiderwebs. Only her red braid and the waves of something dark that emanate from her form almost like mist.

"What is that?" Genevieve asks.

Katharine presses her lips together grimly.

"That is Rho."

Arsinoe reaches down and strokes the neck of her horse with a shaking hand. "Are you a good horse?" she asks. He seems a good one, tall and long-legged, with bright eyes and a smart face. His coat is a deep brown from head to tail, except for two white socks on his forelegs. That was why she chose him. The socks reminded her of Billy and his many, many pairs back on the mainland.

She runs her hand down his withers and traces the lines of his armor. It seems there is too much vulnerable flesh exposed. Too much exposed on all of them. She looks to her left, across the hills to where Jules and Emilia wait for the charge. She wishes she were there. But she has one task and one task only and that is to reach Katharine.

Still, she is not alone. Mathilde is with her and Gilbert Lermont, and the troops behind them are vast. Hopefully vast enough to batter a hole right through the opposing queensguard when they charge. Arsinoe will hold back to see where Katharine goes.

"We'll have to be fast," Arsinoe whispers to the horse. "And

I'll try my best not to get you killed if you will do the same. You probably have no idea what I'm saying. But all those years of naturalist training have to amount to something."

There is a jostling in the soldiers near her, and Billy appears, riding through with none other than Pietyr Renard on the back of his saddle. The sight is enough to make her laugh, even now.

"Shouldn't you be on the far-left flank?" Arsinoe asks.

"We're on our way there. I just . . ." He smiles a little, and her chest tightens. It is surreal seeing him in armor with a sword and crossbow. "Well, Renard wanted one last chance to appeal to leadership."

"I should have a horse at least," Pietyr grumbles. "And a helmet."

"A horse so you can run to the enemy?" Mathilde asks. "And there will be no helmet either. For you are no good to us if Katharine cannot see your pale hair. Every soldier in the queensguard must know you for an Arron. They must see you in the colors of the Legion Queen."

"We will see." Pietyr prods Billy in the shoulder. "Take me to the commander."

Billy looks at Arsinoe regretfully. "My last day on Fennbirn and I spend it in service to this git."

She smiles. She wants to reach for him. To hold him right there so they will be at each other's sides.

"I'll see you after."

"Are you all right?" Mathilde asks after Billy and Pietyr have ridden away.

Arsinoe nods. The oracle does not seem frightened or even nervous. Her bright streak of white hair is braided and wrapped around the golden bun on the back of her head, and she wears a clean yellow cape around her shoulders. Between that and her shining white mare, it is almost like she is trying to make herself a target.

"What have you seen?" Arsinoe asks, and looks beyond her to Gilbert Lermont, in a yellow cape of his own. "Gilbert? What have you been able to scry?"

"When I scry, the wine blooms cloudy," Gilbert replies.

"It is the same with me," says Mathilde. "The smoke is just smoke."

When Arsinoe closes her eyes in frustration, Gilbert frowns. "You have let the sight gift languish for hundreds of years, and when you decide you have need of it, you expect it to return at a snap of your fingers."

"I'm sorry," Arsinoe says. "That's not what I meant. It just seems like all of the gifts have strengthened around this generation of queens. Not only the gift of the dominant sister or the victor. Do you think that's an omen? A sign for the Legion Queen? Or for Katharine, and her many gifts from the dead?"

"That is the problem with omens," says Gilbert. "They can often be taken for both sides."

Arsinoe clenches her jaw. She can feel Mirabella there so strongly she would not be surprised to turn her head and find her seated behind her on the saddle. Mirabella, their great protector. She had tried to avoid this to the last. Her final words to

Arsinoe, written on that parchment, were words of peace. And she had died for it.

"Are you truly ready?" Mathilde asks.

"I am."

"One more time in the old ways, then. One *last* time of queens killing queens." She looks across the battlefield, and her expression of serene calm fades. "What is that?"

Arsinoe turns in the saddle just as the enormous rider emerges from the ranks of the queensguard. Waves of blackness radiate from their armor as if it is very, very cold. Waves of blackness like floating ink.

"Oh, Goddess," she whispers, realizing who it is and what has been done to her. Billy cannot face Rho Murtra. Not like that. Perhaps no one can.

She wants to warn him, but there is no time. The moment the rider reaches the front lines, she roars and sounds the charge. Every horse and rebel soldier around Arsinoe and Mathilde flinch as the queensguard cascades toward them.

"The rider!" Mathilde shouts over the sudden noise. "Who is it?"

"It's Rho Murtra!" Arsinoe shouts back. "Or at least it used to be."

On the battlefield, Rho leaves a trail of writhing rebels behind her like a spreading carpet. The length of her sword cuts through them so easily, it is hard to believe they have any bones inside their flesh. Darkness erupts from her mouth and eyes to dive down rebel throats. Not even Katharine wants to think about what is happening before it bursts back out and the soldiers fall.

"What happened to her?" Genevieve whispers. "What did you do to her?"

"Nearly the same thing that was done to me," Katharine says, and Genevieve shrinks back. "The dead queens. They have been with me since the night of the Quickening when I fell down the Breccia Domain." Or rather, when she was pushed. But even that no longer seems to matter. Out on the field, the queensguard soldiers follow Rho. They follow her because she will be victorious. Because she will keep them alive.

"The king-consort," Genevieve says, her eyes searching Katharine's skin for any sign, any glimmers of gray and rot. "And Pietyr. Did Natalia know?"

"That I was truly Katharine the Undead?" She shakes her head. Though she does wonder if Natalia had suspected. She must have sensed that something was wrong. That she was not the same girl for whom she had needed to fake an entire poisoned feast.

Katharine looks again to the fighting, where the cobbled-together rebels are no match against the accurate arrows of the queensguard, their formations of spears. Her soldiers stop haphazard attacks of elemental fire by putting crossbow bolts into elemental chests. They break the ranks of naturalists by cutting their birds down out of the sky. Already her army has bowed the rebel lines. And Rho has sighted Jules Milone and will be upon her within minutes.

"What kind of ruin am I watching?" Katharine murmurs gravely.

"We must raise the order for reinforcements to the flank," says Paola Vend.

"No." Katharine unsheathes her sword. "Hold the rest in reserve. I will go out myself."

"Katharine," says Genevieve. "You should not."

"If I do not, then how will my sister find me?" She looks Genevieve in the eyes and puts heels to her stallion, knowing that neither Genevieve nor Paola will ride alongside. When she next looks back, they will be gone, retreated into the fortress of the Volroy. It is the last place they should go. For that is where she intends to lead Arsinoe.

Her stallion gamely rushes down the hill, a proper warhorse keen to the sounds of screams and clashing steel. But Katharine's heart pounds. The battle is vast. She hardly knows where to begin. And then she sees him across the field to the north. Pietyr, upright and breathing. Conscious.

Pietyr's sword and shield are streaked with red. Even his pale hair is sheeted pink and dripping down the side of his face. He is not a great warrior like her king-consort Nicolas was. But he is doing his best.

"Pietyr!" she shouts, and somehow he hears her. He turns, and for a moment, his eyes alight and they are the only two people on the island. But then his expression turns dark and hard. He raises his sword and goes back to fighting.

* * *

"Raise the signal for the eastern flank!"

Horses and soldiers fly past as Emilia barks orders, and Jules's horse spins a hole into the mud and young grass. She feels every battle cry and every strike of every hoof against the newly thawed ground. Emilia has not stopped shouting since the queen's army charged behind the black mist-shrouded monster in the queensguard commander's uniform. Jules does not remember Rho Murtra being so large. But perhaps it was only the white priestess robes that had made her seem smaller.

The clash of the armies had not been anything like Jules expected: a terrible boom and then a worse flash of silence before the screams and metallic crossing of swords.

"Go!" Emilia wrenches a flag away from a frightened soldier and waves it back and forth, signaling to both sides of the rebel force before dropping it and wheeling her horse beside Jules's. "We have to go! Another moment and we'll be trampled." She grasps on to Jules's arm. For the first time since they met, Jules sees fear in her eyes.

Camden leaps up behind the saddle to avoid the careless feet of people and horses. She is clunky in her armor, and Jules wishes she had not buckled her into it. Better for the cat to be fast and lithe than bound and distracted.

"Where are we supposed to go?" Jules asks angrily.

Rho Murtra, or the thing that used to be her, barrels through the fray like a rolling boulder. One slash of her steel cleaves three rebels through the middle and leaves them in pieces and trailing pink innards.

"Are we to leave our people alone to face that?"

"I was wrong," Emilia cries. "We cannot face her. There is no queen strong enough. Not even Mirabella."

"I'm not running away!"

"You must!"

"What about the rebellion?"

Emilia looks back to the fighting. "There is no rebellion. As there is no Bastian City. And I would not have what happened to Margaret Beaulin happen to you. I will not lose you!"

Jules looks out across the fields of battle, where people lie dying. She watches Rho as she cuts toward them in a rain of blood. Neither of Jules's gifts are Rho's equal. Her stand against Rho would last only long enough for the priestess to hack her in two. She reaches out and draws Emilia close. She runs her fingers along the inside of her palm and feels the lines of the low-magic scars. The lines of the tether. She hears her mother whispering of destiny. She hears Arsinoe. And she knows what she must do.

"Please, Jules," Emilia begs. "You have to run."

Jules takes the knife out from her belt. She reaches back and slips her fingers into Camden's fur for one moment of comfort. Then she grabs Emilia's hand and turns it over.

She slices through the fabric of Emilia's sleeve and works around the arm guards, using her blade to reopen the scars on her arm and hand. Then she does the same to herself, pressing their arms together and letting the blood mingle again. Setting it free.

"What are you doing?" Emilia tries to pull away, but it is too late. "No, Jules! You can't!"

"I'm sorry," Jules says sadly as the curse rips through her. "But this is what I was made for."

She shoves Emilia, tossing her like a doll, and Camden leaps from the saddle, growling. Every bit of bottled rage is released into her blood in an instant, and she kicks her horse, fixed on Rho.

When Jules charges down the hill, at first Arsinoe thinks she is falling. That is how fast she flies. Later, in Arsinoe's memory, it will seem that Jules covered the ground between herself and Rho in one long bound, her horse's hooves never touching the turf. The two commanders come together with their arms raised, teeth bared, and with so much speed that it seems they both must break upon the impact. Instead, when their swords cross, such a great force is released that it sends a shock wave across the battlefield, and levels the entire line in both directions. Including Arsinoe.

She comes to a breath later, ears ringing. Somehow she manages to stay in the saddle as her gelding struggles back onto his feet. For a moment, she does not remember where she is or understand the sights and smells around her. Blood and the filth of gut wounds. Brave, naturalist-urged horses stumbling with cracked spears in their chests, still lashing out hooves to fight even when their naturalist riders are gone.

That collision. That explosion. It must have been Jules and

Rho. But how could Jules have—?

"The tether." She cut it loose. She let the legion curse go free.

Arsinoe scans the battle and quickly finds them, circling each other with blades drawn, their horses fallen unconscious or perhaps even dead and rolled to the side as if they were thrown. Her heart aches for a moment for that good black gelding of Katharine's who carried them through the mountains after the Queen's Hunt. Jules should not have ridden him into war. Goddess knows, he had done enough for them already.

Arsinoe's vision wavers, and she blinks hard; she clenches her teeth against the dull vibration in her ears. All across the battlefield, soldiers come to, looking dazed. It does not seem possible. Jules is so small and Rho such a hulking beast, Jules should have been thrown all the way back to the rebel camp. Pietyr Renard said that Katharine had sent the dead queens into him, and Arsinoe knows that Katharine has done the same to her commander.

It is almost too monstrous to think about.

Arsinoe tears her eyes away from Jules to search for Katharine. Her gaze passes over Billy, and she allows herself one breath of relief. He is alive. A little blood smeared across his jaw, but it does not seem bad, and might not even be his. But Emilia is nowhere near him. Perhaps as a warrior, Emilia can look out for him from a distance, relying on the accuracy of her crossbow bolts to keep him out of danger. Or perhaps she never meant to keep her promise, after all.

"Arsinoe! Are you all right?" Mathilde asks. The seer is unhorsed, and bright red blood leaks down her cheek from a cut above her eye.

"I'm fine. Where's Gilbert?"

Mathilde shakes her head, and Arsinoe sees a body lying not far away beneath a yellow cape.

"Do you see my sister? Do you see Katharine?"

Mathilde points.

Katharine gallops in the midst of a dozen queensguard with her banners flying and flags draped from her horse's reins.

"I'm going for her. Stay back!"

"Wait!" Mathilde grips her leg as a sudden blast of horns rings out from the rear of the queensguard.

Arsinoe does not need to look to know what it is. She does not need to see the frantic soldiers scattering from the direction of the sea.

"The mist," she whispers. "Come to join us at last."

When Pietyr's eyes met Katharine's across the battlefield, he thought that he would freeze. That he would be killed by some queensguard sword, while he stood, struck dumb. But he had kept on fighting. She had called his name. He could read it on her lips. And the look in her eyes was not one of confusion, or hatred at seeing him in the rebel colors. It was only happiness. Relief. Yet Pietyr had kept on fighting.

As he makes his way through the chaos, that is the thought that keeps his sword arm strong and his legs moving forward.

He passed the test. Face-to-face with his Katharine, he had kept on.

For she truly is his Katharine. The moment he spotted Rho riding across the field, he knew that the dead sisters were no longer inside Katharine's skin. Poor Rho. He is the only other person who knows what it feels like to have those dead queens poured into you, and he does not wish it on anyone, not even her.

Pietyr steps over a fallen soldier and gasps; she looks so much like that little priestess that Bree Westwood is always running around with that he is almost fooled. It is hard to hear, and to get his bearings. The whole world is shouting and metal on metal. And on top of that, his ears still hum from being thrown to the ground so hard that he bounced when the legion-cursed queen and Rho collided.

"Hey!"

Pietyr turns as Billy makes his way toward him through the struggling bodies.

"Why are you not fighting?" Pietyr shouts. "Instead of following me like a lost dog? They did not say we had to stay together!"

He dives as Billy swings hard at his head.

"Are you mad?" Pietyr asks before he looks behind him and sees the fallen queensguard solider.

"No, I'm not mad." Billy pulls his blade out. "Also, you're welcome. Where are you sneaking off to in such a hurry?"

"I am 'sneaking off' somewhere I am less likely to die."

"Come on," Billy tilts his head. "Come back the other way."

"Do you see what's happening the other way?"

"You have to serve your purpose."

"And what are you going to do about it?"

To his astonishment, the mainlander comes forward, sword swinging. It is an unpolished display—bad form, a poor grip, with less chance of cutting him than had he used a butter knife—but Pietyr stumbles backward.

"You idiot!" Pietyr shouts, and then they crouch as an arrow strikes near their feet. They wait out the volley together, shields over their heads as arrows sink into the dirt like rainfall.

For all his talk of poisoner glory, Pietyr never imagined he would be in a fight like this. The sights and smells of the dying do not bother him. But the chaos—the panic and the disorder—it makes his breath come faster and sweat prickle the back of his neck.

"Blast these random volleys! Give me an arrow guided by the war-gifted. At least they always hit their mark."

"You'd rather be hit?"

"I would rather be hit clean than pinioned to the ground by an arm or a leg," he snarls, and feels a moment of empathy for the Deathstalker scorpions that he pins to his lapel.

Billy comes out from behind his shield. The wooden edge is stuck with an arrow. He breaks it off with his foot.

"You say you're slinking off for safety," he says, "but you're heading in the direction of Arsinoe. Tell me why."

Pietyr's eyes narrow. Perhaps the mainlander is not so stupid after all. He is headed for Arsinoe. But not for the reason the boy thinks. Arsinoe is his best chance to get to Katharine. He does not know what will happen to her today. He only knows that he needs to be there when it does.

Billy misconstrues his narrowed eyes and rushes him again. Their shields bash, and Pietyr clenches his fist to stop its vibrating.

"Are you not forgetting your sworn target?" Pietyr asks. "In case you missed her, Rho Murtra is right over there." Across the battlefield, the rebel lines have already begun to flag as the shouts of the warrior captains are ignored and formations break and scatter. He is running out of time.

Pietyr's small dagger is out of his sleeve and sunk into Billy's side so fast, he even impresses himself. Billy's mouth drops open to form a small surprised O.

"I am sorry, Chatworth," he says as he lets go of the handle, leaving it stuck. "But I have to see her."

He turns and dashes through the fighting, leaving the mainlander to fall to the ground. He hopes he will not take it personally. He does not see how he could when the blade was not even poisoned.

It is not hard to find Arsinoe. She stands out from the rest in her black clothes and silver armor, and the furious scars slashed across her face. She is on horseback in the middle of a group of soldiers who are apparently there to do all of the fighting for her. He cannot tell if they are trying to cut her a path through the queensguard or simply keep her safe, and Arsinoe does not seem to care. All of her focus is downfield on Katharine.

Across the field, the riders around Katharine push close. They form a steering wall and take her horse by the reins, pulling on his bit so that his neck must twist nearly to his shoulder. In moments, they have her, and turn back for the Volroy just in time to evade the mist, creeping across the battlefield from east to west.

INDRID DOWN

High Priestess Luca hears the cries of the battle when it begins. The stomping and clashing, constant as a hum. Through her high window in Indrid Down Temple, she catches glimpses of circling hawks and falcons: familiars fighting alongside their naturalists.

Outside her door, her guards have fled to linger on the lower floors and wait for news, or perhaps to abandon their post completely. She does not care. One way or the other, the battle will be decided. A queen will take the throne, or the dead queens will keep it. And Luca's time within that conflict is over.

She pours herself a cup of tea, for it is still cold on this upper floor, and nearly spills it when the entire temple shakes to its foundation. An elemental is what comes immediately to mind. An earth-shaker. But not even Mirabella could have produced that kind of shock from the distance of the battlefield.

When she hears the hurried footsteps approaching, she

turns, thinking it a guard coming with news. Instead, Bree and Elizabeth fly through her door.

"Luca, are you all right?" Bree asks. "What was that?"

"You would know better than I would."

"Whatever it was, it nearly knocked me down the stairs." Elizabeth rushes to the High Priestess and throws her arms around her. Her plucky little woodpecker flies right into Luca's hood.

"He has returned," Luca says, and squirms as Pepper roots around the nape of her neck.

"Pepper, get out of there!" Elizabeth calls the bird back into her sleeve; he emerges a moment later atop her head. "Yes, he's returned."

"And he delivered his message?"

Elizabeth looks to Bree; they nod.

"But there was no return message?"

Bree shakes her head, and Luca sighs. "Well," Luca says. "I suppose Arsinoe means to deliver it in person."

Perhaps not wanting to think about what that message might be, Bree moves through the room and starts stuffing Luca's belongings into a sack.

"What are you doing?"

"What we should have done long before this. We are getting you out of here."

"No. You girls cannot risk yourselves for me. If Queen Katharine wins the day, she will know who did this."

Bree's expression is all elemental fire.

"We know the risks. We are not children anymore."

"And if anyone asks, we'll say we took you out of the city for your safety," Elizabeth adds. She helps Bree with the packing, filling another sack with jewels, clothes, and trinkets. Luca gathers up her personal journal. Whatever else remains, she must trust that the priestesses of the temple will preserve it for her.

"Talk in the Volroy grows wild," says Bree. "I half expect that Lucian will order one of the maids to stab him through the heart rather than face capture by the enemy."

They shoulder the sacks, and each takes one of Luca's elbows. But she hardly needs the assistance. Her legs suddenly feel years younger.

"I would not worry about Lucian," she says, and chuckles. "Poisoners have a flair for the dramatic, but few Arrons are brave enough for it. Natalia was the only one of them worth her salt."

"You sound like you miss her," Elizabeth says.

"I do miss her. My old adversary. If she had not been killed, it never would have gone this far, let me tell you."

She sees the girls exchange a humoring glance. She may be the High Priestess, but they are of another age. And perhaps they are right. It is young women now who bleed upon the battlefield. Young women who will lead them, no matter which side prevails. There will be no more puppet queens.

"Why did you bother saving me?" she asks. "Why did you not leave this old relic to her fate?"

"There is certainly a case to be made that you earned that

fate," Bree says, brow arched. "But we love you, Luca. And we will still need you if we are to get past this madness. You may be old, but you are no relic."

Luca takes Bree's hand and squeezes it. There is still vital blood in her veins. The Goddess may yet have a role for her to play in the future of the island. Or they may be taking her through tunnels and darkened alleys, out of the temple and out of the capital, all the way out of Fennbirn's story. After the life she has led, and all she has lost, Luca is surprised to find she will be happy either way.

When Genevieve rides her frothing horse directly into the castle, she nearly runs right over the top of her brother and cousin.

"Antonin! Lucian!" She looks from one frightened, exasperated face to the other, and notes that they are both carrying velvet bags. "What are those? Do you intend to steal from the Volroy and take to the road like common thieves?"

"Yes," Antonin replies. "And so must you. Go now and take what you can. Thanks to the strategic thinking of Rho Murtra, our way back to Greavesdrake is cut off. We will be lucky to make it through the city and onto the road to Prynn."

"You mean to abandon Greavesdrake? It is our home!"

"Greavesdrake will be burned out by day's end," Lucian snaps. "Have you seen the rebel numbers?"

"Have you seen our commander?" Genevieve counters. "And what about the Queen Crowned? No matter what happens we must remain with her."

"Would you rather advise, or would you rather survive?" Antonin asks.

She sets her jaw stubbornly, and he approaches her horse to put his hand over hers on the reins.

"Sister. I know you would do what Natalia would do. And if Natalia were here, she would stay with Katharine. But she was blinded by that girl. Blinded to her faults. What she should have *wanted* was to live to fight another day. Come now, we have to hurry."

Genevieve sits numb in the saddle. "You are too late. The mist has already made the battlefield. Queen Katharine is retreating here. She will be here within moments."

"All the more reason for us to move swiftly."

For a blink, Genevieve considers helping him onto the back of her horse. Galloping away and never looking back.

"Outside, our soldiers are fighting against naturalist beasts and war-gift-guided knives," she says. "That they should be swallowed up and torn apart by the mist is—"

"Terrible," Antonin whispers. "But there is nothing that we can do."

Genevieve shakes her head. She tugs her hands gently away.

"Genevieve—"

"No. I cannot go. You are right, Antonin. The Arrons must survive. But at least one Arron must remain also with the queen."

"Genevieve!" Lucian takes hold of her leg. "If the queen survives, we will return! But if the rebellion overtakes her . . .

they may spare Bree Westwood and even old Luca, for love of the elemental. But we three, we will burn in the square!"

"Then I will burn." Genevieve swings off the horse, her hands trembling. She is not brave by nature. Not like her sister. She hands Antonin the reins. "Take my mare. You will have a better chance on horseback."

THE BATTLEFIELD

"Queen Arsinoe!"

She looks over her shoulder. Pietyr Renard is making his way to her. There is blood on his hands, and some on his shoulder, but otherwise he seems unharmed.

"You," she says. "What are you doing here?" She cranes her neck to search around him, but Billy is nowhere in sight.

"He stayed behind," Pietyr says, reading her expression. "He said he had his own business to take care of."

"Not with Rho. Not with *that* Rho."

"He knows. He knows; do not worry. He said he would remain, to help."

"But not you."

Pietyr smiles. "Not me."

Arsinoe studies him a moment. He is panting and sweating. Outfitted in rebellion gear. She woke him from unconsciousness and probably saved him from a slow, unaware death. But he is still an Arron, and she half expects that his next move will be to leap upon her and try to cut her throat.

"They've taken Katharine behind the lines," she says.

"Probably all the way into the Volroy, to get away from that." Pietyr nods to the southwest, where the mist creeps through soldiers, swallowing them whole and spitting them out in pieces.

"What does it want?" Pietyr asks with disgust.

Arsinoe watches as retreating queensguard fighters run straight into it in a panic. Not all come out the other side. After the battle ends, she wonders whether they will be able to tell which of the soldiers fell from a blade and which to the mist.

"You can't have thought it would sit this one out," Arsinoe says.

"You cannot have thought that I would," says Pietyr.

Arsinoe looks ahead grimly. The mist lies directly in her path, a white shroud biting at the edges of the battle like a dog pulling at the edge of a tablecloth.

"Jules and Emilia hoped it was Katharine that the mist was after. But if that's true, it doesn't seem opposed to snacking along the way." She glances at him. "You don't seem afraid."

"Nor do you."

"I think Mirabella is there. I think she'll protect me. You know what I mean to do, Renard."

"I do."

"And you won't try and stop me?"

"I mean to come with you. Whatever happens, I need to be there."

She smiles without showing her teeth. "Ready to jump onto the winning side, of course."

"Believe what you wish."

Arsinoe hesitates, her hand on her sword.

"Please," he says softly. "I have earned this. There will be no peace for me if I am not there."

She motions to the back of her horse. "Climb on if you're coming."

After a beat of disbelief, he holds his hand out, and she helps him up. The mist has crept over the ground between them and the Volroy like a blanket. There is no way to go but through.

"We might be torn inside out the moment we step inside it," Arsinoe says. "Or at least you might. Did Mirabella like you?"

"Your sister is not in the mist," Pietyr says in her ear. He clutches her around the waist. "But no. Though we never really spoke."

"I don't know that would have made much of a difference." Arsinoe kicks her horse forward, and wishes she had the naturalist gift to make him brave.

Mirabella, if you're there, look after me one last time.

Emilia can hardly breathe. The blood leaking down her forearm and the ache in her chest mean nothing.

Jules cut the legion curse free.

She crawls across the ground, getting to her feet as fast as she can after Jules shoved her down. Jules and Camden are already halfway down the hill.

"Jules. Jules, look at me!" But she does not really want her to. Jules's spine and shoulders jerk with the curse, and when her head turns, Emilia sees her lips stretched so far over her teeth that it seems that they must tear.

If Jules and Camden were to turn back, they would rip her to shreds, drive steel and claws deep into her chest. But she is not the most enticing target on the field. It is only thanks to Rho Murtra that Emilia is still alive.

"Jules!" she shouts weakly. "Jules, don't!"

Down the hill, Camden leaps upon the first person she reaches. The poor queensguard soldier does not even have time to scream. Jules draws her sword but does not seem keen to use it. Instead, she appears to be driving her horse directly into Rho's, and between his terror and her naturalist gift, the gelding will obey.

There is something both terrible and beautiful about watching Jules race toward all that blood and pain, so fearless and full of anger. And lacking in a plan, just like her friend Arsinoe. Emilia does not know how the two of them survived together for so long.

As Jules and Rho meet, Jules urges her horse to make one final leap, and Emilia opens her mouth to scream.

She wakes up on the ground. And she is not alone—the blast leveled every nearby soldier in a broad circle. Warm blood drips from her nose and runs down to her lip. After a moment, she can hear again, sounds muffled behind the ringing, and she gets to her feet on legs that feel like she has drunk a barrel of ale. The brief pause in the battle is over and stunned sword arms begin to swing. She has to get to Jules. She must find her queen.

She swivels and sees her, already on her feet if indeed she was ever off them. The poor gelding and Rho's massive battle charger lie motionless, their bodies forming a boundary like an arena as the two warriors circle each other in the center. Waves of darkness seep from Rho like fog. The flesh of her forearms are rotting and green. Though Emilia has never been particularly pious, the white priestess hood on something like that seems pure blasphemy. No warrior in Bastian City could stand against such a monster. Not Emilia. Not even her mother. Only Jules.

THE VOLROY

Arsinoe holds her breath as she and Pietyr plunge into the mist. She closes her eyes, and Pietyr's arms squeeze tighter around her middle. But after a few steps, it seems they will not be torn in two.

"How will you know which direction to go?" he asks.

"I don't know," she replies. It is a stupid question, anyway. Everyone on Fennbirn knows that the mist brings you where it wants. Or where you are meant to be.

"Is it always so cold?"

"Yes," she says, though this mist does not feel at all familiar. Not like it was when she was a child in the boat with Jules and Joseph. Not like passing through it on the way to the mainland. This mist feels like a fist waiting to close, so thick she can hardly see the brown coat of her horse beneath her.

"Where is everyone? We must not be alone," Pietyr says just as the horse stumbles. He goes down on his front knees, pitching Arsinoe and Pietyr off over his head.

Arsinoe scrambles to hold on to the reins as Pietyr grasps on to her waist.

"Don't! I can't lose the horse! I can't lose him!" She drags herself up and touches his nose. The poor frightened gelding is breathing hard. She pats his neck, and it is wet with sweat. But he does not bolt. "Good boy, smart boy," she whispers.

"Dear Goddess," Pietyr says from behind her. He stares at the ground, at the thing the gelding stumbled over. It is a body. Or at least it was. Twisted and torn and bent, it is hard to tell whether it used to be woman or beast.

Arsinoe steps back and trips. When she tries to get up, her hands shove inside something wet and warm.

"Another body."

Pietyr helps her to her feet. "Or the rest of the same one."

She pulls the horse close. Her fingers are slick, painted with red and gore to the wrists.

Everywhere they look, on all the ground they can see, are bodies or pieces of bodies. Beside them, several queensguard lie on top of each other coated with blood, like they were piled onto a platter. And to her right, a skinned arm, the muscle and sinew exposed all the way to the disconnected shoulder.

"We have to get out of here," Pietyr says.

"Don't panic," she snaps. She knows better than anyone how long the mist can wrap you in its grasp. They could wander forever. Until they starve or lose their minds. By the end, they could be begging the mist to twist them apart. But there is no point in saying so to Pietyr. "Take my hand."

He takes it without hesitation despite the gore, and they begin to move forward. She counts a hundred paces in the same direction before she begins to suspect they should have reached the Volroy's outer gates. Then she counts a hundred more, passing scattered corpses of horses and soldiers. Pietyr's breath is fast in her ear.

"I do not remember the Volroy gates being so far."

"They aren't. Something's wrong."

"Why must you say that?" he hisses.

"Would you rather we ignore it?" she growls back.

She breathes in and the mist coats her throat and sinks into her lungs. It swirls around them in curious bands.

"Oi! Is anybody there?" someone calls out.

She and Pietyr turn. The voice could have come from anywhere.

"Yes! We're here!" Arsinoe cries. "Over here!"

The young queensguard soldier stumbles into view. Her eyes are bewildered, and she still carries her sword, the tip dragging along the ground.

"Are you real?" she asks. "I couldn't find—I cannot find—anyone. . . ."

"You found us," Pietyr says. "It is all right now."

The girl does not look convinced. But she drops her sword. And when she does, the mist swirls in and tears her apart.

Arsinoe screams. The horse pulls the reins from her hand and gallops off, his hoofbeats gone in an instant.

One half of the girl is missing, including her head. Her other half, with one arm and one leg still attached, lies twitching in the dirt.

"Do you still think Mirabella is in this mist?" Pietyr asks. He grabs her by the shoulder and shoves her toward the girl's body. "This is what is spread upon the battlefield. This is what will cover the entire island! Right now, somewhere behind us or in front of us or around us, everyone you know—it could be happening to them!"

"Who do you think you're talking to?" She jerks away and hits him hard, the back of her fist against his chest. "I know that!"

"Then do something about it! Get us out of here! But do not let go of me." He tightens his grip on her hand. "I think you are the only reason I am not"—he nods to the body at their feet—"in pieces."

"What would you have me do?" Arsinoe asks. "Mirabella was the one who could face the mist. She was the elemental; I'm just a poisoner like you. So why don't you do something?"

His icy eyes snap to hers.

"You are not just a poisoner, Arsinoe. Nor are you merely a naturalist. You are a queen."

She takes a deep breath. Queen she may be, yet the mist presses in on her like a weight. At any moment, Pietyr will be snatched away from her into the white, and she will be alone.

"I know the mist," she says quietly. "And I know who made it. And I am a queen, though not like any queen the island has seen before. We none of us were." She reaches for her small sharp knife. She remembers Mirabella's last letter.

Me to face down the mist. Katharine to be the vessel. And you to banish them with low magic.

"There was only ever one thing that I was good at." She links her arm through Pietyr's and draws the blade across her hand. "And I won't be ashamed of it anymore." She holds her hand before her face and lets her blood drip down her wrist as her voice grows louder. "The dead queens started this fight. But it is the living ones who will finish it." She bares her teeth and slams her palm into the soil.

A great wind rushes down, and Pietyr ducks close, trying to cover her. The mist churns, and voices and cries echo from inside it. Perhaps it is Illiann. Maybe it is Daphne. But though she strains, she does not hear Mirabella.

She closes her eyes and presses her hand harder into the ground, and suddenly the air is light. She opens her eyes. They are in the courtyard beyond the front gates of the Volroy.

"How?" Pietyr asks, rising slowly.

"Don't ask questions. It's where we were meant to be." Arsinoe rises and runs ahead, into the fortress.

Katharine is in her room beside the fire when she hears Arsinoe call her name. It has been so long since she has heard her voice, and she is surprised to find that the sound is a relief.

The castle is nearly empty; there will be no members of the Black Council and no soldiers to impede her. All that remains is to choose the place.

Katharine touches the knives at her waist, her dear, poisoned blades. Though against Arsinoe, the poison does not matter.

The dead queens who remain with her slither furtively into her blood. They prod gently, meek without the strength of their numbers.

"Hush," Katharine whispers to them. "It is almost time for you to face my sister."

THE BATTLEFIELD

Emilia lies frozen in place as she watches Jules and Rho Murtra circle each other. Arsinoe was right. Jules is beyond her. There is nothing she can do, to help, to protect, to stop what is coming.

"Emilia!"

She looks to her right and sees Mathilde. The oracle has taken an arrow to her shoulder but fights on bravely, shoving soldiers back and waving her sword arm to signal rebellion flags. At her order, the reserves come, spilling from the northwest hill like ants. Watching them, Emilia feels a tightness in her throat. They are so brave. Despite the mist and despite the monster the Undead Queen sent for them, they do not flee.

"Mathilde!" Emilia struggles to her feet. Mathilde is unhorsed, and her yellow cape is stained dark with mud. Many of the oracles have fallen, their colors easy to see in the dirt. But a few still fight on.

"We have to hold the line," Mathilde shouts. "Draw the western flank of queensguard thin!"

Emilia nods. She remounts her horse and catches a passing mare for Mathilde.

"Wait," Mathilde says when she is in the saddle. "Look."

Downfield, Billy stumbles through the battle, one hand pressed to his side and the other barely fending off attacks. His armor and clothes are soaked with red.

"Foolish mainlander," Mathilde says. "He should have stayed nearby. If you lead the charge with the reserves now, you may be able to buckle the flank."

Emilia looks between the queensguard, drawn enticingly thin, and Billy, on one knee and bleeding heavily. Downfield to her left, Jules and Rho begin to trade blows. There are so many places she would wish to be and no point in letting this moment of glory pass when the boy is practically dead already.

She raises her sword arm, and the war gift sings in her veins like the Goddess herself. She knows what it will feel like, crashing through the ranks. She can feel the strike of them against her knees, and hear their moans on the edge of her blade.

She squeezes her eyes shut and bellows. "Curse you, Arsinoe!"

"What are you doing?" Mathilde asks.

"Charge the flank without me. Go!" She turns her horse and races to Billy in fast strides, her sword sweeping down to cut through queensguard at the vulnerable place near the elbow. She relishes what fighting she may have all the way to the mainlander.

"Billy!"

"Emilia, thank god," he says as she pulls him into the saddle. "It was Renard. The bastard stabbed me when I tried to stop him from going after Arsinoe."

"Thank your god in your own country," she says, her heart lingering with the fight even as they gallop out of it. "Today you should thank my Goddess."

They look back together as the horse takes them out of the fray. In the confusion of the mist, fighters scatter. They turn on each other, tripping friends and allies in the hopes of buying time. Everywhere the white touches them they scream; they fall to the ground with backs full of blood.

"The mist," Billy says in horror. "What do we do about the mist?"

Emilia faces forward and kicks her horse hard.

"That is up to your Arsinoe now."

Camden prowls the border of Jules and Rho's contest ground marked off by the fallen bodies of their mounts, killed when they first collided. But even without the cougar, no one would have disturbed them. For who would dare?

They strike and parry, strike and parry, their show of speed unnatural. The clang of their weapons crossing would vibrate any other fighter to her knees.

The only sounds are grunts and fierce bellows, the legion curse leaping high and the dead queens knocking it back, every impact hard enough to crush bones. Over and over, they come together and are thrown apart, yet the only damage they show was taken before the encounter began: ribbons of blood down a legion-cursed arm, a speckling of rot across an undead cheek.

The clearing around them grows as those fighting nearby stop to stare. But even the spectators flee when the mist comes.

The dead queens land a fearsome blow and send their opponent rolling. At the sight of the mist, they screech and use the priestess's war gift to wrench the battle-ax out of the ground. With two weapons, they greet their two enemies.

The legion curse attacks, slashing with sword and short dagger, using the war gift as a shield, but the dead queens are not afraid. They lash out, their rage their strength, cutting, bashing, stomping until they hear bones snap.

When the mist curls around their legs, they feel its chill. But they are still not afraid. They sweep their ax through the mist like they will cleave it in two.

They are distracted. They do not see her get up and brace on one leg. They do not see her leap, making the broken bone shatter.

The sword and the dagger sear into their flesh and pierce deep large holes that pour dead, black blood, and the dead queens drop the ax to try and hold themselves inside.

They leak out into the air, sensing Katharine nearby, and fly to her, pouring out of Rho as the body of the priestess collapses to the dirt. They leave her, and the hated Legion Queen, behind. They do not look back when the mist sweeps in to tear the empty sack of Rho Murtra to shreds.

THE VOLROY

Arsinoe shakes her cut hand, sending droplets of blood spattering against the Volroy's stone floor.

"Here," Pietyr says, and hands her his handkerchief.

"Those poisoner manners." She wraps the cut. "I'm glad I never learned them."

They walk together, deeper into the Volroy, and Pietyr keeps her abreast of the turns. He whispers which rooms are which and tells her where they might try. She lets him do it to feel useful. He does not know that she once lived a life through Daphne's eyes and knows pathways through the castle that he has no idea of.

They round a corner and come upon a small green space, a walled garden that Arsinoe remembers well.

"What is it?" Pietyr asks when she lingers.

"This was the Blue Queen's favorite garden. Illiann, she used to sit here for hours."

"How do you know?"

"I know lots of things that I shouldn't know." She looks at him sideways. She should not be going to Katharine with him. It does not matter that he said he would not interfere or that he swore to overthrow the crown. Hearts in love are unpredictable, and once he sees Katharine, all of his promises may be forgotten.

"Am I going to have trouble with you?"

"I told you you would not."

"The word of an Arron?"

"It means more than the word of a Milone."

"I doubt that," Arsinoe says, and snorts. But the Milones have done their share of wrongs and kept their share of secrets. Just like the Arrons. And like the temple.

"You should be more worried about Katharine, in any case. You know what she is. How strong she is, thanks to the borrowed gifts, and how good she is with weapons. You know she is likely to kill you."

"We are likely to kill each other," Arsinoe says, her voice hard. "Yes, I know."

She takes a deep breath. She hears Mirabella and Jules saying how foolhardy she is. How she never thinks anything through. But they would only say that because they love her. Deep down, they know as well as she does that this task can fall to no one else.

Quick as a cat, she draws her knife and shoves Pietyr against the wall, pressing the edge to his neck.

"If I were smart," she says, "I would kill you. So tell me why I shouldn't."

"Because I am an ally. Because I swore I would not stop you."

She presses the blade harder against his skin.

"Liar."

Pietyr grimaces at the pressure of the knife, but he is not really afraid. He looks at her with his usual amount of disdain.

"Then I will tell you the whole truth to prove that I am not what you say."

"The whole truth?"

"In order to reach you on the battlefield, I had to stab your boy, Billy."

For a moment, she cannot believe what she has heard. Then she pulls him forward and slams him back into the wall, hard enough to make him believe she has the war gift.

"You what?"

"I did not kill him. But he refused to let me by. He seemed to think I had nefarious plans for you. He is rather gallant for a mainland idiot."

"You stabbed him?"

"Yes. But I did not kill him."

"How do you know? How do you know for sure?"

"A poisoner knows the body," he says. "We know where to cut to make you feel it. We know how deep to make the blood run. And we also know how to keep you alive, to prolong the suffering."

"If there was poison on your knife, I swear—"

He shakes his head as much as he is able to without being cut.

"There was none. The weapons were provided to me on the march, and I have been watched and searched regularly. When would I have had the chance?"

Arsinoe holds him for a long moment. Then she steps back, and Pietyr rubs at his neck.

"I did not have to tell you that," he says. "But I am being honest. So please believe me when I say I will not interfere with you and Katharine. I just need to be there."

Honest. The word does not even fit in his mouth right. But Arsinoe puts her knife away.

"You can't stop me, Renard. It would be a waste of your life to try."

He nods, and she walks past the garden, pressing her finger to her lips when footsteps sound down a corridor. She flattens against the wall and grabs the servant by the collar as soon as he turns the corner.

"Where is the queen?"

"He is a kitchen boy," Pietyr says. "He might not know."

"She—she is in her rooms." The boy points skyward and to the west. Arsinoe lets him go.

"Good. This can all end like it used to in the old days. With queens in the tower."

Arsinoe is almost there. Katharine can feel her coming. Her angry, middle sister. Arsinoe is coming, and she has purpose:

to do what Mirabella promised she would.

She will not want to kill you, the few dead queens whisper. *She is weak.*

"She will," Katharine whispers back. "For what I did. For sending the others into Rho Murtra to grind Jules Milone's bones into the mud."

The only thing left to decide on is the place.

It should not be here, in these rooms of striped silk and brocade, clumsy furniture, and tea settings. Rooms that reek of ease and civilized capital business.

It should be somewhere stark and wild. Where Mirabella can see.

Katharine goes to the door. She calls down to Arsinoe. And then she hurries up the stairs to the door that leads to the battlements.

When Arsinoe bursts out onto the battlements, she is unprepared for the dizzying height, worse even than when she clung to the side of Mount Horn. She squeezes her eyes shut. When she opens them, she sees Katharine, standing across the rooftop. The Undead Queen's arms are bare and full of poison scars. She wears a black, corseted gown. And she looks almost happy to see her.

Arsinoe is not sure what she expected, but seeing her is a shock. After Pietyr's descriptions of the dead queens, she imagined Katharine half rotten, her skin blackened and showing glimpses of exposed bone. She thought Katharine would simply charge—that they would charge each other—and there would be an end to it. Now, despite her anger and her hands clenched in fists, she cannot bring herself to simply walk across the rooftop and strangle her little sister to death.

"You came," Katharine calls. "I knew you would. She said you would."

"Don't speak of her."

"But you received it? The letter she sent?" Katharine's eyes flicker hopefully to Arsinoe's small, sharp knife. "You know what you have to do."

"Aye," Arsinoe growls. "I know what I have to do." She clenches her fists. "Come and face me!" She squeezes the knife handle and waits, her breath hard, her pulse in her ears. But Katharine does not move. It only makes Arsinoe angrier, this calm exterior, this act. She did not come all this way to butcher a fawn as it slept. She wanted a fight. It has to be a fight.

"Come on!" she shouts. "You're a joke in that crown. A giftless queen. When you found out that I was a poisoner, didn't you think to ask old Willa? Didn't you want to know that you were nothing but a weak-gifted naturalist? A weak, pathetic, nearly giftless naturalist, like I always thought I was. We were supposed to have each other's childhoods, Katharine. Though I'd like to think I'd have handled yours better than you have."

"It does not matter what I was," Katharine says, frowning. "I am something different now. I know that you are angry—"

"Angry? I am more than angry!"

It is not working. Down on the battlefield, people are dying. Her friends are dying. Arsinoe lifts the knife. And Pietyr steps out from behind her.

Katharine rushes forward two steps.

"You are something different, Kat," he says. "You are right about that."

"You are well." Katharine smiles, and her eyes shine. "You are well again."

Arsinoe seethes at the happiness on Katharine's face. She does not deserve it. She deserves cruelty. Pain. She should be allowed to feel nothing but regret. Arsinoe turns to Pietyr and puts her hand on his chest.

"He is well again," she says. "You tried to kill him, and I woke him up." She walks around him. When she trails her hand down his back Pietyr nearly jumps out of his skin, but to his credit, he stays quiet.

"He's not here to return to you, Katharine. He's here to declare that he is with us. With me." She steels herself and grabs Pietyr's face, kissing him hard. Then she shoves him away and runs for her sister.

Katharine knows that the kiss was not real. But it gave her sister the courage she needed. As Arsinoe runs at her, Katharine puts her hands up. Arsinoe's knife swings in a slicing arc. It stabs through the meat of Katharine's hand, lodging between her ring and pinkie finger.

She cries out as the dead queens hiss. They want to twist Arsinoe's head around on her neck. But Katharine swallows them down.

"You killed her!" Arsinoe shouts through clenched teeth. Her knife shakes in Katharine's flesh and saws into it deeper.

"When she loved us more than the crown. More than the island!"

From the corner of Katharine's eye, she sees Pietyr, looking on in misery. "Queens do not get to have loves like that," Katharine shouts.

As they struggle, she feels the pain in Arsinoe's eyes like it is her own. She wants to tell her what happened to Mirabella. That Mirabella had asked Katharine to kill her, to protect her from the invasion of the dead queens. She wants to tell her that it was still her fault because she could not protect her. But if she does, Arsinoe will lose her nerve. She is more like their older sister in that way. And besides, despite the blade in her hand, Katharine almost enjoys the fight. This is what she and Arsinoe do, without Mirabella to mediate between them. It is what they have always done, even back at the Black Cottage.

Arsinoe shoves Katharine back, and wrenches the knife free.

"Why are you looking at me like that?" Arsinoe pants. "What's wrong with you?"

"Cut me," Katharine cries. "Kill me or cut them out of me. There has to be an end to it. An end to the line of queens."

She cradles her hand as blood runs freely down her arm. Arsinoe stares at her in exasperation, exhausted already from the stairs and from whatever she faced upon the battlefield. Below them, and all around them, the mist blankets entire buildings like a covering of snow. Coming ever closer to devour them.

"You brought this on yourself, Katharine. All of it."

Katharine's face falls. Not all of it. She had begun the game as much a pawn as the others. But enough of it is her doing that the rest does not matter.

"I wish we had not been born here, Arsinoe. I wish things could have been different. But I think Mirabella was right. And we were put here for a reason."

"Why didn't you say this before?" Arsinoe asks. The knife hangs in her hand. "Why not when she was still alive and we could have done something?"

"I did not feel it before. I am a queen. It is not in my nature to admit defeat. It is not in yours either."

Before she can say more, there rises such a cry from the battlefield that she and Arsinoe both turn. She knows what that sound was. So do the dead sisters, who swell in her blood, preparing to welcome home their kin. Katharine turns to Arsinoe with wide eyes.

"You must do it now! We are out of time!"

"What are you talking about?"

"If they return to me, I will not be able to control them!"

"Listen to her, Arsinoe!" Pietyr shouts. "Banish them, now!"

Arsinoe unwraps the bandage around her palm as the dead queens arrive in a whirlwind. The black fury of them swirls around Katharine like a horde of stinging insects. Katharine clamps her mouth shut and squeezes her eyes closed. But they always find a way back in.

Katharine drops to her knees. The dead queens are so angry. They tear at her face and arms, trying to claw their way in. They will swarm her mind and steal her body for good.

"Get away from her."

The pain eases. It disappears from her neck and chest, bringing relief like a cool breeze. Katharine opens her eyes. Arsinoe is coming to her across the rooftop, her hand extended and bleeding, parting the cloud of dead queens like smoke. She has carved into her hand the same rune that Pietyr had carved into his when he tried to banish the queens back into the stones.

"That will not work," she says as Arsinoe kneels beside her.

"It will when I do it." Arsinoe takes Katharine's hand. She works fast with her knife, carving the rune upside down, so the two will seal together. She holds out her palm.

Katharine grips her sister's hand. The feeling of the queensblood mingling is unlike anything she has felt before. Beyond the dead queens' gifts. Beyond the elation of the crown etched into her forehead. Her body convulses as the last of the dead are thrown out past her lips to flow onto the rooftop. They slither like ink to rejoin the others, and Arsinoe and Katharine rise.

The dead queens are not strong enough to take form. They linger in the air, boiling like water, and for the first time, Katharine is able to glimpse who they once were. Faces and hands fight to remain, pressing out from the cloud. Echoes of black hair drift like seaweed. She sees braids and the hints of gowns, dresses from times long ago. They were no different than Katharine and Arsinoe once. Their ends no less unfair than Mirabella's.

"They're past saving," Arsinoe murmurs, reading Katharine's thoughts through their joined blood. "We have to banish them. Permanently."

"Look out!" Pietyr cries as the body of Rho Murtra climbs over the battlements.

Not all of the queens gave her up after the mist was done with her. After it left her shredded and torn from a hundred cuts. After it hollowed her eyes. A few of them were clever, and suspicious. And after the mist had eased, they climbed back inside the dead priestess like a suit of armor.

Arsinoe flinches as the thing that used to be Rho raises an ax and brings it down hard on the stones. Katharine pulls her sister out of the way, and they fall against the rooftop, scuttling backward as the dead queens jerkily advance, clumsy inside the dead skin.

"What in the Goddess's name is that?" Arsinoe asks.

Katharine clings to her as they stare wide-eyed at the horror Rho's body has become.

"It must be stopped," Katharine whispers, and Arsinoe lets go of her to carve another rune into her other hand.

Before Katharine can object, she darts forward, quick as a cat.

"No!" Katharine scrambles to her feet and moves to help, but Pietyr takes her shoulder.

"Please, Kat," he says. "Let me." He dashes past her and throws himself onto Rho's corpse. A sound comes from deep inside the rotting, greening skin, almost like a wheeze, a bellow from lungs full of holes.

Frozen, Katharine watches as Arsinoe ducks the swing of an undead arm, trying to press her hand against the corpse's forehead. Pietyr hauls the arm back, but he does not see Rho's other arm swing hard with the ax.

"Stop!" Katharine shouts as it catches Arsinoe in a glancing blow, the blade slicing into the meat of her hip. It sends her flying, crashing to the stones, to roll all the way against the wall of the battlements. Katharine runs to her.

"You are bleeding."

"Yes," Arsinoe says, and grimaces as Katharine helps her up. She flexes her hands, squeezing more blood from the runes. "But I still have enough." She takes a deep breath and heaves off away from the wall, leaping again for Rho's corpse as Pietyr grapples with the dead queens who still hold fast inside it. They rake their undead fingernails down his perfect cheek and he growls and shouts in pain.

"Arsinoe, the ax!" Pietyr wraps his arm around Rho in a crushing embrace and Arsinoe kicks hard against the hand that holds it. She must kick twice more before the ax clatters to the stones.

"I need the head!" Arsinoe bares her teeth. But as she tries to reach it, seeking to climb Rho's massive arm as if it is a tree branch, the corpse jerks its neck and connects with Pietyr skull to skull, sending him to the ground. Katharine holds her breath as Rho's darkened, broken hand wraps around Arsinoe's throat. She will see her sister's windpipe crushed. See the life ebb out of her.

Katharine runs forward. In one fast, smooth motion, she scoops up the ax and swings hard, with a guttural howl. Then she blinks. The blade is buried in the corpse's chest. As the dead queens stare at her in shock, Arsinoe rises and slams the rune into Rho's dead forehead.

The last of the dead seep out, the corpse's jaw hanging as if dislocated. It takes only a moment, and then it collapses into a pile of meat and empty eyes. Katharine, Arsinoe, and Pietyr stand over it, breathless.

"Don't ever, ever make something like that again!" Arsinoe shouts at Katharine, and starts to laugh, bent over with one hand on her knee, the other pressed against the deep cut in her hip. Pietyr begins to chuckle, too. In the face of the reanimated Queensguard Commander, they have momentarily forgotten about the cloud of the dead hanging in the air.

But Katharine has not. Her eyes flicker to them as the dead queens contract, desperately holding themselves together. They need a queen in order to remain. They need a body. And they sense that Arsinoe has been weakened enough.

Katharine does not have time to warn her. She jumps to her feet and throws herself in front of Arsinoe as the dead queens dive for her throat. The impact of them knocks her off her feet. The brush of the battlement stones against her shoulder is surreal as she goes over the top of it, hearing Arsinoe scream as she goes over the edge as well. But Katharine, always the smallest, is also the quickest, and kicks Arsinoe against the wall. The last thing she sees before she plunges into the mist is Arsinoe, holding tight to the Volroy stones. Safe.

Arsinoe clings to the side of the Volroy, legs dangling, her neck twisted as she watches Katharine and the dead queens fall into nothingness. Katharine had saved her. She had saved her. And she fell.

"Kat," she whispers, and then she shouts. "Katharine!"

"Give me your hand!"

She looks up. Pietyr is leaning over the edge. With a groan, she reaches up and grabs him, wincing at the sting of the rune in her hand.

And behind her, the dead queens scream.

"Pietyr! Pull me up!"

He tries, but he will not be fast enough. She knows that by the terror in his eyes.

Arsinoe kicks; her feet scrabble against the stone, unsure whether she is trying to climb or to keep the dead queens away. She dares to look over her shoulder and sees them coming, their form stretched in inky arms and elongated legs.

"I'm not going to make it," she shrieks. "Let go!"

She pulls against his grip, the blood making it easy to slip loose.

"Wait!"

Arsinoe looks over her shoulder again.

The mist is rising, racing up alongside the dead queens. It

swoops up above them and dives back down, swallowing them whole and tearing them apart, spitting wisps of blackness into the sky. Arsinoe and Pietyr freeze as they stare at the battle, the dead queens shrieking, becoming a maelstrom of writhing arms and bared teeth, as the mist wraps around and around them.

The dead queens do not stand a chance. The mist devours. The mist protects. Arsinoe sees the queens of old, hidden inside its depths. She sees Illiann and even Daphne. She feels Mirabella's might as the mist crashes against the Volroy like a thunderstorm. She recognizes Katharine in the sharp, twisting quickness as it slices strands of darkness and casts them off in ribbons. She sees them fight, for her and the island, until all that remains of the dead queens are tatters and ashes floating in the air.

When it is over, the mist disappears. It does not roll back into the sea. It does not retreat. It simply evaporates and fades until there is nothing left to see.

"Arsinoe," Pietyr says, grimacing. "Give me your other hand."

She does, and he pulls her up and back over the side onto the rooftop, where they collapse together.

"It was them," she says, panting. "Mirabella and Katharine."

"It was them," Pietyr agrees, and knocks his head against the stone. "And now it is finished."

THE BATTLEFIELD

One moment, the mist is everywhere. The next it draws back, fading like it never was, and Emilia turns her horse and races in search of Jules.

All across the battlefield, soldiers are wakening. They wander together, helping their wounded, casting fearful eyes on the havoc that remains. So many are dead, twisted around or torn apart, that it is a relief to see a few felled by arrows or a spear, for at least that can be understood.

Emilia urges her horse past them all, jumping the dead and dodging the living, on her way to the clearing where Jules lies. When she reaches her, she pulls the reins so hard that her poor mare skids.

"Jules!" She takes Jules's face in her hands as Jules swivels bloodred eyes toward her. She does not need to look at Jules's leg to know it is ruined. Her trousers are soaked with blood and lie too flat on the calf. The leg is turned the wrong way below the knee.

"Jules, you fool. What have you done?"

"I did what I had to do," Jules says through clenched teeth. She reaches up and touches Emilia's face. "And I'm all right." She smiles. "I'm all right. The curse, it's—" Her eyes flutter, and she loses consciousness.

Emilia pulls her onto her lap.

"Help us! I need help for the queen!"

Rebels come. They bind Jules's wounds tightly and load her and her cougar gently onto horses. As Emilia weeps, Mathilde comes limping to her side.

"What did we do?" Emilia asks. "What did we make her do?"

Mathilde looks sadly after Jules and Camden, borne away on the rocking backs of the horses. Her eyes cloud. And then, she smiles.

"Only what she was meant to do."

The healers take Jules's leg while she sleeps. Emilia was right: there could be no saving it. And Emilia remains with her until she wakes.

"What happened?" Jules asks as her eyes crack open.

"You saved so many," Emilia replies. "You made yourself a legend. A legend, and a queen."

Jules slips back to sleep, and Emilia leans down to kiss her on the forehead.

"Don't worry, Jules. I will be here when you wake. And forever after."

Arsinoe and Pietyr emerge from the Volroy in a daze. Inside, the castle is still quiet, nearly deserted. But outside is carnage everywhere they look. As they stand blinking before the outer gates, Arsinoe is surprised by the warm nudge of a muzzle against her arm. It is her good brown horse, returned, his white socks splattered with red.

"Hey, boy." She reaches up underneath his forelock and scratches his forehead as Pietyr calls to a nearby rebel soldier.

"Where are the commanders?" he asks. "Where have they taken the Legion Queen?"

"They've taken her to the city. Healers have gathered in the square to help the wounded."

Arsinoe nods to Pietyr, and they quickly mount the horse and ride at a canter for Indrid Down Square. As they go, they pass reunions of all sorts. Some joyous. Many with tears as news of the fallen spreads among the survivors.

"Where is she?" Arsinoe asks, turning the horse in all directions. "Where—?"

Someone waves to her from the crowd. Luke. Good Luke, with his face bloodied and a bandage wrapped around his shoulder. He smiles when she looks at him and points across the square to a hastily assembled tent.

They ride to it, and Arsinoe jumps off the horse. Jules and Camden lie inside, with Emilia seated between them.

"Is she—?" Arsinoe asks, and Camden chirrups softly. Arsinoe's eyes catch on Jules's missing leg, and she swallows.

"She will be all right," Emilia says. "She did it. And you did it."

Arsinoe bends and takes Jules's hand. "How? How did she stand against Rho?"

"She cut the legion curse free," Emilia says. "But she is fine. It is gone."

"Gone?"

Emilia shrugs. "Perhaps the curse was never a curse. Ask Mathilde. She has many strange seer thoughts on the matter. But look there." Emilia gestures over Arsinoe's shoulder.

Billy stands on the outskirts of the makeshift camp, his shirt in tatters and a large swath of bandage wrapped around his abdomen. But he is alive.

And so is Arsinoe. She sees the relief and gladness wash over his face as she holds tight to Jules. But when she stands up to go to him, he steps back.

He is leaving, like he said he would. And if he touches her again, he will not have the strength to go. So she smiles, eyes wet from exhausted tears. He smiles, too, and raises his hand.

"So long, Junior," she whispers.

THE LEGION QUEEN

In the days and weeks that followed the end of the Queens' War, as it would come to be called, many changes took place in the capital and across the island. Jules recovered, with help from Arsinoe and Emilia, and learned to walk with a crutch. The legion curse had indeed disappeared, and she was herself again, while both of her gifts were allowed to flourish. She as yet wore no crown, but everyone called her the Legion Queen.

Neither she nor her council took up immediate residence at the Volroy. The grand towers seemed too representative of the queens gone by, and Jules and the rebellion had no interest in repeating the mistakes and corruption of the past. The line of the triplet queens had strayed too far off course, and now the time of triplet queens had ended.

Shortly after the battle, Paola Vend and Renata Hargrove were found and placed under temporary arrest, along with

Genevieve Arron. Of Antonin and Lucian Arron, no trace was found. Rumors swirled that they are in hiding somewhere in Prynn or that they have fled the island entirely now that the mist is clear and the way is open.

Slowly, the rebellion disbanded. Soldiers returned to their homes to rebuild. The naturalists, and Cait and Ellis Milone, left the stronghold of Sunpool for Wolf Spring as the elementals returned to Rolanth. But not all abandoned the city they had helped to rebuild, and these days, Sunpool is a vibrant place of varied gifts.

As for the mist, it is not only at peace but gone completely. No longer will it protect the island from the outside world. No longer will Fennbirn be hidden from mainland travelers, and the true test of the Legion Queen and her advisers will be navigating the change.

In the quiet streets of the early-morning capital, Arsinoe and Jules walk together as they often do, getting away from the bustle. They must go early before there is anyone to share the pavement with. Since Jules lost her leg, Camden refuses go ahead or behind. She insists on being pressed to Jules's side.

"You're getting pretty good with that crutch," Arsinoe says.

"I had been using this leg less anyway. It was never quite the same after I ate all that poison."

They meander down to the harbor and head north along the docks full of ships. The boats still stay close, not venturing out of the island's sight, but soon enough the fishers will brave the deeper waters, and traders will dare to find the mainland.

As they walk, they look up to the northern cliffs, where a tall flame burns, surrounded by polished black stones and fresh flowers. A memorial to Mirabella. On the roof of the West Tower, a similar flame burns for Katharine.

Arsinoe reaches down and scratches Camden between the ears. She misses Braddock. She has not seen him since she went to the Black Cottage shortly after the battle. He was still there, with Willa, and there he will remain until Willa believes what they say about the queens and formally leaves her post.

"Who are you going to leave in charge while you're away?" Arsinoe asks. "Luca?"

"Why? Because she's the oldest?"

Arsinoe chuckles. Mirabella's friends, Bree and Elizabeth, returned to the capital with the High Priestess a week ago.

"No. Because she's the most widely liked."

"She tried to kill you, remember," says Jules. "With that plot during the Quickening."

"But she didn't."

Jules frowns. Then her expression clears, and she shrugs.

"Well, anyway, I asked her for advice, and she wouldn't give it. She wants to remain with the temple. She wants to stay near Bree and Elizabeth. And I think that's all she wants."

"So many changes."

"And more to come. Emilia means to travel to every city with Mathilde to hear what the people say. Or she might just send Mathilde."

"She doesn't want to leave you."

Jules shrugs again and blushes.

"How are you two?" Arsinoe asks. "Are things . . . ?"

"I'm not going to be marrying any mainlanders, if that's what you mean." Jules takes a deep breath and stops walking, hopping slightly to readjust her crutch. "I won't really be a queen, you know. It's all going to be different. You'll see."

"Will you live in the capital, when we get back?"

"I don't know. I'd like to go home to Wolf Spring. Emilia didn't want to abandon Indrid Down to its own so soon, but she or Mathilde will always be here. And I want to be near Fenn and Luke. Matthew and Caragh."

"Maybe you could lure Braddock down to live in the fields near the house?" Arsinoe asks.

They reach the end of the docks and turn back. They may pop into the inn on the corner for a few soft-boiled eggs and some fresh warm bread, like they sometimes do. Or stroll through the market and watch the merchants polish their wares. Above them, the tall black spires of the Volroy stretch into the sky, not a monster anymore casting a wicked shadow but only a building, and Indrid Down is only a city rather than a nest of enemies.

"Will you come with me to the square?" Jules asks.

"Not this morning. I told someone I would help them with something."

"Queen Arsinoe still has her secrets."

Arsinoe laughs. She gives Camden a pat on the haunches and slips away, down side streets and through alleys until she is back at the Volroy gates. The boy waiting for her steps out of the shadows. He does not raise a hand in greeting. He does not even take his hands out of his pockets.

She joins him without a word, and they make their way through the quiet castle, up and up and up the stairs of the West Tower.

"Are you sure you're ready to do this?" Arsinoe asks, and in answer, Pietyr takes a breath and takes the last of the steps by two, out onto the roof.

It is his first visit to Katharine's memorial. The priestesses who tend it have been dutiful, the ring of black stones laid out with care and the wreaths of poisoned berries and blossoms fresh. Someone has even left a live scorpion in a jar.

"Her flame burns high," Pietyr says, and Arsinoe looks to the north.

From up there, so high above the city, Mirabella's and Katharine's flames do not seem so far apart, as if the sisters are together in their burning.

"We fought so hard," she says. "And still, two of us are dead. What was the point of it?"

"The fight," Pietyr replies simply. "The fight was the point." He bends down, his elbow resting on one of his knees as he watches Katharine's flame. "I wish it would burn forever."

"I wish that, too."

But nothing is forever, of course. Not even on Fennbirn, where for an age the mist held time itself hostage. Eventually, the priestesses would let the fires go out. Then they would be lit again on festival days or on the days commemorating the battle.

And one day, there would be no flames at all.

"I should have—" Pietyr says, and his voice breaks. Arsinoe puts her hand on his shoulder. After a few moments, it stops shaking, and he wipes his eyes. "I should get to the square." He stands up and takes a slow breath. "Someone has to advocate for Genevieve's release."

"That won't make you very popular on the new council."

He chuckles. "I do not think there was any chance of that, anyway." He turns to go, and his eyes cloud when they land on the space where Katharine went over the edge. Arsinoe knows he is seeing those last moments in his mind. Wishing he had caught her, even for a second.

Then he blinks, and they walk together down the stairs.

"Are you coming to the square, Queen Arsinoe?" he asks when they reach the bottom.

She moans. "Stop calling me that."

"But it is what you are. What you always will be. Queen Arsinoe. The last of the true queens of Fennbirn. Your legend and your popularity will grow. Perhaps even outstripping the legend of the Legion Queen."

She says nothing, and he sighs, looking back up the stairs.

"I wish there were something more that I could do for her," he says. "Something besides look after her snake. I hate that no one really knew what kind of person she was—how kind and shockingly gentle. How clever. All she ever wanted was to make us proud. And the island will remember her reign as that of a monster."

"No they won't. You're here. You'll make them remember."

"How can you say so?" he asks. "How will anyone believe me after what she did?"

"I don't know what Katharine was after she came back from the night of the Quickening. I only know that, in the end, she was my sister."

Pietyr shoves his hands back into his pockets and walks away.

"Hey," she calls after him. "I'm sorry I kissed you."

He turns his head, just enough for her to see the sharpness of his jawline.

"Not half as sorry as I am!" he shouts, and Arsinoe laughs.

EPILOGUE

The ship rocks slightly in the water as the last of the supplies are brought onboard. Arsinoe shifts her weight from foot to foot, keeping balance as she stares out at the horizon. For the first time, the prospect of leaving Fennbirn does not frighten her. Ships have come and gone for weeks without incident. And she feels that link between her and the island, snapped and flapping loose, deep inside her chest.

"Maybe I shouldn't go," she says as Jules joins her by the railing. "Maybe it's too soon."

"Too soon for what? The new Black Council is nearly set. Mathilde's letters from the road are good and tranquil, in true Mathilde fashion. Even Braddock is settled with Grandma Cait and Ellis. You've run out of excuses. You ran out of them weeks ago."

"You must really want me gone."

Jules laughs. "If I thought you were going forever, I would

be locking you in the Volroy cells instead of preparing to sail with you."

Camden stands to put her paws on the rail, and Arsinoe buries her face in the cougar's fur. "What if he doesn't want me there?"

"I can't hear you when you talk into my cat."

Arsinoe raises her head. "What if I hate it? I do, I hate it there."

Jules makes an impatient face. Her eyes narrow at movement from inside Arsinoe's pocket.

"What is that?" She looks inside, and a tiny, speckled chick pokes its head out and chirps.

"Grandchick," Arsinoe replies. She strokes the fluffy feathers. "Harriet hatched a brood not long ago. I thought Billy should know he's a grandfather."

Jules laughs.

"For a poisoner, you do make quite the naturalist." She reaches down, and the chick rubs its head against her finger. "This chick's home is on Fennbirn, you know. So Billy had better accept our offer to be our ambassador. We're going to need him if we want to reintroduce the island to the world without a war."

Arsinoe arches her brow. "He might refuse if he suspects the only reasons we're offering are so his family is taken care of and he and I can be together."

"We're asking him because he is the best. Our most trusted mainland ally."

"Our only mainland ally."

Jules shrugs like it does not make any difference. And Arsinoe supposes it does not. If Billy agrees, they could have everything they hoped. And it does not feel like she deserves it.

"How can I be alive when they're dead, Jules?"

"How can you ask that?" Jules leans against the rail and pokes Arsinoe in the chest with the top of her crutch. "If Mirabella were here, your vest would be on fire right now."

"And Katharine?"

"She saved you. That wasn't an accident. So yes. If she were here, she wouldn't set you on fire but nor would she put you out."

Arsinoe laughs softly. It is a strange feeling, to not be needed anymore. To be able to go and be certain that Fennbirn will never call her back.

"The island is home, you know, Jules? I don't want to lose that. I don't want to lose you."

"You can never lose me. But you're free. You're not a queen anymore; you can come and go as you please. The island will always be here." She claps Arsinoe on the shoulder, and she and her cougar face out toward the open sea.

"Now let's go find your boy."

ACKNOWLEDGMENTS

Thank you to everyone who has come with me to Fennbirn, who has journeyed with the queens across four novels and seen them to their ends. I cannot express to you what an honor it has been to have you with me, and how grateful I am that you're still here. It means the world that you have lived (and died) and loved (and hated) and won and lost with these queens. Thank you.

In case you haven't heard me shouting about it, my agent, Adriann Ranta Zurhellen, and my editor, Alexandra Cooper, are the most incredible agent and editor ever, and I will fight you if you disagree. Also, Adriann and Alexandra, I don't know how to thank you properly. I'm going to try, but maybe I could just buy you both ponies? I think you would look very fancy on them and maybe they would be good for commuting. You are both brilliant. I would be lost without your savvy advice and uncanny ability to make my terrible words better without making me cry because my words are terrible.

There were many, many people who helped this final book take shape: Jon Howard, Robin Roy, Gweneth Morton, thank you for your eagle eyes, solid sense of story, and command of the English language. Audrey Diestelkamp, Jane Lee, Tyler Breitfeller, and Jace Molan, thank you for being incredible marketing professionals and social media moguls and also being all-around great people. Alyssa Miele (congratulations, editor!) what are we going to do without you? Olivia Russo, you are a dream publicist, and I am so glad I've been able to lean on you and call you late at night when I have travel issues (though I do apologize for that call!). Sari Murray: thank you for putting up with me while Olivia is away. ☺ Bess Braswell: you rock. It's just like, a fact. Aurora Parlagreco, Erin Fitzsimmons, Cat SanJuan, John Dismukes, and Virginia Allyn: you have made this series so amazingly beautiful! Amy Landon, your voice has made the audiobooks absolutely shine. Thank you. A huge thank you to Rosemary Brosnan and the entire team at HarperTeen for unbelievable support.

Thank you to everyone at Foundry Literary + Media, and to Kirsten Wolf and Allison Devereux at Mackenzie Wolf.

Thank you for Crystal Patriarche and Keely Platte at Book-Sparks PR! You guys are awesome.

Thank you to April Genevieve Tucholke for encouraging texts and always being up for an escape room.

Thank you to Susan Murray, for remembering my characters

when you rarely remember any characters except for the ones from *Don't Tell Mom the Babysitter's Dead.*

Thank you to my parents, for raising me and making sure I didn't die and stuff. Also for the many delicious casseroles.

And as usual, thank you to Dylan Zoerb, for luck.